THE NO.1 BESTSELLING SENSATION
NICOLA MAY

STARRY SKIES
in FERRY LANE
MARKET

HODDER

First published in Great Britain in 2021 by Hodder & Stoughton
An Hachette UK company

1

A CIP catalogue record for this title is available from the British Library

Paperback ISBN 978 1 529 34648 0
eBook ISBN 978 1 529 34649 7

Typeset in Plantin Light by Palimpsest Book Production Limited,
Falkirk, Stirlingshire
Printed and bound in Great Britain by Clays Ltd, Elcograf S.p.A.

Hodder & Stoughton policy is to use papers that are natural,
renewable and recyclable products and made from wood grown in
sustainable forests. The logging and manufacturing processes are
expected to conform to the environmental regulations of the
country of origin.

Hodder & Stoughton Ltd
Carmelite House
50 Victoria Embankment
London EC4Y 0DZ

www.hodder.co.uk

For Georgia, Trinny, Jake & Amy

'If you do not love too much, you do not love enough.'
Blaise Pascal

PROLOGUE

'I've told you before, Mum,' Star Bligh said irritably. 'I don't want you doing this if you're stoned.'

Ignoring her daughter, the woman with braided grey hair carried on laying out the well-worn Tarot cards.

'I can see a man,' Estelle Bligh said slowly. 'In fact, I can see two.' Her long, slim fingers began to circle the crystal ball in front of her.

'Huh. Isn't that just your wishful thinking?' Reverting to her sulky five-year-old self, Star began to twirl a strand of her long blonde hair around her finger.

'Shhh,' her mother hissed, then went on. 'Choose wisely, for one of them may break your heart . . .' a dramatic pause ensued '. . . and the other may *shake* it to the core.' Her Cornish accent trailed off in an ominous whisper.

'I don't suppose you saw Skye in your crystal ball, did you?' Star asked. 'I mean, that was the reason for my coming up here this early – thinking that my wayward daughter might have sought solace here with her even more wayward grandmother.'

Estelle tutted. 'She's a big girl now, Steren. You really do need to let her go.'

'Let her go? She's only seventeen, Mum.'

'And at that age, you were a single mother with a one-year-old, already out working all hours at Sibley's.'

Star looked up at the metal clock in the shape of a black cat that was hanging on the wall. 'Noo, is that the time?' She shimmied sideways out of the bench seat in her mother's kitchen and went to fetch her coat and hat. 'I need to get back to the market,' she said, and shivered. 'It's bloody freezing in here. How do you stand it?'

'Oh, to me it brings back lovely memories of all three of us cuddling up under a blanket when our Skye was a baby.'

'Yeah, right. Those happy days when we had no money to mention, and you still convinced me that having a baby when I was in my last year at school was the right thing to do.' Star couldn't keep the bitterness out of her voice.

'That's not fair.' Estelle looked pained. 'Do you regret it now?'

'Of course not,' Star snapped. 'I just don't want to see Skye following in my footsteps. She needs to have a life before she even thinks of starting a family.'

'You're a great mother to her, love. A much better mum than I ever was to you.' Estelle gave a sigh.

Star looked up at the ceiling to suppress her tears. 'Anyway, don't you want to be moving to a proper house, now that you're getting older?'

'And leave this perfect little commune – are you mad? As for the temperature, I've got proper electric heater things now. Haven't sussed out how to work the timers on them, that's all.'

Star looked out across the amazing clifftop view to see the horizon cutting the early October sky and steel-grey sea perfectly in two. Seabirds on the wing, ready to dive down and catch their fishy breakfast, squawked in anticipation. There was no denying that the Hartmouth Head residential static home park was set in an incredible location. And despite having been subject to 'trailer trash' taunts from some of the kids in her schooldays, Star thought that being brought up in such a close-knit community, and against such a stunning backdrop, had had its advantages.

'Can't your new boyfriend do it?' she asked now, grateful for Skye's regular updates on her grandmother's unpredictable love life.

'Sort the heaters, you mean?' Estelle raised her eyebrows meaningfully, then laughed. 'Harley's about as useful on the DIY front as a chocolate teapot.'

'Maybe if you dated someone who wasn't just out of college . . .'

'For your information, he's thirty-two.'

'Oh, just the thirty-year age gap this time, then.'

'You're just jealous. When's the last time you had any fun, eh, my girl?' Opening the door to her static home, painted a dark green that reflected her pagan love of nature, Estelle picked up and lit the half-smoked joint that was resting in an ashtray on the steps of the decking area. Then, after taking a large drag on the fragrant tobacco, she said, 'I named you Steren because it means Star. Now that your daughter is grown and can stand on her own two feet, don't you think it's time for *you* to start shining?'

Chapter 1

'Try this.' Big Frank Brady placed a small sugar-dusted pie in front of the woman who was sitting on a high stool across the cafe counter from him.

The clattering of cutlery as a couple finished off a huge fried breakfast and the shrieking of a toddler having a tantrum in the corner were only slightly drowned out by Audrey Hepburn singing 'Moon River'.

'She's singing your song, Kara Moon,' Frank teased the pretty redhead. Then the towering, dark-haired Irishman, who had owned and run Frank's Café on the Hartmouth Estuary seafront for the past eleven years, went over and twiddled with his beloved jukebox in the corner.

'So,' he said, coming back to the counter, 'what do you think of the mince pie? I'm testing it out ready for the Christmas trade.'

Licking her lips, Kara took a big bite into the succulent-looking pastry. She began chewing, then shuddered and made an ugly face. 'Ew! That taste, it's so bitter.' She reached for the water bottle in her bag and washed down the alien-tasting filling fast. 'What the hell have you put in there?'

'Thought I would try an age-old, revered mince pie recipe. You are my guinea pig.'

'It's only just October,' Kara objected in her faint Cornish accent.

'You know me – I like to be ahead of the game. I found it in a drawer at my old mammy's place after she died, God bless her, and then came across it by chance yesterday in the back kitchen. It had mice teeth-marks all around the edge.'

'What – the mince pie or the recipe sheet?' Frank laughed his deep throaty laugh as Kara continued, with a huge grin. 'Or maybe you just put a dead mouse in it?'

'No, just a slosh of Guinness, as well as the usual brandy.' He took a bite himself, then gagged. 'Jesus! Me old dear must have been on the black stuff herself when she made these, so she must.' They both laughed. 'My Monique already said to just get some of the home-made mincemeat from Alicia in The Sweet Spot. I think she's right; it'll be a lot easier.'

'Your Monique is *always* right,' Kara said, 'and sensible too. I'd follow her advice if you want to keep any of your customers.' She swallowed a bit more water before exclaiming, 'Shit! I need to get going. I've been waiting on an extra delivery of gypsophila and it should be arriving soon.'

'How's it going up there at the market now that you're Miss Passion Flowers herself?'

'Really good, thanks,' Kara said happily. 'I'm so lucky to be working at something I love, and now that the business belongs to me, I cannot tell you how good it is not being ordered around by Lydia Twist. Old Twisty Knickers was a horrible boss.'

'Living the dream, young Kara. And you deserve it, you really do.'

Kara glanced through the cafe window and saw the *Happy Hart* car ferry heading across from Crowsbridge to the Hartmouth quay.

'Talking of things I love, I'd better take Dad and my Billy a coffee whilst they load on the cars,' she said. 'It's cold work on that crossing this time of year.'

Frank placed four takeaway cups in front of her in a holder. 'So, that's you, your dad, your fella and Skye sorted. I think I've got the milk and sugars right.'

'Brilliant, thanks.' Kara paid and made her way to the door. Frank ran around the counter to hold it open for her.

'Feck it!' the big man said suddenly.

'What's up?'

'There's me going on about them mince pies and forgetting I needed to talk to you about something important.'

'That's OK. Let me quickly message Skye and ask her to open the shop up a bit earlier. She can take the order in then.'

While Kara did that, Frank served two new customers with coffee, then came to sit down opposite her in one of the American diner-style booths. Checking her phone, Kara was relieved to see a thumbs-up emoji from her apprentice.

'It's about my brother's boy, Conor,' Big Frank revealed. 'To cut a long story short, he needs somewhere to stay for a little while and I wondered if he could rent your flat – the one above the flower shop, I mean. It is still empty, isn't it?'

'Is he in trouble?' Kara asked instinctively, knowing full well what a colourful family Frank heralded from. In fact, Monique moving him down to the south-west of England had probably saved the big Irishman from a life of crime. Selling hooky booze in the guise of a 'blackcurrant cordial' or 'special iced tea' was his only vice these days.

Not even flinching at her comment, Frank replied, 'He's not now.' Then he put his huge hand on top of Kara's pale freckly one and added, 'And you know I would never put you in a difficult position. He's a good lad, I promise you.'

Kara trusted Frank like family. 'The flat is empty, yes. I use it more as a stockroom and hadn't even thought about renting it out, to be honest. But why's he not staying at yours?' she asked.

'He's a youngster, like you – he'd be bored stiff living way up on the moor with me and Monique. Let me know how much you want, and I'll pay you three months upfront. Cash, of course.'

Kara thought about it. 'It's not very plush and I've only got a sofa up there at the moment, so we'll need to get a bed . . . and it needs a good clean throughout.'

Frank patted her arm. 'Just tell me what you need, little lady, and I'll get it sorted.'

'OK, if you're sure. Any idea when he wants it from?'

'Yesterday.' Frank grinned his lopsided grin. 'You know us Brady boys, we don't mess around.' He stood up. 'Come on, let me get you some fresh coffees. These will be cold.'

Kara took a sip of hers. 'They're still OK. Don't worry.'

'Grand, grand. Right, I've got to get everything ready for my end-of-summer-season party on the quay.'

'Will there be fireworks again?'

'Oh yes.'

'You're so good, doing that every year.'

'I'm not sure if I'll make it to the Pearly Gates though, as I do have an ulterior motive. True, it's a thank you to the locals for coming here throughout the summer, but it's also a PR ploy to remind everyone that I'm still here all winter long.'

'That's allowed and we'd all come anyway. Right, I really must go.'

'I'll catch up with you later re the logistics of the flat. And thanks a million, Kara.'

As Star drove to the end of Ferry Lane, she noticed Kara about to hotfoot it up the hill towards the market. Tooting loudly right behind her, she stopped and beckoned her friend over to her Smart car. 'Get in,' she called. 'I'll take you.'

'You scared the life out of me,' Kara told her, climbing in carefully so as not to spill the coffees she was holding. 'What are you up to, tearing around this early, anyway?'

'Skye didn't come home last night. I know she's officially a grown-up now, Kar, but I wish she'd had the decency to let me know where she was. I didn't sleep a bloody wink.'

'Oh, love. Well, she's at the shop now. She's just messaged me. Is this the first time she's done this – stayed out all night, I mean?'

'Yes, but—fuck!' Star braked suddenly as a stray melon toppled from a box that Charlie Dillon was carrying and hurtled their way. It was only thanks to her quick reflexes that it avoided being crushed under her wheel.

Kara jolted forwards, causing hot coffee to spill out of the cups she was clutching and onto her jeans. 'Bloody hell, mate. Be careful!'

'Don't you be having a go at me too.' Star suppressed a sob as she pulled up outside the florist's.

Oblivious to all this, Charlie Dillon bent to retrieve the runaway fruit and stuck it up his jumper, along with another one. 'Don't get many of these to the pound,' he said in a falsetto voice, mincing around, and then catching sight of an old lady looking, he quickly put them back in the box.

'Oh, Star, I'm so not having a go. I've got to do an early hotel drop, so how about we meet for lunch at Tasty Pasties, and you can tell me what's really the matter. Say twelve thirty, all right?'

'You know me so well.' Star smiled weakly.

'What is it they say? Sister from another mister, or something like that.' Kara put one of the coffees in the car's drinks holder and got out. 'Get that in you,' she said. 'I've already had a sip and there's sugar in it, but it's wet and warm.' Then waving goodbye, she turned and made her way through the glass-fronted door to her personal domain: the beautiful and sweet-smelling florist's called Passion Flowers.

Chapter 2

Star yawned as she made her way inside STAR Crystals & Jewellery, the market unit she had rented and run in Ferry Lane Market for the past six years. Gagging at the sweetened coffee, she then cranked up the heating. She hated the winter, mainly because it reminded her of those freezing days living in the static home with her mother and a young baby. The memories of all three of them cuddling up together under a blanket were not quite as romantic as the version her mother had fondly recalled. Probably because Estelle Bligh had been warmed through with brandy or cannabis at the time, Star thought grimly. The experience had done one thing: made her determined that, as soon as she could afford a place of her own, she and her beloved only child Skye would never be cold again.

Oh, how hard she had worked to create her own little business and forge her way in the world. Steren Bligh had always been a grafter. As soon as she was old enough, she had put herself on the bus to work on Saturdays and after school at Sibley's, the newsagent in Penrigan that was owned by her great-aunt Florrie and her great-uncle Jim Sibley.

The childless churchgoers had always looked out for their pretty little fair-haired assistant. And when she became pregnant at just sixteen years old, despite their Christian beliefs – or perhaps because of them – they had not turned their backs on her; on the contrary, they had taken care of both her and the baby. The couple had kept Star's job open, and they'd also made sure that, when Estelle was working at her 'witchcraft' as they called it, and couldn't babysit, Skye was fed and cuddled in the flat upstairs. Their great kindness allowed Star to carry on working her regular shifts without having to find money for childcare.

Their generosity also meant that Star could save up her wages to buy beads, silk threads and fastenings. Then, staying up as late into the night as possible before her eyes shut without her permission, she would make bracelets and necklaces to sell on Penrigan Beach and along the pier on a Sunday to the many visiting holidaymakers. Putting Skye in a makeshift papoose and ably managing to dodge the council do-gooders, the young entrepreneur did excellent business, with her little white-haired bairn proving a valuable attraction. To the coos of 'what a gorgeous baby', her basket full of trinkets was soon empty, and her money belt was full.

This routine continued until she finished her exams and began helping out more in the newsagent. By then, Flo and Jim were allowing her to sell her handmade jewellery from a stand next to the magazine rack, and she also sold her wares at as many arts and craft fairs as she could fit in around her shifts.

Everything changed when her beloved great-uncle Jim dropped down dead the day before he and Florrie were due to retire. He was just seventy-five.

The Sibleys' retirement plan had been to close down their business but stay living in their modest flat above the newsagent and donate the space below for charitable and church causes. It wasn't until they had both passed away that their heirs – Star, Skye, the RSPB, and the local church – would receive their legacies. However, after Jim's untimely passing Star received her generous legacy in advance: the sum of £20,000, which Jim, with the full support of his wife, had left Star in his will.

When the lease of the much sought-after unit on Ferry Lane Market came up for sealed bids, Star's dream of a shop and a home of her own came to fruition far sooner than she could ever have imagined. With the money, she put down a deposit and six months' rent to start with, and was able to buy everything she needed to set up her business.

STAR Crystals & Jewellery was sandwiched between her best friend Kara's Passion Flowers florist shop and the Hartmouth Gallery run by Glanna Pascoe. The feisty stall-holder not only exhibited the works of some quite well-known local artists but she also painted seascapes herself. And it was with inward delight that Glanna now acknowledged that the tourists who religiously came to Hartmouth for their holidays had started collecting her work, too.

Here in Ferry Lane Market, Star was completely content. She could get everything she needed from the shops and stalls. The rich variety of products made sure you could fill up your shopping bags here for a bargain price and have plenty of choice – as well as banter from the Dillon family's fruit and veg stall opposite at no extra cost.

Ferry Lane Market was like having the whole world in one small community, and she loved it with all her heart.

Star often thought that if it hadn't been for the passing of her dear great-uncle, three generations of Bligh females would still be living all on top of one another in the small park home up on Hartmouth Hill. When she had inherited the gift of money from a man she had looked up to and loved, and with the blessing of his dear wife, she felt that the universe had been listening to her dreams and that she really did have a guardian angel.

Turning on the display window lights against the gloomy autumn day, Star's phone beeped with a text. *My battery went last night, sorry, mum. At work, can't talk. C u later xx*

Star let out a deep breath of relief. If the world were powered by the angst teenagers caused their parents, there would be no need to worry about global warming ever again, that was for sure. As the heater at her feet began warming her up, she set about unpacking the new order of precious stones and crystals, which she would use to make jewellery for her sparkly new winter and Christmas gift collection.

Chapter 3

Star placed herself on a high stool at the window counter in the Tasty Pasties shop. She was waiting for Kara to finish with a customer and join her. Realising that she'd left her phone back at the shop she frowned, then relaxed. Sitting here at the big front window gave the best view in Ferry Lane: the pasty shop was positioned right at the top of the market with an uninterrupted view down the hill to the estuary. It also offered the most wonderful cooking smells as Philip Gilmour, the eccentric and flamboyant owner of Tasty Pasties, insisted that his five exclusive varieties of pasty, including a new vegan one, were all prepared and cooked on the premises. The recipe, he declared, was so secret that even he had forgotten what was in it!

Living off his spoils in one of the big houses high on Hartmouth Hill, the owner was rarely spotted, except on the occasional market day. It was Mrs Harris, aided and abetted by the casual employ of university students, who had worked there and run the place ever since Star could remember. The sixty-something woman's uniform consisted of a branded white hat and dress, with a blue and white striped half-apron, which only just reached round her plump waist to be tied up. Red-cheeked and big-bottomed, she was possibly the most jovial woman on Ferry Lane Market, if not in the whole of Hartmouth.

Tasty Pasties was the only shop that didn't have an outdoor stall on market days. The eleven other unit owners would set up their stalls every Friday and Saturday, whatever the weather, and sell their wares. There was an eclectic mix of stalls to suit both tourists and locals alike. On Star's side of the street, you could not only find Passion Flowers and the art gallery, but an artisan bakery, Clarke's the butchers and a second-hand books and records stall. On the other side, the units were made up of the Dillon family's fruit and veg stall, a clothes stall that sold all sorts of wonderful vintage items, Nigel's Catch the fishmonger, The Sweet Spot belonging to Alicia, selling home-made fudge and local honey including the Honeysuckle Honey made at Bee Cottage, and one stall that was loaded with antiques.

Star never tired of the buzz and exhilaration that the Friday and Saturday market days brought with them. They were also the guarantee of good sales of her bespoke jewellery, especially leading up to Christmas and special days like Valentine's and Mother's Day.

With Star wishing she had put longer than just a *Back in 30 mins* sign on her shop door and no phone to amuse her, she began tapping her nails, always kept neat and short for jewellery-making, on the high counter. Her eyes were drawn to the sign on the wall next to her that she had read so many times before: *The Cornish Pasty*. There was a picture of a shiny-looking pasty next to the title and its history:

This tasty treat has been a documented part of the British diet since the 13th century, at this time being devoured by the wealthy upper classes and royalty. The fillings were varied and rich: venison, beef, lamb, and seafood like eels, flavoured with rich gravies and fruits. It wasn't until the

17th and 18th centuries that the pasty was adopted by miners and farmworkers in Cornwall as an easy, tasty and sustaining meal while they worked. And so the humble Cornish Pasty was born.

Star was baulking at the thought of eating an eel-filled pastry, when Kara came bounding in. 'So sorry, the manager at The Dolphin caught me as I was leaving, wanting to discuss wedding flowers. I did message you. Fancy a large one?'

Star shook her head in mock disapproval as her friend laughed. Without waiting for an answer, Kara quickly bought two of the warm pasties. She presented Star's on a paper plate with a plain white serviette and a bottle of water, saying, 'You're looking tired. This will perk you up, girl.'

Star looked at the pasty and turned up her nose. 'Original? I wanted a vegan one,' she said, straight-faced, winding her up.

'I'm not even replying to that.'

'I need to be healthier. I eat far too much rubbish at the moment, and how many calories are in this, do you think?' Star said.

'There's nothing of you.' Kara tutted.

Star ignored her. 'A huge spot came up on my chin the other day. I never get spots!' She shoved the gorgeous-tasting treat into her mouth, then shut her eyes in ecstasy. 'Oh – my – God. I forgot just how scrummy the meat ones are.'

'How are you feeling now, anyway?' Kara asked.

Star's face dropped. 'I'm all right. It's just – well, I saw Mum earlier and you know how that annoys me, just seeing her sometimes. I left her at eight thirty this morning and she had a spliff on the go already. I'm also worried about Skye.'

'Why? She seems so happy. Loves her new job working

with me and she's great at it. She's a good kid, Star.' An unofficial apprenticeship at Passion Flowers had been the natural choice for the youngster, once her A levels were done with. Although she was artistic, Skye had no gift for jewellery making, unlike her mother.

'I'm looking at part-time floristry courses for her too,' Kara added, 'which means she will eventually obtain a proper qualification that will take her anywhere she wants to go in the business – even around the world if she so fancies.'

'Aw, thanks, Kar. Maybe I'm just over-thinking everything. I don't want her to muck up like me – getting pregnant so young. I don't even know where she was last night. She won't let me follow her on Instagram. She's such a pretty and private little thing.'

'Even I get that. She doesn't want you cramping her style. Though to be fair, you are the coolest mum in Cornwall, in my view.' Kara's voice softened. 'You've obviously talked to her about – you know, stuff?'

'Yes, of course. I even suggested that maybe going on the pill wasn't such a bad idea at her age and her reply was that she wasn't stupid.'

'There you go then. Compared to what we used to be like as teens, she seems pretty bloody sensible to me.'

Star had a sudden flashback to her smoking and drug-taking days when she was just sixteen, and shuddered at the thought of how her little one had been conceived.

Kara carried on talking over her friend's thoughts. 'She's had so much love from you. And from me and Florrie and Jim, when he was still around, bless him. And your mum too, believe it or not, has played her part in Skye's upbringing.'

'Hmm. That's what I'm worried about.' They both laughed.

Kara took a bite through the feather-light pastry coating, swallowed, and said, 'Maybe now it's time for you to stop worrying so much about your daughter and find somebody for yourself.'

'That's exactly what was left ringing in my ears earlier. It's like someone has called my romance angels in without me even asking for them. Mum laid out some Tarot cards, looked in her crystal ball and said she could see two men: one would break my heart apparently, and one would shake it or something like that. I reckon she was making it up as she's desperate to see me with somebody.'

'Well, you deserve every happiness – and it's not as if you were hit with the ugly stick, is it?' Kara looked at her friend's poker-straight, long white-blonde hair, flawless pale skin, perfect little nose and rosebud lips that looked like they had a baby pink lipstick on them even when bare of make-up. Her petite and toned frame made her seem a lot younger than her thirty-three years.

'Who says people can't be happy being single?' Star shrugged.

'You know what I mean.'

'And as for my looks, I kind of think they've been a hindrance. I want someone to see the real me. What's beneath the veneer. Love me warts and all. Does that make sense?'

'Is that why the most serious relationship you've had was with Danny Ball when you were fifteen, do you think?'

'Thanks for that, Kara. Just because you and Billy the Kid are now love's young dream.'

Kara saw the misery in her friend's sapphire-blue eyes. 'Oh, Star, I'm sorry. I'm not exactly the guru on relationships, am I? I mean, how long did it take me to get rid of bloody Jago and then to realise Billy was The One, hey?' She put her hand on top of her friend's. 'I do understand about Skye though.'

'How could you understand?' Star said hotly. 'You can't, Kar. Not until you've had a child yourself will you get it. Skye has been my life: I *have* to do right by her. As a single parent, even more so. I remained single out of choice. I didn't want to bring in a man who might have interrupted her life and disturbed it. I had enough of that with Mum whilst I was growing up – a stream of deadbeats and bullies coming in and out of our lives. I don't know, maybe it's now that Skye doesn't need me like she used to, I feel a loss of purpose.'

'Oh, mate,' Kara said, 'you're right. I don't understand fully, but I'm glad you've told me so I can hopefully support you through what you're feeling.'

'She's also started to ask more questions about her dad too.'

Kara's eyes widened. 'Are you going to tell her the truth?'

'You know I can't, not yet.' Star produced a tissue from her sleeve and blew her nose. Pushing her plate away from her, her face pained, she added, 'Also . . .'

'Go on,' Kara urged.

'I know it was just a one-off with Jack in the summer, but he was the only man I've felt anything for in a long time. I still think about him.' Star paused. 'A lot. Am I mad, Kar, for still hankering after him?'

'Not mad, no. What was it he said to make you go all girly when you first met at the market that day? "The heart has its reasons which reason knows not", or something like that?'

Star poked out her lip. 'Blaise Pascal. What a quote – and well remembered, mate! I just know he really liked me, and I still can't comprehend why, when you saw him in New

York and he had a broken arm and bruises, that he said to say sorry to *me*. There are so many unanswered questions. But he still hasn't responded to any of my messages.' Star looked at the clock on the wall. 'I'd better get back.' She pulled on her midnight-blue long velvet coat and white cashmere beanie.

Kara got set to leave too. 'Dear old Grandad Harry used to say that when you are going through life's tough stuff, to say to yourself, "this too shall pass". God, I miss him.'

'I know you do,' Star said. 'And that too will pass, or get easier with time, at least. When I think of dear old Uncle Jim, what gets me through is realising how lucky I was to have him and memories of him and Auntie Flo both. Good memories. I just need to believe that the universe will work its magic if me and Jack are meant to be, and in the meantime, maybe you and my mum are right. Perhaps it is time to think of Steren Bligh's wants and needs right now.'

As Star waved and shut the door of STAR Crystals & Jewellery behind her, Kara saw her boyfriend Billy Dillon and his twin brother, Darren, carrying a mattress across the road towards the staircase that led up to the flat above Passion Flowers.

'Ah, there you are, sweet cheeks,' Billy Dillon called over.

'All right, Moony?' The bald and chunky Darren Dillon was puffed out.

'What are you doing with that mattress, you two?' Kara wanted to know.

'Frank asked if Daz had a spare bed at his place,' Billy

explained, 'so I've quickly run up to help him move my old one into here.'

'Ah, right. He doesn't mess about, does he, Big Frank.'

Billy wiped his sweaty brow. 'And when exactly were you going to tell me you had a mystery man moving into the shop flat, eh?'

'I only found out myself a few hours ago.'

'Well, just get that gorgeous aris of yours up those stairs and open the flat door for us, will ya,' Billy said cheekily. 'This mattress is bleedin' heavy and I don't want to do meself a damage.'

Chapter 4

'Auntie Flo, are you there?' Star shut the street door behind her and made her way up the uncarpeted winding wooden stairs to the flat above Sibley's, the former newsagent. Finding the old lady asleep in her worn green wing-back armchair, newspaper open on the crossword page, Star said, 'Ah,' out loud. A fire was glowing in the grate. The six o'clock news was blaring out from the TV. The rubber-ended pencil Florrie had been using had slipped out of her fingers and on to the floor. Florence Sibley's hair was a natural silver-grey, cut short in no particular style. Her day dress was designer, her tights thick and her moccasin slippers were lined with sheep-skin. A budgie with a bright yellow fluffy-feathered head and cobalt-blue body was pecking away at a cuttlebone that had been wedged through the bars of his cage. On seeing Star, he started to fly around his cage, chirping, 'Hello, hello, hello, hello.'

That and Star turning the main light on woke Florrie with a start.

'It's only me, Auntie Flo. I've got your fish and chips, and hello hello to you too, Boris.' Star walked across the small sitting room and put the two greasy parcels down on the dining table.

'Friday, already,' the old lady said sleepily. 'Can you believe it, dear. How was the market today?'

23

'Windy and cold, but I sold a few bits from my new collection, so it was worth the frostbite.'

'It does seem to have got cold earlier this year. Aren't you wearing those gloves I got you from the church fete? And turn that main light off, will you, dear. The side lamp will do.'

'It's too dark in here, Auntie.'

'Save the pounds and the pennies will take care of themselves.'

'I think it's the other way around. And you have the money, so I don't know why you do this.'

'I also might live until I'm a hundred and ten, which is another twenty-five years, so be a good girl and do as you're told.' Star knew she would never win this argument. Apart from her legacy, any spare cash the couple had once had would more often than not go into the church collection tin on a Sunday morning. Frugal in their personal life they might have been, but throughout her childhood, her great-aunt Florrie and great-uncle Jim could not have been richer in kindness and spirit.

'*Good girl!*' Boris's screech was drowned out by some sort of firecracker being let off in the street below.

'Bloody kids! They start selling fireworks earlier and earlier these days. Me and Jim, we got them in the shop a week before Bonfire Night and that was that,' Florence Sibley huffed.

'Aw yes, I loved the sparklers. Uncle Jim used to take me to the beach in the dark so I could write my name with them against the real stars.'

'So he did.'

'*Bloody kids!*' Boris screeched again.

'And you can pipe down, bird.' Florence Sibley's sadness came out as a snap. 'Put the cover over him, will you, love?

That'll shut him up, although it doesn't always work now.' She reached for the beaded chain around her neck that Star had made for her and pushed her spectacles up over her nose.

With the threadbare cloth covering the birdcage, there was silence for a second, then they heard, *'Load of bollocks.'*

'Boris!' Star couldn't contain her laughter. 'I bet the Women's Institute ladies don't know you have such a rude man in your life.'

'I bet the Women's Institute ladies wished they *did* have such a rude man in their life,' Florrie said more cheerfully. 'I must remember to curb my tongue in front of him. Luckily, he's yet to shock the vicar.'

'Who have you have been saying "bollocks" to anyway, Auntie?'

Florence Sibley chuckled. 'It used to be to that Piers Morgan fellow on the breakfast programme. One minute I loved him, next minute he made me come out with that. Mind you, I do like that Naga Spaghetti on the other side. She always wears such beautiful clothes.'

'It's Munchetty, Auntie.' Star couldn't wait to share that gem with Kara. She walked through to the small kitchen to get some salt, vinegar and ketchup, calling out, 'Talking of clothes, is that a new dress you're wearing?'

As Star returned and placed the condiments on the small table with its embroidered tablecloth, Florrie undid the tightly wrapped paper parcels containing their fish suppers. 'This dress is from the charity shop – two pounds fifty it cost me. Armani, so I'm told, dear. And no need to holler, I've got my hearing aids in.'

'Well, it's very smart. How's it going down there anyway?'

'Seeing as I have given them our old shop floor for free,

it's all very friendly. I pop down to say hello every day, but just work the two mornings a week now. Means I can still do the church flowers on a Tuesday, go to my WI meeting on a Wednesday and help with the homeless lunches on a Thursday.'

'You're eighty-five and work harder than me,' Star teased.

'"Poor is he who works with negligent hand, but the hand of the diligent makes rich." Proverbs ten, verse four.'

'Amen,' Star said seriously, then, 'Sorry I turned out to be such a heathen.'

'You are a guiding light, my dear niece. You give me the greatest joy and you don't have to do this every Friday, you know, especially in the winter. I don't like to think of you driving on those windy roads. They could be icy or all sorts.'

But Star had kept her promise to her Uncle Jim, that if he were to die before his beloved wife, she would look out for her aunt. And so, with her knowing that the couple religiously had fish and chips on a Friday, Star was adamant that this tradition would continue. Depending on what she was doing she would either drop them off or stay and eat with Florrie at the flat. Now that Skye had passed her driving test, the girl would very occasionally borrow her mum's car and make the short trip from Hartmouth to Penrigan to see her great-great-auntie Florrie, cod and chips in hand.

Star helped herself to a chip. 'I like our catch-ups,' she said, 'and anyway, it's Frank's end-of-summer party on the quay in Hartmouth tonight and I'm not in the mood for socialising.'

'There's nothing that would give me greater pleasure than seeing you married to a lovely young man, you know.'

'Not you as well! Maybe we should both start praying for one, then.' Star stuffed another chip in her mouth.

'We haven't said grace yet,' Flo Sibley chided.

'Grace.' Star stuck her tongue out at her aunt and laughed.

'Naughty. You're your mother's daughter, you are. Saying that, how is the lovely Estelle?'

'The same. Another toy boy and still smoking dope with her morning coffee.'

'My poor sister, God rest her soul, would be turning in her grave at the antics of her only child. Saying that, if Lilian had been around maybe things would have turned out differently.' The old lady perked up. 'That reminds me, Steren love, I said I'd dig out some photos of your beautiful grandmama when she was your age. I'll have them here for when you come next week. If you want to come, that is.'

'I'd love to see those.' Star poured a glass of ice-cold full-fat milk from a large floral-patterned china jug. Milk and fish and chips had been a long-standing Sibley tradition, one which Star had tolerated when she was growing up, but actually rather liked now. 'Cuts through the grease, see,' Uncle Jim used to tell her. Whether that was true or not, she never knew.

Florence Sibley said sadly, 'Tragic, the way we lost our dear Lilian. It's not really surprising your mother is such a lost soul. I keep thinking I must go up and see her, but the last couple of times she gave me such short shrift, as she thinks I am going to preach at her, that it never ended well.'

'Oh, Auntie, she knows where you are.'

'I guess so. Now come on, child, let me say my bit and we can eat up properly.'

'*Bollocks!*' came from the cage.

Chapter 5

'Look at you two rocking around the clock tonight.' Kara laughed at her dad Joe and his girlfriend Pearl, who were attempting to jive to the music that was blaring out from Frank's speakers on the quayside.

'I love all the old tunes that Big Frank plays.' Pearl launched her wide and perfect smile. 'Makes us feel young again.'

'Plus,' Joe Moon added, 'it's helping us not to freeze to death from the cold easterly that's blowing in. It'll be a rum old crossing tomorrow, I reckon.'

'Are you working all through the winter then, Dad? I thought you were going to see if Daz could take some more crossings from you.'

Pearl dug her partner in the ribs. 'Go on, Joe, tell Kara what we're thinking of doing.'

'That sounds interesting.' Kara pulled her scarf tightly around her neck and stamped her feet on the concrete in an attempt to warm up.

'Yes, well, I do want to take some time out,' her dad told her. 'Look, why don't you and Billy come round for Sunday dinner and we can tell you more about it.'

'This'll warm you up.' Billy appeared from the cafe carrying two polystyrene cups. 'Hot blackcurrant, so the big man informs me.' Seeing that Joe and Pearl had joined them, he gave one to Pearl and one to Kara, who took a sip and grimaced.

'Wow. How much gin is in here?'

'Get it down you, girl. You deserve a drink after all that furniture moving.'

'Dad and Pearl have invited us to Sunday roast at Bee Cottage. Is that all right with you?'

Billy put his hand to his stomach. 'Only if Pearl promises to make one of her world-famous morello cherry pies.'

The big lady pretended to be serious. 'Mmm. I usually only take menu requests on a Tuesday, but I'll see what I can do.' She lifted Joe Moon's gloved hand and kissed it, 'Thanks for the drink, Billy. Come on, my Joey. Let's go inside the cafe and warm through.'

Kara took a tentative sip of her hot cocktail. 'Do you think the shop flat is good enough for Frank's nephew? I mean, it needs decorating and—'

'He's a bloke,' Billy interrupted. 'He's got a double bed and a big sofa, a fridge for beers and a power shower, all paid for by Big Frank. I mean, what more could he ask for? In fact, I might move in with him myself.'

Kara mock-swiped her beau. 'Oi! But you're right. I've done it at mate's rates too. I thought we could use the money for a holiday this year?'

The handsome ferryman kissed his girl. 'Let's make that holi*days* shall we? A couple of weekends away and maybe a week somewhere hot.'

'I can't wait.' Kara squeezed his hand, then checked her phone and reported, 'Star's decided to stay and have fish and chips with her auntie. I was just saying it's time she got out more, and this party would be a perfect opportunity.'

'Maybe she will come down later. Don't push her. She can be so fragile at times.'

'You're right.' Kara inwardly swooned at her twenty-six-year-old boyfriend's emotional maturity. 'It looks like half of Hartmouth are down here tonight.'

'Probably for Frank's punch and the hot dogs as the fireworks are usually touch and go.'

Kara laughed. 'Yes, Frank doesn't know the meaning of the words "health and safety". I'm sure it's because he gets them from off the back of a lorry.'

'The fact that the hooch is free all night means nobody will be complaining. Just get ready to duck when the main man sets the rockets off.'

'Is that my big Irish ears I can feel burning?' The cafe-owner came up behind them and put a huge hand on both of their shoulders. 'Word has it that my charming nephew is on his way. He'll be getting a full-on Cornish welcome, so he will. He loves a good craic.'

'The flat's kind of set up now,' Kara said. 'I was going to say that I've left a key under the mat so he can dump his things, then come down to join us if he wants to. You said he was getting a taxi from Penrigan station, right?'

'Yes. That's so thoughtful. Thanks, Kar. I'll drop him a quick text now.'

Star parked her little Smart car up behind her shop. She had enjoyed spending time with her aunt, as Florrie had been on particularly good form this evening. The thrills and spills of the fireworks display down at the bottom of the hill lit up the sky, reflecting darts of coloured light across the dark sea. A variety of *oohs* and *aahs* from the crowd that had amassed down there were carried on the biting wind.

Star wasn't dressed for such a cold night and, despite Kara's pleas, couldn't be bothered to go in, get changed and head out again. Especially now that Skye had texted to say she was having a rare night in and had put a couple of logs in the log burner ready for her return.

As she opened her car door, the security light at the back of the flat next door switched on to reveal a figure in a black hooded Puffa jacket appearing out of Kara's empty upstairs flat and running down the stairs. It was far too tall to be Billy and far too late for a courier. She froze, thinking it must be a burglar. From the safety of her now locked car, she slid down in the seat and bravely shouted out of a crack in the window into the darkness: 'It's too late, I've seen you. And I'm calling the police.' Trying Kara, then Billy to no avail, she quickly dialled 999. The lone figure was by now running at speed down Ferry Lane. 'Yes, looked like he was heading down to the quay. Yes, yes. Six foot, I reckon. Black jacket, blue or black jeans. Stripy scarf. Nike trainers, I think.'

Her heart still racing, Star opened the door to her flat, hurried in and quickly double locked it behind her. 'Skye, I'm home,' she called, directing her voice down the corridor towards her daughter's bedroom, and was surprised at no reply. On walking into the lounge, she saw why. There was her beautiful light-haired girl, earbuds in, phone to her side, sound asleep on the cream rug in front of the log burner. She was also happy to notice that she was wearing the silver swan-shaped earrings with tiny pieces of amber for eyes. Crafted with love and care for her daughter's seventeenth, using the gift of creativity that had kept her sane during the sometimes lonely periods of bringing up an only child with little support.

Star smiled wistfully to herself. When she had been Skye's age, she hadn't had the luxury of burning the candle at both ends. The only time she was up all hours was when she was woken in the night to tend to her toddler's needs. Looking at Skye now, she still couldn't quite believe how she had managed to produce such a kind and lovely human being. Or maybe she could. For by sacrificing her own needs, she had created an environment of such love and stability that Skye had grown up to be secure in herself, with inner strength and showing no fear of being exactly who or what she wanted to be.

Star often wondered whether the fact that her daughter had grown up without a father figure would impact on her in later years. Time alone would tell.

Not wanting to disturb the girl, or alert her to a potential burglar in their midst, Star went to change into comfy clothes, then laid herself down on the purple velvet sofa and sighed contentedly, looking around her. The flat was light and airy with a large oblong living room and a corridor to the rear where two similar-size double bedrooms were situated. She had scarcely been able to contain her delight when, on being shown around by the estate agent, she discovered that the recently modernised and spacious bathroom not only contained a roll-top bath but a huge walk-in shower too. The park home in which she had been brought up had its own redeeming qualities, but space wasn't one of them.

Compared with the rest of the flat, the kitchen off the lounge was small but functional. What made it special to Star was that the plain white tiles were interspersed with blue painted stars and moons in varying degrees of fullness. She had painted every wall white. A couple of abstract colour prints adorned the facing walls of the main room, and the dreamcatcher she had made herself hung in front of the big bay window that overlooked the market. A clock with a painting on its face of a white silk-robed angel ticked quietly, and candles of all shapes and sizes were placed around the room. Two of Skye's favourites were burning, their familiar musky aromas filling the space and creating a comforting ambience along with the glow from the fire.

Star didn't own the flat or the shop, but her uncle's inheritance had given her a buffer to pay her rent and take over the lease. With her business now flourishing, money worries were a thing of the past, and that felt so good. Yes, she had to work ridiculously hard to keep it all afloat, but now that her online business had really started to pick up, with customers from all over the world loving her birthstone jewellery range, she felt that she had turned a corner. She was already working on new designs to expand her collections and was enjoying every moment.

Star remained eternally grateful to Jim and Flo for drumming it into her to split her money three ways whenever she earned any. 'A third for the tax man, a third for saving and a third for living' was their mantra. At the time she had found the idea so dull – and as soon as her jewellery started flying off the market stall, she had wanted to spend everything on herself. Later she came to realise that what they had said made so much sense. Living was expensive, especially bringing up a child in a twenty-first-century world full of gadgets. Savings gave her a comfort blanket. The money boost aside, it was her strong work ethic that had got her to where she was today, fuelled and inspired by her aunt and uncle's regimental running of the newsagent and their passion in doing so. She used to nag them for not going away on holiday, but now that she worked for herself, reality had hit, and she herself had not been away for years. Star had convinced herself it was because she lived by the sea anyway. And on a summer's day, walking along Penrigan Beach, you could actually be anywhere in the world, it was so stunningly beautiful.

Her next goal was to be able to afford her own place, ideally to get a mortgage on the shop and flat if it ever came up for sale. And also to venture abroad soon, if she could find someone to mind the shop and market stall for her for a week, that was.

Just then, Skye began to stir.

'Darling, why don't you get up and into bed,' her mother said.

'What's the time?' Skye replied sleepily, smacking her dry lips.

'It's only nine-thirty but it's market day tomorrow and you need to be up early.'

'OK.' The teenager got up slowly, clumsily kissed her mother's cheek, and with an 'I love you, Mum', headed off to bed.

Star checked her phone. Nothing from Kara or Billy about the suspected intruder. She went to the back door and peered out across to Kara's flat: still in darkness with not a policeman in sight. She then pulled up the wooden slatted blind and opened one of her front windows. The fireworks had stopped, but on craning her neck to see as far as she could down to the estuary, the sight of a police car moving slowly through the end-of-season party masses made her feel decidedly uneasy.

Monique Dubois was just opening the big grey dustbin to the side of Frank's when she clocked the familiar face of his nephew. You could tell instantly it was a Brady. Handsome.

Broad-shouldered, with dark brown curly hair and brown eyes that told you nothing, unless he liked you. He was now walking slowly and deliberately as he mixed in with the crowd. Through her colourful life working in many countries and with a whole range of characters, she had encountered many faces that looked hunted – just like Conor Brady's did right now.

Ushering the young man down the outside brick stairs into the back kitchen, the half-French woman closed the door against the wind, kissed Conor cheek-to-cheek three times before saying, '*Viens* – get in here near the heater. What eez it? You've only just arrived, *non?*'

'The woman who owns the flat left a key out so I let myself in. Her nosy bloody neighbour only thought I was breaking in – said she was calling the Old Bill. I can't be dealing with them, not at the moment. So much for going incognito.' Conor looked stressed.

Blue lights could now be seen flashing down the hill as a police car navigated its way through the crowd down Ferry Lane and parked up alongside the cafe. Grabbing a tea towel, Big Frank precariously carried the big cauldron of unlicensed alcoholic punch from the cafe counter into the back kitchen and plonked it on the side next to an unsmiling Monique and his white-faced nephew.

'Jesus, lad. What's happened? The police are right outside.'

'*Fais pas d'histoires,*' Monique told her long-term lover in a brisk voice. 'It's just a misunderstanding. Some neighbour thought Conor was breaking into Kara's flat. I will deal with it.' She untied her apron to reveal a stylish all-in-one black jumpsuit. Formidable and in her late fifties, she was one of those women with such effortless style that she could have pulled off wearing a bin liner. Taking a deep red lipstick from her pocket she reapplied it expertly to her full lips without a mirror. Then, after patting the back of her platinum-blonde shoulder-length hair, she readjusted her bra to reveal a small amount of cleavage. Before she set off through to the cafe counter, in her sexy French accent she informed the nervous-looking Brady uncle and nephew: 'Gentlemen, leave this to *moi*!'

Chapter 6

'Why waste your time using the aubergine emoji when we've got the real thing here?' Darren (Daz) Dillon addressed the Saturday market day crowd, whilst waving the offending vegetable in the air.

'Leeks as long as Usain Bolt's . . . legs.' Charlie, Daz's father, intercepted. ''Ere, missus, what did you think I meant? Half a kilo for just one Cornish pound, cheaper than Harrods.'

On seeing Conor appearing from the side alley of Kara's shop, he called out, 'All right, lad? You must be a Brady, by the looks of you. Same build and everything. We thought you was coming last night.'

'Er yes. I didn't quite make the fireworks. So, you know my uncle then?'

'Everyone knows Big Frank,' Charlie's wife Pat put in before twirling closed a brown paper bag full of fragrant local tomatoes and handing it over the display to her customer. 'Want some garlic? We've got bulbs in for a special price today.' She popped one into the woman's carrier bag. 'Right, so that's two pound ten, just call it two quid. Have a nice day.'

She turned to greet the stranger and was quite taken by the handsome young man in front of her. 'Well, just look at you – so this is Frank's nephew. Conor, ain't it?'

'That's right.' Conor was amused by this family's East End vibe.

'Welcome to Happy Hartmouth,' Pat Dillon said, pronouncing her aitches for once and for his benefit. She threw him a sly wink. 'And please do excuse my old man, he has the manners of a barbarian.' With a wiggle of her huge square bottom, she walked back inside to fetch another box of cauliflowers.

'Are you staying long?' Charlie asked, filling a scoop with potatoes and weighing them.

'Er, the plan is for three months at the moment.'

'You working with your uncle then, lad?' Charlie tipped the spuds into his customer's shopping bag and took the bananas she handed him to weigh. They settled up and the next person, a man who ran a local B&B, asked for some of the sprouting broccoli to use for his special soup. The work never stopped, Conor noted, and the queue here moved quickly with three people serving.

'Haven't got that far yet either,' he answered.

With his own shady East End upbringing, Charlie Dillon knew to pry no further. 'Well, if you need any fresh veg, I'm your man, and me and my Pat, well we often go to the Ferryboat, the pub down the front on a Saturday night, and you'd be welcome to join us any time.'

'Thanks a million. I appreciate that.' Conor walked off, then looked up in search of the STAR Crystals & Jewellery sign. At the flower stall beside it he spotted a slight blonde girl handing bunches of carnations expertly wrapped in pretty pink tissue paper to a middle-aged man.

'Three bunches of carnations for ten pounds, a fiver each. Every colour.' Skye's sweet Cornish voice rang out like a silver bell against the rough London accents of the Dillons.

A shivering Star was outside concentrating on unwinding a ten-foot white extension cable. When the cable was long enough, she shut her shop door up on it and plugged in the electric fan heater at her feet.

She was just bending down with her back to the street making sure the lead was not a trip hazard, when a voice with a deep Irish accent said, 'You don't shout out to the punters like the others then?' This woman had really riled him with her nosiness last night. But if they were to be neighbours, and with Frank's insistence that Star Bligh was not a troublemaker, Conor paced his response accordingly.

On realising who it must be, Star froze to the spot in the hope that the man would just go away. She had finally got through to Kara in a panic last night, gibbering that she thought someone had broken into the florist's flat and telling her friend that she had called the police, only to learn that it was Big Frank's nephew who'd come to stay for a few weeks. Star was absolutely mortified.

Conor cleared his throat loudly and, realising that he wasn't going anywhere, Star reluctantly turned around and found herself looking into the soft brown eyes of someone who could win a place on any catwalk in the world.

'Or maybe you just prefer to sing like a canary?' Conor said, now faintly amused and slightly taken aback by the beauty of the nervous-looking blonde in front of him.

Star stared back at the friendly face, took a deep breath and said, 'Very funny.' Attempting to regain her composure, she began tidying some earrings on a rack.

'Conor Brady.' The man held out his big hand. Star lifted a gloved one and just gave him an awkward wave from across the market stall.

'Steren Bligh, but most people call me Star.'

'Everyone except your mammy, you mean?'

Star couldn't help but smile. 'True – and my great-auntie.' Just the presence of this man had caused the speech she had prepared to become lost in translation. She began to gabble nervously. 'I am so sorry about last night. It's just Kara didn't tell me you were coming, and no one is ever near those flat steps as it's been empty for months and . . . oh God. I didn't get you in any trouble, did I?'

Conor looked at the young woman in front of him, so petite, so vulnerable, and suddenly felt as if his heart might actually leap out of his chest and cling to her.

Not realising that she didn't need to say another single word to him, Star carried on desperately. 'I just don't want this to be awkward between us as Kara tells me we are going to be neighbours for a while now. What can I do for you to forgive me? How about a crystal or a necklace for somebody special in your life?' She gestured at one of her star-shaped display stands.

Conor's lips were full, his smile lopsided and sexy. Star noticed also that he had just one deep dimple on his right cheek. Damn those butterflies that were doing somersaults in her stomach. Tall, handsome men never usually had this effect on her; normally she was attracted to short men with less attractive but characterful looks. However, she could already feel Conor Brady's energy, and it made him so much more than just a face full of perfectly formed features.

'I know exactly what you can do,' Conor lowered his voice and leaned into her, 'Star Bligh.'

'You do?' Star said, entranced.

'Yeah. You can take me out for a drink.'

Star felt her pale cheeks go pink. 'How do you know I'm single?'

'And how do you know I meant that sort of drink?' The Irishman grinned.

Star faltered. 'It's . . .'

'It's non-negotiable, that's what it is,' Conor butted in. 'Now, how about I meet you in the Ferryboat tomorrow night, shall we say seven o'clock?'

Chapter 7

'Oh my God, Kar, you didn't warn me how handsome he was.'

Kara was loading the dishwasher in her apartment overlooking the estuary, her mobile resting between chin and shoulder. 'Get down, James Bond!' she shouted. Star moved her ear away from the handset. 'Sorry, Star. The bloody cat keeps jumping up on the worktops lately. Anyway, I thought you only fancied ugly men, but from that tone you've obviously changed your mind. And with all the goings-on last night, I haven't even met this Conor myself yet.'

'I don't know what it is, there's just something about him. An energy. And I like it.' The animation in Star's voice came over loud and clear.

'Saying that, you've always had a bit of a thing for Big Frank,' Kara pointed out, closing the dishwasher door.

'I think that's the glint of bad boy in him, not his face or physique.'

'You're funny.' Kara giggled. 'Hang on a sec, Star, Billy's waving a menu at me. Yes, get a large Meat Feast and some of those warm cookies. We've got salad and coleslaw in the fridge,' she called. Billy put his thumb up and went back into the lounge to order their takeaway. 'Sorry about that. Come round for some pizza and a glass of wine if you like.

I've persuaded him indoors to watch *Strictly*, so that's our Saturday night sorted.'

'It's not even three months yet and you're like an old married couple already.'

'Good, isn't it?' Kara laughed. 'Anyway, back to you and the sexy one. So, did you say sorry to him?'

'Of course I bloody did,' Star ranted. 'I'm still cross that you didn't tell me he was moving in and then none of this would be an issue. I wouldn't have got spooked and called the police and I wouldn't be going for a drink with a complete stranger tomorrow night.'

'Don't be arsy. I didn't tell you as it all happened in such a blur. I had hardly any warning myself. You were sad at lunchtime, it was a busy market day and then you were at your auntie's in the evening, so I didn't get the chance. And it's all OK now. Over and done with. Monique spoke to the policemen and explained how it had all been a terrible misunderstanding – that Big Frank had been moving stuff into my flat to help me out and it had been him that you had seen. He only started running down the hill because he had the fireworks to light. Conor just kept out of the way, then went back up to the flat at midnight when the coast was clear.'

'That makes it all a bit weird though, don't you think? Why not tell them the truth?'

'Frank has assured me that everything is kosher. Just said it was best that his nephew wasn't seen by the police down here for a while. That the reason he is down here in Cornwall is to be incognito. I do trust Frank.'

'I do too. But now I'm intrigued to find out what Conor has done. He could be an axe murderer, for all we know.'

'I very much doubt it. Anyway, you can ask him over that

drink, can't you? It's exciting and I want to know every single thing about it.'

'I love the way you are so blasé about it all. He basically said that me taking him out for a drink was the only way he would ever forgive me.'

'You've got to admire his balls, I guess.' Kara laughed rudely, adding, 'And I'm really impressed you are going, mate.'

'I'm still not sure if I should though.'

'Give me one good reason why you wouldn't meet him.' Kara blew a kiss at Billy as he came into the kitchen, poured her a glass of red wine, then took the bottle back through to the lounge.

'Well, what if he really likes me?'

'I think you're more worried about you liking *him*,' Kara replied wisely.

'Don't be clever with me.' Star hesitated. 'Should I go, then?'

'Yes! You must. Have a drink, have a chat. How lovely to be in male company. It's been too long, and you really do deserve some fun, mate.'

'What about Jack?'

'*What* about him?' Kara harrumphed. 'Jack is in New York. Jack has a girlfriend! If Jack cared, he would have contacted you. Stop overthinking it and just enjoy the moment.'

Billy appeared, leaned over Kara's shoulder, and spoke into the handset.

'Just get him drunk, Star, take him home and shag him senseless. Now, are you coming down for a glass of Shiraz and a Cha-cha-cha with us, or what?'

47

Chapter 8

'Now I don't want you getting me drunk and taking advantage of me, you hear?' Conor placed the large glass of white wine down in front of a nervous-looking Star and took a seat opposite her in the little wooden nook next to the open fire.

She shook her head in mock horror. 'In your dreams, but thanks for the drink. I don't usually have a large one.'

Conor smiled. 'And don't be opening me up for innuendo already, little one. I'm pulling out all my gentlemanly stops here.'

Star remained deadpan. 'Well, as long as that's all you pull out this evening.'

Conor put his hand to his forehead. 'That one just slipped out, sorry.'

'Ha ha! I bet you say that to all the girls.' Star felt instantly comfortable as they laughed in unison.

They both took a drink. 'You look nice,' Conor added casually.

'Thanks.' Star blushed. It had taken her over an hour of taking clothes from the wardrobe, trying them on, throwing them off, only to end up in the outfit she had put on in the first place. She wanted to look good, but also as if she hadn't made too much of an effort. It was, after all, just a chilly Sunday night in a quiet local pub. So skinny blue jeans, a cream cowl-neck jumper and her knee-high black suede boots had made the cut. Her steel-blue eyes were smudged with a navy eyeliner and black mascara, while her midnight-blue velvet coat always made its own entrance, and a dash of light pink lip gloss finished her look off perfectly.

Conor caught sight of her silver drop earrings in the shape of dolphins.

'Dolphins, eh? Frank was telling me you sometimes see them off the coast here.'

'Yes. Penrigan Point is a good area to spot them. I saw some once. It was magical.' Star felt sad. 'I never seem to find the time to go up there now.'

'Wow. That's so cool. They come just in the summer when the water is warm, I guess?'

'Sometimes in the winter too,' Star replied knowledgeably. She cocked her head to the side. 'You don't strike me as a man who likes nature.'

'That's a very sweeping statement on a first meeting. So, what do I strike you as then?' The handsome Irishman smiled his lopsided smile, causing his dimple to fire up, then took a drink from his pint of cloudy cider, with a grimace. 'Jesus, this'll put even more hairs on my chest.'

Glad of the diversion, Star agreed. 'Yes, the locals call it Red Apple Ruin.'

'They've all gone home for a lie-down by the look of it,' Conor noted, making her laugh. 'Is it always this lively in here?' He looked around. The pub was empty save for two men quietly chatting at the bar and another couple deep in conversation in one of the window seats.

'The Ferryboat does amazing roasts on a Sunday, so it's rammed at lunchtime, and in the summer it's a huge tourist spot, but it's end of season now, and it is bloody cold.'

'All the seafaring memorabilia around this place reminds

me of where I used to live in Ireland. I'm a country boy at heart, really.'

'Yes, I love the lobster-pot lights in here. The pub is so old and it's kept its original look.'

'Unlike London where it's now all fancy wine bars and gastro pubs.'

There was a short silence. They then both went to speak at once. 'You go first,' Star said, taking a large mouthful of wine and looking right at him. There was no denying that Conor Brady was jaw-droppingly good to look at. His plain round-necked black jumper accentuated his wide muscly back and shoulders and went well with his dark blue jeans, which were snug and trendy. Star could see that his designer trainers were expensive but understated. She loved the way his hair tumbled all over the place above soulful eyes of a molten chestnut brown. Add in the accent and he would make even the most reticent of romantics swoon.

Conor cleared his throat. 'Did you know that dolphins are able to see beside them, in front of them and even behind them because their eyes are placed laterally, one on each side of the head?'

Star smirked, the alcohol already loosening her tongue. 'You'd better come back in your next life as a dolphin by the sound of it then.'

Conor laughed loudly and lifted his glass to tap hers. 'Very good,' he said, 'but you still didn't tell me what I struck you as.'

'Hmm.' Star thought for a second. 'OK – first impressions. A lovable rogue. The kind of guy I'd warn my daughter about. Your reputation already precedes you, I'm afraid.'

A shot of electricity ran through her arm as Conor took her hand across the table. 'It wasn't a good start for us both, was it? Look, I'm so sorry if I scared you. Some random man in a black hoody appearing from nowhere must have been terrifying.'

'Aw. That's sweet of you but I'm the one who's supposed to be apologising to you. I could have got you arrested.'

'Yeah, and nobody likes a grass.' Conor patted her hand, then noticing the look of horror on Star's face, he reached up and put his finger gently on her button nose. 'I'm joking, beautiful. Look, I haven't actually done anything wrong. Kind of ironic really that I should get accused of a house break-in because that's the very reason I'm here. A real-life break-in took place at a big house in Kilburn, that's in north-west London where I was living, and it was pinned on me. The Bradys have a reputation of being able to look after themselves where I come from, so it was a surprise that some dodgy gang should have tried to set me up. Star, I'm no more a thief than you are.'

Star listened in silence as he added hastily, 'Don't get me wrong, I'm not a saint and I don't turn down knocked-off gear if I get offered something I want, but I don't go looking for it. I'm certainly no hardened criminal and I wouldn't go into someone's home and rob them. To me, that's despicable. However, they did a good job of putting me at the scene when in fact I was tucked up in bed in my shared flat watching a film.'

Realising he was from the same pod as his uncle, both in type and demeanour, Star relaxed. His blatant honesty was refreshing. She didn't condone petty crime, but it didn't shock her. Having her whole life been party to her mother selling home-grown weed had put paid to that. This sideline had introduced the girl to an array of dubious characters, one of whom, according to her mother, had been Star's own father.

'Poor you,' she said now. 'That must have been so worrying.'

'Yes, and expensive. Every scrap of my savings went to pay for a lawyer. My Da and Frank had to chip in too. Thank God justice prevailed.'

'At least you had some savings. So, what do you do for a job?'

'I did a business degree but ended up running a small landscape gardening firm. I soon realised that being stuck in an office wasn't for me.' Conor scratched his head, making his curly hair even more untidy. 'Unfortunately, that's all gone now,' he said. 'To raise money I even had to sell my van and my tools.'

'So why run away from it all?'

'I needed to clear my head. Get away from toxic people, from obsessive thoughts of revenge. Frank and Monique are great and I feel safe down here.' He took a big drink from his pint glass. 'So, that's me and my story: at thirty-six years old I've come to a picturesque estuary town with a bag full of hope, empty pockets, and a heart open to anything.'

Star put a hand to her chest. 'Aw. That's tough stuff. I'm sure I can find some people who may want their garden landscaped, their lawns mown, their bushes trimmed even.' Steren Bligh shocked herself at this subliminal flirtation.

'You're sweet.' Conor suddenly looked slightly sad. 'Talking about it has brought the enormity of it home. In fact, it's made me question where home has ever been really.'

'Well, I know it may sound cheesy, but Hartmouth is a place full of kindness. People look out for you here and the few who might not aren't worth your time anyway. If they know you are related to Big Frank too – well, you'll be more than fine.'

'That is good to hear, thank you, and from what I've seen and who I've met so far, I'd agree with you.' He lifted his empty glass at Star. 'Another drink?'

'It's my turn.'

Conor ignored her and made his way to the bar, coming back to put her wine down in front of her and ask, 'Talking of bushes that need a trim, how's yours shaping up at the moment?' The Irishman's face remained straight.

'I'd rather talk about dolphins if you don't mind.' Star appeared outwardly calm but couldn't deny that if this man did ask her if she wanted to go back to his, she would most certainly be showing him her very unkempt lady garden. What was happening to her? It was as if she had suddenly been put under the kind of love spell that her mother would cast whenever there was a full moon and Estelle was in search of an intimate connection. Which was quite often.

'I also have an interesting fact about dolphins,' Star said. 'Hang on, I just need to google it so I get it right.' She read from the screen. '"*Dolphins are one of the most spiritual animals in human culture . . . their instinct surpasses that of all other mammals so they only bestow guidance and protection to the chosen few.*"'

Conor cautiously took a drink of his fresh pint of cider, then looking right into Star's eyes, he said with no hint of a smile: 'I knew I came here for a porpoise.'

Mid-sip, Star nearly choked. Her head went back, and she shook with laughter. Every time she tried to contain herself, she started laughing again. Tears ran down her cheeks, taking her mascara with it. When she was able to talk, she wiped her eyes with a tissue from her pocket. 'I really must stop drinking,' she giggled. 'I'd forgotten how good it was to laugh!'

'And there's me thinking it was just my wit causing such mirth. Your eyes look even bluer when they have tears running through them, you know. You are a stunning girl, Star Bligh.'

'Yeah, yeah. I've heard that before. Beauty is just skin deep, Conor Brady.' She over-pronounced his name.

'Well, if it makes you feel better, you don't fool me one little bit. I can tell that under that perfect exterior you are a complete and utter bitch.' The Irishman smirked.

Star let out another tinkly laugh. 'At last I've been rumbled.'

'Seriously though, why hasn't someone as gorgeous as you been snapped up already?'

'That question! I have a daughter, she's seventeen. I guess I've put her first.'

'Ah, OK. I think I saw her earlier, she is the spit of you. On the flower stall, right?'

'Yes, that's my Skye.'

'Cool name too.'

'So, call me a freak, but I haven't had a serious relationship since she's been around really. You?'

'Not a freak, just protective.' Conor sounded knowing.

'My mum, Estelle – which yes, also means star in French – wasn't and isn't much help. I was always the adult where she was concerned. But I don't want to talk about her, or me, for that matter.'

'There's a whole planetary vibe going on there. What's your granny's name – is it Cloud?'

'She died before I was born.' Star blew out a noisy breath. 'On the same day as my grandad, actually. Her name was Lilian.'

'Jesus, talk about me putting my big foot in it. I'm sorry. Feck it.'

'It is what it is. A very sad tale and one I do my best to accept and get on with now.' Star shrugged.

'So, I've been married before,' Conor blurted out in an attempt to divert the attention of the pretty woman in front of him. 'She was called Maeve,' he went on when he saw that Star had pulled herself together and was listening. 'Even saying her name leaves a bad taste still. We met at school in Ireland. Back then it felt like she was the only girl in the world for me. Twenty-one we were, when we tied the knot.' His own face now looked sad. 'I have a son, Niall. He's eleven.'

'How lovely,' Star cooed. 'I've always wanted a little boy. What happened? If you don't mind telling me, that is.'

'She cheated on me with a mate. It was either kill him or get away from the little town I grew up in, so I never had to look into their deceitful eyes again. My dad arranged for me to stay with family in London. We divorced. I'm still in touch with my lad, on FaceTime and stuff. I send him presents.' His voice tailed off. 'But it's not the same as being there with him, you know.'

Star put her hand on top of Conor's. 'You've been through it too, haven't you?'

'No, it's grand. I get on with it. I would hate for any of them, especially my son, to know I was in any kind of trouble though. I've always paid my share for his upbringing, which is another reason why I hope to find my feet here and start earning again quickly. Frank was a diamond paying for your mate's flat upfront. I intend to pay him and my Da back every penny I owe them.'

'I thought you were only here for three months?' Star queried.

'Before Big Frank met Monique, he used to put on a funny singing voice and belt out that old Paul Young song

"Wherever I Lay My Hat That's My Home." Who knows what life will bring with it, eh?' Conor drained his second pint of cloudy cider. 'So, you say you haven't had many relationships, but you must have had some flings?'

'Er . . .' Star took a large gulp of her wine as a flashback to the summer and wild sweaty sex with Jack Murray washed over her. An urge to run came over her. 'Do you know what? It's been great, Conor, but I really must get back. I've got work tomorrow and two glasses of wine on an empty stomach is a lot for me and I—'

'I didn't mean to pry.' Conor looked perplexed. 'Tell me to shut up. I'm a nosy bastard. How about I walk you up the hill? I mean, I am your real-life boy next door now.'

Star stood up and started putting her outer garments on at speed. 'No, that's OK. I er . . . I need some air. Thanks for the drinks and it's been lovely to meet you.' She almost ran towards the door. Conor grabbed his own coat and followed her out into the freezing night.

'Star, wait.' His long stride allowed him to catch up with ease. 'Hey. I'm sorry if I upset you.' He awkwardly pulled his coat on and dragged his hood up over his curly locks. 'I need a thought-to-mouth filter, I reckon.'

It was only 9 p.m. but Hartmouth's seafront was eerily quiet and dark, apart from the fairy lights that Big Frank had put up around the cafe and along the estuary wall for his party. With heavy cloud shrouding the moon, not even one star was poking itself through to brighten the mood. A few clangs, creaks and moans could be heard from the resting boats in the estuary. Even the seagulls had gone to bed early by the sound of things. As they reached Frank's, Conor took Star's hand, shuddering. 'Jesus, it's fecking Baltic out here.' Then without warning he pulled her right into him.

'What are you doing?' Star wished she'd left that second glass of wine alone.

Then, feeling her resistance lessen, Conor wrapped his massive frame around her, engulfing her in one huge belter of a man hug. Slightly concerned that every last little bit of breath was coming out of her and would leave her like a deflated balloon, Star inhaled deeply. Oh, how good it felt. To be in the arms of someone, to feel the connection that a great big warm and meaningful hug brings.

She broke away and stared up at Conor's slightly worried face. His relief was obvious when she spoke. 'I'm not sure who needed that more, you or me,' Star said. 'The thing is though, Conor Brady, I'm not ready for anything.' Her voice was slightly slurred.

Conor held on to her hand tightly. 'You don't have to be,' he whispered, then grinned. 'It's all written in the stars, anyway, Miss STAR Crystals & Jewellery, isn't it?'

Star looked up at him. 'Are you ever serious?'

'Not often – and even less so when I like someone as much as I do you.'

Chapter 9

Billy sat in the comfy armchair right next to the roaring fire in Bee Cottage and cradled his stomach. 'That was incredible. But I feel like I'm gonna puke,' he said piteously. Since getting together with Kara, they quite often came to the Moon family home for a Sunday roast.

'That's what happens when you have two pieces of my morello cherry pie and mix it with red wine, young man. I told you one helping was enough, but would you listen?' Pearl shook her head. 'I'll get you an indigestion tablet, hang on.' And she left the room.

Kara sat on the floor at her boyfriend's feet, head against his legs. The orange of the fire lit up her face in a warm glow, and the comforting crackling sound made it hard to move. 'We'd better go,' she said eventually. 'I've got a funeral tomorrow and the flowers are needed by ten thirty.'

Billy groaned as he got to his feet. 'OK. I wonder if I can get done for being drunk in charge of a tugboat. I had far too much to drink last night too.'

'You'll be all right after a good night's sleep.'

'Who says we are sleeping, sweet cheeks?' He pinched her bottom.

Joe appeared with a tea towel in his hand. 'Have you one sec before you go, Kerry?' Her dad and Billy were the only ones who called her Kerry, taken from her full name Kerensa, meaning 'love' in Cornish. She followed him into the kitchen while Billy stayed behind and messed about with the fire, before putting the guard up in front of it.

Checking that Pearl was out of sight and earshot, Kara's father whispered, 'I want to propose to Pearl – and soon. But I'm not sure how. I want to make it really special. Pull out all the stops.'

'The divorce has been finalised already then? That was quick.'

'You say quick, but it's taken me twenty years to get around to dealing with it. And it was so easy, not to mention cheap, seeing as your mother and I have lived apart for two decades. Lord, I should have done it ages ago. Bloody Doryty.' He shook his head.

'Well, it's over now and I am so excited and happy for you, Dad. Pearl is like her name, a precious gem.' Kara thought for a bit, then: 'I know! How about Christmas Day, putting the ring in the Christmas pudding?'

'No, that's too clichéd. I was thinking more like—'

On hearing Pearl clattering down the stairs with a box of tablets for Billy in hand, Kara quickly turned to pretend she was getting a glass of water.

'What are you two whispering about down here? I can see guilt written in both your faces.'

'Err. Umm. It's someone's birthday Christmas Eve, isn't it?' Joe piped up.

Pearl smiled. 'OK, I'll let you off then, but if you are plotting something, remember – no fuss. You know me, I don't like a fuss about *nuttin'*.' She gave Joe a smacking kiss on the forehead as Billy appeared in the kitchen and gratefully took one of the indigestion pills.

'Dad, I'll call you tomorrow, OK?' Kara gave him a sly wink and a hug. 'Thanks for a lovely dinner, both.'

Billy held on to Kara's arm as they walked down from Bee Cottage towards Ferry Lane.

'That was a nice evening.' Kara's breath plumed out like a dragon's into the freezing air.

'Yes, it was. I am so chuffed your dad wants me to captain the *Happy Hart* now too. I nearly choked on my roast potato when he said it.'

'You've worked so hard and I'm proud of you.' Kara put her head on Billy's shoulder for a moment. 'And I'm proud of Dad too. He needed to let it go and the fact that he's promised to stand in when we want to go on holiday makes it perfect.'

'How lovely that he and Pearl found each other so late in life,' Billy mused.

'Look at you, being the old romantic.'

'You bring out the soft in me, you do.' Billy squeezed her bum. 'But I'm not complaining. Someone needed to.'

'Yeah, my very own Romeo.' Kara laughed.

'We'd better go to my old man and woman's soon though. You know what Mum's like.'

Kara put on the accent of Pat Dillon. 'I never bleedin' see ya nah you've got that treacle tart on yer arm.'

'You are so funny when you try and use Cockney rhyming slang, Kerry Moon. You just say "treacle" and I think you are exaggerating, just a bit.'

'I'm glad you told me that it meant sweetheart as I didn't

know what to think when I first heard your dad say it.' She reached for Billy's hand as they headed down the steep path of Ferry Lane towards the estuary.

'Poor old Darren cops it worse than me though, as she contradicts herself by going on about him *not* having a bird.'

'So, Darren's not seeing anyone at the moment then?'

'Well, seeing is a loose term. He's usually just shagging around, you know that. Now Twisty Knickers has left town and Lady Rachel from the big house sent him packing, I think he's having something of a dry spell. He's been a bit miserable lately, to be fair.'

'Oh, that's no good.'

'Yeah, he's been like that ever since I moved out of the flat and into yours. I don't think he likes being on his own.'

'I didn't even think of that. We must ask him round more. Do you think he'll be OK taking on some more shifts on the ferry too?'

'I hope so.'

'I never thought Dad would slow up,' Kara said thoughtfully. 'I couldn't believe it when he came out with it.'

'Yeah, but it's tough work out there in this weather, whatever age you are.'

'I'm so pleased for them. Pearl finishes working for good at the hospital on Christmas Eve, so they can just be together in retirement looking after the bees and the honey production. Plus, the garden alone at Bee Cottage is a full-time job, especially now Grandad Harry is not here. Billy, guess what Dad told me tonight? He wants to propose to Pearl – and before Christmas too.'

'He's not hanging around, is he? They're a bit like us two: when you know, you know.'

'Look at that wine making you all gooey, Captain Dillon.'

Billy laughed. 'You will refer to me as that at all times from now on, Kerry Moon.'

'You're mad,' she tutted.

'More money too, so that's a result, but I need to get responsible now. Daz can share tug duty, which is useful, but when he's off I will need someone else to load the cars and take the money, et cetera.'

'Shouldn't be too hard to find someone, should it?'

'Hmm.' Billy mused. 'Out of college holidays I'm not sure.'

Suddenly Kara dragged Billy into an alleyway in the marketplace and put her finger to his lips. Hoping it was some kind of fantasy she'd been hiding from him, Billy sucked her finger into his mouth and put a hand firmly on her left breast. She smacked him away and said, 'Shh!'

Star and Conor had stopped just by the side alley that led up to the Passion Flowers flat. 'Listen!' Kara hissed.

'I need a piss.' Billy stepped from foot to foot.

'Well, thanks a million for such a great night,' they heard Conor say, and Kara was delighted to hear the sincerity in his voice.

'I was supposed to be treating you, remember?' Star replied.

'That means we will just have to do it again then, won't we.' Kara made a little squeaking noise of delight at the Irishman's smooth reply. 'Do you not want me to see you right home? I mean, there's some nasty characters who lurk around these parts.'

'Get in, lad,' Billy said out loud, causing Kara to pinch his hand and make him stifle a cry.

'Ha! I think I can manage the ten metres on my own, but

thanks for asking.' Star was already walking away from the big man.

'So, do you want to do it again, then?' Conor called after her.

The slightly drunk Billy, now badly in need of the toilet, had had enough of playing hide and seek. He appeared out of the alleyway, leaving Kara with no option other than to follow.

'"Do it again, Star, you know you want to",' Billy mimicked with a belch.

'He's drunk, sorry.' Kara took in the full gloriousness that was Conor Brady. 'I'm Kara, your landlady, and this is my slightly over-served boyfriend, Billy. Sorry we haven't met properly before.'

'Hey. Good to see you – and that was kind of my fault, I guess.'

'No, it was mine for being such a snitch.' Star turned round, adding, 'OK, I'm going to bed.' She then hotfooted it down her alleyway, shouting back as she went, 'Thanks, Conor. Night, all.'

'All OK up there for you is it, mate?' Billy nodded towards the flat above Passion Flowers.

'Yeah, grand, grand. Honestly.'

'Well, just shout if you need anything,' Kara told him.

'I will. I have your number.'

'I'm in the shop every day bar Sunday, so just pop your head in.'

Billy took hold of Kara's hand possessively. 'See you around, pal.'

By the time Conor had got to the top of the metal steps leading to his new place, Star was inside, door closed and outside light off.

He had hoped that a change of scene might cause a change of direction to his life, but he just hadn't seen it happening quite this quickly. Yet despite the obvious chemistry between him and the ethereal Steren Bligh, it looked like he might have his work cut out trying to get her to love thy neighbour in the way he imagined.

Chapter 10

'You're home early, Mum.' Skye walked out of her bedroom with her tablet in her hand, her white-blonde hair tied up loosely in a scrunchie.

'Aren't I a good girl.' Star smiled.

Skye shook her head and tutted. 'So?' She removed her earbuds. 'How was your date?'

'It wasn't a date.'

'Yeah right. You haven't made that sort of effort since Uncle Jim's funeral.'

'Well, that's not a good comparison is it, really.'

'You know what I mean. You look a little flushed. What have you been doing?'

'It's cold out there. Anyway, I haven't got time for a boyfriend.'

'Who are you kidding? All you do is sit up here making jewellery and binge-watching period dramas.'

Star didn't dare admit that she was mainly doing those things to distract her from worrying about Skye and waiting for her to return home safely.

'And are you drunk?' her daughter persisted. 'I've never seen you drunk before.'

It was true. Her own mother, who was always drunk or stoned, had put paid to any desire on Star's part to lose control, especially since she'd become a mother herself. 'I had two glasses of wine, that's all, madam.'

Syke looked at her phone. 'Anyway, that's Tegan messaging. I'll see you in the morning, yeah? Love you, Mum.'

'Love you too, darling.' Star kissed the cheek her daughter offered and walked through to the kitchen to put the kettle on.

She couldn't help but smile at what had just happened. Porpoise! There was no denying that Conor Brady was hot. He was also very funny and the bad boy part of him kind of aroused her. Why couldn't she just have said, 'Yes, Conor, I'd love to see you again.' She had felt a spark, but not the immediate and powerful connection she had felt for Jack Murray, the day she had first caught sight of him across her market stall. That same evening they had made passionate love in the kitchen, the bathroom, the hallway and then in her bed. It had taken Star a week to get round to cleaning the shoe marks off the hall paintwork where she had wrapped her legs tightly around him and given herself into complete ecstasy. She remembered having to move a table and put flowers on top of it so that Skye didn't notice.

Star had to admit that that some sex would be nice. It must be around three or four months by now since that unforgettable night with Jack, which had awakened something in her that had been dormant for far too long. Maybe that was it? She hadn't had sex for so long that when she and Jack had got together, the connection had only *seemed* that much stronger. 'Hmm,' she said aloud. Conor had thrown a pebble into the pond of her brain and the ripples it was causing were preventing her thoughts from making much sense right now.

Taking milk from the fridge, she made herself a calming

cup of hot chocolate. Afterwards, she curled up on the sofa and found a meditation track on YouTube. As she listened to the hypnotic sounds of rain and birds calling through her phone speaker, her eyes closed and her thoughts became clear.

She had chosen not to question Jenifer, Kara's sister and Jack's previous work colleague, about him again as she feared that if she did so, the scary woman might literally bite her head off.

When the truth came out, Star had learned that it was in fact Jen who had sent Jack over from New York to stay at Kara's newly set up Airbnb so he could spy on Pearl. This was because Jen suspected that Pearl was planning to woo Joseph Moon with the sole aim of making a claim on his daughters' inheritance.

Star flipped open her laptop. 'One last time and I mean it,' she said aloud. She glanced at her sent messages. Four of them. All to Jack Murray and none of them having received a reply. And yet when he had bumped into Kara in New York, he had made a point of asking Kara to tell Star that he was sorry. This gave her hope. There was unfinished business between them, and she just knew that there had to be a simple explanation for his lack of response.

Her logic said to drop it, but she couldn't. What she had felt for Jack Murray was too powerful to ignore. She then asked herself: what if this was Skye or even Kara asking for her advice? She would tell them to stop clinging on like this, to have more respect for themselves – but this was different. She *couldn't* let go. It was almost as if the agony of him ignoring her satisfied a painful need in her – brought her subconsciously back to her young isolated self. To the long, lonely days of sitting on the benches on Penrigan Pier or at

Hartmouth Head car park, waiting for her mother's various lovers or lecherous drinking companions to either have left or crashed out on the sofa.

She checked the time. It would be 4.30 p.m. in New York – if he was still in New York, that was. Knowing that he didn't use social media, and that the personal email address she had originally used for him and his phone number were no longer active, her only option was to contact him via his work email. It was her only hope of ever getting hold of him. With the words 'one last time' running through her head, she began to type, *Dear Jack* . . .

Chapter 11

'Ah, Miss Bligh,' boomed Big Frank. 'Good morning. I hear you were out on the town with that nephew of mine last night.'

'You can't do anything round here these days without someone knowing,' Star said grumpily, standing at the counter and staring at the menu. She had a headache and felt out of sorts.

'Don't tell me he's upset you already?' Frank carried on refilling the coffee machine.

'No, he hasn't upset me,' Star said ruefully. 'Quite the contrary.'

'Grand, grand. Ah, here comes that Kara Moon now.'

Kara pushed open the glass door, bringing in with her a gust of wind and a scattering of leaves. 'Bloody hell,' she gasped, 'if I'd realised it was this windy, I'd have worn a hat.' She patted down her unruly ginger curls and made her way to the counter to stand beside Star.

'Want a coffee?' Star asked her. 'And I'm having some toast to settle my stomach. I had two large glasses of dry white wine last night and I feel really dodgy this morning. Have you got any paracetamol, mate?'

'Two glasses, that's an aperitif for me.' Frank put two slices of brown bread in the toaster.

'May I have a large toasted crumpet with strawberry jam

and clotted cream, please?' Kara took her coat off and threw it on the nearest table.

'Kara, did you really say clotted cream?' Star had gone pale. 'It's eight o'clock in the morning!'

'Oh, no – is it really? I didn't realise dairy products cared what time they were eaten,' Kara said cheekily. 'I'm enjoying my curves now, doncha know.'

'And so you should be, you scrumptiously voluptuous woman. I'll get this.' Star put her card against the contactless terminal. 'Being such a Skinny Minnie has its own disadvantages. I'm sure that's why I feel the cold so much, you know.'

Big Frank laughed to himself behind the counter. He would never understand women and their incessant worries about weight.

'I'm hungry for badness this morning and I'm even more surprised you weren't last night.' Kara lowered her voice. 'I know it was dark, but he's fit as a butcher's dog's dog, isn't he? I love my Billy, but bloody hell, that Conor is *super*-hot.' She handed Star a box of Nurofen.

'All right, calm down. Thank God you're having a crumpet, or you might internally combust.' Star made a fuss of taking one of the tablets as Kara went into inquisition overdrive.

'I want every detail. Is he as good as he looks? Is he funny? More importantly, what do you reckon? Was it a date? Do you fancy him? And the biggest question of the lot, do you want to shag him? I can't imagine for one microsecond that's a no!'

'Bloody hell, Kar, give me a minute.' Star shoved in a piece of the brown toast and Marmite that Frank had just delivered to their table. It was not until she had finished her mouthful that she blurted out, 'To begin with, quite honestly, if he had said he wanted to have sex in the toilet I would have considered it.'

'I knew it!' Kara shrieked.

Doing his best not to listen, Big Frank carried on cleaning the coffee machine.

'But hang on,' Kara continued, 'when I saw you, you scampered off like a frightened rabbit.'

'Right – yes. Truth is, I was SO pleased to see you and Billy.'

Kara stared at her. 'Why? You're not making any sense now.'

Star tried to explain. 'I don't want to just jump into bed with someone. You know what I'm like usually, I don't even like opening my legs for a smear test.'

At this, a now grimacing Big Frank hotfooted it through to the back kitchen while Kara put her crumpet back down on the plate.

'And look what happened with Jack when I shagged him after ten minutes of meeting.' Star went to take another bite of her toast. 'He cleared off, used me! And despite all that, and ignoring my messages, he has been etched on my mind ever since.'

'Jack was different though,' Kara said gently. 'He had a girlfriend; it was what is known in the trade as a one-off shag.'

'You don't know that.' Star became agitated.

'Oh, mate, please don't tell me he is the reason you are hesitating.'

'OK. OK. I thought of him *again* last night.' Star confessed miserably. 'And it gets worse. When I got in, I was a bit drunk,' she made a little groaning noise, 'so I emailed him.'

73

It was Kara's turn to groan. 'Oh no!'

'This is the reason I like staying sober.'

'Well, you've done it now. You're not the first and you won't be the last to do that so there's no point beating yourself up about it.'

Star looked like she might cry. 'It didn't even get through to him. The email address he had when he worked with your sister, well, there was an out-of-office automatic response saying he'd left the company. There were no more details. So that's it now. Short of loitering around outside the Dakota Building in New York, where I can only assume he still lives, I have no means of contacting him.'

'Good.' Kara licked clotted cream from her top lip. 'Mmm, this is so lush.'

'Good?'

'Yes, good, Star. It's obviously not meant to be. Forget about him now and have some fun. Wasn't it your mum who used to say to us when we were teenagers that in order to get over someone, you had to get under someone else?'

'And look what happened when I listened to that advice. Hello, Skye!' Star finally managed a smile. 'I know what you're saying is right but "The heart has its reasons which reason knows not" and all that.'

'Yeah, OK, but maybe just change the word "heart" to "fanny" on this occasion and give him a chance.'

Star couldn't help but laugh. 'You're so wrong.'

Big Frank was back behind the counter and, with his huge shoulders shaking with mirth, he eavesdropped as Kara told her best friend, 'Conor is obviously into you and he's right here, right now. He's not some unavailable bloke who is miles away and involved with someone else.'

'I suppose you're right. It scares me though, Kar.'

'I know it does, but rock the new cock, I say. Looking at the size of him, I bet he's got a huge one too.'

Ducking down behind the counter, Frank was by now silently crying with laughter.

The redhead drained her coffee. 'Shit, is that the time? I need to get to work.'

'What are you like?' Star shook her head at her friend. 'And wait a sec, I drove down, so come up with me.'

Kara was just fiddling around to locate her seat belt when her fingers encountered something on the floor of her mate's Smart car. She held up a neatly hand-rolled cigarette to her nose and took a sniff. 'Weed? I thought your dope-smoking days were over, missus.'

'Give it here.' Star grabbed it and put it in her bag. 'Skye borrowed the car last night and said she wanted to visit Mum. You wait until I talk to the pair of them!'

'How do you know Estelle gave it to her?'

'My mother thinks nothing of shoving ten tons of toxins down herself but she still insists on using those organic unbleached brown papers. Of course it's her.'

'Don't be too hard on Skye,' Kara said. 'She's just experimenting. Think what we were like as teenagers – and well before we were her age.'

'Exactly! And you don't want her turning up at work stoned.'

'Star, mate, I think you're overreacting. She probably has an odd joint with her mates.'

'You really don't understand, do you?' Star burst into tears.

Nicola May

'Oh, darling. What's the matter?'

'I try to do everything right. It's been hard not having a proper mum to support me, and I don't even know who my fucking dad is. I have never met my maternal grandparents either. My grandad was a shit, evidently. I actually hate her sometimes – Mum, that is – for not being there for me, and as much as I adore Skye, it's been so hard. And now she's smoking bloody weed!' The tears came again.

Kara put her hand on her friend's knee. 'I do hear you. My mum running off when I was thirteen was hard enough but at least I have my dad, so I can't even imagine what it's like for you.'

'Thank God literally for Uncle Jim and Auntie Flo, even though I don't believe in the big man upstairs.' Star managed a watery smile. 'They did their best, but they were busy too. I feel like I'm losing Skye and I don't think I can bear it.'

'You will never lose her; she loves you too much.'

'And what if I do fall for Conor – and what if he leaves me, just like my grandparents and Jack *and* Uncle Jim did? Just like everyone fucking does.' A wracking sob tore through her.

Kara leaned across to her trembling buddy and held her. On seeing the car parked up near the end of the ferry quay, Billy ran over to say hi. Kara quickly pointed to Star, at which he made a sad face, stuck his thumb up and left them be.

'I wish I could take some of your pain,' Kara murmured to Star. 'I'd wrap it up and throw it far out into the sea where it couldn't hurt you any more. I know words probably won't help at this time, but you are kind and beautiful and so loved, Star Bligh. And if it counts for anything, the moment I set eyes on you at our first day of school at Hartmouth

76

Primary, I knew we would be friends forever.' She carried on awkwardly rocking Star across the car seat as if she were a baby. 'I've got your back, mate. What was it we used to say? "Secrets to the grave" and all that?'

Star put her head up, mascara streaked down her pale cheeks, fronds of damp hair stuck to her face. 'I love you, mate,' she said.

'I love you too. And I will *never* leave you. And when we are grey and old, if I do go first and I'm still holding on to all your bloody secrets, I will come back to haunt you.'

Star managed a grin as Kara finished with: 'Now, are you OK to drive?'

'Yes, better now,' Star sniffed, pulling some tissues from her coat pocket and blowing her nose loudly.

'What are you going to do about the joint?' Kara asked.

'Maybe we should just smoke the damn thing ourselves,' Star said and they both laughed. 'But no, don't worry. I won't do anything crazy. I will speak to Skye, calmly. I think my issue is more to do with having a mother who gives her granddaughter drugs than my daughter smoking them, to be honest.'

'Billy's at a five-a-side tournament tonight so come round mine for dinner later if you both fancy it?'

'Thanks for the offer, but I really need to go and talk to Estelle.'

Chapter 12

'Conor, lad!' Charlie Dillon shouted, catching sight of the tall Irishman making his way into Passion Flowers. 'How're you doing?'

'I'm doing just grand, thanks.'

'Glad to hear it. Right, Conor, I've something to ask you. My son Billy could do with some help down at the ferry crossing, if you're still looking for a job?'

'Really? That's such good timing, I was literally just going over to Crowsbridge to the Jobcentre.'

'Ah, so we got to you in time then. Billy's twin brother Daz, he's being soft, says he's ill so is not working today. Right, so nip down asap, Conor, and Billy will show you the ropes. Him and Joe will be so grateful, I'm sure.'

'Thanks a million, Charlie.' Not daring to confess he had suffered from seasickness in the past, Conor pushed open the glass door to Passion Flowers to be greeted by a smiling Kara, watering can in hand.

'Everything OK?' she asked.

'Yeah, yeah, the flat is more than comfortable, thank you. And Charlie Dillon tells me your Billy could do with some help on the ferry.'

'That's right. Billy was going to call you about it today; we didn't realise you were looking for work, sorry. Both Star and Frank have been on our case.'

'There was you thinking I was on a happy Hartmouth holiday. Now that would be nice.' He coughed. 'By the way, how is the blonde bombshell? I popped in to see her at her place yesterday and she called through from the back saying she was busy. I hope I haven't upset her.'

'Family stuff, not you. Give her a couple of days.'

At that moment, Skye appeared from the back of the florist's with a face like thunder carrying a large display of brightly coloured autumnal flowers. 'I'm just taking these down to the hairdressers,' she said curtly.

'Perfect. And well done, they look fantastic,' Kara praised her.

The young girl managed a smile as Conor held the door open for her.

'Teenagers!' Kara carried on topping up some of the metal buckets of flowers with water.

'Yeah. I shall have one of those soon myself,' Conor told her.

'You have children? That's nice.'

'Just the one son, Niall. He's back in Ireland. He's almost twelve going on eighteen himself, so he is.'

'Aw,' Kara said, and when Conor just stood there looking awkwardly at her she asked, 'Did you want anything else whilst you're here?'

'Yes, please. Can you tell me if there are any flowers that Star really likes? And um . . . I don't want to pressure her, so maybe you could drop them in to her and just say that Conor says hi.'

'Hi – is that it?' Kara raised her eyebrows.

'That's pretty weak, isn't it?' Conor acknowledged.

Kara nodded. 'How about "Let me know whenever you fancy that drink"? I mean, if I received flowers with that message, I'd find it hard to say no.'

'Nothing to do with my Irish charm then?' Conor teased.

'Well, if only I'd known that all it would take to make a woman happy was a bouquet of flowers, I'd never have been single.' Much more cheerfully, he scribbled some words on the back of the Passion Flowers gift card and made his way towards the door to leave.

'Um, Conor,' Kara called after him, sounding embarrassed. 'I'd love to give them away, but . . .'

The big man turned around. 'Jesus! What am I like, eh? So full of finding work, that's me today.' He reached for his wallet and pulled out a debit card. 'It's because I didn't have them in my hand.'

Kara's face remained expressionless as his debit card was refused. She felt relieved when he spoke first.

'It's been declined, has it?' Conor felt himself reddening. 'Shit, I haven't got any cash on me either.'

'It's OK. Go and see Billy and get some work booked in. You can owe me for these.'

'Are you sure? I can get them another day, when I have the cash, it's fine. How embarrassing.'

'I'm one hundred per cent sure. Catch up soon, Conor.'

As Kara watched the handsome stranger walk out of the door, she tried not to judge him. He was Big Frank's nephew after all, another lovable rogue. And most people had hit on hard times in their lives before. He was just going through one of those. But why did she feel suddenly uneasy? Was Conor an example of 'there's no such thing as an ugly face, just an ugly person'? He certainly could talk the talk, but could he walk the walk? And it was her friend's very fragile heart at stake here.

Wrapping the assorted coloured dahlias in some blue tissue paper, she tied a big white bow around them and, popping in his note, hoped for so many reasons that her gut feeling was wrong on this one.

Chapter 13

Star felt pained as she drove past the familiar Hartmouth Head residential park sign and up the hill towards her mother's place. Skye had admitted straight away that Granny Bligh had given her the joint but promised her that Estelle had never given her one before. The girl had been intending to smoke it with her friends at the weekend and only noticed it was missing from her pocket when she awoke that morning. She was horrified when she realised that the incriminating article could well be lying around in her mum's car.

To the girl's surprise, Star handed over the offending 'herbal' cigarette to her, saying that if Skye was going to do something like this, she would rather know about it. She then warned her daughter to be careful as it was more likely to be the tobacco she would get addicted to. Smoking was the easiest thing to start, but the most difficult thing to give up. Star had learned this first-hand from her own teenage experience of smoking and working in a newsagent where the glossy packets had tempted her all day long with their promises of sophistication. It was different now that the dull-looking, rebranded packets came with such stark health warnings.

Star's logic for the way she was handling this incident was that if somebody was hell-bent on doing something, they would find a way to do it anyway. Her honest form of parenting had always worked with her daughter in the past. Growing up so close in age, it had felt hard to create a boundary between friend and mother, but Star hoped she had just about managed it. And despite this little hiccup, she did feel that her daughter was a credit to her. She would just have to believe that their love was strong enough that Skye would always want to be part of her life; would never abandon her once she knew how big the world was outside the confines of Hartmouth and its close-knit community.

Star was surprised when she arrived to find her mother sitting in a deckchair on the strip of decking outside her static home. Wrapped around her was a black blanket with white stars on it. Estelle had a glass in one hand, a cigarette in the other. A nearby candle was offering a small flicker of light.

'What on earth are you doing out here?' Star asked. 'It's bloody freezing.' She pulled the hood of her coat up over her ears. Waves crashed noisily against the cliffs below. One seagull cawed its lonesome lament. The moon again was covered in cloud, the sky black. The bass beat of reggae music could be heard thumping out from the next door neighbour's home.

'No woman, no cry,' Estelle Bligh sang out woefully. 'No woman, no cry.' Her head was lolled to the side. She had a small bruise and cut on her left cheek.

'Let's get you inside, shall we,' Star said. On the rare occasions she did visit now, finding her mother drunk or stoned had become the new norm.

'He's got no woman now. Bastard! He's left me, Star. Harley – he's gone and pissed off. We had a fight. Said he'd always wanted to go to Thailand. Did he invite me? Did he fuck.' Estelle took a slug of her neat brandy. 'So he's going to live in a hut on a beach where he can,' her voice rose to a screech, '*find himself.* Oh, what a cliché. Oh, what a total plonker!'

Star took the glass from her mother's hand and stubbed the cigarette out in the ashtray on the decking steps. She then manoeuvred Estelle inside, where it felt just as cold as out on the steps.

'Mum, I can't believe you haven't sorted out the timers on these heaters yet.'

'Stop moaning at me. Look, there's an electric fire there for now. Pop that on.'

'It looks ancient – are you sure it's safe?'

Estelle Bligh huffed. 'Stop worrying, Steren, I got it off eBay and it works lovely.' She plonked herself down on the sofa. Star sat down next to her. Taking in the warmth from the electric fire and the familiarity of the caravan she had spent so many years living in, the younger woman suddenly felt a weird sense of peace.

'I took Auntie Flo fish and chips last week,' she told her mother.

'Huh. Just because she's a God-botherer doesn't mean you'll go to heaven, you know. And haven't you enough to do without driving over to Penrigan to see that old bag?' Estelle coughed loudly without putting her hand to her mouth. 'No wonder I never see you.'

'You know she's not an old bag,' Star replied calmly. 'She's digging out some photos of Grandmama to show me. Of her when she was the same age as I am now.'

Estelle sat upright. 'What about me? I don't even have any photos of my mother at that age.' Her voice was almost childlike. 'Will you get one for me, if that's all right with Florence?' She swallowed. 'Mummy would have been eighty-three tomorrow, you know. And she would have loved you.' A lone tear began to run down her face. 'I never forget her birthday. Forty-five was no age for her to go. For them both to go.'

'And being left without a mother in your early twenties must have been awful,' Star added gently, feeling Estelle's pain in her own heart. Unable to imagine how Skye would ever cope if the same happened to her at such a young age.

'At least I could stay living here without them mithering me. There's always a silver lining,' Estelle wiped the tear away roughly with the back of her hand.

Fetching the blanket from the bench in the kitchen, Star loosely laid it around her mother and back over her own legs, in readiness for the tragic story which was sure to follow.

'Ironically, I was in Thailand myself then, travelling the world for a year and having the time of my life. I'd worked at the fruit-picking farm and saved like mad, put every penny away.' Eyes closed, a smile crossed Estelle's lips. 'Did I ever tell you this, darling?'

'Yes, you did, Mum,' Star replied patiently. 'Many times.' She braced herself for the next bit.

'Six months in I get the news that my father has struck my mother, causing her to fall and knock her head on the kitchen side. Instant and painless her death would have been, so the coroner said. Bullshit! Get me another drink, Steren, please.' Star ignored her request. 'At least Mum didn't have to find Dad hanging in Penrigan Caves, but then if he hadn't "accidentally killed her" – that's what he wrote in the note he left for me – both of them most probably would still be alive. Where's my drink!' Tears were now running down Estelle's face again as her mood changed. 'I don't know how much more I can deal with. Harley wasn't perfect, but he was good company and I'm not getting any younger.'

'Oh, Mum.' Star sighed. 'How about I make us both a nice hot chocolate and you get into bed.'

Estelle huffed. 'There's no milk. Can you make me some toast, please?' she wheedled. 'Like you always used to, with peanut butter and jam.'

Resignedly, Star went and did as her mother asked. 'What are you doing here anyway?' Estelle added suspiciously as her daughter presented her with her gooey-looking snack. 'You never visit me unless you want something.'

'I just wanted to see you, that's all.'

'Liar. Never let a fool kiss you or a kiss fool you, Steren Bligh.' Estelle sprayed toast crumbs as the words came through her, without thought. 'You hear me?' the woman slurred.

'I hear you,' Star replied, her memory jolting back to the two men her mother had also predicted her meeting not so long ago. 'Now get that down you and get some sleep. All will seem brighter in the morning.'

Skye was in the kitchen pouring herself a glass of water when Star let herself in and threw her keys on the side. 'What's going on with you then?' she asked her daughter. 'Three nights in on the trot, are you ill?'

'Funny. Work's busy, that's all.'

'Ooh.'

'What's "ooh" supposed to mean?' Skye gave her mum a look. 'And where have you been anyway? On another date?'

'No, to see your grandmother.'

'Muuum! Please don't say you had a go at her?'

'I didn't mention it actually, seeing as the new toy boy is already an ex. She wasn't very happy about it. I hope you're not going to use her as your drug dealer again, are you?'

Skye rolled her eyes. 'Oh yeah – I forgot. Talking of dates, it looks like lover boy is keen.' Nodding her head towards the sink, the teenager stalked back to her bedroom.

Star picked up the beautifully wrapped bunch of dahlias, her favourite flowers, read the message that came with them and saw that he had put his phone number on there too.

How about that drink you owe me and soon? Conor x

Chapter 14

Star was up a stepladder reaching for a box of silver necklace clasps when the wind chime that she had placed against the shop door tinkled to alert her of a customer.

'Won't be a sec,' she called down, wobbling slightly.

'I think I've seen that peachy little bottom of yours more times than I've seen your face.' The Irish accent made her freeze for a second. She made her way carefully down and turned to face the beauty that was Conor Brady.

'But I'm not complaining.' He smiled The Smile, causing Star to fixate on his one dimple and become temporarily mute. 'Just checking you got the flowers then?'

Star ran a hand through her hair. 'Yes, sorry. I meant to text you last night and I fell asleep.'

'Sweet dreams about me, I hope.'

Star laughed. 'You're relentless. And the flowers, they're beautiful. Thank you so much, you really shouldn't have.'

'Oh, I really should. I mean, however else am I going to get that drink you promised me? After all, Kara told me that the dahlia flower can mean finding a balance between adventure and relaxation.'

'Did she now? But it's market day tomorrow and I've got so much to do that I have time for neither of those enviable pursuits, unfortunately.'

'So, it's not a flat no then?' Conor Brady's tone was that of a man who wasn't used to being turned down.

The wind chime tinkled again as a girl with long jet-black hair and multiple piercings arrived and started to look at the earring display stand on the counter.

'I'll be in touch, I promise,' Star said briefly to the waiting Irishman, then turned to assist her customer.

'OK, and I'll sure be up for the craic when you're ready for either of those . . . pursuits, that is,' Conor said and left the shop.

With a pink face, Star served her customer then went through to her work table in the room at the back of the shop. She had bought it off eBay and loved the fact that it was covered in chisel marks and had nonsensical writing all over it, plus a variety of coloured pen doodles. The table was perfect for her jewellery-making venture. Linking her phone to her portable Bose speaker, she searched for the download of *The Very Best of Enya* album. Kara had always said that she had an old soul; Star's outlook on life and her choice of music were certainly not typical for her thirty-something years. She herself knew that it was because Estelle always used to have music playing in their cramped home, whatever time of day or night, and these melodies had stayed locked in her memory vault.

As the haunting sound of 'Only Time' drifted around her little workroom, she shut her eyes for a second. What was the worst that could happen if she dated Conor Brady and fell for him? she asked herself. Maybe she had just been holding on to Jack because there was nothing else to hold on to. Maybe what she had felt for him was just lust, because they certainly had had a lot of sex in a short period of time. Sadly, that's all it had been, just one evening of passion. In fact, she hadn't even woken up with him the next morning as Skye had been out with a friend and was due to come home. Star remembered feeling guilty and flustered as she passed her daughter in the hallway almost the very second after he had left to go back to Kara's flat down on the estuary. Jack had been staying in the room her friend had been renting out as an Airbnb then. Rushing to the bathroom, Star had climbed into a hot bubble bath with a huge grin on her face, thinking over and over what had just happened.

Love at first sight was surely a myth, she thought now. Yes, they had clicked, had even finished each other's sentences at one point. And who else had even heard of Blaise Pascal, let alone be able to quote back her favourite ever saying: *The heart has its reasons which reason knows not.* Star whispered the words to herself and felt her breath quicken as she relived the touch of Jack's hand as he had stroked her neck before kissing her for the very first time. He had smelled so good too. And his shoes . . . Fickle it might be, but shoes mattered to Star, and Jack had been wearing good trainers.

She had always believed that when the time was right, the universe would open up and her love angels would send her the man she was supposed to be with. But Jack was not only thousands of miles away but had been in a relationship already; surely her angels wouldn't make her chance at love that complicated? And if he had felt anything for her, he would surely have followed it up and been in touch with her. He had told Kara to tell Star that he was sorry. Why couldn't he have sent a message to tell her that himself? And now that she didn't even know where he worked, short of flying to New York in the hope that he might still live in a block of flats overlooking Central Park and then camping outside until she saw him, her options were decidedly limited. And anyway, that idea was perilously close to stalking.

Maybe it was time to let him go from her thoughts. Was that possible? Could you really do that? she wondered. If you didn't love someone, surely the memories of them would fade. Like when your heart felt as if it was breaking, and then one day, you suddenly realised you hadn't thought about that person for a long time. 'Only Time' would tell. Star sang along to the final lyric of the Enya song. Time was definitely a healer, but it was also a funny thing. You wanted it to go fast when you were sitting in a school classroom during a boring lesson or at a desk in an office doing a job you hated, or freezing on a platform waiting for a train to arrive. Then sometimes you ached for it to go slowly, like those delicious few hours she had spent with Jack.

Star made herself a coffee, then went back to fixing a light green peridot stone to the delicate necklace she was creating. She loved it when she had moments like this, alone with her thoughts whilst she became absorbed in the work she was so passionate about.

Jack again crossed her mind. Could she really love him after just one meeting? It couldn't be possible, surely? If she was honest with herself, Star didn't think that she had ever been in 'real' love with anyone, so how was she to know?

This was her fault for not putting herself out there after having Skye, she decided. Yes, she had felt devastated when Danny Ball had dumped her in her teens at school, but had that been love? At the time she had thought so, experiencing a heartbreak so painful that she had thrown herself into a destructive spell of drinking and smoking weed. This reckless path had led her to become involved with an older married man, and soon it was 'Danny who?' The fact that her new lover was twenty-eight made it all the more exciting, as did having sex in his car, with his insistence that it was their secret and that no one should know about them. An experienced lover, he had taken her to sexual heights she had not known existed. He gave her free weed from the stash he regularly scored from her mother and even money for cigarettes.

It had all seemed like some kind of distorted fairy tale until the day she told him she was pregnant. His expression had changed then, become frightening. He said he would have known if the condom had split. Told her that she was a lying little bitch. Had then swiped his hand across her cheek so hard he had cut her skin and created a bruise so colourful she had to keep her hair pulled around her face for over a week so that nobody would notice. She wept, begged, promised him that she was not sleeping with anyone else and that he was her everything. For fear of repercussions, he immediately gave her cash for an abortion, even drove her to the private clinic she was to go to. Then he ordered her never, ever to contact him again. It was over. He would find somewhere else to get his weed. And if she ever tried to communicate with him in any form, he would deny even knowing her name.

Star had been just sixteen years old. She was also five months pregnant at the time, as her irregular periods and tiny flat tummy had given her no indication of what was going on within. It was Estelle who, on seeing her naked one day, had suspected and gone out to buy her a pregnancy test. And when the result was positive, it was Estelle who told her that she would accompany her to the doctor straight away so that she could get all the pre-natal care she needed.

Flashbacks to the day when, thanks to her mother's intervention, she had found out she was pregnant, were so painful. It had seemed like the end of her world then. Not only was she losing the man she had become totally obsessed with, but she was also now going to be a mother at just sixteen years old. When Estelle asked who the father was, she had lied, telling her that it had been a casual encounter with another teenager, a holidaymaker on the beach. She said she didn't even have the boy's number or surname, so they would never be able to trace him.

Once Star had had her scan and could see just how well formed and far along the little baby was inside of her, there was no question of an abortion; she was going to have this baby. This decision was the one her mother had convinced her was the right one, despite Star going on to doubt it for the next four and a bit months of her pregnancy. It wasn't until the tiny five-pound wrinkly and screaming red baby was handed to her with her big round blue eyes and wispy white hair, that Star and Estelle Bligh instantly fell in love. And from that day on, little Skye Lilian became the fourth generation of Bligh women to live in the dark green static home high up on Hartmouth Head.

Chapter 15

Star could hear Boris chirping as she clomped up the uncarpeted wooden staircase to the flat above the former newsagent shop. She arrived at the top to find Auntie Flo throwing the shabby cover over the noisy bird.

'Phew, that's better. He's been full of it today, naughty bird. This might quieten him down a bit, but I'm not promising anything.'

'Have you had a good week, Auntie?'

'Hang on, let me put my ears in. I took them out to shut Boris and the world out for an hour. Bloody marvellous they are.' The old lady reached for her hearing aids on the side. Today, she was wearing a brightly patterned shift dress. There were all sorts of whistles coming from her ears for a second, which Boris then took on himself to replicate.

'You can get new ones of those, you know,' Star said, concerned.

'Bird or hearing aids?' Florence Sibley said wittily. 'Why would I waste my money? These National Health ones work perfectly well once I set them right.' The screeches carried on as she continued to fiddle, adjusting the settings.

'You've got a new dress by the look of it,' Star said loudly.

'Fifty pence from downstairs. It's D&G, this one.'

Star laughed. 'I love that you know more about fashion designers than me.'

'Fashion designers, dear? I'm just saying what's written on the label. Are they a good shop then? I much prefer M&S.'

Star went through to the kitchen and plated up the two warm and white parcels. The mouth-watering aroma of fish and chips began to fill the room.

'You're eating with me again, I see,' Auntie Florrie noted. 'To what do I owe this pleasure?'

'Probably me wanting to shut the world out too for a while.'

'Oh, duck, what's wrong? The oven's already on low, pop our dinner in there and let's sit by the fire for a second.'

Star put her head back on Uncle Jim's winged armchair opposite her auntie, no barrier between them, the glowing fire to their side. She let out a big sigh. 'Where to start.'

'Take your time, my dear.' Florence Sibley reached for the chain around her neck and put on her spectacles, nearly dislodging the hearing aids. 'You're looking well – whatever's going on with you?'

'It's just . . . well, Mum and Skye and men.'

'The plural of "men" makes me slightly nervous there.'

Star managed a smile. 'With Mum it's situation normal really. I don't see her enough and feel guilty, but when I do see her, she is usually in such a state and sometimes I feel I can't carry on pulling her through everything. It's not my job, is it?'

'No, it's not your "job" but this love lark has a lot to answer for, doesn't it. Your mum is a grown-up and she has all the tools to take responsibility for herself. She smokes that muck, she drinks. But I daresay she has a lot she needs to escape from in that mind of hers. It's such a shame, Star, love. I told you I can't relate to her when she is the way she is now. But I pray. I always pray.'

96

'She told me the story about Grandmama and Grandad for the millionth time,' Star said quietly. 'It doesn't get any easier to hear.'

'I know, sweet Star. We have all suffered in our own way and I have been so lucky that I had my faith to see me through.' Auntie Flo sniffed. 'I found the few photos I have of dear Lilian if you'd like to see them.' She produced an envelope, which she had pushed down the side cushion of her chair.

'Aw.' Star was surprised and pleased. 'She looks like me.'

'The spit of you. Thirty-three she was when that photograph was taken – the same age as you are now, in fact.' Flo's voice went into a whisper. 'My little sister,' she mused. 'Fifty years ago. In a way it seems like yesterday. Proof that life is very fleeting.' The old lady paused. 'And it has moments you must seize.' She shut her eyes to allow a vision to flash through her mind of her husband Jim kissing her under the pier at Penrigan, when the tides used to go back way further than they did now.

'So how old would Estelle have been then?'

'Can't you just call her Mum?'

'Sorry, Auntie. I do try when I'm with you.'

'She would have been just twelve years old, I think. Look, here's one of your gran and her.'

Star looked at the pretty little blonde girl staring back at her from the faded photograph, so innocent and happy looking, with no idea of what was to come. Poor Estelle.

'I see you and have to double-take sometimes,' the old lady went on. 'It's just as if our Lilian has walked into the room again.' Florence Sibley wiped away a tear. 'Grieving is a process. We have to do it properly, take the time, or we will never settle in our souls. It's been a long time now, and

I have processed it – something I'm afraid your mother never did. I tried to encourage her, but she refused to take the help she was offered. Just stayed in that caravan on her own seeing and doing God only knows what. Me and your uncle tried to be there for her, but she was in her own little world up there on the Head.'

'She still is,' Star replied. 'That's so interesting about grief and getting it out. A bit like me being at school and someone telling me that if I didn't cry about something sad it would go back inside and drown me.' Star let out a tinkly laugh. 'How weird. I never understood that until now.'

'So true. That's why I'm glad that you still feel you can come and talk to your old auntie. Your mum did right by sending you our way, at least. And nothing fazes me. Nothing at all. You know that.'

'You don't even have to say it out loud.' They both sat looking at the fire for a while before Star broke the comfortable silence, letting all her worries flow out in a sudden stream of words.

'I'm frightened that Skye will leave home and not come back to me. I've met a man and he seems really lovely, but you know Jack who I told you about? I still have feelings for him, and I don't know if they are real or whether I've built him up into something that I shouldn't have because I'd had no one to love for such a long time.'

'Slow down, my dear. That's a lot going on in that pretty head of yours. Let's break it down into bite-size chunks, shall we? I mean, you wouldn't try and eat an elephant in one go, now would you?'

'Pretty boy,' Boris squawked.

Florence tutted at the budgie's antics, then carried on. 'It's obvious that Skye adores you. You have created a foundation of love, trust and respect with that child. Yes, she's going to find her own way in life, but that umbilical cord between mother and child will never be broken. Wherever she is, your hearts will be forever joined, and you will always be with her and she you.'

Star felt a lump forming in her throat as her wise auntie continued. 'And as for your affairs of the heart, only you can be the judge of your feelings. That Jack had a girlfriend, didn't he?' Star nodded. 'I can't condone that, but it happened, and your feelings are your feelings. And sometimes they need all kinds of managing.'

Star shifted slightly in her seat. So strong was the urge to make love to him, she hadn't even cared that he had a girlfriend.

'You spoke about another man?' Florrie Sibley never missed a trick.

'Yeah. Big Frank Brady's nephew is staying in Hartmouth for a bit. He seems genuinely nice. We went for a drink and he wants to see me again.'

'Me and my Jim used to go to the pub a lot when we were courting. I used to have a Babycham and he would have a pale ale. We both used to smoke like bloody chimneys in the sixties.'

'Well, I never would have thought that!' Star laughed. 'You're a dark horse, you are.'

'The Good Lord looked after us. Well, our lungs anyway.' It was Florrie's turn to laugh, then her face dropped. 'He was such a good man, your Uncle Jim.'

'I know,' Star said. 'He really was.'

Florrie's face then lit up again at memories of her beloved husband. '"If I make it to three score years and fifteen, I'll be happy," he would say, and he did. Died to the day on his seventy-fifth birthday. All his affairs were in order. He even gave me a bigger kiss than usual in the morning before he went down to sort the paper orders. Had told me to stay in bed for an extra cup of tea. I reckon he knew.' She became brisk. 'Anyway, he wouldn't want us to dwell on it, this life is for living. What's this new chap's name?'

'Conor. His name is Conor, and I do like him, Auntie.'

'Well, that's a good start. Is this one single?'

'Yes.' Star smiled. 'And Irish.'

'Oof, he'll be giving you all the blarney then. Sexy too, I bet?'

'Auntie!'

'Not everyone will abandon you, Star. And if you don't give anyone a chance, well, what a sorry life that would be.'

'Where did that come from? I don't remember Mum abandoning me, if that's what you meant.'

'Physically she didn't, no.'

A quiet 'Oh' was all Star could muster.

There was a short silence, the only sound the ticking clock on the mantelpiece – a present for Jim from Flo when they had reached forty years of working at the newsagent together. She had joked that as she had always been the boss, it was up to her to buy it for him as there was no one else who would.

'What would be good for you to understand though, Star, is that there is a strong contrast between love and fear. I know you don't always agree with my Bible bashings, but the Apostle John said, "There is no fear in love; but perfect love casts out fear, because fear involves torment. But he who fears has not been made perfect in love."'

'How do you remember all these verses? And what does it all mean in heathen terms, exactly?' Star asked, feeling a warm rush of love for the old woman in front of her.

'The Apostle John is saying that it is impossible for love and fear to harmoniously co-exist. When real love hits, there will be no fear. When I met my Jim, it was as if nothing else mattered anymore. I just *knew*. In fact, I would have taken a bullet for him and him for me. And even when he was unable to give me children, it was still OK. We had Estelle, you and our Skye to fill that void. How blessed were we.' She looked right into her niece's eyes. 'Don't be afraid to jump in. Let love win. It usually does.'

Star got up and went to stand behind her auntie, putting her arms around her and nuzzling into the back of her hair as she used to do when growing up. 'I am so lucky to have you in my life.'

'Come on, that's enough of all these maudlin meanderings. Let's get our chippy tea in us, shall we? I might even get you to say grace.'

'Grace.' Star laughed loudly as her auntie heaved herself up, harrumphing and trumping at the same time.

'Pardon me!' Boris shouted from under his cover.

Chapter 16

'Have a look at my Brussels sprouts, ladies, fresh from the farm. Lovely and big, ain't they?' Charlie Dillon winked at a blushing pensioner in her eighties. 'We've got artichokes too – some call 'em fartichokes but what can you do. Better out than in, eh?' Charlie was enjoying himself, in full swing as the open-air market sprang into life on this first Saturday of November. 'Just eight weeks until the big man will be coming down your chimney, ladies. If you fancy some juicy dates for Christmas, just call on me.'

Pat Dillon tutted. 'I didn't think you could sink any lower.'

'How low, how low, how low can you go?' Charlie Dillon faked a limbo under his fully stacked fruit and vegetable stall. His wife laughed and made a face at him. 'Here, have you heard from Daz?' he asked.

'Yeah. He texted me earlier, said he's had to help our Billy out on the ferry today.'

'For fuck's sake,' Charlie grumbled. 'The van needs unloading.'

'It's all right, we'll manage.'

'I dunno what's wrong with the lad lately. I know he had the flu but he's turning into a right pansy. When I worked Covent Garden Market with my old man, even if we'd had nine pints the night before or a dodgy curry and were shitting through the eye of a needle we would still just turn up and get on with it.'

'Sometimes you are so disgusting, Charlie. Look, as I said, Daz is working with Billy today, so for Gawd's sake give it a rest. At least he's grafting.'

Despite her words, Pat Dillon too was concerned. Her twin boys had always come to her in the past when they were troubled, but she knew she couldn't pressurise either of them as it was a fine line between prying and supporting. And the worst thing she could do was to alienate Darren and push him away. She didn't want to worry Billy about his brother, but it was getting to that stage. In fact, she was surprised that Billy himself hadn't noticed and mentioned it already. But then he was totally smitten with Kara Moon, and for that Pat was happy. She liked Kara and knew she was a good 'un. Her Billy's wild days seemed to be behind him now and there was every hope that she would get the grandchildren she had always longed for sooner rather than later.

The *Happy Hart* had just disgorged a string of cars, which were now making their way up to Ferry Lane to park in the market car park. It was a fun and lucrative time to be a stallholder in the months leading up to Christmas. For budget reasons, the council left the Christmas lights permanently up, and someone somewhere had already turned them on, which added to the festive atmosphere. With the market in full sparkle, there was definitely an air of magic about the place.

A few stalls over, Star was scrabbling about on the ground to turn her little heater up, when the familiar and sexy accent she hadn't heard for over a week spoke.

'So, Miss Star Crystals and Jewellery. On a scale of one

to ten, just how much have you missed me?' Conor mimicked her soft Cornish accent and answered his own question with a high, coquettish, 'Eleven,' and laughed at his own joke.

Her face beaming, Star emerged from under the table in her little white beanie hat and thick blue jacket. A smudge of Bitch Perfect Charlotte Tilbury lipstick that she had stolen from her daughter's bedroom that morning highlighted her lips.

'I heard you crying yourself to sleep every night across the stairway, no doubt thinking, is that gorgeous Irishman ever going to brighten up my day again?'

Conor would never admit it to anyone, but it had taken all his resolve to stay away from Steren Bligh, knowing that if he were to rush her, there would be no moving forward with any kind of relationship.

'I was at home counting the money I've been saving by not taking you for a drink,' Star replied cheekily. Her auntie had made her feel so much better about the whole scenario. She really did have nothing to lose by just having fun. And now she was feeling relieved that she had stopped herself from making the first move and texting him the night before to ask what he was up to.

'Anyway, this is short but sweet, just like you, but I need to run. Billy said I could have a lie-in, but I can see the ferry loading now. Here.' Conor placed an envelope in her hand, then headed off at speed down Ferry Lane towards the estuary quay to board the ferry float.

Taking off her sparkly woolly gloves and sitting back down on her little stool so as to warm her legs and feet, Star tore open the envelope. Inside was a greetings card with a quote on the front from the famous Irish poet and playwright Oscar Wilde: *The very essence of romance is uncertainty.* Inside was a very badly drawn picture of a dolphin and written in scribbly capitals: *I TOLD YOU I WAS HERE FOR A PORPOISE*, followed by a smiley face, and *How about a walk on Sunday morning. Meet 10.30 at Frank's? Conor x.*

Star laughed out loud. Romance? She'd almost forgotten what that was. But Conor Brady got ten out of ten for trying on this occasion.

'All right, Billy boy?' Conor said gaily. Then, 'Shite, are you on your own, mate? You should have called me. I thought Darren was here with you first thing on a Saturday.' A tired-looking Billy was just shutting the back gate of the car ferry and heading for the tug to set off across the estuary to Crowsbridge Quay. A cold east wind was whipping around their ears. Small waves were lapping against the side of the ferry float. Seagulls circled in the hope they might be a fishing boat about to dump some scraps over the side.

'Nah, he's had to help out my old man and woman evidently. He texted this morning and I'd promised you a lie-in. It's fine. These early crossings are easy Hartmouth side on market day; it's the Crowsbridge end with them all piling over from about now that I need the help with.'

'Has Kara's Da totally finished for the winter now then?'

'Yes. He's ready to rest his sea legs, he told me. He's going to help me out when I go away and stuff though, so it's a win-win for me really.'

'Aye aye, skipper, and all that then.' Conor laughed.

'Exactly! And a full-time job for you – if you'd like it, that is? Daz has only ever worked part-time anyway.'

'Billy, I will bite your hand off, so I will. That is just the best news, thank you.'

'Every other Sunday off and one day a week off to my choosing, if that's OK by you?'

'I'm over the moon, I tell ya.'

'Just don't let the customers see you puking, eh?'

'Jesus, there was me thinking I'd got away with that.'

'Darren hasn't got good sea legs either. Star told him to chew raw ginger. He finds it so vile, it stops him thinking about being ill.'

'She has all the remedies, that one.' Conor nodded. 'But I'll try that, for certain.'

'Yeah, watch her, she'll be putting a love spell on you next.'

'Here's hoping.' Conor pulled his hat down over his ears causing curls to spill out in a funny shape. 'Sunday, you say. I may have a commitment tomorrow, shite.'

'Tomorrow is fine. Daz has promised me he'll be here.'

'Grand.'

Billy reached inside his money bag and pulled out five crisp ten-pound notes. 'Here's a nifty as an advance. I pay every Friday straight into your bank account and at that point I'll deduct this. I just need all your details.'

'What a man! Can I be a pain and ask you for cash instead of using my account? I could do without my overdraft sucking it all up.'

'Course. Why don't you just invoice me, then you can sort your own tax out, be self-employed. That would help me out too. Less paperwork, although I'll do my part with the insurance and so on, so you're looked after.'

'If you're sure. Ah, this is just the best thing to happen. I can't thank you enough.' Conor put the black leather money belt that Billy had handed him over his shoulder. 'Actually, whilst I remember, take a tenner back as I owe your Kara for some flowers. Tell her it's for Star's bunch, will you?'

Billy nodded, took the money, and went to get the *Happy Hart* on its way.

Conor jumped on board and was just pulling on his gloves when he heard his phone beep in a text.

Your persistence has won over my resistance. Oscar would be delighted, I'm sure. See you tomorrow. She had signed off with the icon of a star and x.

A new job, a new home, and a date with the most beautiful woman that had crossed his path for a long time. Conor Brady began to whistle while he worked.

Chapter 17

Star was just closing her flat door behind her and about to head downstairs when she heard a motorbike noisily revving outside of her market unit. Already late for her date, she ran downstairs, straight past the motorbike and down Ferry Lane to the estuary front and Frank's Café. As she got to the end of the market stalls, the motorbike pulled up alongside her and the rider pulled off his black visored helmet and shook out his hair slowly and deliberately as if in some kind of romance movie.

Star started laughing. 'Oh my God, I didn't realise it was you.'

'And I must have totally missed you walking past me. I wanted to surprise you and save you walking down the hill.' Conor Brady smiled his lopsided smile. 'Here.' He handed her an old green open-faced helmet. 'Hop on.'

'I thought we were going for a walk and I haven't been on a motorbike for years and—'

The voice of Florence Sibley suddenly crossed her mind. *'Don't be afraid to jump in.'*

Star took the old-fashioned helmet, popped it over her white beanie hat and allowed Conor to do up the strap. Leaning in closely, she could feel his warm breath on her face. Just the nearness of him and his leather-gloved fingers touching her neck caused the butterflies to awaken in her stomach, alerting a need she hadn't felt since Jack.

'Why can't I have a trendy helmet like yours?' she asked.

'Because it's the only spare Frank has.'

'I didn't even know he owned a motorbike.'

'We are men of mystery, we Bradys. Part of our appeal, don't you think?' Conor said, stepping back.

Star felt herself reddening. 'I'll only get on this thing if you go slowly, you hear me? And if I bash you once, that means go slower and if I keep bashing you after that, that means stop. OK?'

'OK.' A look of amusement spread across Conor's face.

'Where are we going anyway?'

'It's a secret.'

'Thank God I wore jeans. Why do men never think about practicalities?'

'I guessed even you wouldn't wear a ball dress on a walk.' Conor smirked. 'Now, will you just get on the fecking bike.' Star did as she was told. 'And make sure to hold on tight to me and not my rucksack or you'll be off and on the floor quicker than your knickers if I have my way.'

'What did you say?' But the din of the motorbike engine starting up drowned out her words.

Conor took Star by the hand as they walked up the steep path towards Penrigan Head. 'See? I told you we were going walking.'

'I'm surprised I can actually put one foot in front of the other after going through those country lanes on that bloody bike.'

Conor laughed. 'I wasn't going that fast.'

'You've got a visor! My cheeks were wobbling so much they were playing a tune.'

'Now *that* I would like to see.' He peered at her bottom. Star tutted. 'You're a rude boy.'

'And you have a dirty mind.' Conor pulled her arm. 'Come on, let's get to the top. We can have a coffee there to warm us up.'

After fifteen minutes of solid walking, they reached the end of the cliff path, which flattened out to reveal a jaw-dropping vista. The grey winter sky mirrored the calm sea below, where coastal birds bobbed up and down on the white-tipped waves as if on some watery fairground ride. On spotting a shoal of fish darting under a rocky shelf at the bottom of the cliffside, the birds dived at them, shrieking their approval.

The couple set up camp between two large rocks and sat down on a blanket that Conor had stored in his rucksack. Star sipped a coffee from a flask that Conor said he had found tucked away in a drawer in the kitchen above Kara's shop.

'Nature lover and Boy Scout,' Star said. 'I have got you wrong on so many levels.'

'It's not only you who likes to think of themselves as more than just a pretty face, you know,' he told her.

Star nursed the plastic cup warming both her hands. 'It's so nice to get out of that wind.'

'True. It's also nice to get out of "that London",' Conor added.

'I bet. It is so quiet down here, but I just love the sea and the open space. Makes me feel alive,' Star said dreamily. 'I get an energy from nature like nothing else.'

'I hear you. I grew up in a beautiful setting in Ireland

too, but life happens. London happened.' Conor sighed. 'But I'm here now and at least I have bagged myself a job already.'

'Billy took you on, then?'

'Yes, full-time too, even though he'd already sussed my seasickness. I've renamed the tug the *Happy Hurl.*'

Star couldn't help laughing. 'That is so funny, but the good news is the crossing is short so at least you can recover each time the car float is filling up again.'

'It hasn't physically happened yet, thank goodness. Not a good advert for the business if it does though, is it, a so-called ferryman heaving over the side?'

'Holding a sapphire may help with the motion sickness. Or chew some ginger even.'

'Already on the ginger, thanks to you.'

'Ah yes, Darren is the same. Good! At least some people listen to me.'

'I kind of get it about the natural stuff working, but do you really believe all that guff about crystals and healing or do you just kid people to make them feel better about them-selves?'

'Said the real-life charlatan to the crystal jeweller.' Star took a sip of coffee. 'And yes, Conor, I do believe in it.'

Conor looked up and out to sea. 'OH . . . MY . . . GOD! Quick!' Taking Star's cup, he rested it on a rock, then dragged her by the hand towards the cliff's edge where he stopped and pointed to the ocean below.

'Look, look! Would you believe it?'

Star made a little shrieking noise. 'A dolphin! In November too. Wow.' She squeezed Conor's hand.

'Well, I told you I was here for a porpoise.'

'Don't you set me off again.' Star stared down at the creature who appeared to look up at them, turn, then disappear into the waves. 'A Harbour Porpoise,' she said. 'Goodbye, little fella.'

'Yes, also known as Phocoena phocoena.'

Star couldn't stop giggling. 'You're making things up now.'

Conor reached to his pocket for his phone, then read aloud: '"*The Harbour Porpoise, also known as Phocoena phocoena, is one of seven species of porpoise. It is one of the smallest marine mammals. As its name implies, it stays close to coastal areas or river estuaries.*"'

'Let me see.' Star took his phone off him. 'OK, OK, so you're right, but what I can't believe is that we've seen one today.' She shivered.

'When I attempted to draw that dolphin in the card, I thought it was such a long shot that this would happen, but it was the sole reason I brought you up here in this cold. Just in case.'

'Really? That is so sweet.' Star felt the defences around her heart crumble a little.

Conor moved his feet from side to side to try and warm himself. 'Yes. I spoke to Billy and he said it was doubtful, but you did say yourself that they'd been spotted in the winter sometimes. It must be a sign, mustn't it, my little magical one.' He paused. 'Now come here, you.' He pulled Star's petite frame into him. 'I didn't realise quite how short you were.' He put his flat hand on top of her hat.

'Five foot four is average for a woman. You're just a giant.' Star closed her eyes, put her head against the softness of his jacket, and for the first time in a long time she actually felt properly 'held'.

It was only when sporadic spots of rain started falling that Conor broke free. The sky had quickly turned a slate grey. Seabirds were now making their complaint at the turning of the weather and were circling above the cliffs, ready to find shelter.

'Oh, feck. I thought we'd miss the rain.'

'The very essence of Cornish weather is uncertainty,' Star informed him.

'Witty as well as beautiful, eh? In that case, I guess we'd better head back down before we get soaked.' Star shivered again. 'Come here.' Conor pulled her to him again and instinctively pressed his mouth against her now wet nose. Suddenly oblivious to the deluge of rain, he placed his full lips on Star's delicate mouth and kissed her. A kiss so slow and precise that at that moment Star Bligh realised that, whatever this sensation was, whatever his lips brought to her, come rain or shine, she wanted more of it.

When they eventually broke free, she said breathlessly, 'Conor Brady, what on earth do you think you're doing?'

'This.' He leaned down and kissed her again.

A massive fork of lightning went from sky to sea, followed quickly by a huge rumble of thunder, which reverberated around the clifftops, sending the bobbing seabirds to the cover of cliff ledges. Sheets of rain were now aiming at them in all directions. Star's hair was hanging like rats' tails from under her hat, but she didn't care. Ignoring the storm, she kept her arms tightly around Conor's back, looked up at him and spoke.

'You know I said the other night that I wasn't ready for anything?'

'It was just a kiss, this surely doesn't count.' But Conor's sparkling eyes were speaking the same language as hers.

'Well, I think I may be ready after all.'

'I knew it wouldn't take long.' Conor smirked then held her gaze as Star made a funny face at him. 'But I can't make you any promises, *a stóirín*.'

Rain was now trickling from each strand of his curly fringe. He grinned his boyish grin as Star brushed his lips with hers once more.

'I prefer it that way,' Star whispered, then breaking away she started running down the sandy cliff path, shouting back through the rain: 'Last one back to the bike buys the pasties!'

Chapter 18

Billy sprinted up the metal stairs to his old flat two at a time and bashed on the door, shouting, 'Daz! It's me. I forgot my key. Hurry up, I'm freezing my balls off out here.'

His twin brother opened it, then without a word walked back into the lounge. The football coverage had just started for the mid-week match between West Ham and Tottenham. From ten years old, the twins had never missed watching a match together when their beloved Hammers were playing. Their dad, an ardent season-ticket holder, would take them to every single home game as soon as they were old enough to enjoy it.

'Blimey, it looks like a bomb's hit this place.' Billy looked around in dismay. The usually tidy lounge was scattered with pizza takeaway boxes and crushed-up cans of lager, and the small open-plan kitchen area was stacked with dirty plates and mugs. There was a distinct smell of a full rubbish bin about the place.

'Don't you start,' Daz growled. 'Dad's already been up here, screaming and shouting at me for not showing up for work today.'

'Thank God I've got Conor on the ferry now or I don't know how I'd be coping either,' Billy agreed.

'Yeah, why don't you stick the knife in too, eh.'

'Shit. I didn't mean to have a go. It's just . . . you've not been yourself lately. You're a grafter usually. So what's going on? I don't get it.'

'It's nothing.' Darren Dillon slumped down on the beanbag and looked up at the huge flat screen that they'd fixed on the back wall of the spacious lounge when Billy had been living with him. He opened a can of cold lager and began to drink.

Frowning, Billy sat down on the sofa behind him. Something was definitely wrong. His brother had become almost hermit-like over the past few weeks. Daz had never been one for exercise, but it was obvious to see he wasn't looking after himself now in any shape or form. He had put on weight. His West Ham shirt had a food stain down it. Even his normally shaved head had growth coming through and he was sporting a scruffy beard, which shocked Billy, who was used to seeing his twin clean-shaven, smart, and smelling a lot more fragrant than he did today. The only thing that was shining bright was the diamond stud in his ear. The boys had always been seen as chalk and cheese, with Billy's almost black hair cut into a trendy style with a floppy fringe and his lean body the opposite to his brother's soft one. But what they did share was a wild and wicked sense of humour, and unconditional love and respect for each other.

'I know since I've moved in with Kara, I haven't seen a lot of you,' Billy tried.

'I'm happy for you, mate. It's not that. Look, can we just watch the match together like old times?'

'Are you ill?' A feeling of panic gripped Billy.

'Nah, I'm all right.'

'Are you in trouble then?'

'Bill!'

'Is it a woman?' Darren shut his eyes as if to contain himself, but his younger brother by two minutes didn't let up. 'I didn't think you cared about that Lydia Twist or Miss Fancy Pants from Crowsbridge Hall – I thought they were just mindless shags.' He thought then exclaimed, 'Ah, I know what it is! You really were in love with Lydia Twist, and she moved away. Is that it? That *is* it, isn't it.' Billy knew if he just kept pushing, Daz would eventually snap.

Darren leaped up from the beanbag. He was shaking. 'Bill. Can you just shut the fuck up for a minute? Please. Actually, why don't you just fuck off home. I'm sick of the lot of you. Mum wanted the old man to come over tonight too. Can't you all just leave me *alone!*'

Feeling a sudden anger, Billy grabbed hold of his brother's shoulders and stared deeply into his matching indigo-blue eyes.

'I know you better than you know your fucking self,' he said.

'No, you don't.' Darren's eyes were welling up.

'Whatever it is, we go through it together – like we always have. I promise you that. Darren, you're my twin. My other half, for God's sake!'

Darren's bottom lip wobbled. He kept his brother's gaze for a second, then pulled away and slumped back on to his beanbag. 'Just be here, can you?' he said quietly.

Billy opened a beer, pulled up another beanbag and, touching elbow to elbow with his brother, began to watch the match.

Chapter 19

'Honestly, Kar, I'd forgotten how fantastic good sex makes you feel,' Star said as the two of them started their second lap of power walking around the perimeter path of Duck Pond Park. 'I've gone from wanting Skye to always be around me, to now loving it when she says she is staying out at Tegan's, so she doesn't know what I'm up to. What sort of mother have I become?'

'A horny one by the sound of it,' Kara replied. 'What a difference a year makes, eh? Me finding love with Billy and you . . . well, I guess it's not love yet, but getting it on with the handsome Irishman.'

'I can't believe how quickly it all happened.'

'I'm just so pleased that you've moved on from Jack.' There was a silence, which Kara broke. 'You have, haven't you?'

'Jack was different. I can't . . . well, look, Conor is such a laugh. We have so much fun together. He can cook too, which is a bonus, so I quite often go round to your flat next door for food. I feel like I'm getting so fat.'

'Nonsense, and it won't do you any harm if you are putting on a pound or two. What's Skye said about it all?'

'I think she's just loving the fact that I'm not constantly chasing to find out where she is and moaning if she's late home, to be honest.'

Kara checked her Fitbit. 'Surely nearly two miles of power walking equates to a cake of some sort.'

'That's not bad for a lunch break. What's the time, anyway? I put *Back in 1 hour* on the shop door and I want to have a quick wash before I start again.'

'We can finish the lap,' Kara said breathlessly. 'Conor's doing well with Billy too. Daz is not pulling his weight at the moment, so thank God Conor came along when he did.'

'He came in like a wrecking ball.' Star suddenly started singing.

'I'm not sure I can get used to you being this happy.'

'Do you not sometimes spontaneously sing, and the words are kind of relevant to what's happening in your life?'

'I've never really thought about it, but I'm going to from now on, obviously. A wrecking ball though?'

Star laughed. 'Anyway, it's about time I felt like this. Even though I've got this new person in my life now, weirdly I feel so much freer.'

'And long may it continue, I say.'

'I never really ask you about Billy, just assume you are still love's young dream.'

Kara was puffing hard now. 'Yes, in fact it's the nearest thing to perfect I think I'll ever find.' And as two swans swam up to the side of the pond next to them, she panted, 'Aw, we love our swans. Wasn't it you who told me they mate for life?'

'Yes. They are also a symbol of motherhood,' Star added. It was Kara's turn to go quiet.

'Oh my God, Kar, you're not, are you?'

'Not yet.'

'Which means you're trying?'

'Practising, we like to call it, but don't say a word to anyone.'

'I'm so excited.' Star made a little screeching sound. 'I've always wanted to be an auntie like you are to my Skye! So, you're not planning to get married first then?'

'I was thirty-four in September; I need to get a move on.' Kara sighed. 'I think I'm nearly in the older mother category already.'

'Oh stop, you're still a spring chicken.'

'Pearl, you know she's a nurse, well, she told me that the medical term for a pregnant woman aged thirty-five and over is senile gravida.'

'Oh. Well, you're not over thirty-five, so just keep practising, I say. And you can still get married. I love a wedding! The last one we both went to was Clara Southgate's, wasn't it? How on earth did she bag someone so bloody handsome? At school I don't even remember her having one decent boyfriend.'

'I think she only invited us to the evening do to show off and also to inform us that he was almost as rich as Richard Branson.'

'Yeah, you're right. I refuse to attend an evening do ever again after that one. I'm nobody's afterthought. There should be an addition to evening invitations stating: *You weren't good enough to come to the main event. I just needed to up the numbers to make us look even more popular and interesting.*'

'What are you like?' Kara stopped walking and looked at her Fitbit. 'Anyway, let's see, eh? I don't want to upstage Dad and Pearl.'

'Blimey, so much news.'

'He hasn't asked her yet, so that's between us for now.'

'I'd so love another baby one day,' Star said wistfully.

'Play your cards right with Mr Ireland and maybe you will.'

'I don't think he's the settling down kind. He's already said he couldn't promise me anything.'

'Oh. Right.' Kara was suddenly serious. 'Joking aside, be careful, won't you, Star? With Conor, I mean.'

'I'm not stupid, mate.'

'I didn't say you were. But he's a Brady. He will be clever.'

'Clever at what?' Star asked. 'The only thing I've got worth stealing is my heart, if that's what you mean.'

Kara grabbed her friend's arm. 'I don't know what I meant. Come on. We'd better get back to the market so that daughter of yours can have a lunch break.'

Chapter 20

At the tinkle of the STAR Crystal & Jewellery wind chime, Star walked through from the back to find a familiar customer standing in the shop.

'Morning, sassy Star,' said the much-loved Joe Moon, father of Kara.

'Hey, Joe. How are you doing?'

'Fine thanks, pet. But I need to be quick. I told Pearl I was just popping out to get some fruit and veg. We are picking up a new dog from the RSPCA centre in Penrigan at lunchtime.'

'Aw, Kara didn't mention it.'

'No, we only saw this little beauty a couple of days ago. I will invite Kara up later to meet him, and you're always welcome too at Bee Cottage, you know that.'

Feeling warmed by his affection, Star said, 'So, come on, details please.'

'He's a black Labrador, an oldish boy – nine, I think they said. His owner had died and well, Pearl took one look at his sad little greying face and that was it.'

'An old lady used to come into Sibley's when I was working there. She had a Labrador, told me he literally used to eat everything, other dog poo included. The breed are renowned for it evidently.'

Joe laughed. 'Ew, what have we signed up for?'

'Does he have a name?'

'Yes, Bob.'

'Bob the Dog, that's funny.'

'We can't change it now; he's been Bob all his life so yes, Bob the Dog *Moon* is coming *soon*.' Joe looked pleased at his rhyme, then remembered and said, 'Down to business, my girl.'

Star put her hands flat down on the counter. 'Yes, so what can I help you with today, sir?'

'A ring.'

'An off-the-shelf kind of ring or a bespoke one, perhaps?'

'Bespoke?'

'Yes. I can create one to whichever design you like. You choose a stone, and we work on a design and I make it for you.'

'Well! I never knew you did that, young 'un. Proper job, that is. It's a special ring, see.'

'A special ring.' Star nodded. 'OK, so a special ring I shall make for you.'

'It's a secret too.'

Star thought it so sweet that he didn't want to let the engagement cat out of the bag.

'So, when do you need it for?'

'As soon as you can do it really, please.'

'Now, what do you reckon would suit your Pearl? I assume it is for her. You haven't got some fancy woman hidden somewhere?'

'She'd have my guts for garters if I did, can you imagine?' They both laughed. 'Trouble is, I dunno what I want. I haven't really thought about it.'

Joe Moon's well-cut white hair gave him a distinguished look against his handsome, weathered face. He was a prime example of a man who had at last found contentment in his life, and being in his early sixties he still had plenty of time ahead of him to enjoy it. Star felt such a love for the familiar face in front of her. She had grown up with Joe as a father figure in her life. In fact, she'd been labelled 'Daughter Number Three' in the Moon household. Knowing that she had no dad of her own, Joe had always shown her a care and kindness that went way beyond any of her other friends' dads. No fool, Star realised that part of this was due to her strong friendship with Kara, which had no doubt helped Joe's daughter through the difficult times when her mother Doryty Moon had left Joe and their two daughters in the lurch.

There were times when Star felt envious that Kara had such a lovely father. And it now looked as if Pearl was turning out to be the best stepmother her mate could ever have wished for, too.

Star had a flashback to when her mother had sat her down on the outside steps one balmy July night when she was just five years old. She remembered vividly having got sunburn on her shoulders and it felt so sore it was making her cry. Her mum, drunk from the huge jug of iced sangria she had been sipping from throughout the day, had made up a combination of aloe and raw honey and was dabbing it gently on her daughter's back with cotton wool.

'Where is my daddy?' Star had asked.

'He's dead to me,' was the reply. 'And to you.'

For years Star had understood that her daddy was dead. When anyone asked, that's what she had told them. Even Auntie Flo and Uncle Jim had no clue who he was. It wasn't until she reached thirteen that she asked her mother about him again. With a cigarette in one hand and a neat gin with ice in the other, Estelle had thought for a moment, then replied, 'Oh, it was some guy I met and we had sex under Penrigan Pier after getting stoned on the beach. I didn't even know his name.'

'Mum, is this true? You weren't a teenager then but a grown-up!'

'And? Does bloody age dictate where and when you can have it off? Does it, daughter?'

'You told me he was dead.'

'I had to pretend he was,' was all the woman could muster. 'But I wanted you, Steren, I wanted you more than anything in the whole damn world. I loved you, I still do. I always shall.' With that she had fallen back in her chair and promptly passed out, leaving Star having to take the lit cigarette from her fingers and the glass from her hand before it tipped down her front or fell to the floor.

'So, what do you reckon then?'

Star jumped back to reality at Joe's question. 'Firstly, and I'm guessing you might not have this, do you know the size of the finger you want it to go on?'

'Oh, bloody hell. I didn't think about that. First time around, well, Doryty had already chosen hers. I just had to hand over the money.' He made a face. 'Cost me an arm and a leg, that one did. And not just in jewellery.'

Star nodded understandingly. 'OK, maybe you can quickly trace a ring she already wears on whatever finger you are choosing it for? Or maybe she wears one on the same finger of the other hand?'

'Leave it with me. I'll sort it, or I'm sure my Kerry will help me somehow, if I can't.' Joe peered at the selection she had on offer. 'Looking at some of these you have on display, I was thinking of maybe getting something a bit different. I mean, a pearl in the ring would be the ideal, but do you think that's a bit cheesy?'

'Not at all, it will be a unique choice. A pearl will get questions and compliments about it as she'll probably be the only person who has one.' Star had a thought. 'Hang on, let me get something.'

She went through to the back to get her folder of past designs. When she came back Joe said fondly, 'I know you can keep a secret.'

Star put her hand over his. 'I can't tell you how happy this makes me, Joe. Pearl is such an amazing lady.' She did a little shimmy just as the wind chime went off again.

'Dancing on my arrival now, are you? That shows I must be special.' Conor Brady smiled The Smile, causing her to catch her breath and grin widely. 'Hello there, Joe.' Conor acknowledged him politely. 'Sorry to butt in but I'm on a quick ferry break and just wanted to tell Star that I'm cooking dinner tonight for her and me, seven thirty at my place.'

'Oh, are you now?' she piped up. 'Great. Should I bring anything?'

'Just your sweet and beautiful self. Goodbye, all.' The wind chime signified his departure.

'Star Bligh! He's smitten and so are you by the look of you.' Joe had noticed her blushing face. 'It's about time, love, and he seems like a good lad. It'll be you getting engaged next at this rate.'

'Hardly. I've only known him for a few days.'

'All I can say is when you know, you know. I took one look at Pearl's beautiful face and well, the rest is history.'

'Hmm. Well, knowing or not, we'd better get on with this or she *will* be having your guts for garters and it will be Bob the Dog shouting "Fetch" to you.'

Chapter 21

'Dinner is served, madam.'

Star's chin dropped to the floor at the sight of Conor appearing in the kitchen in just an apron and nothing else. His peachy bottom was dancing in front of her as he stirred a steaming saucepan on the hob.

'To what do I owe this pleasure on a Tuesday evening?' she asked from her front-row seat at the kitchen table.

'So, I checked the calendar, and it is four weeks today since I first set eyes on that beautiful woman who works in that Ferry Lane Market place – and in my book that's worthy of my speciality dish and some kind of anniversary toast.'

Star was very touched. Men didn't do this sort of thing, did they? 'I'm impressed.'

'Mrs Harris from the pasty shop will be here in a minute, so if you could just drink up and leave, please.' Conor carried on stirring his pot.

Star got up and pinched his bum. 'You are annoyingly funny, as well as bloody sexy, do you know that?' She pushed herself up against Conor's bare bottom, placing her hand around and up the front of his apron.

'Ah, I see madam would rather go straight to the dessert, would she? Or how about some kind of long hard sausage for starters? I know of a very succulent Irish variety.'

'I would insist on a "try before I buy" kind of basis for a delicacy of this nature.'

Conor gasped at her touch, put down his spoon and switched off the heat. 'Your wish is my command, Ms Bligh. How can I refuse?' Turning, he put his arms loosely around Star who, on looking up into his eyes, ripped off his apron then slowly and seductively began to make her way down the big man's body, kissing every inch of flesh as she did so.

'Mention of a dolphin wins them over every time,' Conor teased her.

'And I have been known to bite right through a sausage,' she said dreamily.

'Ooh, my little *stóirín*.'

'My big bad leprechaun.'

Chapter 22

Jack Murray shut the door to his Upper Westside Manhattan apartment, brushed off a few stray snowflakes from his thick black hair, then kicked his shoes off and hung his overcoat on the rack in the hallway. Glad to be home, he went through to the sleek designer kitchen, poured himself a red wine and flopped down in the living area, where he turned on a huge flat-screen TV. Wondering why all the lights were on, he scratched his bushy beard, relaxed into the grey leather sofa and took a deep glug of the comforting alcohol.

It had been a stressful day on Wall Street. In fact, every day was stressful since recently starting his new job in the financial district of New York. Working in the money markets was rewarding in one way but so fickle in others. Thinking of the clients he had worked with, he had rarely experienced the sight of money bringing happiness to any of them. The opposite, in fact: he had seen a lot of the wealthy and successful fall. Addiction was a common enemy. Cocaine had no regard for the destruction it wreaked, its victims in thrall to its malevolent power, fellow brokers included, who thought they were Wolves of Wall Street like Leonardo DiCaprio when in fact they were the complete Wankers of Wall Street.

Jack was grateful that his only vices were a fine Bordeaux and at the moment a wannabe actress who went by the name of Riley. He would be the first to admit that the fact her father happened to own this flat in the sought-after Dakota Building had been one of the deciding reasons for them moving in together. New York rentals were expensive, and if Jack were to eventually follow his dream of giving up the nine to five to concentrate on writing a successful Hollywood screenplay, he needed every leg-up he could get. Paying Riley's father a peppercorn rent was a real bonus.

When he was offered his dream job in New York working for a shrewd cookie by the name of Jenifer Moon, he had been thirty-five, a man in his prime. Ready to face the world and whatever it offered or asked from him. He hadn't expected to meet somebody quite so quickly. It was a case of life happening to him when he was busy making other plans. Also, he had anticipated a bigger bonus than the one he had actually received, so his chance of taking time out had not yet come to pass. Yes, the money trappings allowed him a great lifestyle – but was he really happy? He would much rather be finishing his new screenplay and getting it off to agents, but the vicious circle of work, sleep, eat and repeat had become robotic, and he a kind of robot. Jack wanted to make a good impression at the new firm so was working flat out, which meant he was so knackered when he got in, usually after a drink with his colleagues, that writing was the last thing on his mind.

'You're late.' A shrill American accent broke his peace.

Slightly startled, Jack raised his eyes and his voice. 'I thought you were out with Brooke tonight?'

'I couldn't be bothered in this weather. Cabs are so slow today and the traffic is terrible. I'm in the bath. Come join me if you want to.'

'I'm just having a nightcap to wind down.'

'Oh, come on, spoilsport. Bring it in with you.'

Jack went over to the window and looked out. Huge snowflakes were falling in front of his eyes, landing on Central Park and the sidewalk below. Despite the darkness he could make out a group of young guys shrieking in delight as they chased each other in a snowball fight. What was it about snow that reduced even fully grown men to children? Probably the same reason a barbecue turned them into the next MasterChef.

After the day he had had, he was quite happy to settle down in the warm and shut the noisy world out.

New York never slept, but tonight, the sirens and traffic seemed muted, as if the elements had allowed the city to doze off, just for a second. He flicked on the television to find an effusive weatherman waving around facts and figures about how rare snow like this was at this time of year, and how the city could expect another heavy fall of it from midnight.

'Jack! Come to me.' His girlfriend's sulky tones caused Jack to make a face. Knowing he would pay for it later if he didn't, he turned off the TV and walked through to the bathroom, glass in hand.

Riley Roberts, 'real name not stage, honey' was luxuriating in the huge copper standalone bath, up to her neck in a veil of thick bubbles. At twenty-five, her body was fit and toned. Her blonde crop made her resemble a young Gwyneth Paltrow, but instead of relying on her natural beauty, her lips had been enhanced and her eyelashes lengthened.

'Oh, you're empty-handed,' she said, those plumped lips curling.

'Sorry – you should have said.'

'Did you call the orthodontist today?'

Jack felt his anger rising at the familiar mantra. 'How

many times do I have to tell you. My *very slightly* crooked bottom teeth are staying.'

'And how many times do I have to tell *you* that they are so not Hollywood, doll. Imagine if your screenplay is a hit and I'm walking that red carpet with you. I can't be doing all the smiling at the press on my own, now can I?' Riley lifted herself up out of the water to show off her small pert breasts. 'Are you drunk? You look drunk.'

'I had two glasses, this is my third.'

'I expect Caitlin was there flirting with you all?'

'Yes, the Caitlin who is very happily married to Dominic was there, but not flirting.' Jack sighed. 'If you're going to start being ridiculous again, I'm going back in to watch the end of the film I started last night.'

'Fillum.' Riley mimicked his English accent. 'I don't know why you can't say movie like normal people. So, who else was there then? Ruby? Calista?'

Jack noticed the half-full bottle of Chardonnay resting in the portable wine cooler on wheels he had got her last Christmas. 'Why are you asking me for a drink, when you have plenty here already?' For a moment he felt tempted to empty the icy contents over her head.

'That's right, be horrible to me. I'm darn sure you wouldn't speak in that way to that witch you met in Cornwall last year. "Oh, Star, you're so beautiful. Oh, Star hi, show me your crystal shop and around this quaint little village. Oh, Star, put a love spell on me."'

Jack ran a hand through his hair. 'Wait a minute, where did that come from? Every time you have a bloody drink you—'

'I've just been lying here thinking about it. I'm surprised the bathwater isn't boiling.'

'I'm not getting into this. I have changed my numbers and every email address. And now I've left Eddison's, she doesn't even have a clue where I work. Riley, please stop this.'

His fingers automatically went to the scar on his forehead, a reminder of the drunken row when Riley had discovered a message from Star – saying nothing too incriminating, thank goodness. But his incensed girlfriend had pushed him in her fury, and he had lost his footing, cracked his head on the coffee table and fallen awkwardly enough to break a bone in his forearm.

Jack Murray had never before been a cheater or philanderer. Born to Emma and James, both GPs, he had had a blessed upbringing, and with two younger sisters, he knew how to treat and respect women. He had had two serious relationships before Riley. One straight out of uni with a sweet half-Italian girl called Maria and another in his late twenties with Jacqui, a teacher, who had actually done the dirty on him and been unfaithful, saying that if he hadn't been married to his job, it never would have happened.

Looking back, he realised he probably wasn't in love with either of them as on neither occasion had his heart been broken. He and Maria just drifted apart, and with Jacqui, despite agreeing that she was right in what she was saying, he was more annoyed that she had cheated on him than that they were splitting up. He had been in London then, living with her in a rented flat in Old Street; an easy commute to the City and his finance job. As they parted ways, he stayed where he was and she moved in with her new lover to the flat above the dry cleaners at the end of their street. Talk about rubbing his nose in it.

Jack went over to Riley and leaned down to kiss her on the forehead. 'Let's not fight. Please.'

Riley turned her head away. 'Just go and watch your movie, Jack. I need more time to think.'

Relieved that his feisty lover seemed to have calmed down slightly, he walked back through to the living area and began flicking through the many channels on offer. His thoughts turned to Star. It was as if the light in his heart had been turned on when he had met that girl. He just had to glance across at her pretty little face behind her market stall and *bam*, there she was, spouting a quote from Blaise Pascal. The one and *only* romantic quote he knew from anyone really. And he had Maria, his first lover, to thank for that – although he never confessed to Star how he knew it. While they were both studying Mathematics at Oxford, fellow nerd Maria had given him a book explaining amongst other things Pascal's invention of the original calculator. In the front of it she had written, *The heart has its reasons which reason knows not.*

His logical brain couldn't accept all or maybe any of sweet Star's 'power of the universe' theories, but it had seemed quite strange that this one quote had set off both their initial conversation and huge physical connection. She had told him that she believed there were such things as love angels who led you to the right partners at the right time in your lives. Maybe she was right?

Jack felt a stirring at the memory of their lovemaking that day. It had felt so natural and right to want to make love to her. Like a primal instinct. The fact that he was cheating hadn't even crossed his mind. It was the best sex he had ever had in his life, adventurous and fun. It had also caused feelings to go through him that he had never thought possible. He had liked Star too. Her soft, gentle nature. Her honesty. She had touched on her slightly wobbly heritage, the opposite of his stable one, and it had made him like her even more. Made him want to protect her. However, later that evening when he had gone back to his Airbnb to find Kara still up, and he had chatted to her on the balcony, the overriding feeling then was guilt. There was he, in a live-in relationship with Riley, two years down the line, and whilst he was making love to another woman, Riley had been frantically trying to get hold of him. Her parents had had a car accident whilst staying at their holiday home in Barbados, and were in intensive care on the holiday island.

He had flown home immediately to do everything he could to help. Held Riley when she needed it. Realised that there was a soft centre underneath all her bravado. Realised that he did love her too.

Things went back to normal, and all was well until the day she found the message from Star. Riley had been lying next to him on the sofa, fiddling with his phone to find some music to play through the apartment's expensive speaker system when it had popped up. Just a simple *A little hello to the big apple. Hope the silver screen is still calling,* then the emoji of a star with an x for a kiss.

He had explained to his girlfriend that Star was a friend of Kara's who was running the Airbnb and that she had offered to show him around Hartmouth because Kara was busy. The kiss was what had thrown Riley though, and like a dog with a bone, her extreme jealousy had taken over. She had found Star's shop online and was beside herself that there was no phone number listed on the website. The night of their big fight, she was trying to get Jack's phone off him to call Star directly and ask her what the hell was going on. Later, mortified by his accident and knowing that she was responsible for his injuries, when with a guilty tongue he assured her again, ten times over, that he and Star had not had sex and that he would delete and block the woman from every form of communication, Riley promised that she would never bring it up again.

He thought often of Star, her sweet spirit, her tender touch, the bolt of lightning that had gone through him when he first set eyes on her . . . but his life was here. Here in New York. He wondered what would happen if he were to pitch up in Hartmouth and see her again – but who was to say that she would want anything to do with him anyway, after he had cut her out of his life and failed to keep in touch. There were finance companies dotted around Cornwall, of course, but if he moved back to England they wouldn't give him a salary anywhere near what he was earning now. And then he thought of how it would be, living by the sea and writing his screenplay in a life with less stress. Maybe he could manage down there. He had to admit that staying at Kara Moon's B&B looking over the water had given him such complete peace. And to be in the same country as his parents and sisters again would be so lovely.

It was their turn to be at Riley's parents' this Christmas. The couple were fully recovered from their injuries, aside from her mother having a slight limp from her badly broken leg and her dad now having a deep gangster-type scar across his neck, which would no doubt be treated by the best plastic surgeon in California where they lived, once the time was right. So, Jack wouldn't get to see his folks again until at least Easter now. The wave of homesickness that swept over him was halted by the sound of Riley walking purposefully up the hallway.

Quickly putting the TV on to a channel, he stared at the screen. It was showing an old black and white Hollywood movie. The glamorous actress in a feather boa with cigarette holder in hand was crying as she entered a hotel. A young porter rushed to her side to take her bags and, with a slow voice like Forrest Gump, said, 'If you don't mind me asking, what's troubling you, ma'am?'

'It's not a what, it's a he,' the actress said in her brittle voice.

'Well, like I say, lady, if you do not love too much, you do not love enough. He musta bin a lucky fella.'

'That is just the sweetest thing.' The officious character took a drag from her cigarette holder. 'Did you make that up, boy?'

'Jeez no, I'm not that clever person who says things like that. My old boss, he was the one with brains. He told me about a man called Blaise Pascal, he evidently had all the right things to say to the ladies. I don't even know who he was, ma'am.'

Jack's mouth fell open and then stayed open as Riley appeared in the doorway wearing a complete white underwear set, stockings included; smudged red lipstick and teetering on her highest Louboutin heels. Sexily strolling across the room, she put her expensive shoe up on the sofa and, making sure her crotch was right next to her boyfriend's face, growled, 'Let's just fuck, Jack.'

Saying nothing, Jack pulled her gently down on top of him and with the words of Blaise Pascal and thoughts of Star Bligh and her love angels running through his mind, he made love to his young fragrant girlfriend on a cold snowy November night in New York City.

Chapter 23

'Here she comes, the jolliest girl in the whole of Hartmouth,' Joe Moon greeted Star at the front gate to Bee Cottage.

'Your Pearl or Mrs Harris from Tasty Pasties should get that award, I reckon,' she replied.

'Well, it's good to see a smile on that pretty face of yours for once, whoever's putting it there.' The wise ferryman opened the gate. 'Quick, come on in out of this cold. They're forecasting a big storm for later – like the one we had nigh on twenty years ago. Trees down, the lot.'

'Ooh good. I love watching the lightning. But let's hope it doesn't strike Mum's caravan like it did back then. Do you remember?'

'Oh my goodness, yes. I had to come and collect you and my Kerry from school. They rang as no one had turned up to collect you both. I drove us up to Hartmouth Park and found your mum getting into an ambulance with a broken arm. She'd panicked when the lightning struck, rushed outside and missed her footing on the steps.'

'That's right – so you did. Those schooldays are kind of happy memories – well, apart from Mum causing another drama.'

'We even stopped the ferry for a day. Now that is unheard of. How is your mum these days?'

'Miserable, stoned, unreasonable. Same as normal, really.'

Joe gave Star's shoulder a squeeze just as Kara pulled up outside in her Passion Flowers work van. The redhead got out and slammed the door behind her. 'Sorry I'm a bit late. That new receptionist at the Hartmouth Bay Hotel, God, can she talk. I got a christening flowers order from her today though so that's good.' She lowered her voice. 'Has Pearl gone?'

'Yes, yes.' Joe kissed his daughter on the cheek. 'But we need to hurry. I've no idea how long it takes to get that hair of hers done.'

There was a loud woof as Joe showed them into the kitchen and an overweight black Labrador with hints of grey around his whiskers came bounding towards them all.

'Oh, look at you! Hello, Bob the Dog.' Star knelt down and fussed him. 'What a handsome boy you are.'

'I forgot you hadn't met him yet.' Kara patted the hound's back as a trail of drool came out of his mouth and onto the kitchen flagstones. 'Ew. Not sure what's worse, that or Grandad's dog Bert and his toxic farts.'

'I miss that old Jack Russell as much as I miss your grandad,' Joe said, putting three mugs next to the kettle. 'Seems like an age they've both been gone, can't believe it's only a matter of months.'

'I know. I still feel as if Grandad is with us,' Kara said. 'That all of a sudden he will appear on his old trike, get Bert out of the basket on the front and march up the garden to his shed, then give the chickens some apple cider vinegar.'

'And Bert will come in here, release one of his silent but deadly smells and clear the kitchen.' Joe's shoulders shook with laughter.

'He will be with us again soon when Harry's Rose starts coming up in the garden,' Kara told them, thinking back to the seeds he had left her to plant next to the Agatha Christie rose that represented his dear late wife, her Granny Annie.

Joe swallowed the lump in his throat. 'Be keeping an eye on all of us, he will. We'll have to behave ourselves then.'

'I reckon he'd kind of prefer it if we didn't.' Kara smiled as Bob grabbed her trainer from the doorway and padded off with it to another room. 'The dog's listening to him already, see?'

'Right, let me make you both a hot drink. Will coffee do you?' Joe asked.

'Could I have a herbal tea instead, if you've got one, please? I've gone off coffee lately.' Star removed her coat and scarf and put them on the back of one of the kitchen chairs.

'Green Tea and Mint is all we've got, that do you?'

'Lovely.'

'Have you got the ring gauge?' Kara asked as she looked in the fridge to see if there were any goodies they could snack on.

'Yes, in my pocket.'

'Let's quickly do that first then.' She handed Star a little Babybel cheese to eat.

Joe carried on making their drinks. 'Her rings are in the musical box on her dressing table in our room. You want the gold one with the single ruby in it. She's definitely not wearing it – I checked as she left.'

The girls went upstairs. 'I feel as if I haven't seen you properly for ages,' Kara said as she started to look through Pearl's jewellery, taking care not to disturb it too much.

'I've been busy making Christmas stock and making whoopee with Mr Ireland, so I have.' Star affected an Irish accent. 'Sorry, we must sort something. I thought just that this morning.'

'Yes, we must.' Kara looked at her. 'I suppose it's silly to ask how it's all going?'

'Sex is how it's going. Lots of it. It's great he has your flat, a place of his own. Skye loves having the freedom, and my going next door also means she doesn't have to know what her harlot of a mother is up to.' Star grinned.

'So, he doesn't take you out then? Me and Billy thought maybe we'd see you in the pub this weekend. I miss you.'

'We always have the intention of going out and then just end up in bed and getting a takeaway. Or he cooks for me. I get the impression he's saving up. He owes his dad and Frank a lot of money since his court case.'

'And me actually. He still hasn't paid me for the flowers he got for you.'

'Oh.'

'Mate, I don't want you getting hurt. Are you sure he's seeing you for the right reasons?'

'Kara. It's all good.'

'If you're happy that he doesn't take you out and it's just sex then great, but I just . . . Oh, I don't know. I'm slightly miffed he hasn't paid me for the flowers, to be honest.'

'Just ask him.'

'I don't like to. I know he's in debt but now you've told me he's splashing the cash on takeaways.'

'I get most of them.'

'Star!'

'I offer – after all, I'm fine for money. I'm just helping him out, Kara. I know you would do the same for Billy.'

'I don't trust him.'

Star's voice began to wobble. 'Can't you just be happy for me, Kar? Not everyone is like your ex. Jago bloody Ellis, now he *was* a thieving bastard.'

Kara felt tears pricking her eyes, but her dad calling up the stairs to tell them to hurry up put a halt on her emotions. She took a deep breath. 'Let's get this ring measured, shall we?'

'All done?' Joe presented the girls with their hot drinks.

'Yes. Sorry though, Joe, I've no time for a drink after all,' Star blustered. 'I've been here much longer than I expected.'

'I'll give you a lift back down to the market.' Kara hastily went to get her coat.

'No, thanks. I need some fresh air.' Star threw her coat on and went out of the door. 'Bye, Joe!'

'Oh, Dad, I've upset her,' Kara said when the cottage door slammed.

'Why?'

'I said I didn't trust Conor.'

'That girl has been brought up on her wits, and Billy could sniff a bad 'un out from ten miles away. What's more, you know Frank. He's like family to us. I think you may have got this wrong.'

'Maybe I have. Oh dear.'

Joe pulled his daughter into him. 'Come to your old dad. You're never too big for a cuddle, now are you? Me knowing you inside out, back to front and a little sideways too, thinks maybe my Kerensa Moon here is a teensy weensy bit jealous that she hasn't got her best friend at her beck and call any more.'

'That's what Star said too. I didn't consciously think that.'

'We can't all be Sigmund Freud, can we, my girl. And all families have rows. She's been more like a sister than your real one ever used to be, so just make some time for each other. It will all come right, I'm sure.'

Chapter 24

Billy groaned with pleasure as he sat and put his feet up on the comfortable new sofa that he and Kara had just had delivered to their Ferry View apartment that weekend. 'God, this is so lovely compared to that old saggy two-seater you had in here.'

'Isn't it. I just want to doze off every time I get on it. Drink?'

'A beer, please. What's for dinner?'

'I can't be bothered to cook so as it's nearly the weekend, either we run out for fish and chips or we have pizza again.'

'Pizza is perfect.'

'I'm such a bad girlfriend.'

Billy tutted. 'We are a partnership.'

'I asked Star why we never see her out and about with Conor,' Kara called through from the kitchen.

'Oh yeah, what did she say?'

'That they are always getting takeaways too.' She walked through with Billy's beer. 'What do *you* think of Conor?'

'I think he's great. He's a hard worker, totally honest with me. Very funny. I like him.'

'Oh. OK.' Then Kara began to blurt out, 'I was just worried that he's using Star and also he bloody owes me for some flowers, and I know he's been skint but that doesn't sit right with me, especially as you are his boss now.'

'Oops! That's my fault.' Billy reached into his jeans pocket. 'Here, he gave me a tenner and I forgot to give it to you.'

'Shit, Billy.' Kara was stricken. 'Bloody hell, poor Star, I was such a bitch to her earlier.'

'Sorry, sweet cheeks, I've had a lot on my mind. It was so cold and windy out there today and Daz didn't show again so I had to do the tug all day. Poor Conor was freezing his bollocks off out the front; at least it's a little warmer behind the wheel.'

'You said Darren didn't show? Hmm.'

'What does hmm mean?' Billy took a slug of his beer.

'Your mum said that he wasn't on the stall today as he was helping you.'

The wind, now whistling across the estuary at a rate of knots, was causing torrents of rain to sporadically rattle against the balcony doors. A huge flash of sheet lightning suddenly lit up their compact living area.

Kara flinched. 'Here comes the storm. Is James Bond in, do you know?'

Without acknowledging her, Billy jumped up as if the lightning had struck him. A look of panic was on his face.

'Did Daz really say that?' he demanded. Kara nodded. 'Where's my phone?' He fumbled for it in his jacket pocket and dialled his twin's mobile. He couldn't get through. 'I've got to go to him. Kar?'

'What's the matter?'

'I can feel it, something's wrong. Fuck! It's Daz, I just know it.'

'Do you want me to come with you?'

'No, no, I'll call you. Keep your phone handy. Order the food.' He kissed her on the forehead, snatched up his keys, slung on his work coat and boots and headed down the stairs. As he ran to his van, a massive gust of wind coming right off the sea knocked him sideways. The slashing rain stung his face.

Billy abandoned the van in the market, then two by two he shot up the metal stairs to his old flat above the family's fruit and vegetable shop. The last time he had had an intuitive feeling of dread like this was when they were teenagers and Darren had fallen off his pushbike cycling back from the pub and had smashed his face up. He knocked loudly and rang the bell. 'Daz! Daz, bro! Are you there?' The crash of a dustbin being blown over and sent down the hill shocked him, as much as the next crack of lightning and resounding clap of thunder did. If the belief that God was moving His furniture was true, he certainly had brought in a big bloody wardrobe tonight.

Billy rummaged in his pocket for his keys, his cold wet fingers hampering his desire to get the door open and see if his precious brother was all right. Once inside, he slammed the door to against the wind and raced into the lounge.

Darren Dillon was lying face down on the floor with his mobile to the side of his face. He was breathing. A voice on the end was speaking slowly and calmly. 'I'm still here. Take your time. You're through to the Samaritans. Has something happened that has made you want to call us today?'

'Oh hello. Sorry, sorry. I'm his brother. I've got him now. I've got him. Thank you so much,' Billy gasped and ended the call.

'Daz?' Billy sat his brother up; Daz's head lolled on to his shoulder. He stank of alcohol.

'What have you taken? Have you taken anything? What have you done? I'm going to call an ambulance.'

'No,' Darren managed. 'I'm just really, really shpisshed.'

151

With that he hurled right over Billy's left shoulder and all over the rug in the middle of the wooden floor.

Billy laid him on his side in the recovery position, then fetched his duvet and put it over him. He went through to the kitchen to find an empty half-bottle of whisky. The whole place was in an even worse state than when he had come round the other day. It smelled like a refuse tip. In the bathroom he checked the medicine and toiletries cupboards for tablets of any kinds, putting some paracetamol in his pocket as he did so. He also raked through the bathroom bin for any drug packets and ran to both bedrooms to see if there were any in there either.

He walked back into the lounge to check that his brother was still on his side and that his breathing was OK. It was shallow. He paced around a bit. Darren so wouldn't want a fuss, but what if he was dangerously drunk, what if he did need an ambulance? What if they couldn't get through because a tree was down? He googled to see if there was any helpful information about what to do if someone was very drunk, but he didn't know whether Darren was just drunk, or dangerously drunk. He had only been sick the once and his breathing wasn't too shallow – or was it? Were there levels of shallowness? His mind racing, Billy raced into the kitchen and frenziedly tipped up the kitchen bin and scanned littered surfaces for any other empty bottles. Billy knew he needed assistance. He didn't want Kara coming out in this weather, so should he phone his mum or dad? Then he breathed a sigh of relief. He knew exactly who he could call.

Pearl was there within minutes, skidding up on to the pavement below on her pea-green scooter and hurrying up the steps to bang on the door.

'You caught me perfectly, my little darling, just as I was leaving the hospital,' she said, and immediately Billy felt a great relief. 'I told Joe I'd be a bit late 'cos of the weather, but I sailed through. OK, let's see what's happening here, shall we?'

Billy rolled up the spew-covered rug and threw it over the top of the outside stairs, out into the elements and somewhere that no one would fall over it in the dark. Meanwhile, a calm and professional Pearl checked over Darren.

'You did everything right,' she told Billy when he came back. 'Your brother is just very drunk, as you said. But he can stay here. He needs a warm bed and plenty of fluids as soon as he's able. And I don't mean Jack Daniel's.' She laughed quietly. Billy smiled.

'Good job he called you,' she went on. 'The bigger danger would have been him going on to his back and choking on his vomit.'

'He didn't call me, but with our twin sense when Kara told me he hadn't been to work, I just knew. But he did call the Samaritans.' Billy's voice wobbled. 'I thought . . . I . . .'

'It's all right.' Pearl put a reassuring arm around Billy's shoulders. 'Calling them – well, that's a positive thing. He's obviously ready to talk about whatever it is that's troubling him. Now come on, let's get him into bed.' A comatose Darren Dillon allowed the nurse and his brother to clumsily carry him into his bedroom, where they heaved him onto the bed, laid him on his side and rested a pillow behind him, so he couldn't roll over.

Leaving a bowl on the bed and a pint of water next to him, Billy and Pearl went back through to the lounge, which stank of alcohol and vomit.

'Will you stay here?' Pearl asked. 'I think it would be wise, just in case he needs you.'

'Yes, I will. I'll call Kara now and let her know what's happened. She's rung me twice already, bless her.'

'And Billy,' Pearl looked the young man in the eye, 'this stays between you and me unless you say otherwise. I understand.'

Billy gulped. 'I knew you'd take away all the drama. Mum would have gone into hysterics. Dad would have got angry.' Her kindness made him feel like he was going to cry.

'Talk to him,' Pearl counselled. 'Find out what it is. I've seen and heard many scenarios during my thirty years in hospitals and I've realised that the only thing in the whole world there is not a solution for is death. Whatever it is he'll be all right. You'll be all right. And you can always come to me to talk, you know that.'

As Pearl made her way carefully back up the hill to Bee Cottage on her scooter, dodging the gusts of wind, Billy messaged Kara, who was concerned but fine, then went in to Darren, who suddenly shot up in bed and managed to vomit directly into the bowl that Billy and Pearl had put near to him.

'Bill? What you doing here?' His voice was croaky. Billy put the bowl on the floor and handed him the loo roll that Pearl had also put on the bedside table. Darren then promptly burst into tears, tears that should have been shed long ago, and now that the dam had been burst by alcohol, he just couldn't stop. Billy sat on the bed and just held him, not saying a word.

'I need to tell you something,' Darren sobbed finally, his breath hitching. 'I'm sorry I'm so drunk.'

Billy felt the same fear go through him as when he had thought his brother might be ill or worse. He waited with his heart pounding.

'I will tell you what's wrong and you're going to laugh at me, and you might even hate me. And Dad will go apeshit, I know.' Darren made a noise between a laugh and a cry. 'I'm an iron, a poofter. Call me what you like.' Darren grabbed the pillow next to him and put it over his face. 'I'm gay, Billy,' he said in a muffled voice. 'Gay.'

Billy pulled the unnecessary barrier away. He was super-calm. 'Is that it?'

'You what?'

'Daz, I'm so close to you I know when you need to take a shit, don't I, and you me. You've never had a bird, not even at school. Yes, you shagged the Penhaligan tart and Lydia Twist, but neither of those were going anywhere. That was obvious.'

'Lydia fell for me, big time.'

'No shit, Sherlock. That's obviously why she went away. Kara and I had already worked that one out. I was just waiting for you to tell me.'

'After Lydia, I realised I had to be true to myself and other people. Everybody hated her but well, she was actually quite decent underneath all her demons. I hurt her.' Darren sniffed again.

'Are you going to be this sensitive all the time now you've admitted you're a big wuss?'

Darren managed a smile. 'You're not allowed to say things like that.'

'I can say what I bloody want to you. You scared the shit

out of me! When I heard the Samaritans at the end of the phone, I thought you had tried to top yourself.'

'Mate, they've been amazing.' Darren groaned and took a drink of water. The smell of sick was making him feel queasy again. 'I have rung them a couple of times. Just to talk to someone, you know. No judgement, no fear. Even in the middle of the night, a calm voice is at the end of that phone.' Saying this made tears run down his face.

'What did you expect me to do though, really? I love you, Daz. Love is love. You're attracted to men, so what? That doesn't change our relationship, not one bit. You're still my brother.' He hugged Darren.

'What about Mum and Dad?' Daz asked fearfully. 'Us having grandchildren is all Mum goes on about on the stall.'

'Me and Kara have got that covered, and if you meet someone and want a family, well, you can do that too. The options are there. Actually, Conor was telling me the other day that one of his best mates in London is a single social worker, and he's just adopted a little boy. Times have changed, mate.'

'I know Mum will handle it, but Dad won't be able to cope.'

'He might surprise you. Weren't the Kray twins gay or one was bisexual – and he's obsessed with their story. And anyway, it's your long-term happiness here that's important. It's your life, Daz. And what other people think of you is of no consequence. People who love you will always be there for you, whatever you say or do.'

'Will you come with me when I tell them?'

'If you want me there.'

Darren gulped down the rest of the glass of water in one. A huge rumble of thunder felt like it shook the bedroom.

'Bloody hell.' Darren laid his head back on the pillow. 'I didn't realise the weather was so bad.' He was feeling dreadful. The room swam and his head ached.

'You didn't realise what your name was earlier, so it's good to see you a bit more like yourself.' Billy smiled. 'You'll soon be feeling better. Will you go back to London or stay here, do you think?'

'We don't all run around dancing on Gay Pride floats and drinking in Soho, you know.' It was Darren's turn to smile weakly. 'In fact, us gays are really quite prevalent in the south-west, according to my dating app.'

'That was a stupid comment.' Billy sighed. 'Sorry, bro.'

'It's fine and I'm not going anywhere. Not yet. It's family, innit.' They both laughed. 'And now the only place I am definitely going to is sleep. I feel so rough.'

'Do you want me to stay?'

'Nah. Get back to Moony – and thanks.'

'For what?'

'For being such a fucking cool brother.'

'I won't say a word, not even to the missus.'

'No, I want you to tell her. I want her to know, but please don't say anything until I've told the old man and woman.'

'OK, but you do the talking when you're ready to anyone else, not that it's anybody's business really. But in future, bro, don't suffer in silence. I'm not going anywhere. Well, unless you start supporting Tottenham, that is.'

'You dick.' Darren grinned sleepily. 'I'm sorry I scared you. I was frightened of losing everyone, you see. Especially you. But I need to do this. I need to be me.'

'Yes, you do. Never forget we are twins, Daz. One for all and all for one and all that. After all, we lived together for nine months before anyone else even met us.'

'I bet we even caused chaos in the womb, poor old Muv.' Darren laughed, swung his legs out of bed, felt very dizzy, then somehow managed to right himself and groaned, 'I so need a piss.' Billy quickly moved the bowl of sick in time for Daz to stagger off to the bathroom.

Kara had replied to his coming home message with a pizza emoji and a big kiss. He shouted out: 'Don't worry about work in the morning. Get yourself together and tidy this shithole up.'

'Just pass me my feather duster,' Darren shouted camply back, then appeared in the lounge to see Billy putting on his coat. He hugged him and said in his normal voice: 'You're my fucking hero, Billy Dillon, do you know that?'

Billy felt a warmth go right through him. 'Jesus, you'll be singing Mariah Carey to me next. Now fuck off back to bed.'

Chapter 25

'Dirty stop-out,' Skye said when she bumped into Star coming down the stairs from the flat above Passion Flowers. They both then laughed. 'Have a nice day, Mum,' the girl went on. 'It's good to see you looking so happy – and I truly mean that.'

Star just about managed a quick, 'Thank you, darling,' before hastily running up her own stairs, unlocking the front door and rushing to the toilet, where she vomited.

She ran the shower until it was hot, smothered herself with her favourite almond and vanilla body wash, then put her head back in the soothing jet of water, making an *mmm* sound as she did so. Feeling better, she thought back to what she'd eaten last night. She'd only had one glass of wine with her meal, so it must have been the oysters. She had never been that keen on them, but Conor had insisted on the aphrodisiac starter, not that they needed any kind of encouragement in that department. Wiping her mouth, she went to the kitchen and got herself a glass of water. She felt shattered. All the late nights and lovemaking were beginning to take their toll on her. She had told Conor that, as much as she loved having fun with him, tonight she was staying in, sitting cosily in front of the log burner and re-watching *Normal People*. Which, she had told him, was almost like being with him anyway as Paul Mescal, the sexy male lead,

159

reminded her of a younger version of him; plus it was full of raunchy sex scenes.

Throwing on her dressing gown, she made herself a hot water and lemon and was just going through to the bedroom to get dressed and ready to go down to the market, when her phone beeped in two messages.

One was from Conor with an image of the Pussycat Dolls and his words, *Bet you wish Paul Mescal was hot like me.* Star shook her head and smiled. For someone who appeared so big and confident, underneath he had his own deep-rooted insecurities. The other was her mother saying, *Can you come?* Having received this message on many previous occasions, Star rang her immediately, to hear sobbing. 'Steren, Steren, can you come?' She could hear the slur in Estelle Bligh's voice.

'Mum, is it urgent? I've got to open the shop in a minute.'

'He's dead. Dead.'

'Who is, Mum?'

'Steren, can you just come, please?'

Star said patiently, 'Let me ask Kara if Skye can watch my shop for a bit and I'll whizz over.'

Finishing off her now lukewarm water and lemon, Star quickly checked her emails. On seeing Jack's email address amongst them, she felt a surge of energy fly from the top of her head to the bottom of her toes. Then realising it was her sent box she was looking at, she blew out a calming breath then stood up ready to leave. Jack Murray had gone. But why, in that case, did she still feel that he was so close to her?

Chapter 26

Jack Murray finished off a Zoom meeting with his colleagues in London, put his feet on the desk and looked out of his huge glass-fronted office at the skyscrapers opposite. He could see many more Jack Murrays, clones in the corporate world. Suits and desk lights on, typing or engrossed on the phone. Making or losing dollars; most of them probably wishing they were somewhere else instead.

Raindrops had started to trickle down his seventeenth-floor window, crossing and dancing with each other as they dripped their way down to the sidewalk below, where sirens blared and pedestrians ran for cover with multicoloured umbrellas or bags or folders over their heads. He fell into a daydream of being back in Hartmouth, sitting in Kara Moon's apartment, looking out of the balcony doors at the beautiful harbour estuary and writing his script . . . then was brought back to reality by his secretary putting a call through on his landline.

'Jack, Riley for you.'

'Thanks, Chloe.' He cleared his throat. 'Hi, Riley. What are you doing, calling me on my office line?'

'Just checking you're at work. Joke!' Jack sighed inwardly as his girlfriend justified herself with: 'I know you don't always pick up your mobile, that's why – and this is important.'

'Go on.'

'Brooke has asked if I'd like to go for a long spa weekend in the Hamptons with her sister and one of her girlfriends, so I'm going.'

'Right. So you've phoned to tell me, not ask me. When?'

'Not this weekend, but the next. Oh, Jacky darling.' Jack cringed at her nickname for him. 'You're always harping on about wanting some time on your own and now you've got it.'

'I didn't say anything, did I? Of course you must go.' Then with a flash of Star Bligh's pretty face entering his mind, without thinking the words flew out of his mouth: 'I've been thinking about visiting my parents before Christmas anyway as we are going to yours this year. This gives me the perfect chance to do that.'

'Oh.'

'Riley, don't start,' he warned her. 'You know you can't bear going there as it's so quiet where they live.'

'OK, OK, you go and pay your duty visit. Absence makes the heart grow fonder and all that jazz. Anyway, gotta go. I'm being called for my audition. It's only for the goddam chorus, but the show has got an A-list top-dollar lead. See you later, honey.'

'Break a leg . . .' Jack murmured but she'd already gone.

Chapter 27

'Mum, you're not making any sense. Who's died?'

On arrival at the static, Star found Estelle Bligh sitting in front of the old electric fire nursing a mug of whisky. 'And you can't fool me into thinking there is coffee in that mug.'

'I'm not,' Estelle said truculently. 'It's just there's no clean glasses.' She clumsily put her drink down on the table, then lit a half-smoked roll-up that was sitting in the ashtray. Star opened the window.

'Don't let all the heat out!' her mother whined.

'Then put that bloody thing out whilst I'm here,' Star said. 'I've got to go back to the shop, and I'll stink of smoke. I'm also not feeling a hundred per cent today.'

'Always about you, isn't it?'

Star closed her eyes in the hope it would also shut her mouth and prevent it from saying what it really wanted to.

'Your father has died.'

'You've got me all the way up here to tell me that the man I presumed dead for thirteen years has actually died.' Star felt her throat stinging. 'You could have just told me on the phone, I would have come at lunchtime or after work. Anyway, I thought you didn't know him, let alone care about him?'

Estelle started sobbing. 'I loved him. I loved him, Star. He was the love of my life.'

'So what was his name? You owe me that at least now.' Gripped by nausea, Star rushed to the toilet. She came back white as a ghost.

'I made him a promise that whatever happened, I would never tell a soul.' Nervously playing with the grey braids in her hair, Estelle took another slurp of whisky.

'I'm your daughter, *his* daughter – what harm would it do? He's dead, for God's sake! Come on – I want to know.'

'Oh, fuck off, Steren. What do you know about anything?'

Star felt the anger rising within. 'What I do know is that I *will* fuck off – and Skye will fuck off too, and you'll be left a lonely old woman up on the hill, smoking weed, getting pissed and shagging ridiculous men. I've had it with you, Mother.' She swept up her coat. 'My father is what we are talking about here. Not any man. He's half me and a part of your grandchild.'

'In genetics he may be, but I raised you, my girl. Nurture over nature is what matters.'

'You raised me, you say?' Star's voice was shrill. 'Hardly! If it wasn't for Uncle Jim and Auntie Flo, I'd probably still be here, sitting next to you on that stinking sofa, wasting my life like you've wasted yours.'

By now she was spitting with rage. 'You made me have Skye too, a decision with your own interests at heart! Sixteen, I was. Still a child myself. You wanted a new baby, with the hope that maybe you could treat her better than you ever treated me. But luckily *I* knew how to be a mother!'

Estelle laughed. 'There, that's the fire, that's the fire I gave you. Good girl!' She then stood up calmly and, grabbing her daughter's chin, stared right at her. 'And it's lucky that you *do* know how to be a mother, as by the look of you, you're going to be one again before too long, and you'll need more than St Patrick to help you with the next one.'

Without even stopping to ask her mother what she meant, a sobbing Star ran to her car, started the engine and drove right to the top of Hartmouth Head and into the car park, close to the bench that sat facing out across the endless ocean. As a child, this had been one of her thinking places. She knew the wording on the brass plaque fixed to the bench off by heart. It read: *In Loving Memory of Diggory Pickett 1950-2000. He swore by and at the tides who took him away to his final watery resting place.* Here was where she would take refuge from Estelle and the small space that she shared with her.

Ignoring the cold, Star opened the car window and inhaled lungfuls of fresh sea air. No one was about to see her as she felt her boobs and put a hand on her stomach. She didn't feel pregnant. She couldn't be pregnant. So infrequent were her periods that she couldn't even remember when she had last had one, certainly not since she'd been seeing Conor, that was for sure. Yes, it was irresponsible not always using a condom, but he had assured her he had recently had a sexual health check and she had lied, saying that she hadn't had sex for years so definitely had a clean bill of health. They had been enjoying abandoned, latex-free sex, with Conor always pulling out in time. This had always worked without fail if she hadn't used a condom before. Ironically, the only time she had got pregnant was when Skye's father had insisted on using them, and one had obviously split.

Yes, Star decided, she had felt a little bloated lately but that was because she was now eating regular, hearty meals with Conor. In fact, she had never eaten so much or had so much sex in such a condensed period of time in her whole life. Sod Estelle's premonitions. The only baby she was having was a bloody food baby.

She would keep her word and stay away from her mother too. How could the selfish woman not realise how much hurt she had caused her? Yes, she may never have known her father, but he was still her blood. Him dying wasn't a matter of grieving for him per se, but more about grieving the relationship she could have had with him. And how dare Estelle keep his identity to herself! Especially now.

Star shut the window and turned the radio on. Pat Benatar singing 'Love is a Battlefield' blared out through the speakers. Reaching over, Star found a random pack of tissues in the glove box and blew her nose hard. Love in its many guises was definitely just that – a battlefield. Relationships were hard. Especially the one she had with her mother, who sadly had only ever managed to care about the relationship she had with alcohol and drugs.

Chapter 28

'Here she is.' Kara engulfed Star in a big hug. 'I've set up camp on the back window seat and am so looking forward to one of Frank's lunches, aren't you?'

'Big Frank's Burgers are on special today too, ladies,' the Irishman called over, then went back to making coffees at the machine.

'It's so good to see you.' Kara had a proper look at her friend's face as they sat down with their drinks. 'Are you all right? You look like you've been crying. Oh, mate, what's up?'

'Mum – and, well, my dad too.'

'Your dad? What?'

'He's dead, Kar. And I know I never even knew his bloody name, but it still feels kind of weird. I've always hung on to the thought that even without trying to find him, I would just meet him one day.'

'Oh my God, that's huge,' Kara breathed. 'I'm so sorry. So is Estelle finally going to tell you who the mystery man is, now he's gone?'

Star sighed. 'Who knows what will come out of that addled mind of hers.'

Kara clasped her friend's hand over the table. 'Give her time. Maybe she is grieving for him in her own way.'

'Yes, she kept on that he was the love of her life, but it was still situation normal up there. She was drunk and on the wacky baccy. We had a huge row. It's just so hard. I love her, but I hate her at the same time. I want her to change but I know she's got to want to change herself. I feel so bloody responsible for her.'

'What would happen if you suggested her getting some sort of help?'

'Oh, Kar, you know I've tried.'

'Yes, sorry.'

'Everything is just a big drama with her, heightened by the alcohol and drugs. I worry for her health too. Saying that, I was really sick this morning. We had oysters last night – I don't know why I agreed to eat the pesky things. Estelle even insinuated I was pregnant.'

'Shit! Did she?' Kara gave Star a long look. 'Do you think you are?'

'God, no. I can't be.'

'She was right with Skye though, wasn't she, and you didn't have a clue then either.'

'Mate, don't say that! I haven't had a period for months, it's fine.'

'Er, isn't that what happens?'

'No, you know what I mean – they are so irregular. I keep thinking I must see a doctor about that too, but it's been the same all my life. Months without. They used to say it's because I didn't eat enough.'

'You've certainly been eating loads lately from what you tell me.'

'I know – Conor is a bloody feeder. I need to diet. You know me, get over a size six and I start to panic.'

'Can't say I know the feeling.' Kara smiled. Then she said sensibly, 'Maybe do a test, at least that'll put your mind at rest.'

'I can't even bear the thought. I know I said I wanted a baby, but be careful what you wish for and all that. It would be such bad timing. We are so not at that stage. It's just fun at the moment. Pure fun.'

'And there's me hoping I will be pregnant soon. Mind you, we've only been trying for a few weeks.'

'Life – it's a funny old game sometimes, isn't it?' Star picked up the Specials menu and blew out a breath. 'I don't think I can go for a burger. I still feel a bit queasy.'

Kara ordered their food and came back to the table. 'I know what I had to say and it's so important. I owe you a massive apology. Conor had given Billy the money directly for your flowers. I am so sorry I doubted him. And for being a complete bitch to you at Dad's the other day.'

'It's forgotten and yes, Conor is a rogue of sorts, but he's not the sort to shit on his uncle or on his own doorstep. The more I've got to know him, I realise that. He's a lovely man. Underneath all the macho exterior he's sensitive too.'

'Is he The One?'

Star took a sip of her fizzy water and thought about it.

'Too long to answer.' Kara smiled.

'I really like him but . . .'

'He's making you smile, and you haven't mentioned the J word for a while so that can only be a good thing.'

At that moment Big Frank appeared with a huge burger for Kara and a buttered jacket potato for Star.

'Enjoy, ladies! I hope that nephew of mine is behaving himself. Any problems, you just let me know, Miss Bligh, and I'll box his nose.'

Star grinned. 'He really is behaving perfectly, Frank. He's a breath of fresh air, to be sure.' She ended her sentence with the Irish accent she loved so much.

'Ha! You're picking up the lingo already. Grand, grand – and I hear he's doing a good job on the ferry too. I like that I can keep my eye on him from here.' Frank laughed his deep throaty laugh. 'He's the son I never had myself, that one.'

Star started picking at her potato as Kara took a huge bite into her burger, dripping sauce down her chin as she did so. Finishing her mouthful, she exclaimed, 'Talking of the ferry reminds me: there is something else massive I needed to ask you!'

'Go on.'

'So, you know that now, like Billy says, I am officially a jetsetter?'

Star laughed. 'Oh yes, how could I forget about your surprise trip. Australia, Spain and the Big Apple in three weeks wasn't it? Not that you haven't mentioned it before.'

'Jealousy so doesn't become you.' Kara grinned. 'So, Billy and I want to get a long weekend away in before the Christmas madness. Daz had agreed to man the tug. And Conor is obviously fully on board, excuse the pun.' Kara took a swig of coffee. 'Anyway, back to our holiday. We are going to rent the spare room out for Airbnb to get a bit of cash in whilst we're not here – might as well – so could you possibly throw a bit of food down for James Bond while we are away? Once a day is fine. I'll let the guest know – if we get one, that is. The keys will be outside in the key safe Billy put up, so that's sorted, but if you don't mind them having your number in case of emergencies, that would be so handy. That's it really.'

'Of course I don't mind. Pleased to help. Where are you planning on going?' Star yawned.

'To Prague, possibly. The Christmas markets will be on, and it looks magical. Or if not there, Cologne maybe.'

'How wonderful. I so want to go away.'

'Well, you must. Don't do what I did and wait too many years. Just book something. Perhaps you and Conor could go somewhere together? I can keep an eye on Skye and maybe Pearl could watch the shop for you. I bet she'd love that when she retires after Christmas Eve.'

'Maybe, but that's ages away and he might not even be around then.'

'Oh yeah, I forget he said he might only be here a few months.'

'He seems to be loving it here though.'

'With you on his arm, how can he not, dear friend. Right, we'd better go. An hour's gone already.'

'My darling daughter will be having a tantrum having to run between shops, so yeah.' Star drained her water.

'If you want to talk more about your dad, I'm here.'

Star frowned thoughtfully. 'I mean, I have my own reasons for not telling Skye, so I do kind of get Mum's point of view.'

'But that doesn't make it right or easy, does it?' Kara stood up and kissed Star's cheek. 'It's been lovely.'

'Yes, it has.' Then Star fretted, 'I will *have* to tell Skye; I can't have her feeling like I am today.'

'In your own time.'

'Yes, yeah. I need to think about it.'

They waved at Frank, who was busy serving another customer.

'Let's arrange a drink soon too, just me and you, like the old days,' Kara said. 'And with your mum, let her settle down a bit and maybe when the time is right for her, she *will* tell you.'

'I hope so.'

'And Star, for your own peace of mind, get that test.'

'I will. I promise.'

Chapter 29

'Aye, aye, Cap'n.' Conor high-fived Billy as he arrived at the Hartmouth ferry quay to start their day.

'Thanks for coming early, mate.'

'Nah, it's grand. I was home alone last night, so got some sleep. And will you just look at that sunrise.'

Billy nodded, then went on, 'Joe liked to jet-wash the float down at least once a month and it certainly needs doing today.'

The winter sun, like a fiery orb, was just raising its head where the estuary met the sea over the craggy cliffs towards Hartmouth Head. The sky was a kaleidoscope of reds, oranges and yellows, a colourful backdrop to the dark silhouettes of seabirds soaring over the still grey sea below, looking out for their fishy breakfast. The low tide caused little waves to lap gently against the quay wall. The silence of early morning offered a peace and stillness that was unavailable later in the day.

'Going to be a bright day, I reckon. I can deal with the cold, if it's sunny,' Billy said, his words coming out in clouds.

'You sound like a proper old sea dog.'

Billy laughed. 'Less of the old, mate. I've got ten years on you, haven't I?'

'Ha, don't rub it in. I need to get exercising again. Me and Star seem to be eating our way through life at the moment.'

'Eating, you say?' Billy grinned, making Conor smirk. 'Kara made us some bacon rolls up, fancy one before we get going?'

Billy pulled out the old fold-up red chairs that had been in the tug for decades and set them up on the float. As they sat clasping their coffees with gloved hands, the young ferryman cleared his throat. 'It's been quite a week, turns out my brother's gay.'

'No big deal there, though, is it?'

'Nah I guess not, but for some reason Daz wanted me to tell you as we are all working together.'

'How did your folks take it?'

'Mum was fine, but Dad has taken it hard. He's such a man's man and he can't get his head around the news. This is crippling Daz. It took so much courage for him to come out to them. The atmosphere has been so bad on the fruit and veg stall that he's quit and is going to be doing more shifts on here. He can manoeuvre the tug and you can stay out on the float. Gives me a break, so I'm all for that.'

'Your Da'll come round. Your family seem tight.'

'I hope so.'

'And I don't mind what I do on here. I'm just happy to be working. In fact, life is pretty good all round at the moment.'

'Star's a great girl, isn't she?'

'Yeah, she is. I'm not sure where we're heading but I do like her a lot.'

They ate in silence until a huge seagull swooped down to try and steal the last bit of roll out of Conor's hand.

'Jesus, they scare the life out of me, so they do.'

Billy was amused, then remembered: 'There's something else I meant to say. Me and Kara are away next weekend, so you and Daz are in charge, if you don't mind. Joe said it would do the pair of you good to do a few runs on your own.'

'No problem. Going anywhere nice?'

'Yeah, we decided on Prague, plenty of good beers there and Kara is so excited about seeing the Christmas markets. You'd have thought she'd want to get away from them, being stuck in one all week. Anyway, I can't wait.'

'Nice one.'

'We've got a bloke booked into our place in the Airbnb room too. Star will go in and feed the cat, but again, just in case he's a weirdo, keep an eye and ear out, can you? We lock our bedroom, but you never know.'

'Good bit of extra cash coming in, I get it. And don't worry, I'll make sure my presence is felt if needs be.'

'I know what I meant to ask you,' Billy added suddenly. 'Have you any idea how long you will be staying down here in Hartmouth?'

'Well, I see no point in leaving, if that's a good enough answer for now.'

'Course it is and I'm sure Star will be delighted.'

The big Irishman shrugged. 'She's a woman. Who knows what's going through her pretty mind.'

They both laughed. Screwing the lid on his Thermos flask, Billy stood up. 'Right, we'd better get moving. This deck ain't gonna clean itself.'

Chapter 30

Star sat at her crafting desk and linked her phone to her Bose speaker. As Enya's music started to fill the cosy workroom to the rear of the shop, she had to make sure that she didn't start to daydream too much. She had a very special ring to make for the equally special and soon-to-be Mrs Pearl Moon.

When Star was little, her mother used to rock her on her lap and sing along to the mournful lyrics of Enya's 'May It Be'; the song had forever instilled in her a feeling of peace. The first line contained the word 'star', hence its relevance to both Estelle and her daughter. But whatever the reason, this and other mindfulness-inducing music was one thing she could thank her mother for introducing her to. When it got to the line about a promise living inside her, Star looked across at her handbag and tears started to flow down her cheeks. Tears for the row she had had with her mother, tears for her lost father, whoever he might be, and fear for the results of the pregnancy test that was sitting unopened inside her bag.

Yes, she had to admit, she had a very slight tummy, and yes, looking at her usually small breasts, they too were a bit fuller and more tender. Maybe she had been kidding herself it was all that eating, or all the sex hormones flying around that might have caused her boobs to feel a bit sore, or even that she was due a period, as that used to happen sometimes too. Finally, she had to face the fact that those symptoms could mean that she was pregnant. But for today, she was going to sit in her workroom and do what she loved because once that baby-shaped cat was out of the bag, all hell would be let loose.

Conor was great. But – there was a *but*. Almost like being on the verge of the best orgasm you'd ever had, but not quite getting there. Like having your favourite ever haircut – but getting home from the salon and wishing you'd had the fringe cut that tiny bit shorter. Like deciding on a Mr Whippy ice cream cone and saying no to the flake. So nearly there and yes, being with Conor was nice, but who wanted something that was just 'nice'? Something that was not quite enough?

Star imagined weeing on that little white stick and getting a negative result. Would she feel upset? Maybe she would for one small moment, because she had always wanted another child. Star shut her eyes and imagined the word *pregnant* looking back up at her. She had so much to achieve still, and would a child get in the way? And would Conor want to stay with her? What's more, would *she* want to stay with *him* if he wasn't The One? But then how could she possibly allow another child to grow up without a father figure? This was becoming a rather awful generational pattern. How would Skye feel? Auntie Flo too!

Whatever happened, Star decided she would have to deal with it, and she would. It was Monday, a quiet day in the Ferry Lane shops. She could hold on to whatever 'promise was within' until later. She would finish Pearl's ring and then go upstairs to the flat and just do it, do the test, get it over with and worry about the consequences after.

Just as she was searching for her smallest pair of pliers in the wooden tray in front of her, she came across a little piece of pretty pink-flecked rhodochrosite crystal. She smiled at those love angels of hers presenting this to her right at this particular minute. She had encouraged Jack to give Kara a pair of earrings made out of this very crystal, to thank her for his stay in Hartmouth. He himself had thought it was a bit over the top, but knowing what a bad mental state Kara had been in at the time after her break-up with the horrible Jago, Star had insisted.

Coincidences like this often happened to her and made her believe in the power of the universe even more. She reached for one of her crystal leaflets and read, *Rhodochrosite can guide one in the quest for happiness, help one move forward after a period of doubt, and express love towards others without fear of rejection.* She thought sadly of Jack, who had rejected her. They had without a doubt both experienced strong feelings, but it had been a one-off. A wonderful memory of sex on a summer's day with a beautiful man. So yes, Jack 'I'm a bloody Englishman in New York' Murray could fuck off now. Maybe her expectations of love had been too great. Nobody was perfect. Nothing was perfect. The whole episode with the short, bearded one was a 'could have been', rather than a 'would have been'. What was the note he had written for Kara too, when he gave her those earrings, something like *no more 'I wish', but 'I will'*?

Maybe, whatever the outcome, this was the new start she needed in her quest for happiness. This was her time now. She *would* and she could! No more hankering after someone who had so little regard for her. Someone who couldn't even reply to a simple email message. There was never a good enough excuse for somebody not messaging you back. If people wanted to make time for you, however busy a life they had, they would.

Fingering the crystal and saying aloud, 'May it be, indeed, Enya,' Steren Lilian Bligh reached for her handbag, turned the shop sign to *Back in 15 mins* and headed up the stairs to the flat – and her destiny.

Chapter 31

'So Skye, you're all sorted, aren't you?' Kara rushed into Passion Flowers to make a last check on her able assistant. 'Why oh why did I arrange to go on holiday on a market day!' She opened the till to check there was change in there for the rare cash-paying customers. 'I've kept it simple, so say no to bouquets until Tuesday unless it is very urgent, then of course you must do it, but all hotel deliveries can wait.'

An impatient Billy was waiting outside in his van ready to drive them to the airport. He tooted to hurry her up.

'Dad and Pearl are going to swing by later on and tomorrow, and if they need to jump on the stall and help, do let them.'

'Kara,' Skye said calmly. 'You've written it all down for me. I've done many a market day. I will close Sunday, and Monday is always like a morgue, so stop worrying. Just go and enjoy yourselves, will you.' The teenager ushered her boss towards the door. 'Mum is next door, so I will be fine, and as you say, Joe and Pearl will help me if I need it. I'd love to run a flower stall myself one day, so this will be a perfect opportunity for me.'

'Aw, well, that's a great ambition. OK, call me if you need me, promise – but I will text you each day anyway. Bye.'

Kara signalled to Billy that she just had to run quickly in to see Star. He held his hands up in despair. He liked to be at least an extra hour early to an airport, he had told her, so there was time for him to have a couple of beers in Departures to calm his pre-flight nerves.

Star came through to the front of the shop as the wind chime signalled a customer.

'I've gotta be quick as Billy's outside,' Kara said in a rush. 'I just wanted to say, James Bond has been fed and watered so don't worry about today, but if you could do once tomorrow, Sunday and Monday morning that would be good. The Airbnb guy's name is Ralph, he looks hot on his profile photo, but try not to catch him in the shower.' She added archly, 'You do have a history with my previous guests.'

'Guest,' Star corrected, now having a vision of Jack Murray in her mind that she really could do without.

'Anyway, he's arriving this afternoon and leaving really early Monday morning. I will give him your number and message you his, just in case he needs to ask you something. Anything else?' Kara asked herself.

'Key code?' Star queried.

'I checked the spare key is in the box and that it's the same 1066 code as before and um . . . that's it, I think. I've left him Frank's vouchers for breakfast, and tea and coffee is on the kitchen side.' Billy tooted the horn again. 'I'd better go. He'll be going crazy out there.' Kara looked more closely at her friend. 'You seem quiet, are you all right?'

'Yes, just a bit tired, that's all.'

'Can't believe I forgot! The test – did you do it?'

'Yes. It was negative, thank goodness.'

'Phew, yes, complete relief, I'm sure. Sorry, been so full of it getting ready for this trip. See you Monday. I'll text you and thank you SO much for doing this.'

Star's 'Have fun' got lost in the tinkling of the wind chime.

Walking back through to her workroom, Star put a hand on her rounded abdomen. Damn her mother being right again! Star had never lied to her best friend before, but Kara had been in a rush and the truth was, Star wanted to keep things to herself for now. Herself and the little person growing inside of her. Team Bligh. For once she told Conor – in fact, as soon as she told anyone – life as she knew it would be so very different and she wasn't ready for that just yet.

Turning her mind to the job in hand, she reached for the little red jewellery box that housed the engagement ring she'd made for Pearl. She had put her heart and soul into making it perfect for dear Joe and couldn't wait to see what his fiancée thought of it when he popped the question. She reached for a miniature brush from her toolbox and, removing it from the box, delicately began to wipe at the bespoke sparkling piece. Its white gold double band studded with diamonds displayed a single freshwater pearl and her suggestion of a delicate flower made from a pink shell finished the second band off perfectly. Once clean, Star held up the exquisite piece and admired her handiwork. 'Shit,' she then muttered aloud, waving her hands about excitedly as she searched for the little spiritual card she had calligraphed earlier to include with the ring. On one side a plain red heart, on the other, the words, *Pearl: a person or thing of great rarity and worth. The gems of the sea are believed to offer protection to the wearer, as well as attract good luck and wealth. Moreover, pearls speak of the wearer's purity and integrity.* She popped it in the box and sighed contentedly. Job done.

Star then brought up the calendar on her mobile phone and started counting the weeks with her fingers. Her due date would be July sometime, she reckoned. Conor had only been here a matter of weeks, so it was pretty easy to calculate the delivery date even without her having a last period date to work from. Clever little eggs she must have, ovulating in a magical way. Her body had thought Conor Brady was The One obviously, even if she wasn't feeling it, and this surely must count for something. The love angels had sent him, and this was the reason: for her to have another, much-longed-for child.

Star began to convince herself that all was well. Conor was single, great to look at and a hard worker; also, being a dad already, on paper he had some great credentials. And a summer baby would be nice, no freezing cold night feeds like she had had with Skye. Then: 'Oh God,' she said aloud. Her worst thought was that Conor would be really angry with her. But as with everything, it took two to tango and they had agreed not to use condoms. So risky, looking back. Also, Conor was a self-confessed traveller. It was all right saying you wanted to stay in a place because you liked it, but not because some local girl had trapped you by getting pregnant. Which wasn't the case at all – but what if he thought that?

Star made a little huffy noise and picked up her phone again. Whatever, she would make it work. She had managed with Skye and she'd been only sixteen then. She was a grown working woman now, and if she had to do this alone then she would. She could do feeds in the workroom, maybe get an assistant. Anything was possible.

She dialled her doctor's surgery. 'Hello? Yes, I'd like to make an appointment with the midwife, please . . . That's right, she hasn't seen me before . . . Tuesday at 8 a.m. is perfect. Thank you.'

Chapter 32

Star had nearly finished setting up her stall and was hoping that a busy Friday market would help her take her mind away from her situation. Opposite, Charlie Dillon was tipping a pile of ready-cooked beetroot into a large bowl. His usual black beanie hat with an embossed carrot on the front was pulled well down over his ears and he was looking preoccupied.

Star went across to select an apple for breakfast. She had got over her feelings of queasiness on waking earlier this morning.

'No Daz today, then?' she asked casually. Star was finding it really hard to understand Charlie's reaction to his son coming out. If Skye were to tell her she was gay, Star knew she would embrace it – and her – with open arms.

'No, he's down on the quay what with our Billy being away.'

'Ah, right. I've missed his smiley face in the market lately.'

Pat Dillon was putting a handwritten *Organic Parsnips* sign at the front of a pile of the vegetables. She looked pained as her husband said darkly, 'Yeah, well, he's made his choice.'

'We all make choices, Charlie, and they're not always ones that other people agree with. You see, now Skye is a teenager, I've begun to realise that a bit of wiggle room is required, especially where so much is at stake.' She picked a juicy

Orange Pippin off the front of the stall, and placing a 50p coin on the green baize cloth in front of her, walked back to her own stall, head held high. Was it any of her business? No, it wasn't. But Darren was a friend and via Kara she had heard just how much he was hurting from his father's response or lack of it.

Back in the workroom, a couple of text messages beeped in. One was from Conor saying, *Hello stranger, fancy some Friday night fun?* But all of a sudden the fun felt like it had to stop. Sex with him was joyous and spontaneous, but the creation of a new human being could, ironically, spell the end of both of those things. She took her gloves off to answer.

I promised Auntie Flo fish and chips as it's Friday
Spoilsport! How about after?
I need to be up uber early for Saturday market day too

The Irishman went quiet. The other message was from Estelle. Star had made no contact with her mother since her outburst, had ignored her messages and calls knowing that if she answered when she was still feeling so angry, she might end up never seeing Estelle again. And that was something she didn't want to happen.

Star, it's me. I'm sorry x

Star reread the text. Estelle Bligh had never apologised to her in her whole life. Overwhelmed with both the response and the hormones now juggling around inside of her, Star started to cry. Rather than having a go at Charlie, maybe she should be less of a hypocrite and deal with her own problems first. Who was she to judge the man? They were not her feelings, nor her battle. She looked at her mum's text again. Yes, sorry sometimes was the hardest word to say, but with the fragile state she was in at the moment, Star knew that she needed to sort herself out and be feeling calm before facing the dramas to come. She and her mother had said some dreadful things to each other, but Estelle had hurt her badly and Star wasn't quite ready to forgive.

Star decided she would let her mother stew for a little while longer and reply when she was good and ready. And when the time was right, they could re-establish their skewed relationship equilibrium as they had done countless times before.

A new customer had just come in. Wiping her eyes, she put on a false smile and came out towards the counter.

There in front of her, his face hidden completely by a bunch of flowers, was Conor. He pulled the bunch down as if playing peek-a-boo with a child and just stared at her for a second, then realising she had been crying he dropped the gift on the counter, leaped over the counter gate and pulled her into a huge bear hug. 'What's the matter?' he asked. 'I knew something was wrong.'

'It's OK. I had a row with my mum, that's all.' Star couldn't stop the tears from coming again. He continued to hold her. 'I need to get outside and man the stall,' she said weakly.

'They'll come in if they want anything and the only suspected criminal around here is me so I doubt if anyone will steal anything.'

Star broke free. 'Sorry. It's just, my dad died, and I know I didn't know him, and the row with Mum was big and—' She stopped.

'And?'

Star bit her lip. She just couldn't say the words. Instead: 'I'm tired, Conor. I just need a good night's sleep.'

There was relief in his voice. 'I'm so sorry to hear about your Da, that's very sad. Do you want to talk about it?'

187

'Not now.'

'OK,' he said gently. 'How about I leave you be for a couple of days and, weather dependent, we meet for a walk on Sunday? It'll have to be after lunch as we are running the ferry till one o'clock. We could see if our old mate Phocoena phocoena is up on the Head, maybe?'

Star managed a grin. 'I'd like that . . . and Conor, it's not because I don't want to see you, it's . . .'

Conor held his hand up. 'No need to explain. We all need some time out. Daz asked if I fancied a drink tomorrow night, so I will have a few of those cloudy numbers with him, so I will.' He grinned, jumped back over the counter gate into the body of the shop and picked up the beautifully wrapped bunch of flowers. 'Here y'are,' he said. 'Stargazer lilies for the brightest little Star in Ferry Lane Market.'

'Aw, look at you being all romantic.' Star put her nose to them. 'They are gorgeous, thank you.'

'No, you are gorgeous and thank *you* for being just the way you are, tears, tantrums and tiaras included.'

'Even Auntie Flo told me that you will have kissed the Blarney Stone.'

'Well, you can tell Auntie Flo only the very lucky few receive my gold star jibber-jabber.'

Star smiled. 'I must pop over and see her later. Get her fish and chips.'

'Can't Skye do it again this week if you're tired?'

'No. It relaxes me, seeing her and Boris.'

'Boris? Don't tell me she's found a fella!'

'No, he's her potty-mouthed, or rather potty-beaked, swearing budgerigar. Proper hilarious, the things he comes out with. I should video him on my phone so you can hear.'

'Well, maybe I can come up and meet the pair of them

in the flesh and feathers one of these days. And the legendary Estelle, of course.'

'Then you would run for the hills.'

Conor leaned across and kissed Star's forehead. 'Nah. I'm not going anywhere. See you Sunday and no more tears, OK?'

As he disappeared back down through the crowds now forming in Ferry Lane Market, Star noticed the Oscar Wilde quote on the card she had put up on the shelf beside her: *The very essence of romance is uncertainty.* She thought it wasn't only the essence of romance that was uncertain, the very essence of bloody life was too.

Chapter 33

Jack parked his hire car where Kara had instructed then took his suitcase from the boot, tapped the 1066 code into the key store, unlocked the big front door and made his weary way up the stairs to Number One, Ferry View Apartments. His mate Ralph had said that yes of course he could use his Airbnb profile, as long as he promised not to wreck the joint and would come clean if an awkward situation arose as he didn't want to lose his high guest rating.

It was a great relief to Jack to find out, after sending a couple of messages, that Kara would be away with Billy while he was there. After all, the whole point of him coming was to surprise Star, and knowing how tight the two young women were as friends, that would have been nigh on impossible if Kara saw him first. He could have booked in at The Dolphin up the hill, it looked like a really nice hotel, but his memories of staying here in this apartment earlier in the year were so good that he wanted to relive them. The uninterrupted view of the estuary from the front room was what had sold it.

He put a couple of bottles of water in the fridge, then on opening the balcony door to take in the beautiful vista before him, he stretched out his arms and released a sound of pure pleasure. New York had been bitterly cold when he had left; the snow had gone, but a smoggy freeze had remained –

almost as chilly as the farewell he had received from Riley, who had had the jealous (and accurate) hunch that he wasn't really coming to England to visit his parents. It wasn't a complete lie as he had flown in a day early and had met them for dinner at the Heathrow hotel he had stayed in last night, saying that he had business meetings in Plymouth today and Monday, so was making the most of a little Cornish break. A photo of them together over dinner had appeased Riley, who said how sorry she was and that she probably wouldn't contact him again now as she was off to the Hamptons with her friends and would be busy herself.

All these lies. He wasn't proud of them, but it was easier than trying to explain that he had come all the way across The Pond to see if the feelings for a girl he had been with for such a short time were real or just a complete fantasy. His practical GP parents would think he was being foolish, while his girlfriend would probably push him out of the window of the Dakota Building. But something inside was telling him that he had to do it. Hearing that Blaise Pascal quote in that film had been too much of a coincidence. Star believed that people were drawn together for a reason, something he had found ridiculous initially, but despite trying to make a go of it with Riley, Steren Bligh had remained on his mind. And why, at that precise moment in his life, did old Blaise have to pop his circa four-hundred-year-old head up again?

After the long drive he had just had from London, the November rain when he stuck his head out on to the balcony brought with it a crisp Cornish breeze and a much-needed breath of fresh air. It was so nice to be back in Blighty. To be back amongst nature rather than the concrete jungle and constant pressure of the Big Apple and his life there. It had also been so wonderful to see and hug his mum and dad.

It made Jack realise how much he missed them, and also his sisters, who sadly had been unable to make it last night due to work commitments.

The sea was calm apart from a few wrinkly waves when the light wind hit its surface. On noticing Kara's dad's little yellow and red tug pulling cars over on the ferry in the distance, Jack smiled fondly. He loved the sound of gulls, a comforting signal that he was by the sea. As he watched, a couple of guys in a dinghy pulled up alongside a yacht, then one climbed aboard while the other whizzed his way back to the quay. It was so relaxing, Jack thought. He literally could estuary watch all day.

'Hello, James Bond.' He was effusive in his greeting as the black and white cat came tearing through his cat flap then purred around his ankles. 'I'm sure I can find some treats in the kitchen for you.' He went through to the compact kitchen area and found a packet of Dreamies next to the kettle. There was also a box of cat food with a note from Kara saying, *S. Once a day is fine, honestly, just load him up with 2 sachets. Thank you! See you Monday, K xx.* When Kara had told Ralph a.k.a. Jack that a friend of hers called Star would be coming in to feed the cat in the morning, his heart had started beating at a million miles an hour. It was a perfect scenario; he didn't even have to try and find her or convince her to see him. She would just be there.

A text brought him out of his daydream. It was from Kara, checking he was in and all was OK, and if he had any questions, to just shout. He was just about to ask what had happened to Sid Vicious, the terrapin who had lived here back in June, when he suddenly realised that he was in fact moonlighting as Ralph Kaufman from San Francisco and not Jack Murray, an Englishman from New York.

He looked around the apartment. It had changed, felt like it had more soul. Was more lived in, with its new comfy sofa and different pictures. A photo of her and Billy Dillon, the young ferryman he had briefly seen when he was here last time, was on the shelf where the terrapin tank had once been. The couple looked really loved up. He was so pleased; Kara was a great girl. On opening the cupboard in the bathroom, he realised that young Billy must have moved in already too. That was fast work. Jack felt an urge to chat to her and find out what was going on. The chance to do this when he had returned home had obviously been halted with Riley's jealousy and him wanting to keep a wide berth of everything connected with Hartmouth in order to try and save his relationship. He also noticed some wonderful photos of Kara in Barcelona, New York and Australia. She looked so well and happy, it was a delight to see.

Kara's sister, Jen, with whom he used to work, had told him the dates when Kara would be in New York and had asked if he could deliver something to her. She explained that it was a message and a ticket to spur her younger sister on to the next leg of the travel journey, which Jen had secretly arranged to allow Kara to open up her horizons. This had pleased Jack greatly, especially as during his short visit to Hartmouth he could see that his hostess was struggling after a break-up. This was when he had imparted his *No more I wish, but I will* message to her. Yes, Kara Moon had made an impact on him too, but in a very different way to her best friend.

Jack looked at his watch. It was 2 p.m. and his stomach was telling him he was hungry. It would be breakfast-time in New York, and he was used to having a large bagel delivered to his office around this time. Unpacking could wait, he decided. Pulling a bobble hat over his thick black hair, he made his way downstairs, out of the Victorian apartment block and began to walk along the crazy-paved promenade towards Frank's Café.

'Good morning,' came a greeting from a big Irishman. 'What can I do you for?'

Jack was grateful the man didn't recognise him from before.

'A ham and cheese toastie and a black coffee, please.' He was the only customer aside from a young woman with a pushchair sitting in the very back booth. The jukebox was belting out 'You've Lost that Lovin' Feelin'.

'Sure. Sit down and I'll bring it over. Sugar?'

'No, thank you.'

Frank began to sing along with the tune as an effortlessly elegant woman appeared at the doorway. Frank ran around the counter to open it for her.

'*Mon chéri.*' She kissed her lover cheek-to-cheek three times. 'You forgot your wallet, and I thought you might need it.'

'Aw. You drove all this way from home? That's so sweet.'

'I am hungry too. You can make me an omelette. No cheese.' She looked out of the window to see the car ferry just coming into the quay. 'Your Conor is in charge today, I see.'

'Yes. Billy's away with Kara so our boy is loving it, especially now he's won over the seasickness. Star gave him some sort of potion, so he tells me.'

'They seem very happy, he and Star, *non?*'

Jack's ears pricked up and homed in on the conversation. Damn those Righteous Brothers singing so loudly.

'I wouldn't be surprised if he never left here, you know. He seems smitten,' Frank said, beating some eggs in a bowl.

'He needed a good girl to sort him out.'

'Yes. I think they are perfect together. What's more, we could do with a wedding down here. I've still got all those beers that Roger the Dodger delivered last Christmas to use up before their sell-by date.'

'Bah! You are so romantic, Frank, not!' Monique swiped at him with a tea towel.

And as Big Frank laughed his throaty laugh and scooped his pretty partner into his arms, Jack Murray felt more like crying – into a glass of Dodgy Roger's beer.

Chapter 34

'I recognise those footsteps. Oh, Steren love, thank goodness you're here.'

Star walked into Florence Sibley's lounge, two warm bundles of fish and chips in hand, to find her auntie on the floor on her knees with her arms reaching right behind her.

'Jesus, Auntie. What are you doing down there?'

'Don't you be taking our Good Lord's name in vain now, my girl. Just help me up.' Star put their dinner down on the table as Florrie went on. 'I found this nice young man on the Internet. Enrico, his name was. Had wonderfully droopy Spanish eyes. Yoga for old fogies is his class. Anyway, I got in this position before the news and now I can't get out of it.' The old lady chuckled naughtily. 'Thank God I popped a TENA Lady in after *Countdown*.'

'Silly cow,' Boris squawked from his cage.

Star, unable to suppress her laughter, gently lifted her auntie to her feet. The old lady let out a ricochet of farts of relief as she slowly uncurled her aching limbs.

'I was joking about the incontinence pad bit,' she imparted breathlessly. 'I've the bladder of an ox, your uncle used to say to me.' And then she limped off to the toilet. When she reappeared, Star had set the table and had tended to the fire so that it was now crackling comfortingly in the grate. Their fish and chips were keeping warm in the oven.

'Remind me to bring some more logs up for you before I go,' Star said.

'Stop fussing, please. Come on, let's sit by the fire and have a catch-up. I feel as if it's been an age since I saw you.'

'Sorry, Auntie, I've been busy, with work *and* play.'

'Now that's what I do like to hear, and it was lovely to see young Skye last week. You know what she's like though. She's got ants in her pants, that one – could only sit still for five minutes, didn't want to eat with me, rushed off as soon as she felt she could get away with it. I couldn't believe how long her hair had grown.' Florence Sibley then stared right at her great-niece. 'What's wrong?'

'It's nothing.'

'And after nearly thirty-four years of knowing you body and soul and loving you, I think it's much more than nothing.'

Star rested her head on the wingback chair and shut her eyes for a second. She then took a long slow breath in and exhaled it noisily. 'I'm pregnant.'

'Jesus, Mary, Joseph, Mother of God! Not again!'

'Hello, hello, hello, hello,' Boris screeched from his cage, causing Florrie Sibley to jump up and throw the cover over his cage.

'Once is a mistake,' she told Star. 'Twice is a choice.'

'No, it wasn't like that.' Star felt wretched. 'Look, I don't want to go into details, but I thought we *were* being careful.'

'Not that careful, quite clearly. Oh, Star.' Florence Sibley then sat upright in her chair and chided herself with: 'What am I doing? "Do not judge, and you will not be judged." Luke chapter six, verse thirty-seven. I take it the baby is the Irish fella's? And there was me worrying about Skye getting herself into trouble.'

'You and me both.' Star managed to smile.

'And you want to have this baby?'

'I really do.'

Florence softened. 'Well, we had better get ready for another little Bligh bairn in our midst, hadn't we then? How lovely. When are you due?'

'I'm at the doctor's on Tuesday, so will find out for sure then, but sometime next July, I think.'

'Do you feel all right?'

'Bit sicky the other day but I think that was because I ate shellfish. I've been drinking a lot too, poor little thing. I had no idea.'

'It's a bit late to be worry-warting about that now. And what does the King of the Blarney have to say about it all?'

'I haven't told him yet. You are the only person who knows. Estelle did, however, tell me I was pregnant before I even realised. Just like with Star.'

'Of course she did,' Florence Sibley said bitterly, getting up and kissing her great-niece on the forehead.

'My dad is dead evidently. She blurted that out too. We had a huge row as she still won't tell me who he was.' Star's voice went low. 'Not even now he's gone.'

'She never told a soul. And for that reason, as hard as it is, maybe it's better not to know.'

'But I feel I have the right to. I *want* to know.'

'I dare say she's having hysterics about it even though she's probably not seen him for decades?'

'Yes.' Star sniffed. 'I keep thinking I will tackle her about it again when she's sober, but she never is sober these days.'

'If it's meant to be, the truth will come out when the time is right, my dear.'

'Do you really believe that?'

'I do. You're not ready for it yet. And I will pray for you

199

to find your peace with it, as I pray for your mother every day that she may find hers. Do you love him? Conor, I mean?'

'He's a good man. He's working hard for Billy Dillon now on the ferry and we have a lot of fun.'

'Clearly you have fun, but you didn't answer my question.'

'I've only known him seven weeks.'

'I knew in seven seconds with your uncle.'

'Load of bollocks!' came from under the birdcage cover.

'I just found out today that the priest from the Catholic church up the hill passed away this week too. Cancer. Just sixty-one he was, so very sad. That's no age at all, is it?' Florrie said. 'I didn't know him personally, but Mrs Beatty, who comes to my WI group, told me he commanded much respect in the community. Rarely took a day to himself.' The old lady sighed. 'The Dear Lord takes the good ones first, as they are better served in His world, is my belief.'

'Now that can't be true, Auntie, or you would have gone years ago too.'

Florence Sibley tutted, then went to the stove to take out their dinner. They sat at the kitchen table with Star even letting her say grace without a word.

When she'd finished what she could manage of the large portion, Flo put her hand on top of her precious great-niece's. 'This old table has seen family present and past laugh, cry, debate, sing and be merry. And it shall carry on doing this, way into the future. When I go, promise me you'll find a place for it somewhere in your life, where its secrets can soar.'

'I promise,' Star said, and she meant it. 'Thank you for being such a constant in my life, Auntie Flo. But don't you be going anywhere anytime soon, please.'

'You were the daughter Jim and I longed for ourselves and I am so very proud of you.'

Star looked sad. 'Everything will be all right, won't it, Auntie?'

Florence Sibley nodded. 'Of course it will. And if it's not all right, then it is not yet the end.'

'Amen!' Boris shouted from under his cover.

Chapter 35

Jack sat on the sofa eating leftover pizza for his Sunday lunch. His head hurt from the too many beers he had consumed whilst watching rubbish Saturday-night television. He took a sip of his now cold coffee, and gagged. Getting up, he threw open the balcony doors and, not caring about the freezing rush of air, he stared out at the view. It was a surprise to him to note just how many boats were sailing up and down the wide estuary waters. Was there such a thing as Sunday boaters, like Sunday drivers? It wasn't something he could say he fancied in this weather. Although when the sun did pop through, it did feel quite warm on his face. Maybe he should try it before he knocked it. He was sure he had never had this negative attitude towards stuff before he met Riley.

He looked back at his laptop, open at his most recent screenplay. Writing was hard. The screenplay he'd been working on last time he was here had received countless rejections, but he was determined to keep going. And now that he was feeling so miserable, the words for the new script were starting to pour out of him. The male lead was going through heartbreak and it was the first time in his life that Jack could honestly relate to that.

Since overhearing Frank and Monique talking in the cafe on Friday he had decided that he would just hide out at

Kara's place until Sunday. When Star came in to feed James Bond, Jack had held his breath and hid under the duvet, praying that she wouldn't hear his heart beating loudly beneath it. Just the sound of her sweet voice and kindness to Kara's beloved cat made him realise why he was feeling this way. Once she'd left, he would sneak out on the balcony so he could maybe catch a glimpse of her either getting in her car or walking back up the hill to her flat.

That morning, he had heard an Irish accent on the ferry and looking out had seen a tall, dark and very striking-looking man who he assumed must be Star's new partner. The man was the complete antithesis of himself – a five feet eight and a half, pale-faced bearded man with slightly crooked lower teeth and now a scar on his right cheek. He had always felt that he was punching above his weight when he first saw Star – until they had connected over the Pascal quote, that is. And he had finally understood how true those words were, that his ex-girlfriend had written to him all those years ago. Because now, however much his head told him that he didn't care about Star, that his life was in New York, the pull of his heart had been too great to ignore. Maybe he should just see her and tell her how he felt. He had to leave ridiculously early tomorrow; hit the road by 5 a.m. at the latest if he was to make his early afternoon Heathrow flight. So if he was going to do it, he had to do it today. In fact, he had to do it this afternoon.

Just as he was about to come in off the balcony, he heard voices and laughter below. Realising who it was, he shot inside. Peering behind the curtain in a way Agatha Christie's Miss Marple would have been proud of, he glimpsed the towering figure of Conor Brady swinging hands with the tiny, ethereal Star Bligh. They were chatting animatedly as they walked along the crazy-paved promenade, even stopping for a quick kiss before they pushed the door open to the Ferryboat.

Jack slammed the balcony doors shut and kicked the large empty pizza box that was on the floor. How ridiculous had he been, to think that Star would be sitting waiting for him! In fact, he felt embarrassed and shocked that he could have been self-absorbed and obsessed enough to think such a thing. Star had known that he had a girlfriend. And not only had he blatantly gone back to Riley, but he had also ignored Star's messages and then selfishly told her, via the third party that was Kara when he had bumped into her in New York, that he was sorry! No wonder the girl had moved on. He had given her no reason to do otherwise.

Chapter 36

Star wriggled on the pub seat to get comfy as Conor went to the bar of the Ferryboat to collect the two roast dinners they had ordered. She had found herself putting on leggings and a big jumper as she wasn't sure if it was her imagination or not, but since she had found out she was pregnant it seemed like she was ballooning at a rate of knots. It was exactly what had happened to her with Skye. But she had been five months along when she had found out – after Estelle had seen the truth and told her.

She was only a matter of weeks now, but looking at the size of Conor, this was sure to be a big baby. Star winced at the thought. Giving birth to Skye, a tiny five-pound baby, had been painful enough. And Star had forgotten her dislike of being pregnant too. At sixteen, unused to the bump that she thought just made her look fat, she would look in the mirror at her silhouette and cringe. And when all her school friends were dressing up to go to clubs, she was sitting at home in her joggers eating garlic mushrooms dipped in custard! Being older, it would be different this time, she hoped. The hardest bit was going to be telling Conor. Luckily, she had agreed to drive up to Penrigan Head for their walk after lunch, so she didn't have to make an excuse for her lack of drinking at least. She had it all worked out in her head. Conor, suffering from a huge hangover after his night out with Darren, had insisted on food before they had their walk. So, with limited daylight, they needed to eat and get up there quickly. Her plan was to tell him where they had seen the dolphin and kissed. Set the mood. It would be fine, she kept reassuring herself.

'Diet Coke?' Star laughed when Conor returned to their table. 'You must feel bad.'

'I tell you, it's that cloudy poison. I am never *ever* drinking it again.'

'Are you sure you want to go for a walk?'

'Yes, the sea air will do me good.'

'We will need to eat and leave as it gets dark around four now.'

'Sure, sure. I'm just going to inhale this whole plate of food, then I'll be fine.'

'How was Daz?'

'He's grand. Says he feels a whole lot better, now he's being true to himself.'

'Good, and did he mention his dad?'

'Yeah, that's not so good yet. He's hoping with Christmas coming up that it may ease the situation.'

'Families and Christmas.' Star sighed. 'We usually just go to Flo's, me, Mum and Skye. Mum gets drunk and rude and is usually crashed out by the fire before five. Skye recently is just stuck to her phone, so me and Auntie are the only ones who end up watching the Queen's Speech and playing silly games together.'

'Thank heavens for Auntie Flo.'

Star laughed. 'Thank heavens indeed.'

'I love my Irish family Christmases. I have three brothers and a sister. It's quite a party.' His voice became sad. 'But I don't always get to see my Niall any more.'

'Aw, that's tough, but wow having all those siblings. Being an only child has its advantages, but big celebrations is certainly not one of them.' She looked him. 'Will you go back to London for Christmas then?'

Conor hesitated. 'Unless I get a better offer, of course.' He squeezed her knee under the table. 'Pudding?'

'Are you having one?'

'It has to be apple crumble and custard for me.'

'Just a bowl of custard would be good.'

Conor laughed. 'You are so sweet. Custard coming up.' He returned to the table to find Star looking at her phone with an anxious look on her face. 'What's wrong, *a stóirín*?'

'It's my mum. She's fallen over, thinks she might have broken something and wants me to go to her right now.'

'That's OK. I'll come with you. Let me cancel dessert and settle the bill.'

They pulled into the Hartmouth Head static home park slightly blue in the face as Conor had insisted that Star roll the roof back so he could not only see the beautiful coast-road scenery but also allow him some room to manoeuvre his six-foot two frame in her little Smart car.

'Home sweet home.' Star parked outside the only dark green unit.

'Right.' Conor got out of the car. He had no preconception of his girl's mother or where she might live.

Estelle Bligh was sitting on the sofa, drink in hand, with her foot lifted up high on to a cushion.

'So here you are at last!' she snapped ungratefully. 'Did

you bloody walk or something? I took some ice out of my drink and just put it on my leg and wrapped an old tea towel around. It's *sooo* sore. Oh, hello, big boy.'

'Hello, Mrs Bligh.'

'It's Miss and just call me Estelle, please.' The drunk woman looked him up and down.

'Mum! This is Conor. Conor, this is my mum Estelle.' Star began to unwrap her mother's foot. 'How did you do it anyway?'

'I was only wearing one shoe and I slipped down the decking steps. What I needed was a strapping young fella like you to land on, Conor. Steren! Ow!'

The woman's little toe was bright red and slightly swollen. Her breath was acrid with alcohol.

'They can't do anything for broken toes at the hospital even if there is a fracture, I don't think,' Star said, 'so you'll just have to rest it. Did you hurt anything else?'

'Not that I know of. I think the vodka broke my fall.' Estelle tipped her head back and laughed hysterically. 'The vodka broke my fall, get it?'

An apologetic Star looked to Conor who winked at her encouragingly and advised: 'Just a plaster will do. Wrap it around the other toe to keep it stable.'

'I forgot you were a Boy Scout.' Star smiled, heading off to the bathroom cabinet to see if she could find a suitable Band Aid.

'Well, my girl certainly knew how to pick a good father for her children. What beautiful babies you are going to make.'

Hearing this, Star froze in the doorway of the bathroom.

Conor gave a nervous laugh. 'I'm very fond of your daughter, Estelle, but we're not quite at that stage yet.'

'Aren't you? I think maybe she owes you a little chat.'

As Conor gazed over at Star with a look of bafflement on his face, she threw the packet of plasters at her mother.

'Refusing to tell me about my own father and even how he died was a pretty low blow but this, *this* tops even that,' she shouted. 'From now on you are dead to me!' And she stormed out of the mobile home and into her car.

Conor said a hasty goodbye to Estelle then ran off, calling, 'Star, calm down, darling. Talk to me. It's OK, it's all right.' He squeezed himself into the passenger seat.

Without saying a word Star started the car and tore out of the park and on to the coast road. Ignoring Conor's attempts at reassurance and emitting sounds which had never before come out of her, Steren Bligh drove, white-hot with rage, until she reached her chosen destination. Here she stopped and got out. On a cold Sunday afternoon in November with the dark gloam of the night sky already forming she made her way over to her thinking bench. Conor was right by her side.

She looked out to sea as if the familiar view would soak up and whisk away the painful conversation she was about to have. With a massive sob, the words, 'I am pregnant,' flew out of her mouth and into the world, hitting the confused Irishman's ears, causing his mouth to drop right open like some bizarre fairground attraction into which you throw balls.

'How?'

'Do you want me to draw you a picture?' Star sobbed again. 'I am so sorry, but we had the conversation about condoms, and I guess because we were having so much sex, whatever precautions we were taking didn't work, did they?'

'Feck!'

'Are you angry?'

'No, of course not, just a bit shocked, that's all.' He put his arms around her quivering shoulders then took his warm jacket off and wound it around her. 'How far gone are you?'

'I don't know for sure. I'm going to the doctor's on Tuesday.'

'And how are you feeling?'

'I feel fine so far. I was a bit sick after we had those oysters the other night, but I don't think that was baby-connected.'

'Do you want to keep the child?'

'I had to talk to you first, but yes, I do.' Before he could say anything Star began to gabble, 'I know you're a wanderer, I would never trap you. I can manage fine on my own.'

Conor stood up and ran a hand through his hair. 'Let me just take this in, OK, before you start saying things like that. Jesus, Star. I was just getting myself back on track.'

'And that doesn't have to stop. We're not in the Dark Ages. I have a successful business. I don't need your money, Conor.'

'It's not about money, is it? It's about that little human being inside you that needs love and care and to be brought up correctly. And you definitely want to keep it?'

'Please don't ask me that again.' Star stood up, his jacket slipping to the floor. 'I want to go home.'

With Conor now hunched up in the car with the roof closed, they travelled in silence back to Ferry Lane. Star parked up at the back of her shop, switched off the engine and put on the handbrake.

Conor turned to her and put his hand under her chin. 'I really do think the world of you, Star, and I mean that, but I just need to go into my own place and have a big think about this and digest it – and then we can work out what we both do with this news. Do you understand?'

Star nodded. 'I'm so sorry.'

'Apologies not required. I was there, remember? It takes two, after all.' He kissed her gently on the lips, looked down at her tummy then clambered awkwardly out of the car. As he walked up the stairs to his flat over the florist's, he called back, 'Give me a couple of days to get my head around everything. OK?'

Star nodded again, then when he was out of sight she bashed her hands on the steering wheel and through gritted teeth repeated, 'Damn Estelle! Damn bloody men! Damn getting bloody pregnant!'

Chapter 37

Star woke up when the alarm went and looked at the bedside clock. Seven thirty, good – she would have time to go and feed the cat over at Kara and Billy's place and then get back to the shop. A text was already in her inbox from Conor. *Morning beautiful mummy to be. Dinner at mine 7pm tomorrow. Heating will be on full, I promise xx.* She smiled. She was always moaning to Conor that his place was never warm enough. And it was probably better to see him after she'd been to the doctor's anyway, so they would have a definite due date of birth to work to.

'Bye, Mum, see you in a bit!' her daughter shouted as she left, slamming the front door.

Star caressed her rounding tummy and felt worried about telling Skye. It could be even trickier than telling Conor had been.

This should be such a happy time, but it was far from the ideal scenario. On paper: pretty girl meets handsome Irishman and they have a baby. The crucial bit missing from the story was: they fell in love with each other as their relationship developed.

From the outside, it appeared that most couples seemed to do everything in the right order and in the right way. They got to know each other, fell in love, had the most gorgeous wedding, moved into a bright and airy home with a huge garden, popped out two adorable children, neatly spaced, with two sets of amiable and flexible grandparents who helped along the way. But did anybody really have the perfect life? Of course not. This was the unreality of 'reality' on social media, with its filtered experience that made even the most adequate feel inadequate. Once you turned off this fantasy, you saw that every single person was fighting their own battle to stay afloat in this everchanging world.

As Star stood under the shower, she thought about the families around her: were there any who fitted the perfection mould? The Dillons, who had been a tight unit, were now blown apart by the inability of Charlie to accept Darren's sexuality; Kara's mum had left her husband and younger child for another man; and even behind the bright smile of Mrs Harris from Tasty Pasties lay the memory of her husband dying in a fishing boat accident ten years previously. (Although Philip Gilmour, the owner, had once told Star in confidence that the man had been a bully anyway, and that was why Mrs H. was so relaxed and contented now.) There was always a backstory behind the front page.

Life, Star decided – *real* life – was one big board game of Snakes and Ladders. First you were up, and then, just when the final square with 100 on it was within reach, you could land on a big snake and tumble all the way down to the first square again. Nothing was guaranteed in life. When happiness came along, it had to be grabbed with both hands and celebrated, bounced about with joy like a beach ball with friends on a sunny day.

Before too long, Star was making her way down to Ferry View Apartments to feed James Bond. An hour had passed since she had woken up, and by now Conor would be over at the other side on the ferry crossing, which pleased her. She wasn't ready to face him yet and the Airbnb guest would definitely be gone by now. Kara had messaged her last night to tell her that she and Billy had had the most brilliant time and to confirm that the guest was leaving at 5 a.m. today for his return flight. She wrote that she and Billy would pop in and see Star on their way back that evening. Star had been burning for her friend's support but, not wanting to ruin her minibreak, had decided that telling her face-to-face was much the best option.

With all the dramas going on, she was pleased that things had been so straightforward with the Airbnb booking. She actually hadn't heard one peep out of Ralph from San Francisco. She had knocked gently before going in to feed James Bond the past two mornings, but the guest had either been out already or was asleep in his room.

She tapped out the code, 1066, took the key from the safe on the wall and opened the main front door to the Ferry View Apartment block – then was nearly knocked over as James Bond raced out past her, taking her breath away. Once she'd recovered, she trotted up the stairs and politely, as if she was a housekeeper in a hotel, knocked on the apartment door with the back of her knuckle. Pushing it open, believing the guest to have departed, she was surprised to notice a small wheelie case standing by the door. Calling out, 'Hello!' she went into the kitchen and was opening the fridge door to pop in the pint of milk she had bought for the wanderers' return when a familiar-sounding and uplifted, 'Hello, you,' came back at her.

That was the second shock. With her heart beating madly and a huge rush of adrenaline coursing through her veins, Steren Bligh walked into the lounge to see a bearded figure standing in front of the open doors of the balcony, waiting for her.

Aside from the small scar on the top of his right cheek, he was just how she had remembered him. With her eyes and mouth open as wide as the Hartmouth estuary twinkling in the winter sunshine below, she let out a gasp.

'Jack? Oh my God – it's *you*, Jack! What the hell are you doing here?'

Chapter 38

Darren Dillon expertly manoeuvred the *Happy Hart* tug on to the Crowsbridge quay and came out to help Conor usher the cars and one van off.

'You're a bit quiet this morning, mate,' Darren noted as he took his gloves off, lit a cigarette and leaned on the side railing of the float.

'Yeah, I've got something on my mind, true enough.' Conor sighed. 'Big shit, actually.'

'Wanna talk about it?'

'I'm not sure.'

'Remember that I've kept a pretty big secret to myself for a good few years, so I do know how to keep my mouth shut.'

They both laughed.

'Your Bill can't hear about this just yet,' Conor warned him. 'Just so you know.'

'I can respect that, mate.'

Conor looked out to the estuary mouth and took a deep breath. 'Star's pregnant.'

'Oh man.'

'Tell me. I really like the girl, she's great as you know, but I wasn't quite ready for this little bombshell.'

'I can imagine.'

'I really like it down here too, but again, it's a big commitment to start a new life in a place I barely know.'

'You have Frank and Monique and me and Bill already as family and friends, so it's not as if you are on your own.'

'My son is in Ireland,' Conor said heavily.

'And? How often do you see him? Cornwall is not a million miles from anywhere really.'

'I know, I know. I think it's the "where do I go next with Star" thing that's bothering me the most. I don't want to make another mistake. I've only known the girl five minutes.'

'Well, you've made one big mistake, so what's another?' Darren laughed as he took a large drag of his cigarette and blew out a massive ring of smoke into the freezing air.

'Thanks a lot.' Conor jokingly swiped at his arm. 'What's important is herself at the moment. I mean, she's got to go through the pregnancy and have the little mite.'

'Give it the seventy-two-hour rule.'

'That's a new one on me. What do you mean?'

'It's something my old man taught me. Problems that seem impossible, you wait around three days – the seventy-two hours – before doing anything, and then they either don't seem so bad, or something happens to take the edge off the drama.'

Conor said soberly, 'That baby is not going away.'

'Yes, but you may see things a little more clearly.'

'Let's hope your dad takes a bit of his own medicine there, eh?' Conor put his big hand on Darren's shoulder. 'Thanks, mate.'

'Glad to be of help.' Darren gestured at the cars already lining up on the quay. 'Right, let's get back to business – and mum's the word on this, I promise.'

'Ha ha – very funny. Ever thought of being a comedian?' Conor shook his head as he opened the gate and let the waiting customers stream on board the floating deck.

Chapter 39

In winter, Penrigan Pier was only open in daylight hours. Aside from one mobile coffee and snack van at the entrance, all the other food and retail ports were closed up against the elements. Pensioners, reliving their youth and glad of the lack of crowds, could be seen wrapped up warm taking a leisurely stroll along the boardwalk or sitting with a blanket on their knees on a bench in one of the alcoves that ran down the middle of the pier, many with a shopping bag containing a flask of tea and a packet of sandwiches. At weekends, teenagers would hang out in the alcoves smoking, drinking, shouting and play-fighting. The historic Penrigan Pier had most certainly given to the area a legacy of first-time lovers and lasting loves.

'I feel most honoured you've shut up shop for me.' Jack took a sip of hot chocolate, and some foam ended up stuck to his moustache. He wiped it off, then licked his finger.

'Hardly. I need to be back by eleven – one of the joys of running my own business.'

'D'you know, Star, I haven't been on a pier for years,' Jack said. 'Shame it's not all open or I'd have whipped your arse at the Dolphin Derby at the end. Sad to admit, I'll even go for a bit of Bingo in places like this.'

'Me too,' she confided, 'but I would never confess that to Skye. I just thought it would be easier if we came here – and I do love a bench.'

'You're so funny.'

'No, Jack, I think everyone should have a special place to think. I have two. This is one of them. Nature gives me such an energy boost, clears my mind. I can get my thoughts straight when I'm away from people and my phone.'

'Where's the other one then?'

'Up on Hartmouth Head car park near my mum's place. And when I'm down here in town, I come to the pier as it's near my auntie's flat. I've been coming here all my life, in fact. Just sitting and staring and thinking.' She looked at him. 'Have you ever checked out inscriptions on benches?'

'Er, no, can't say I have.'

'Well, I know all the ones here off by heart.'

Jack's own heart skipped a beat at this beautiful woman's quirky ways. She really was something else.

'I mean, read this one.' Star stroked her finger along the engraved plaque attached to the bench they were sitting on. 'This is why I chose to sit here.' She began to read aloud. '"To my Molly. There's never an end to the sea, so why for you and me? Your Ronnie." So sweet. I don't even want to know if either or both of them has died. I prefer to imagine that they are infinitely happy.'

The unobscured view of the dark grey sea blew Jack's mind. The sound of the waves licking the edge of the pier struts was hypnotic, the shelter from the wind in the little alcove creating a sense of warmth and safety.

'I'm not sure if life allows that luxury.' Jack smiled at Star's endearing ways, her innocence and her wisdom. 'I would probably more likely remember this graffiti on here.'

'If we look close enough you might see "Star loves Danny."'

'Did you? Love Danny?'

Star laughed again. 'Doesn't everyone think they are in

love at fifteen?' She then said shyly, 'Your beard looks good shorter.'

'Thanks. I trimmed it especially.' Then Jack cringed at this revelation.

To fill the awkward silence, they started to talk at the same time.

'You go first.' Star was conscious that her hands were shaking slightly. Just sitting next to him in the twenty-minute car journey to the pier had engulfed her with the exact same feeling she had experienced when she'd first set eyes on him in the market earlier that year. Memories had come flooding back; the moment she heard his voice; the passionate love-making in her flat; the soulful connection that she had never experienced with anyone else, ever.

It felt like she was dreaming to have him back here with her, especially when she had expected never to see him again. To see him had been such a surprise, but of the nicest kind. And now she was sitting this close to him, the cloud of connection between them was like a soft golden glow that illuminated them both. Maybe *this* was love.

'Why did you lie and tell Kara you were somebody else?' she asked.

'I er . . . I didn't want my girlfriend to know that I was coming here. She has a habit of checking my messages.'

'Ah, I see. And I thought you were leaving at 5 a.m.'

'Yes, I was but I was tired and it makes no difference to me getting a later flight as I'm not due back at work until Wednesday.'

'Why didn't you let me know you were here? I don't get it.' Star felt hurt.

Jack took another sip from his now not so hot chocolate. 'I'm working on a new screenplay and I just wanted the silence,' he lied eventually. 'I love the peace of this place. The whole estuary thing, it's just gorgeous and so far removed from New York and my life there. I guess it's running away without running away, if you get what I mean.'

'None of us can run away forever, Jack.' Star had found it so hard to put into words what was missing from her relationship with Conor, but this was it. This natural chemistry. The kind of magnetism that drew two individuals together when they met for the first time. A bit like the everlasting bond that her auntie had described between mother and child – this is what she felt for Jack.

As she looked deeply into his long-lashed hazel eyes, he quickly stood up, asking, 'Are you hungry?'

'I can wait.'

'I need something, I'll run up to the food van at the entrance.'

On his return, Jack placed a bag of food down next to him then put his hand on top of Star's, causing a tingle to shoot up her arm and then down to a direct hit on her heart.

'I'm really sorry for being such a coward and not responding to your messages.'

She pulled her hand away. 'Well, yeah. It did upset me, I'm not going to lie.' Star recalled her sleepless nights and feeling of despair at being rejected by the first man in ages who had quite simply rocked her soul.

'And when I saw Kara in New York,' he went on, 'I was so pleased that at least I could pass on some words to you.'

'What happened to you – your scar? And Kara told me that your arm was in a sling.'

'It was an unfortunate accident. Riley, my girlfriend, found one of your messages and went crazy.'

'And hit you?' Star's voice rose.

'No, she pushed me and I fell backwards on to our glass coffee table.'

'That's all right then, sounds like a great relationship.' A memory of her grandmother experiencing almost the same fate, elevated the bitterness in her voice.

'I was the one who was unfaithful.'

Star was stung. 'Like I say, a great relationship.'

'I wanted to contact you so badly, but I promised her that we would make a go of it and that I would change my email address and phone numbers. Anything for a quiet life, really,' Jack admitted. 'You see, I've been with her a while, and life isn't black and white, we all know that. And when I met you, the time I spent with you . . . well, it was amazing. I've never laughed so much. You're beautiful, Star Bligh. You really are. It was the best one-day stand I think I've ever had.'

Star felt the bile rising within her. 'One-day stand,' she repeated, taking in a big gulp of air at the acceptance of that fact.

'I've never done anything like that before, but . . .'

'But "The heart has its reasons which reason knows not" and all that.' Star finished off his sentence with a fake laugh causing Jack to feel that his heart might actually burst out of his chest. Butterflies on acid were now flying round his gut.

'Even if the timing *is* shit,' he blurted out, glad of the diversion of the seagull landing noisily next to their feet and beginning to pace around as if questioning why the food bag had not yet been opened.

'So, you and Riley are going strong then,' Star said flatly.

'Well, let's put it like this, we're going . . . but those love angels you were on about, well, they've called in a handsome fella for you now, haven't they? And with no complications, I bet.'

'How did you—?'

'I saw you on the quay.'

'Ah, right. Yes, Conor's great.' Star automatically put her hand to her bump. 'And yes, it's been plain sailing.'

'I guessed he's Frank's son by the look of him.'

'His nephew.'

'Ah, I thought there was a similarity. So, it's going well for you, is it?'

'Really well,' Star enthused, thinking that she might actually vomit. And then without warning her subconscious took over and the words, 'In fact, so well that I'm pregnant,' suddenly burst out of the 'things I really didn't want to say today box' and into the ether.

'Wow. Congratulations,' Jack managed after a moment. 'You didn't waste any time. Is that a public toilet I see down there?' He rushed off, shouting back, 'Give me a minute.'

With both hands on the small white hand basin he looked up at the water-splattered mirror and tried with all his might to push the feelings of complete despair back down inside. His face was red, his breathing shallow. His heart was breaking. Why had he thought that making a go of it with Riley was the right thing to do? Their relationship was poisonous. And ironically, even now pregnant with another man's child, Star Bligh represented everything to him that was pure, everything he had ever wanted in a woman. But he had lost her, and he deserved to have lost her.

Splashing his face with cold water, he composed himself and came back to the bench where Star was peeking in the paper bag to see what food he had ordered.

'Sorry about that,' he said. 'Too much coffee earlier.'

Star handed him the bag. 'Well, eat up. I should be getting back to the market soon.'

'I don't fancy it now.' Jack waved his hand dismissively. 'I must get on the road, too. Can't be late getting home to Riley. Changed man and all that.' By gritting his teeth it somehow helped to keep the emotion out of his voice.

'No, you must get back to her.' Star felt like she was burning up inside.

On arriving at Kara and Billy's flat, Star was relieved to see that the ferry was mid-estuary and heading towards Crowsbridge. The last thing she needed was that sort of run-in. Not now.

Jack squeezed her leg as he got out of the car. 'It's been so good to see you, and good luck with Conor . . . and the baby.'

'You too, Jack. Take care.'

He turned and tapped on the window. Holding in her tears, Star put the window down. Realising it could be their last goodbye, Jack hung on to it as if his life depended on it.

'I meant to say I heard another Blaise Pascal quote in a film the other day.' The words *'go away'* were screaming in Star's head. '"If you do not love too much, you do not love enough."' Jack's voice quivered. 'Great, isn't it?' He abruptly turned and tore himself away.

'Goodbye, Jack.' Star's voice ended in a sob as she called after him then sped off from Ferry View Apartments as quickly as her little Smart car would take her.

Yes, the timing had been shit, as Jack had said. Time may fly and time may drag, but sometimes time is just a complete and utter bitch.

Chapter 40

'*Dobrý den!*' Kara pushed open the door to her friend's flat above STAR Crystals & Jewellery and made her way inside. 'Why have you closed up so early today?'

'Dobray what?' Star said dully.

'It means hello in Czech. Put the kettle on, Star, I've got so much to tell you. We've had the best time! You must go with Conor. The stalls are amazing, and so are the pretty lights and the food and just everything. And bless Skye, I've just popped in to see her and she's coped fine, so all is well in my world.' Kara then checked out Star's face, swollen from crying. 'Shit mate, there's me completely full of it and you look like the weight of the world is on your shoulders. Go and sit down, I'll make us a cuppa or do you want something stronger?'

'Green tea is fine.' Star sat with her knees curled under her on the comfy purple sofa.

'So, what's up?' Kara joined her.

'I saw Jack.'

'You *what?*' Kara's eyes were wide.

'Yes, there was no Ralph from San Francisco. Jack had used his mate's profile and it was him all along.'

'Oh my God, Star, what did he want?'

'He said he was working on his screenplay and needed the peace.'

'Complete bollocks. Why come all the way to Hartmouth to do that? He could have gone anywhere else. He wanted to see you, obviously.'

'Oh Kar, I don't know what to do. There's something else.' Star bit her lip.

Kara moved to her friend's side and put her hand gently on her arm. 'Is it your mum? About your dad?'

'No.' Star started to cry. 'I *am* pregnant. I was when you asked me the other day but I just kind of felt by not telling anyone, it wasn't quite real. I didn't have to face it.'

'Oh, darling. Have you told Conor?'

'Yes, and Flo – and God only knows why, but I just told bloody Jack.' Star sobbed again.

Kara went to the bathroom and got her friend a wodge of toilet issue. 'Here, blow your nose and let's break this down, shall we? Do you want to go through with it?'

Star nodded. 'Yes, of course I do. I have no excuse not to have a baby.'

'But you do have the choice.'

'I know I do. The thing is, I don't love Conor, but I think I love Jack.' Star's expression showed her torment as she began to ramble on. 'And how can I spend my life with someone I don't love when I love someone else? And it's not as if I don't like Conor – I do, very much – and don't say I might grow to love him because nobody can predict that.'

'Hold on a second, this is considering that Conor is going to stay around.'

'He said he needs time to think things through.'

'That's fair enough.'

'Is it? He went home on his own last night and I just wanted him to come around and hug me.'

'Did you tell him that?'

'No.'

'Men are not mind readers, Star, they need to be told and not just when it's a matter of affairs of the heart. Never forget that the majority of them see the world through testosterone-tinted glasses. My Billy would happily not hoover for a year, if I didn't prompt him.' Kara took a swig from her tea. 'How far gone are you?'

'I don't know exactly. I've got the doctor's tomorrow.'

Kara looked at her friend's tummy. 'There's a little bump already.'

'I know! I reckon it's going to be a monster child. There's part of me that is so excited.'

'There's a lot of me that's so excited.' Kara grinned. 'I'd better hurry up on our mission. They can be in the same year at school then, just like we were.'

Star perked up. 'Aw, that would be amazing. They can play and grow up together just as we did too.'

'It's good to see that smile back. Would you like me to come with you tomorrow?'

'Thanks, but no. I'd rather go on my own.'

'OK. As for Jack, is he still with Riley?'

'Very much so, by the sound of it.'

'Well, leave him to that dysfunctional relationship. He obviously has no balls – whereas Conor appears to have huge ones.'

Star managed a laugh. 'I could talk for hours but I'm so knackered and stressed. I'm going to have a deep bubble bath and a lie down, I think.'

'Good idea. Before I go, did Estelle give you any more info about your dad's death?'

'None. She's getting worse, Kara. I think him dying has

badly affected her. Her drinking is off the scale. She only fell and broke her bloody toe yesterday. She also told Conor that I was pregnant before I had had a chance to break it to him in my own way. It was mortifying.' Star closed her eyes for a second. 'I was so angry, I said . . . I said . . . that she was dead to me.' She swallowed the painful lump in her throat.

'She probably won't even remember that,' Kara comforted her. 'Don't worry. Go and have a nice bath and relax, and let me know how you get on at the doctor's. I'm always just a phone call away, you know that.'

With the click of the front door, a deep-in-thought Star started running a bath. When it was ready, she climbed in, lay back and let the warm water soothe and relax her. And as she began to put things into perspective, a feeling of peace came over her. For amidst all the uncertainty surrounding her, the one thing that she was sure of was that, just like Skye, this baby would be dearly and completely loved.

And at the end of the day, that was all that really mattered.

Chapter 41

'Riley? Riley, I'm home!'

Relieved at there being no answer, Jack left his case in the hallway and walked on through to the lounge, where he noticed a bar of his favourite chocolate on the coffee table and a little hand-scribbled note saying, *Back at eight, enjoy this now, enjoy me later. Missed you x*

Without even taking his coat or shoes off, he let out a big, tired sigh, sat down and was just laying his head back on the sofa when a text came in from his secretary. *Hi Jack. Don't forget you've got a 7.30 breakfast meeting with Saxon's tomorrow, then lunch with McAdams Fuller, so wear a tie.* He sent back a quick thumbs-up emoji and shut his eyes in the hope he would be able to have a nap before Riley got home and started jumping all over him.

The plane journey from London had been long and given him too much time to think. It had taken everything for him to go over and see Star, to tell her how he really felt – and because of his own stupidity, it had all been for nothing. Angry at himself and angry that she was pregnant so soon after meeting someone, he had blocked her number. There was no point in any of it now. Just seeing her beautiful face again as they sat on the pier had stirred up another whole load of feelings. Feeling the warmth of her personality and the obvious chemistry that flowed between them had been off the scale. It had made him realise that he was ready to up and leave his New York life and Riley; but none of that mattered now. If she just had a boyfriend, he could have fought for her, but a baby in the mix too, well that was a whole different ball game.

He looked around him. There was no denying they lived in luxury here, but home sweet home didn't feel like home any more. Seeing his parents had made him realise how much he missed them. Just being in England, where everything seemed smaller, more real, less contrived, was where he belonged. But sadly, the woman who he now realised he wanted to be with, was pregnant with another man's child and seemed very happy.

Why hadn't he just acted on his gut and told Star how he felt when he left her the first time? Why did he think the life he had here was better? The money, the kudos of living in the Dakota Building, the fantasy of a pretty young actress on his arm and him walking the red carpet when his screen-play hit big. None of that mattered any more. All that mattered plainly and simply was a girl called Steren Lilian Bligh who lived above a jewellery store in Ferry Lane Market in the picturesque estuary town of Hartmouth.

Chapter 42

'Are you sure?' Star was stunned, almost speechless, as she sat opposite the white-haired midwife in the treatment room at the Hartmouth doctor's surgery.

'I've delivered enough babies in my time to know you are around halfway through, missy. By my reckoning, your due date if you go the full forty weeks will be March the seventeenth.'

'That's my birthday too!' Star exclaimed, with a flashback to her mother's drunk lips relaying that even St Patrick couldn't help her. Of course, 17 March was St Patrick's Day as well as her own birthday! Estelle Bligh really *was* a white witch.

'I thought I was just getting f-fat,' she stuttered. 'March, that's so soon.'

Star thought back to her tryst in June and now everything made sense. With Conor and her only getting together in October, there was no way it could be his. The startling and undeniable fact that Steren Lilian Bligh had to face was that she was very much pregnant with Jack Murray's baby.

Feeling suddenly faint, she made a funny little squeaking noise.

'Are you OK, dear?' The midwife reached for Star's wrist and took her pulse.

Remembering her yogic breathing exercises from a few

years back, Star managed to centre herself as the matter-of-fact woman in front of her continued.

'Granted, you are a tiny thing, but your bump is still on the small side, so just to be safe I'm sending you straight to Penrigan General for a scan. You would have had one around now anyway. I have seen ladies like this before though, and then all of a sudden they balloon.'

'So just to double-check, are you really and I mean *really* sure? Skye, that's my daughter, was only five pounds when she was born.'

'Steren, I am one hundred per cent certain. Have you felt Baby kicking at all?'

'No.' A sudden panic swept over her.

'Don't worry, sometimes they don't make their presence felt until a bit later.'

'I've read about things like this happening, about women not knowing they were pregnant.' Star gulped. 'I could have gone full term and given birth under my market stall.'

'Situations like these are rare but not unheard-of, you're right. Especially as your periods are so awry. But here we have living proof that little miracles can happen. This baby was meant to come to you.'

'Yes, I do believe he was.' Star smiled shakily.

'He?' The midwife laughed. 'Now that is a confident prediction.'

Chapter 43

'Snow is forecast for later,' Billy Dillon greeted Conor at the ferry quay. 'A rarity down here with our climate.'

'Well, it is December,' the big fella replied. 'And that may make for a perfect scenario later.'

'What do ya mean?'

'I chatted it through with my dad and Frank, and I've come to the conclusion that the right thing to do is to marry Star. No telling your missus yet, mind, or it won't be a surprise.'

'Wow. That's a big leap, man.'

'I want to do right by her, and her bump is already growing really fast. It sure is a big strapping Brady in that tummy of hers. D'you know, Billy boy, I'm really excited now.'

'Have you got a ring?'

'A temporary one. Because as she is the Queen of Jewellery herself, the darlin' girl, I want her to choose something she loves.'

'Man to man, if you weren't having this baby, would you want to marry her?'

Cars started to queue up ready to embark on the float. 'I'd better open the gate,' was all Conor said as a few stray snowflakes began to whirl slowly and sporadically around them.

'She's a special woman,' was all Billy could muster.

'You don't need to tell me that. And is it really all about hearts fluttering and knees trembling? Can't it just be about friendship and mutual respect?'

Billy looked at him and said honestly, 'You're a better man than me, Conor Brady.'

Conor sighed heavily and made his way towards the line of vehicles.

Chapter 44

Star looked at herself in the mirror as she put her mascara on. Her face was definitely getting fuller. It suited her. But despite her now accepting her predicament, she still hadn't found the courage to tell Conor that the baby wasn't his.

The only person she had confided in was Kara, who had solemnly promised that she would not tell a single soul until her friend had told the handsome Irishman herself. But every time Star had braced herself to say something to him, she just couldn't – because she knew that as soon as the truth was out, he would be gone, and she would be alone again. And although she wasn't in love with him, she really cared for him. Really enjoyed her time with him. He had been so careful with her and so loving towards her bump. Even making sure the foods he bought were suitable for pregnancy and that she was in bed early to get enough sleep, so she wasn't tired for work. She owed it to him to tell him, she knew, and as soon as possible, but it was one of the most difficult things she had ever had to do in her life.

Here, inside her, was Jack Murray's baby. The baby of a man with whom she had spent a matter of a mere few hours. The baby of a man who had run back to his girlfriend in New York yet again to rekindle his worthless relationship. The first man she had actually felt that she was in love with, but not only was he unobtainable, he also lived thousands of miles away.

Lightning *had* struck twice. She had had sex with two attached men, Skye's father being the first, Jack the second, and had fallen pregnant both times. Star knew she had created her own karma and now she would have to pull her big girl's pants up, take the consequences and bring up yet another child on her own. She did the calculations and worked out that in another eighteen years she would be fifty-one, still young enough to live her life again after that. So yes, she would just have to suck it up and get on with it.

She had gone over and over the quandary in her mind of whether or not to tell Jack that he was the father of her child, and had more or less decided not to. She feared the revelation would be traumatic, and the inevitable rejection of her too much to bear. What's more, if Riley had pushed Jack so viciously merely by suspecting that she and Jack had had sex together, God knows what might happen if she learned that he'd impregnated an English Rose.

So much deceit was flying around. It was breaking her heart, and it wasn't good for the baby.

She was conscious that she hadn't seen her mum for what felt like an age either. Estelle had betrayed her so greatly that Star wasn't ready to make peace, but was also torn by the knowledge that her mother was not a well woman. The dreadful words she had said – that her mother was dead to her – played constantly over her mind. Alcoholism: an illness that ravaged the body and mind, and which couldn't be cured until the sufferer accepted that they had a problem. Such a cruel illness, and so difficult for those with it and the people around them who loved them. She put her head in her hands and sighed deeply just as Skye came bounding into the room like an excited child.

'It's properly snowing out there now, Mum. Come and have a look! Mum? Shit, Mum, what's the matter?'

Star sat up on her dressing table stool. 'Skye, we need to talk. Sit on the bed, darling.'

'Mum? You're scaring me.'

'No, it's all OK. I should have done this ages ago. Firstly, I want to tell you all about your father . . .'

Chapter 45

'Your chariot awaits.' Conor greeted Star at her flat door and held out his arm.

'What are you doing here?' she asked. 'I was just on my way over to you.'

'I couldn't let a pregnant lady negotiate these outside stairs in this snow, now could I?' Big fat, perfectly formed snowflakes were silently falling; one caught on her eyelash and, noticing it under the outside light, Conor kissed it away. 'Have you got your trainers on and is that coat warm enough? Gloves?'

'I thought we were just going to yours for dinner?'

'Come on, take my arm.'

The big Irishman led her safely down the steps and then on through Ferry Lane Market where their footsteps crunched in the icy white carpet that was getting deeper in front of their eyes. The sparkling Christmas lights looked even more magical against their wintry backdrop and the shop windows were a feast for the eyes with their colourful Christmas goodies displayed for all to see.

'Fresh snow, I love it.' Conor squeezed her hand.

'Me too,' Star agreed. 'We rarely get snow like this down here. What a treat. And that crunchy sound is just so cool.'

They turned the corner to see Frank's Café and the decking area outside completely lit up in pretty coloured fairy lights.

'Wow, Frank's really gone to town this Christmas. It looks magical against the snow. Quite romantic, in fact.' On getting closer she could make out an arch of holly, ivy and mistletoe interspersed with white flashing lights in the shape of stars. Her heart sank at the realisation of what might be about to happen. She started to shiver, saying, 'God, it's freezing out here. Can't we head back now that I've seen the lights?'

'Wasn't it Aristotle who said, "To appreciate the beauty of a snowflake it is necessary to stand out in the cold"?' Conor quoted.

'Didn't he also say that "No great mind has ever existed without a touch of madness"?'

'I shall take that as a compliment.' Conor laughed and carried on leading her towards the cafe.

The promenade was silent apart from a couple of kids having a snowball fight in the pub car park opposite. The sea lay perfectly still as if accepting its new freezing layer willingly. Seagulls squawked their disapproval at this seasonal interference and the various yachts and boats creaked their usual sleepy lullaby.

Without a word, Conor led Star with two hands to stand underneath the arch, then immediately got down on one knee. He looked up into her now watering eyes. Oh, how she had wanted a moment like this, a thought-out proposal in a romantic water's-edge setting with a handsome man. And to top it off, with the picturesque backdrop of snow too. All the ingredients were here for the perfect beginning to a perfect romance – except the only thing that hadn't shown up was her heart.

'Star Lilian Bligh,' Conor began. 'It may have only been a matter of weeks since we first met, but every moment of them has made me smile. You are a beautiful soul and now you are growing *our* little soul inside of you, it's only right that I ask you to—'

BANG!

All of a sudden, a huge explosion reverberated around the night sky. It was coming from up on Hartmouth Head. 'What the . . . ?'

BANG!

Conor grabbed Star close to him as an eruption of orange flames and black smoke could be seen from where they were standing.

Just then, Billy pulled up alongside them in his van and stuck his head out of the open window. 'It's the mobile home park,' he said. 'My mate Larry who lives up there just called me.' He reached out and took Star's hand. 'I was just about to ring you: it's your mum's place, Star. Get in, both of you.'

As Billy screeched into the Hartmouth Head static home park, Estelle Bligh's van was a ball of fire. Sirens could be heard cutting through the freezing night air. Residents were doing their best with fire extinguishers to try and ease the blaze.

'*No!*' Star screamed. '*No!*' as she scrabbled out of Billy's van and towards the green-painted static home that had been in her family for four generations. 'Mum! Where are you? Mum!'

'Star! Don't even think about it.' Conor ran after her, followed by Billy. A fire engine could now be seen making its way as fast as it was able through the snow to the roaring inferno; an ambulance screaming in its slipstream.

Star took her coat off and put it over her face to avoid the smoke. 'Stop! Star, come back!' Conor's voice was urgent. 'You can't go in there.'

But an adrenaline-fuelled Star was only listening to her heart. She suddenly felt Estelle's presence near to her. At the sight of her mother lying alone, motionless in the snow, six foot from the blaze, she fell to her knees beside her on the freezing ground. 'Oh Mum, Mum. I'm here. I'm so sorry for what I said. I love you so much.'

The woman's face was black, her clothes partly burned off her. Her arms looked sore and raw against the whiteness of the ground. Star began frantically gathering up snow and frenziedly throwing it on to her wounds in an attempt to cool them down.

'Star, you need to move away.' Conor started to pull her back from her mother. 'The fireman said if there's another gas canister in there it could blow at any minute. Think of our baby.'

'You came. My little girl came,' Estelle Bligh murmured, then fell back unconscious as a paramedic leaped down to the injured woman's side and called back to his colleague: 'We're going to need an air ambulance to get her to Derriford Burns Unit – and pronto.'

Star kicked her legs in fury as Conor carried her away from danger against her wishes. 'Let me go! Put me down!' Looking at him with a face so contorted with anguish that it was almost unrecognisable, she then sobbed, 'It's not *our* baby, Conor. I'm so sorry. I can't marry you.'

Chapter 46

'That snow went as quickly as it came, thank goodness,'
Florence Sibley said matter-of-factly as her great-niece
appeared at the door to the flat above the former newsagent.
'I've made a chicken pie and mash, your favourite. Sit down
by the fire, duck, and get yourself warm – and just look at
that bump of yours! What have you got growing in there, a
hippopotamus?'

'Hello, hello, hello, hello,' the blue and yellow budgie trilled,
then started flying around his cage, causing seed husks to
shower out and onto the plastic table covering below.

'Even Boris is pleased to see you,' Florrie said comfortably.
'That's his happy squawk.' She sat down opposite the beloved
girl.

'Where's your Christmas tree, then Auntie? You usually
religiously get it out two weeks before the big day?'

'I've lost track of time with all these goings-on. At least
she's out of intensive care now.' Flo's voice was full of relief.

'Yes, thank goodness. They are just the best staff there.
And although Mum is out of the ICU they suggested we
don't visit just at the moment as she's not really well enough
to see people. Luckily, she hasn't got to have any skin grafts
and when she does come home, the nurse at the local surgery
can dress her arms. What's more, she didn't have a mark on
her anywhere else, the staff nurse told me. It was lovely to

see her on FaceTime. Sober. Auntie Florrie, it's been so long since I've seen her like that. She's on drugs for the pain, obviously, but it was almost like having my old mum back.'

'Bless you, my love. I shall thank the Good Lord in my prayers tonight. Do you know what happened yet? The night of the fire, I mean.'

Star let out a huge sigh. 'Yes. I told her not to use it but she still hadn't sorted out the timings on her radiators, so insisted on using this second-hand open-bar electric fire. The fire investigator said it looked like she dropped something on it, which started a fire, which in turn set off the gas canister that she keeps underneath the static for when she has a barbecue. Luckily, she was outside when it went up or she would have been killed, that's for sure.'

'Poor Estelle. We need to think about where she's going to live when she comes out.'

'It's not your worry, Auntie. In fact, it won't be mine either. You know what the community is like up there. They look after each other and the fire has really made them rally round. There's an old van that's been sitting there for years. I went up there with Skye yesterday. Mum's neighbours have aired it and cleaned it top to bottom, a hell of a job that must have been. They've had the services reconnected – electricity, water, flushing loo – and have even given it a lick of paint inside. Everything is in working order now, including the heaters. People have donated their spare bits of furniture, cutlery and crockery, and bought some bits from the Pound Shop here in Penrigan. Tell the truth, I reckon they enjoyed themselves, and Mum will be well set up. All they wanted from me was to get a new bed and bedding, and I'll be glad to do that. So when Mum moves in, everything will be fresh and new. Morvah, who must be at least ninety now, has run up some pretty curtains and Larry, that's Billy Dillon's mate, he's found the exact green paint the other one had and was just finishing off the outside when we were there.'

'That's God in action – the Christian spirit. How marvellous. But if Estelle does need anything, you both know where I am.' Florence Sibley looked right at Star. 'You could do without all this stress in your condition, young lady. You do suddenly look huge though.'

'I know. Probably because I'm due in March.'

Her great-aunt understood immediately. 'Oh, Star. The one from America with the girlfriend?'

'Yep. It's Jack's.'

'Oh dear.'

'I know. And he still *has* that very same girlfriend in America.'

'So does this Jack know that he is soon to become a father, with a baby boy or girl in Hartmouth?'

Star sighed. 'No, and I have no intention of telling him either.'

'Right. And how did Mr Blarney Stone take it?'

'This is the thing. He was just about to propose to me, had it all set up, and then the accident happened at Mum's, which in a way saved me from having to turn him down there and then. But in the heat of the moment when I had just found Mum and thought she was dying, I came out with it. I had to tell him the truth, that it wasn't his baby.'

'You always did like a drama.' Florrie shook her head. 'The poor man.'

'Oh, don't say that. I feel bad enough already.'

'And how did he take it?'

'I don't know. I was in such a state when Mum was carried off in the air ambulance that I rang Kara to come and get me and Conor went back in the van with Billy. I haven't seen or heard from him since.'

'He liked you then.'

'Yes, it seems he did.'

'Your uncle used to say to some of the youngsters in our church who were struggling with love that time decides who you *meet* in your life, your heart decides who you *want* in your life and your behaviour decides who *stays* in your life.' She looked at her great-niece. 'Do you still want him in your life, Steren? Conor, I mean?'

'With behaviour like mine, I don't think that question is for me to answer.'

'And why not tell Jack? I don't understand, duck. Doesn't he have a right to know?'

'It's a bit like it was with Conor: I don't want to force someone to be with me just because a baby is on the way. I want to be with someone for love. As I told you, he came here for a weekend, and gave no indication that he liked me. Mind you, I did tell him that I was pregnant with another man's child. What a fool I've been. Oh, Auntie, how can one human being make so many mistakes in one life!'

'You're getting dramatic again, and it's not good for you. I'll go and dish up our dinner.' Florrie waited a few minutes until Star was tucking into the lovely hot food, hungrily clearing her plate. Then she asked gently, 'Did you not tell him how you felt when you saw him, my love?'

'No, because he dismissed what happened between us . . . now let me remember his words . . . as "the best one-day stand" he'd ever had.'

'Well, it's better than being the worst,' Florrie said, forking some pie into her mouth.

'Auntie! That's not funny.'

The old lady swallowed and had a drink of water. 'It is a little bit. Oh, Star, good communication is the difference between a relationship working or not, but sadly between what is said and not meant, and what is meant and not said, most of love can get lost. It's tragic really.'

'If only I had your sense.'

'I've had years of practice.' Florence Sibley stood up and put her hand on her great-niece's shoulder. 'Now let's have some of my jam roly-poly and custard, shall we? We need it in this weather.'

'Amen!' Boris the budgie shouted from his cage.

Chapter 47

Charlie Dillon was in full swing on the family stall at the Saturday market. 'Order your Christmas veg in now, ladies,' he shouted out to the queue that was forming. 'No need to travel to Belgium, madam, the finest Brussels sprouts are here, go well with your turkey stuffing.' He gave a cheeky wink when he said the word 'stuffing'. 'And don't miss out on our very own five-star Savoy cabbage – the very same those chefs use at the Savoy Hotel in London, don't you know.' The queue was entertained as usual.

Darren tore down the back stairs on his way to the ferry quay.

'Dad,' he acknowledged tentatively as he walked by the laden stall. An expressionless Charlie just cocked his head at his son and carried on serving his customer. A strained-looking Pat Dillon put a fake phone to her ear and mouthed at the young man, 'Call you later.'

'All right, Kara?' Charlie shouted across to her when he had a breathing space. She was busy arranging her Christmas wreaths at the base of her stall. 'Did you hear that Tasty Pasties is up for sale? Never thought I'd see the day when Philip Gilmour would hang up his pink apron and let someone else have a go. Rumour has it he's found a new fella and is running off into the sunset with his pasty fortune. Each to their own, I guess.'

Beside her

Kara took in this comment and gulped. She had minded her own business about his falling out with Daz, mainly to keep the peace as much as possible with the rest of the Dillon family, but it seemed somehow strange that he could talk openly about another gay man, but not be accepting of his own son's sexuality. She calmed herself. 'You interested then?' she quipped.

'Nah, he's not my type, darlin'.'

'Ha ha.' Kara made a funny face at the bald middle-aged man. 'I meant about the shop!'

Beside her, working at her own stall, Star was putting the finishing touches to her display. Despite all the drama, she had still managed to get her Christmas collection together, the various bespoke pieces gleaming beneath the sparkling lights she had positioned all around them. She had given up on messaging Conor, who had chosen to ignore her for days. She hadn't seen him once going backwards and forwards to work down at the ferry and there had been no sign of him in Frank's. She was saddened that he really was being so adamant in his avoidance of her. She missed him. He had become such a big part of her life and now, with no contact at all, her days felt empty again. Especially now with the worry of her mother still being in hospital.

'You all right, Mum?' Skye called from the Passion Flowers stall next to hers. 'Kara has asked me to pop down to Frank's to get coffees and bacon rolls. Do you want anything?'

'Ooh. I'd love one of his warm bacon and cheese croissants, please. Here, let me give you some money.'

'Don't be silly, I'll get it. Coffee too?'

'A decaf please, plenty of milk.'

It had been such a relief when her daughter took the revelation of her father's identity in such an adult way. Star had spared no punches with the story, had told her exactly how it was and who he was. And that she had heard on the grapevine that the man in question had gone to live in Australia with his family around ten years ago. 'I couldn't bear you feeling like I do now, not having any clue at all who my father was,' she had told her daughter, adding that if Skye were to contact him, whilst respecting his existing family, then that was her choice, but she needed to be prepared for rejection if she did so. The wise seventeen year old had just held her mum's hand and told her how sorry she was that her father had been such a bastard, and how lucky she was to have Star as the best single parent a daughter could ask for. She had also been completely cool about her mum having a baby, was very excited, in fact, at the thought of a tiny brother or sister. And when Star told her that the child was Jack's, Skye hadn't batted an eyelid. Had said that she thought Conor was great, but that whatever happened, her mum should follow her heart. It had made Star burst with pride that she had brought up such a balanced and thoughtful individual.

Star turned her heater up under her stall and put both hands on her bump. She had stared at the image on the screen during the scan and couldn't quite believe, despite what the midwife had told her previously, how far along the pregnancy was. When asked if she wanted to know the sex, she had declined, same as with Skye. She preferred the element of surprise and the lack of preconceptions in her mind of what her hoped-for little boy would be like. She and her baby would meet each other in March for the first time properly. A feeling of warmth engulfed her at the thought. A new little bundle of joy to love and cherish and one she had wished for, albeit not in quite these circumstances.

Nicola May

Just having the scan in itself had been sobering. With Skye, her mum Estelle had been involved all along the way. She hadn't seemed quite such a drunk then, or maybe she was and at sixteen years old it hadn't been so obvious to Star. Estelle had been moved back to Penrigan Hospital now and was hopefully going to be allowed back home in a few days. Star would call her at lunchtime to see how she was getting on and ask when would be a good time to visit.

Kara's Christmas wreaths were flying off the stand. 'Great idea to make all those up in advance,' Star called over to her.

'I know,' Kara replied. 'At this rate I'm going to have to ask Skye to do some more when she comes back from Frank's. How are you feeling today?'

'Good, thanks. Cold as usual.'

'Shit, I forgot to give you this! I'm so sorry. Billy gave it to me last night.' Kara handed her mate an orange envelope. 'It's from Conor.'

Inside was a card with a dolphin on the front and the words: *I've been an eejit the past few days, sorry. Let's talk. Pop up after the market. I'll be home by five.*

'Well?' Kara was on tenterhooks.

Star put her hand to her heart. 'I'm going to see him later.'

'Good. I don't suppose you've heard from Jack?'

'Why would I? He thinks I'm pregnant with another man's child. Not exactly a catch in his eyes.'

'I think you should tell him.'

'No! I told you, I don't want a pity plea from any man, and he actually said out loud that he was a changed man and must get back to Riley. What a mess!' Star thought sadly back to her auntie's wise words: *Between what is said and not*

256

meant, and what is meant and not said, most of love can get lost.

How true were those words and how common in relationships. It was ironic really that the one person you shared all your deepest darkest secrets with, not forgetting bodily fluids, was generally the person you communicated with the worst. And then, after many angry words that you didn't mean, you would split up, and the person you had once been so close to became a stranger. There must be a graveyard in the sky full of misunderstandings, regretted words, and lost romantic hopes and promises.

But it was Star's fear of complete abandonment that had been the narrative of her life. She had lived it avoiding the crossfire of emotion; not saying how she felt, because sometimes just believing that she wasn't good enough for someone to want her was easier to accept than the fear of somebody actually *telling* her that she wasn't.

Chapter 48

Conor opened the door to his flat with the smile that had so captivated her from the start of their relationship. 'Madam.' Taking Star's coat, he led her to the kitchen where he had laid the table for two. A candle was burning in the middle.

'I know it's early for food, but I'm starving,' he told her. 'I've just done jacket potatoes with a choice of fillings so you can pick and choose what you want when you're ready. Now, how about a glass of wine – oh shite, what am I saying!' Conor laughed nervously. Star was enamoured by this side of him she had not seen before. 'Fizzy water OK?'

'Stop fussing,' she said. 'Water's great and jacket potatoes even better. I'm eating even more like a horse now.'

'You feel OK? Feck, this is awkward.'

'It is, but let's try not to make it that way.' Star sat down. 'I'm just so sorry.'

'So am I.' Conor breathed deeply, before taking a massive slug of beer from the bottle he was holding.

'I can't believe you were going to propose,' Star said.

'Nor can I.' Conor then relaxed and laughed. 'Thank God I'd just got you a cheap ring, eh? I was going to get you to choose what you wanted, that was the plan.'

Star looked across and took in the handsome face of the tall Irishman sitting opposite her. His kind brown eyes and mad curly hair. His sexy dimple and lopsided smile. 'You're

an amazing man, Conor Brady, and I've had the best fun
with you. You brought me back to life.'

'That'll be all that Irish sausage I fed you.'

Star gasped then started laughing out loud. 'You are *so*
wrong.'

'You love it, so you do. And you do have a beautiful arse.'

'Great sex, I can't deny you that one, and I do really like
you, you know that.'

'And me you. I am so very fond of you, but if we are
honest with ourselves, we were never going to get as far as
walking down the aisle. At least, I don't think so.'

Star started loading her potato with butter and grated
cheddar. 'I reckon there must be couples like us everywhere.
It's kind of friends with benefits who stay together but that
massive rush of passion is not there, that deep, connected love.'

'Don't be going all philosophical on me, it took me all I
had to ask you around for a jacket spud. So,' Conor went
on, 'do you – or more importantly, do I – know who the
father is? I honestly didn't think you would see someone
behind my back. I thought I was giving you the best ride of
our lives and we were hardly out of each other's sight.'

'Oh my God, Conor, no wonder you've kept away, thinking
that. I was hoping Billy might tell you and it certainly wasn't
something I wanted to convey in a message.'

'You know Bill, he's loyal to you as a friend. Said it was
for me to ask you.'

'So, what happened was this. Kara had a B&B guest back
in the summer, Jack his name is. We slept together.'

'Bloody hell.' Conor grimaced. 'I've been shagging you
when you've been pregnant too. That feels kind of weird.'

Star made a face too. 'I honestly didn't know.'

'Come on, you must have.'

'I don't have periods often – I told you that much. Anyway, it's happening. I'm due on St Patrick's Day, and there's no going back now.'

'The irony of that, eh?' Conor sounded deflated.

'Oh. I hadn't thought of it being an Irish celebration day, sorry.'

'So, what does this Jack think about you having his baby?'

'He doesn't know. He has a girlfriend.'

'Ah. Shite.'

'Yes, shite indeed.'

'And I guess it was a one-nighter so you're not that bothered about him.' Conor was thoughtful for a minute. 'Saying that, I'd want to bloody know if I had a child on the way and I'm not going to lie, Star, there was a little bit of me that was kind of excited when we thought the baby was mine.'

'Aw, that makes me sad.'

'Don't be. There's life in this old dog yet and I'm not in the right place to provide for another child, not yet.'

'I don't want you to hate me for telling you this, but I *am* bothered about Jack. Since he left, I haven't really stopped thinking about him. You have been the best distraction but deep down I knew that I didn't feel for you like I felt for him.'

It stung, but after a minute Conor replied, 'Why would I hate you? Honesty shows respect. But you have to tell him what's going on, for you as much as for the baby. True connections don't happen often in this life, Star, and when they do, I think they need to be seized and fought for, I really do.'

Conor put his knife and fork down and stood up. Walking round to Star's side of the table he took her hand and gently pulled her up from her chair.

'What are you doing, you crazy coot?'

Mindful of her bump, Conor Brady wrapped his huge Irish arms around the petite blonde Cornishwoman and gave her the bear hug of all bear hugs. Rocking her gently as if she was a baby, he then kissed her on the forehead.

'I wanted to see you tonight to say that if you ever need me for anything, whatever it is, I'm here for you and Skye and the new little one. I might even put in a stint at babysitting if you ask me nicely.'

Star pulled away from him. 'So, you are staying in Hartmouth then?'

'I'm enjoying the outdoors on the ferry for now, so I am. I've been able to start paying off my debts to my Da and Frank, which is the main thing.'

'You didn't answer my question?'

'I've had the best time with you, my little *stóirín*. The Dillons are a great family, and Frank and Monique will always have my back. And now my boy Niall is getting older I'm hoping his mother might allow us to spend some time together. Like me, he'd love it down here. I know.'

'All good then.'

'Yeah, that's right. But it's you we need to get happy now. And whether it be Jack or someone else, whoever that man might be, they will be so lucky to have found you, and I mean that with all my heart.'

Star looked up at him and whispered, 'Thank you. Thank you so much.'

'You're a special lady, Steren Bligh, and don't ever forget that.'

'You're up late.' Skye came bounding in bringing the cold in with her, not expecting to see her mother sitting in silence on the sofa with a mug of hot chocolate in hand.

'Just having a think about stuff,' Star told her.

'Was Conor OK?'

'Yes, we're still friends.'

'Good, good. And you feel all right, with the baby I mean?'

'Yes, darling.' Star reached for her daughter's hand. 'Thanks for being so understanding about it all.'

Skye came and sat beside her. 'Can I come and see Granny Bligh with you on Sunday?'

'Of course you can. I called the hospital earlier and they said she's so much better. That reminds me, we must get her a new mobile phone. Hers was lost in the fire.'

'Let's do that tomorrow. Oh yeah, I forgot, there's some post for you in the kitchen. One marked *Addressee Only,* with a solicitor's stamp on it.'

'Thanks. I wonder what that is? Did you have fun tonight?'

'Yes, me and Tegan just watched a film. I wanted a quiet one. I can't be doing with a hangover on a market day ever again.'

'Look at you being the sensible one.'

'Well, someone has to be in this family.' The young girl leaned over to kiss her mum on the cheek. 'Night, Mum. I love you.'

'I love you too, precious.'

When Skye had gone, Star suddenly felt completely alone. Yes, Conor wanted to be her friend, but what she herself really wanted was a big spoon, a cuddler and a confidant. A partner to help her navigate motherhood for the second time, to share responsibility and worry, to love her uncon-ditionally. What was it that her mother had said again about the two men she had seen in her crystal ball? She thought back. Yes, that was it: one would break, and one would shake her heart. Sighing deeply at the realisation that Conor must be the shaker in all of this, Star looked down at her phone and found the number she had under Ralph Airbnb. Just to hear Jack's voice would be enough for now. With a trembling hand, she disguised her own number to Unknown Caller and dialled. When the call didn't even go through to a dialling tone, she threw the phone down on the sofa and put her head in her hands.

Chapter 49

A few days later, a sleepy Star pulled on her dressing gown and made her way through to the kitchen to make herself a cup of green tea. She had hardly slept, mainly due to the fact that her mind was troubled by worries for her mother, but also because her little baby had most certainly come to life now and was kicking her when she awoke at five and continued to do so until her alarm went off at six thirty. It had been a bit of a waste of time, her and Skye going to see Estelle at the hospital as she had slept during the whole visit. She looked so peaceful they didn't want to wake her. And that was the thing – she really did look peaceful, not so ravaged by the demon drink or the drugs that were normally swilling around her system.

Pearl had popped down quickly from A&E to see them, informing them that the burns on Estelle's arms were apparently healing beautifully. She promised that she would talk to the team on their behalf and ensure that a district nurse would visit Estelle at home when the dressings were due to be changed, so that Estelle didn't have to fret about getting herself down to the doctor's surgery whilst she was still fragile and recovering. Pearl had also taken Star aside and privately let her know that Estelle had agreed to speak to somebody from the drug and alcohol support unit. Hearing this, alongside all the pregnancy hormones that were flying about inside her, had caused Star to burst into tears. Skye had to go and sit with her granny until her mother had calmed down.

As Star was pouring boiling water on to her teabag, she noticed the forgotten post that Skye had propped behind the toaster. She pulled out the envelope with the solicitor's stamp on it, and as she read the letter inside, her heart started beating fast. It contained the instruction that she was to go to Bright & Company Solicitors today at 1 p.m. 'Today! Shit.' Star put her hand to her forehead. She was to meet a Cedric Bright, Senior Partner, who would explain everything on her arrival.

A solicitor? What did that mean? What had she done wrong? Maybe it was to do with the lease on the shop unit, but Star was sure that had all been sorted correctly and she had definitely not missed any payments. She double-checked the date on her calendar. Good job she had opened the letter when she did. At least the meeting was at lunchtime so she wouldn't miss too much Christmas trade. In fact, she would just ask Skye to pop between shops. Making a little groaning noise, she took her tea through to the bedroom and turned on the shower.

'Steren Lilian Bligh?' asked a voice with a Scottish accent. A tall man with a pinched face, tiny little spectacles and neat grey hair, which was leaving specks of dandruff on the collar of his worn navy suit, greeted Star in the reception of Bright & Company Solicitors. Star nodded. Having found it hard to locate the offices and then a place to park had left her feeling a little sweaty and decidedly anxious. She followed the solicitor into his wood-panelled office where he sat at an antique mahogany desk with a green leather top.

'Could I trouble you for a glass of water, please?' she asked. 'I found it hard to park and—'

'Olivia,' Cedric Bright shouted through to the receptionist who had greeted her. 'Two waters, please.' Star smiled weakly; the man didn't smile back. He would have been far more suited to be an undertaker, she thought. Glad that she would soon have some water to wash down her anxiety and refresh her dry mouth, with her coat still on she sat back in the swivel chair and took the same calming deep breaths that her auntie had once taught her as a child, when she had got in a state about Estelle's wrongdoings.

'Steren Lilian Bligh,' the man repeated. 'Do you have some ID with you?'

She was so glad she had seen the footnote on the letter. 'Yes, my driving licence.' She scrabbled in her bag for her purse.

'Perfect.' The man studied it closely then handed it back to her, peering over the top of his glasses as he did so, advising her, 'Don't worry, you have done nothing wrong.'

Star put her hands around her baby bump and breathed out with relief.

'And with a new family member on his or her way, I see. Congratulations.'

'Um, thank you. So why am I here?'

The man raised his hand, and Star caught a whiff of his stale aftershave. 'Wait and I shall tell you, Ms Bligh.' He tapped a cardboard folder on his desk. Star was now completely perplexed. When he started to talk again, she thought she might well faint.

'I am dealing with the Last Will and Testament of a Reverend Matthew Nesbitt of The Rectory, Church Road, Penrigan, who sadly passed away this month at the untimely age of sixty-one. Our instruction was that a representative from our company, namely myself, would in the light of his death meet you and personally hand over two letters from this file, the contents of which are strictly private and confidential. I will leave you to read them for a wee while and if anything does require any further action from ourselves, then please do let me know.'

'A reverend? Th-thank you,' Star stuttered and, with a shaking hand, opened one of the letters, which was so beautifully handwritten it looked as if it had been crafted by a calligrapher. The other envelope was intriguingly labelled *Open me when instructed to*.

Dear Steren,

You are reading this because I am dead. You are also reading this because you are my daughter. (Star took a sharp intake of breath.) *I am not sugar-coating anything to you here because, as I never heard from you, I believe that Estelle must have kept her word to me that she would never tell a soul, even you, of our indiscretion.*

I am not proud of the fact that I never met you. I am not proud of the fact that I had an affair with your mother. But I wanted you to know that I did love Estelle. However, God had called me, and I loved Him more. I am a priest: that was my vocation. The life I chose. In an ideal world, a man of the cloth would be decent and upstanding, but we all have our shortcomings, for that is what makes us human. Sadly, I failed my faith twice, but I will come to that later.

I always kept a distant eye on you and tried to help

Estelle in ways she would not have known about. I would never have seen her destitute. Yes, I was a weak man, and I chose my spiritual calling over being a father to you. My selfish sexual desires conquered my vow of chastity for a brief interlude when I was in my twenties. Oh, how I loved a wild woman, and your mother was just that. Blonde and exuberant. A little way out and so damn beautiful, she took my breath away.

I met her in the church. (Star's eyes widened. Her mother in a church!) *She had lost her way. Her parents, your grandmother and grandfather, had died a few years previously, but she had never got over losing them. She was distraught, frightened, and she felt so alone. I wanted to help her. For years, I would meet her and we would talk for hours into the night. I would hold her hand whilst she cried, whilst she told me about the wonderful memories she had of them both. I felt her pain.* (Star put her hand to her heart as the words in front of her eyes continued to flow.) *She became my friend, but the problem was she became more than my friend. One night, I met her under Penrigan Pier and we made love. And it* was *making love, Steren. It only happened once. It* could *only happen once, for I loved her. Had it gone any further, I would have had to leave my calling and spend my life with her. She told me that she was using protection, and at the time I believed her. But now I think she hoped that we would make a child. And that is how you came about.*

Shock, the absurdity of it all, made Star start laughing hysterically. Her mother had shagged a priest! But this fake mirth soon turned to grief. Maybe if she had known, she could have gone to church, seen her father in action, got a feel for the man who was half of herself. Poor Estelle. She had been so vulnerable, and it was the Reverend Matthew Nesbitt who had taken advantage; who couldn't keep his rosary beads under his cassock. What a bizarre and tragic situation. All credit to her mum for being loyal to her promise and never jeopardising his position. Also, how very sad that such a beautiful-sounding friendship had to end by them falling in love.

It gave Star joy to learn that she been born of parents who loved each other so deeply, and that Estelle had really wanted to create a child with this man who meant so much to her. She carried on reading.

I am writing this on my deathbed as cancer is taking me to my resting place. I'm leaving a lot sooner than I thought but God only takes us when we are ready. So, I must be prepared when the time comes. Steren, my child, I regret that I have no money to leave you or your mother. It is all with the church, but if I can give you just one thing before I go, it is the knowledge that the most valuable thing you can make is a mistake, because you can't learn anything by being perfect. We all make them, Star, so don't let that be a reason to give up on somebody.

And now, thanks to the magic of a camera with a timer, you may open the second envelope. Please tell your mother that in all the years since we were together, these have never left my side.

Star did as she was told. Inside the second envelope were two almost identical photographs of a young man with neat fair hair, wearing jeans and a checked shirt. He was sitting on the beach close to where the pier meets the sea at low tide in Hartmouth, and laughing, as was the beautiful blonde woman whose head was poking up behind his, her arms loosely draped over his shoulders. What a handsome man Matthew Nesbitt had been, Star thought, and she had never seen her mother look so happy. Turning one of the photographs over, Star gasped. On the back was written:

Dearest Steren, Love comes unseen; we only see it go.

Your father x

She scrabbled to look at the back of the other one.

Estelle, you let go of me with love, the ultimate sacrifice. I never stopped loving you but it's time to say goodbye now and for you to be the person I know you can be. Matthew x

'Wow,' Star said to herself, immediately turning back to the letter.

Star, if my abandonment has caused you to suffer in any way, please forgive me and may God bless you.

Star let out a huge breath. She felt so many different emotions: she felt numb, she felt angry, angry at this man for being so duplicitous. But she also felt elated too, and also somewhat amused that she was a priest's daughter. She took a large glug of water in anticipation of what else there was to come.

271

There is just one last thing I need to tell you. It will come as a surprise, I hope a welcome one. I said I had failed my faith twice. And again, I ask myself: was it really a failure? Because the thing I really want you to know is that you have a half-sister, and her name is Kerensa Anne Moon.

Chapter 50

Even a dull December day seemed magical when you had an uninterrupted view of the ocean. The white sky was still, the sea grey, with little froths of white on the waves near to the horizon. Even the seagulls seemed to be quieter than usual. The Hartmouth Head car park was completely empty apart from a couple of head-to-toe Lycra adorned cyclists stopping to take a look at the view before setting off on their onward adventures.

Sitting on her thinking bench, Star knew she was in a state of shock. Too much had happened. It had been difficult enough to digest the fact that this little baby growing inside her wasn't Conor's but Jack's, let alone discovering that the priest from Penrigan Catholic Church was her father, and now having to take on board the massive revelation that her dear friend Kara was her big sister by just six months, with Kara's birthday being on 13 September! No wonder they had got on so well while growing up. 'Sister from another mister' indeed – that had always been their mantra; in fact, Star remembered having said it just a few weeks ago when she had been feeling overwhelmed about everything in the cafe.

Star tried to get her head around the thought of the Reverend sleeping with two women – and impregnating them – in such close proximity. He had certainly kept to type. Red-headed Doryty Moon, his first lover, and blonde Estelle Bligh, his second and last, were indeed both feisty characters, forces to be reckoned with, although at that point in her life, Estelle had also been very vulnerable. Matthew had professed love for Estelle, while the feelings he had had towards Doryty appeared to be lust, plain and simple. Weirdly, Star could understand. It was no different to her with Jack and Conor. She had feelings for both of them, but those for Jack far outweighed those she had for the big Irishman. Love and lust were very different bedfellows.

Star looked far out to sea. Despite the cold wind whipping up around the cliffs now, she didn't feel the chill, was warmed by at long last knowing who her father was, which helped her in turn to know who she was. She didn't feel sad now that she had never got to know him; she accepted that he was a man of the cloth and, despite his shortcomings in his twenties, there must have been a whole lot of good in him, and for that she could be eternally grateful. Maybe she should go to a service at the church and see if anything was said about him. In fact, if it wasn't too late, maybe she could go to his funeral! Should she tell Auntie Flo? Flo wasn't a gossip so there would be no harm. That's if she believed it at all, of course. Star thought of how her aunt had mentioned his passing just the other day and had spoken so highly of him!

Grief suddenly stabbed through her. Poor Estelle, no wonder an air of melancholy had stayed within her all this time. She had made a sacrifice, let go of the man she loved for his greater good, putting her own happiness aside, and what's more had stayed true to her word that she would never tell anyone what had happened between them. In a bittersweet way, this made Star feel safe inside, now she understood what had happened. And proud of her mother, who had been so strong! It also made her realise again just how hard it was, to find true and lasting love.

Star's thoughts then turned to Kara. The revelation that the Reverend Matthew Nesbitt was Kara's real father would lead to all kinds of repercussions. She had asked the solicitor if there were any other letters that he was giving out, including ones to Kerensa Anne Moon, but of course he was unable to disclose that to her. She didn't go on to share with him any of the contents of her own letters, especially not how she'd just found out that Kara was her half-sister, in case word somehow leaked out to her friend before she heard it from the horse's mouth.

But what if Kara was never told? Star asked herself. Would the responsibility fall on her to reveal this devastating truth? She knew that not only would it destroy Kara, but it would also destroy the wonderful Joe Moon. His relationship with his younger daughter was so important to him. Their bond had become even closer following the trauma of Doryty leaving them for her new lover in Spain. Star had been envious of that bond all her life, especially whilst growing up. Ironically, it now emerged that in fact, the two girls shared the same father!

Whatever the Reverend Matthew Nesbitt had, one thing was the ability to make sure that his secrets were kept safe. Star looked up at the sky and called to her angels. The universe would do right by her, she was sure. She also truly believed that the Reverend Nesbitt would do right according to his faith – that he would let Kara know the truth that she too was his daughter. It would be wrong to give the incendiary knowledge that Kara had a sibling to Star alone, and expect her to keep it all to herself.

The stars were already aligning for at long last she knew what she had wanted to find out her entire life: the identity of her father. As for Kara and Joe, she could only hope that their love, which was stronger than the tides that had taken poor old Diggory Pickett away to his death, would overcome such a shocking revelation.

Poor Estelle. Love was so weird! Why couldn't it just be directed at the most suitable candidate? Why could you not choose who you fell in love with? It would be a whole lot easier to make sure that the course of true love did run smooth if that beating organ within didn't just run riot and do its own thing. Or *was* it doing its own thing? Did the heart actually know more than the human brain? Were its matchmaking skills to be reckoned with? Her gut had always been right in the past, so why not her heart too?

Star was filled by a sense of enlightenment and energy. Maybe for the first time in her life she should stop being fearful of rejection? Maybe for the first time in her life she should listen to her heart and act without fear! Estelle had been prevented from expressing her feelings: because the man she loved had already given his heart to God, so she really had no chance. The thought that her mother had been faced with that huge obstacle to love and happiness made Star's own obstacle of a huge ocean and an abusive out-of-work actress seem far, far less daunting.

Maybe her father's last message from the grave was the only one she had ever really needed. Love had indeed blind-sided her when it had come so unexpectedly into her life, and she was damned if she was going to watch it go.

Chapter 51

Billy was just securing some solar lights around the *Happy Hart* to make it look Christmassy when he spotted Darren walking along the quay. 'It's your day off today, isn't it, bro? What are you doing down here so early?'

'I wanted to see you before you started work.'

'You OK?'

'Mum told me this morning that the old man doesn't want me at their place for Christmas dinner.'

'For fuck's sake! What is wrong with him?' Billy was furious. 'Well, if he's going to be like that I won't be there either. We can all go to Joe and Pearl's for the day, instead of me having lunch there then coming to Mum and Dad's in the evening with Kara.'

'You can't do that to Mum. She's upset enough about it all as it is.'

'So, I'll have to sit there without you whilst he's being a miserable sod and see Mum in tears. Great! One happy fucking Christmas this is going to be.'

'I should have just kept my gob shut.' Darren sighed. 'Can you imagine what he'll be like when I tell him I am seeing someone?'

'Are you? Seeing someone, I mean.'

'Um . . . it's early days.'

'Do I know him?'

'Nah. Nah.'

Billy knew it wasn't the right time to push it. 'I'm pleased for you, bro, and as for keeping quiet, no way. You did the right thing. We'll get through it and I know that Joe and Pearl will welcome you with open arms.'

'Have you seen Star lately?' Daz asked. 'I just wondered how her mum was. I can't believe the baby's not Conor's. He took it well though, considering.'

'I think he was slightly relieved, to be honest. And Estelle is due home this week, I think.'

'She was lucky.'

'She bloody was. Ah, here's my girl, wonder what she wants?' Billy said as Kara pulled up in her Passion Flowers van.

'Just thought I'd say hi/bye in case I'm going to prison, now a solicitor's asked to see me,' she said.

Billy laughed. 'Let's hope you've been left millions in someone's will.' He leaned in and gave her a kiss. 'Call me as soon as you're done, OK? And don't worry, sweet cheeks, I'm sure it's nothing serious.'

Kara waved and tooted at the pair as she headed off up the hill.

'What's all that about?' Darren was now helping to fix up the lights around the float.

'Oh, it's just she got some random letter from a solicitor in Penrigan, saying she was to meet one of the partners there this morning and he would explain why on arrival.'

'Hmm. Curious. You've got me wondering why now too.'

'Gentlemen!' Conor appeared looking slightly the worse for wear.

'You look like shit, mate.'

Conor grinned. 'Just a bit tired, that's all. You didn't warn me about Natalia from the dry cleaners. H – O – T,' he spelled out.

'You didn't waste your time.' Darren looked slightly shocked.

Billy said wittily, 'Not like Daz, who used to shag Kara's fifty-year-old boss, and she was H – R – T!'

'Filth, the pair of you.' Darren couldn't help but smile. 'And there was me thinking you were really hanging out for me.'

Conor scanned the sky then gave Darren a friendly punch on the arm, saying, 'The only thing that's on the turn round here is the weather, my friend.'

A laughing Darren jumped off the float. 'Have a good day you two, I'm off home.'

'It'll be all right,' Billy called after him. 'We'll sort it.'

Star waved at Darren as she pulled up at the quayside and got out of her car.

'Blimey, it's like Clapham bleedin' Junction down here this morning,' Billy greeted her.

'I was going to see if Kara wanted breakfast at Frank's before work, but I can't get her on her mobile,' Star told him.

'She's driving. Got some random letter from a solicitor in Penrigan.'

Star felt slightly sick. 'Ah right, she's gone there now, has she? That's early.'

'She's got to be there for nine but didn't want to be late for traffic on the main road.'

'OK.' She kept her tone casual. Conor blew her a kiss from the back end of the float. She waved back, unsmiling.

'Your mum's coming home this week, isn't she?' Billy added.

'Yeah, yeah. Tomorrow. Right, I'm starving. I shall get Frank to do me one of his legendary fry-ups.'

'You feeling all right? You look a bit peaky.'

'Yeah, just a bit tired, that's all. I'm going to park outside yours, if that's OK?'

'Course it is. Right, I'd better get these cars loaded or we'll be late for the off. See ya.'

'Bye.' Star put up her window, bit her lip and thought for a second. Breakfast could wait but being there for her mate when she was about to receive such life-changing news couldn't. Texting Skye to keep an eye on the shop, she revved the engine on her little car, then swiftly turning around, she headed towards the main road and Penrigan.

Chapter 52

Jack turned his key in the apartment door to be greeted by blaring house music and the squeals and shouts of what sounded like a home full of very drunk young women. Since returning from Hartmouth, he had found himself staying at work longer and longer, and when he and Riley did infrequently dine together, more often than not they would then head off to separate rooms to watch preferred stuff on TV or head out with their different sets of friends. It was as if since his return, a mutual barrier had been put up between them. He was, however, quite relieved and surprised that Riley's incessant whining whenever he was late home had ceased; even her jealousy seemed to have subsided slightly.

New York was great at Christmas time; shop window displays were dazzlingly festive and the smart bars and clubs were buzzing with after-work drinks and parties. Great, if you were in the mood to party that was, but Jack felt like he'd had a bereavement. Nothing seemed to bring him joy of any kind. Seeing Star pregnant with another man's child had spelled the end of something that could have been so great. He kept trying to pull himself together, thinking he was being ridiculous, but every thought led him back to the funny and smart, blue-eyed blonde that was Steren Bligh: the only woman for whom he had felt what he assumed must be love. Why, oh why, had he been such a limp dick!

And how could he fight this feeling? For as hard as he tried it just wasn't going away.

Tired from working late on reports, he decided not to even make conversation with his girlfriend's drunken crew. Instead he sneaked into the kitchen, grabbed himself a cold beer and a pack of pastrami from the fridge and headed to their bedroom to enjoy both. No one had seen him. Sitting propped up on a couple of pillows, he thought about his next step. He had seen Human Resources the other week and they'd informed him that his managers were delighted with his performance in his new role. So delighted, in fact, that now that his initial short contract was coming to a close, would he be happy to sign for another year, commencing just after New Year?

The question was, could he bear another year in New York? Moreover, could he bear another year with Riley? The twelve-year age gap had never proved a problem before, but now that he was approaching thirty-seven, and hearing the boom-boom-boom of the bass beat of whatever song had been cranked up, and her incessant nagging about them not going out clubbing enough, he was beginning to wonder. Living with Riley meant he had a home. But if he were to stay solely for a cheap roof over his head, what kind of person would that make him? It wouldn't be fair at all. And meeting Star had confirmed that, although he did care for Riley, he clearly wasn't in love with the girl.

Maybe it was time to go home? Stay with his parents in Bristol for a while, then find another job and a place of his own back in Blighty. He sighed deeply. At the moment none of the above excited him, especially the thought of living with his parents again, albeit briefly. And the defeated way he was feeling, it all seemed too difficult to contemplate. If

Star was in the mix, then it would be easy. He would pack a bag, book a flight and head to Hartmouth. He would live in a tent in the dunes of Penrigan Beach if he had to. Whisk her off her tiny little feet and tell her again that he was sorry and that she was the only woman for him. That conversation, even if she was still with Conor, he would now be brave enough to have. However, a boyfriend was manageable, but a boyfriend *and* a new baby on the way? No. It was not even an option.

He was just flicking through the TV channels to try and find some British football, when the bedroom door flew open and in came Riley. Lifting up her top to reveal a sexy lace bra, she then popped a nipple out and, after pushing it right in his face, she began gyrating sensually around the bed. 'My sexy little Jack.' She then fell on to the bed and whispered, 'You just wait until they are all gone, I am going to ruin you.'

Before he had time to answer, there was a huge smash from the living room, then an even bigger scream. Pushing Riley to the side, Jack ran out to find Riley's friend Brooke in a heap, sobbing. She had been dancing on the glass coffee table and it had given way. Helping her gently to her feet, he checked her for any big cuts or broken limbs and was both amazed and relieved to find none. Jack then turned the music off. He was feeling furious. 'Your father will want that replaced,' he said grimly and told his girlfriend, who had waltzed back into the room, 'I've had a hard fucking day, Riley, and I want some bloody peace. So, can I suggest you all fuck off out of here!'

'"I need some peace",' Brooke mimicked, the alcohol obviously acting as an anaesthetic to her pain. This made Jack see red. He went to the coat rack and threw every single coat he could see down in front of them. 'Now take which-ever is yours and please leave.'

'Jack, don't be so embarrassing,' Riley flounced. 'This is my daddy's place, not yours, and I can do what I want, when I want.'

'We're going, it's all right.' The more sober of the group began herding everyone out like sheep.

'You staying here?' Jack addressed Riley, who was now staggering in front of him. The front door slammed, and the giggling entourage made their way to the lift.

'You're an ugly, boring pig, Jack Murray. That's what you are.' Riley pointed right into his face.

'That's nice. The spare room's made up; I'm going in there tonight.' He knew not to rise to her taunts when she was in this kind of state.

'Good.' A shower of spit came flying out of her mouth towards him.

Wiping his face disgustedly, Jack said, 'You need to take a long hard look at yourself, Riley Roberts.'

'Look at myself? How about you look at *yourself*, Jack, with your crooked teeth and that bushy beard. My friends think you're lucky to have me. You're punching above your weight, honey. I could have anyone I wanted.'

A vision of a smiling, beautiful and calm Star kissing him goodbye at the door to her flat the day he had first met her suddenly came into his mind. Anger would be futile at this moment. Just four simple words would suffice. 'I am leaving you.'

'Ha ha. Leaving me? What, for that slut in England, you mean?'

'No, Riley. I am leaving you because I deserve better than to be treated like this. I have tried so hard with you. I deleted all Star's numbers and we vowed to try and make it work. But you're impossible.'

'Do you know what? I don't care any more. And do you want to know why I don't care, Jack? Because I've met someone else too, that's why,' she smirked, revealing teeth stained with red wine.

'You're lying.' Jack felt angry rather than hurt.

'I'll show you a photo if you like.' Riley fell back on to the sofa and reached for her phone. 'I met him in the Hamptons, he's called Eric,' she slurred. 'Where's my wine?'

Jack ignored her, but she was not letting up.

'He is far richer and more handsome than you and his screenplay is in the hands of a top film producer. He knows, see. He knows how to do it.' She began to laugh wildly.

Jack bit his lip and sighed resignedly. Maybe the outcome of *their* relationship had always been written in the stars. Riley Roberts' currency was based on looks and wealth, and despite his indiscretion with Star, he much preferred to trade in kindness and integrity.

Chapter 53

It didn't take long for Star to get to Penrigan, even less time for her to spot Kara's Passion Flowers van parked up on the road near to the solicitors. Ordering herself a bacon sandwich and coffee, she sat in the cafe window opposite the door of Bright & Company and waited until her friend eventually reappeared looking white-faced and devastated. Star immediately went to the door and called her name. Almost in a trance, Kara crossed the road and joined her inside the cafe.

Once sat down, Kara began nervously fingering the fake flower table decoration. Her voice was barely audible when she asked, 'How long have you known?'

'A couple of days. I just hoped that the randy rev would have the decency to tell you too. That he wouldn't leave it to me to spill the beans. Oh, Kara, I'm so sorry.'

'It's not your fault, is it? He was the one spilling his bloody biblical beans! Trust my mother to fuck things up again. I hate her so much! Poor Dad.' Kara wiped her eyes and while she did that, Star ordered two cups of tea in order to give her a moment.

'It all makes sense now, doesn't it?' Kara said dully. 'I look like Doryty, so it was never that glaring. Big sister got Dad's looks and slighter build. I'm tall and broad, like *him*. "Our dad". That's bat-shit crazy! We are half-sisters. Skye really is my niece. I just can't take it all in.'

'Did he give you a photo?' Star asked carefully.

'Yes, of himself in normal clothes. He looks so young. He was handsome, wasn't he? He wrote me a letter explaining that although it had been just one night he spent with my mother, she told him that I was his and that she would never tell her husband and, of course, she would never speak about him to anyone.'

'He never needed to have known about you.'

'I know – it's weird, right? But he told me that he paid for my upkeep. Doryty isn't stupid, is she? He probably funded her stay in Spain when I was thirteen, the cheating cow. She'd seduced a man of the cloth because she knew no one would ever find out, and when she discovered that she was pregnant after that encounter, she made sure she was guaranteed a monthly payout. Yes, my mother kept it quiet all right, for her own selfish reasons.' Kara blew her nose. 'No wonder Estelle didn't want you to know either.'

Star sighed. 'Yes. She kept that secret for him and from me all these years.'

Kara took a slurp of tea, then a small smile hit her lips. 'Our father, who art in heaven is a priest – can you believe it?'

'A sinner of a priest at that. There are just six months between us, so he was having a right old time of it. First your mum, then mine.' Star's shoulders shook with laughter. 'Sorry, I can't help myself – it is kind of funny.'

'Do you know if the funeral has happened yet?' Kara asked.

'No. I'd have thought Flo would have mentioned it, so probably not. Maybe they need to find a cathedral big enough to fit all his bastard children in.'

'So, Flo goes to his church?'

'No, but she knew of him.'

'I don't want to go to his funeral. In fact, I don't want to know anything more about him.' Kara was adamant.

'Really? If you have children, they will share his genes.'

'It's too much to take in.' The redhead's voice nearly broke. 'I can't bear it. I didn't even think of that.'

'I know. It's kind of different for me as I never had a father figure like your lovely dad when I was growing up, so in a way it's completed me now I know who helped to make me, even though I will never meet him.'

Kara said brokenly, 'It's the opposite for me. I can't believe it – and how on earth am I going to tell Dad? It will break his heart.'

'Do you have to tell him?'

Kara's head shot up. 'I can't believe you said that, mate. Of course I do! I couldn't keep it in, I wouldn't be able to act the same around him. He's been the best dad.'

'Joe still is the best dad. You could have gone through life never knowing any different. I bet that happens a lot in real life.'

'What a mess. At least Dad has Pearl now. She is so straight talking, maybe she can help me tell him. Or do I just not tell him, as you said? Oh, Star. I really don't know what to do.'

'I've got your back, sister, whatever you decide to do. Just take your time.' Star put her hand on top of Kara's. 'We've always been like sisters from the start. Love can't tell the difference whatever blood is flowing through our veins.'

'What did Estelle say?'

'She's only just home from the hospital. An ambulance dropped her off. I had planned to see her later.'

'How's she doing?'

'Fine, I think. She left me a message saying she has something important to tell me face to face. Maybe having such a life-changing accident has made her realise I should know the truth. It certainly made me open up to Skye.'

'About this?'

Star nodded. 'And about her own father. She took it so well. I think it helps that the wanker lives in Australia now. But I did say that if she ever wanted to meet him, she should respect his current family situation, but that I would never stop her. Of course, I hope she doesn't, but it destroyed me not knowing who my dad was when I was growing up, so she has every right.' She shifted in her chair. 'I'm feeling really tired today. This little mite decides to wriggle around at the strangest times. I'm sure Skye slept when I was sleeping when she was growing inside me.'

'Sorry, Star. I'm in such a state I didn't even ask how you are feeling.'

'Sad is how I'm feeling, mate. With both this and the Jack situation. I'm determined to contact him. I haven't quite got there yet, but I will.'

'He may surprise you.'

'He may be furious, more like.'

'What did he say to me?' Kara thought for a second. '"No more I wish, but I will." So, you should.'

Star stuck out her tongue. 'Like I said, I haven't quite got there yet.'

'This being-an-adult business is hard, isn't it?' Kara placed her hands on her own stomach. 'I think the hardest part of all this is knowing that *my* babies won't have any lineage to Dad.'

'He will love them just the same, Kar.'

'But what if he doesn't?'

'You're being silly now, and whatever happens, I will be right by your side.' Star paused. 'Sister . . .'

'. . . from the *same* bloody mister,' they said in unison and laughed.

'Let me look at the photo he gave you.' Star reached for it, then turned it over. 'Did you read this?' She handed it back.

Kara shook her head and haltingly read the words aloud, '*A constant nurture trumps a fleeting nature. You are so loved, Kerensa Anne. Matthew Nesbitt. Your father (by birth only) x.*'

Chapter 54

Riley pushed open the spare room door then snuck into bed next to a quietly snoring Jack and curled her skinny body around his warm soft one.

Stirring, he took her hand in his, then suddenly remembering what had happened the previous night, he pulled away and sat up, sleepily rubbing his eyes.

'You stink of drink,' he said.

'That's charming.' Riley sat up too. 'God, I feel rough.' She groaned. 'We broke Dad's table.'

'You were acting like teenagers.'

'Jack, were you serious when you said you wanted to leave me?'

'I'm surprised you remembered, the state you were in. And considering that this new guy Eric seems to be providing you with a casting couch, then yes, I was serious.'

'That was a joke,' the young blonde whined.

'Riley, this isn't a game. This is about our lives. Our futures.' Jack's voice softened. 'Look, we can't say we haven't tried. I'm not even angry about you being with someone else, which shows that my feelings for you have changed.'

Riley stuck her bottom lip out like a child. 'I loved you.'

'And I loved you, but even you can surely see that what we did have is over. I feel ready to settle down and ultimately maybe even start a family.'

'You said you didn't want kids.'

'I know – and that's why we worked so well at the start, but maybe it's me getting older, I don't know. Things have changed in my mind. You are at the start of your acting career, we're not growing together, and your jealousy is wearing me out. I can't take any more.'

Riley sighed. 'I suppose you're going back to her, are you?'

Jack was surprised at how level headed she was being. Maybe the hangover was dulling her senses, or maybe it was the wonderful Eric. Whatever the reason, he was profoundly thankful.

'I was never with her.'

'That didn't answer my question.' She swung her legs out of bed, stomped towards the door, then turned back. 'Let's just make this as painless as possible, shall we? When are you thinking of leaving?'

'Before Christmas.'

'That soon? And you'll go off back to England?'

'I have a few things to organise here first.'

'So, you *are* going to her, then?'

With Jack failing to answer, Riley stropped through to the living room, avoiding the big shards of glass that were embedded in the carpet. Spotting Jack's phone on the kitchen counter, a look of devilment crossed her face. Tapping in his security code, part of her side of the deal in trusting him, she searched down his directory. On seeing the name Star Bligh, she sneered. Unlike Eric disguising himself as Erica in her phone, Jack hadn't even tried to disguise her name. A little appreciative nod on seeing that the number was blocked though, was followed by her immediately unblocking it.

Hey Star, she typed as quickly as her fingers would allow.

Just a little note to say that me & Riley are getting married in January. Happy wife, happy life and all that. I wish you well but I'd rather you didn't contact me again. Goodbye. Jack x

'And send!' she said aloud.

Just as she was about to delete the message and block Star's number again, Jack appeared in his dressing gown. Quickly dropping the phone back where she'd found it, she turned to the coffee pot.

'Ah, there it is.' He grabbed his phone from the bottle- and snack-littered kitchen and headed back for the bedroom. 'What a dreadful mess!'

'Yes, what a dreadful mess,' Riley repeated in an English accent under her breath and smirked as she reached down a mug from the cupboard.

Chapter 55

Star pulled up outside her mum's new home to find her painstakingly putting some solar lights around the side of the decking with one hand. Familiar music was streaming out across the park from the second-hand CD player that Star had got Estelle from the market.

'I was worried you wouldn't find me but then realised it's the same green as the other one,' Estelle shouted down as Star got out of the car.

'Here, let me help you.'

'No, no, I want to do it, it keeps me busy. But come on in now.'

In the lamplight Star could see that Estelle's long grey hair had been cut and styled into a sleek bob with blonde highlights.

Star went to turn the music down. 'Your hair is amazing, Mum. You look like Helen Mirren, so beautiful.'

'Thanks. I'm just getting used to it.' Estelle messed it up a bit with her good hand. 'One of the nurses at Penrigan General has a sister who is a hairdresser. She came yesterday and did it for me for next to nothing. I feel like my old self again.'

'You sound like the old you too,' Star said and smiled at her. 'How are your injuries doing?'

Estelle sat down on her sofa and lifted both her bandaged

arms up. 'My right hand is virtually healed now. The left arm will take a little longer and I will have nasty scars, but I know I'm lucky to be alive. The burns weren't deep, just surface. I think it was more the shock that put me in intensive care.'

'And I'm so glad that you are alive.' Star went and sat next to her on the sofa. 'Mum, I'm so sorry about what I said to you before the accident.'

The words *you're dead to me* reverberated around Estelle's mind for a minute, but then she put a comforting hand on her daughter's knee. 'I know we had a row, but I don't remember what you said. I am the one who should be saying sorry to you. Sorry for all the years I wasn't there for you. Sorry that you had to go to dear old Auntie Flo for your love and support. I don't deserve you to be sitting next to me. You should have deserted me years ago.'

'I love you, Mum. I would never have walked away, ever.' Star looked around to see if she could spot any signs of alcohol use, but all she saw was the elephant in the room – her father – who lurked there.

'It's nice and warm in here,' she remarked.

'And not an electric fire in sight.' Estelle smiled to reveal clean white teeth. Her skin looked clearer, lacking its usual blotched red texture. 'Larry, you know Billy Dillon's mate, he sorted the electric radiators in here. Timed to perfection!' She grinned. 'I mean, how kind are my neighbours. I lost everything, but to come home to this, well, there are no words. I owe it to you and to them and myself to get my act together now. You see, I didn't realise I was loved or just how much.' Tears started to flow down her cheeks as she said brokenly, 'I lost all my photos, of you, of everyone I ever cared about.'

'Oh, Mum. Auntie will have some more, I'm sure.'

Seeing that her mother was strong enough for the surprise to come, Star scrabbled in her bag to find the solicitor's envelope. It was time. Handing her mother the black and white photo of herself with her beloved Matthew, she said, her voice shaky, 'It's going to be OK.'

Estelle put the photo to her heart. 'You know? You know about Matthew?'

Star nodded. 'He wrote me a letter. I'll leave it with you to read. There is one thing you should know before you do read it though, Kara is my sister.'

'Oh my God!' Estelle spoke in slow motion. 'Matthew told me he had slept with Doryty – another secret I had to keep. But that was before me, when we were trying to resist each other. Trying not to do the deed, as we both knew that if we did come together it would cement our love and make it all the more difficult for us to say goodbye. I wasn't shocked or angry when he confessed to me. I know how powerful desire can be, especially when it is unsatisfied. As for myself, I have never known wanting like it. Poor Kara,' she sighed. 'And poor dear Joe. I had no idea. Do they both know?'

'Kara knows, as she received a letter too, and she's getting ready to tell Joe. They will get through this. They love each other and that is stronger than anything. And Matthew loved you, Mum. I understand so much more about you now. I'm so sorry. Read what he said to you.' Star took the photo gently from her mum's bandaged hand and turned it over.

'You read it to me,' Estelle whispered.

'*Estelle, you let go of me with love, the ultimate sacrifice. I never stopped loving you but it's time to say goodbye now and for you to be the person I know you can be. Matthew x.*'

Estelle's face was etched with pain. 'Get me a tissue, love.'

Then, after wiping her face and blowing her nose loudly, she said, 'Steren, I was going to tell you everything, but it seems my darling man got there first.'

Star nodded. 'Yes.'

'I also wanted you to know that I've started a programme to help get me off the drink and drugs. I've been clean since the day I went into hospital and I am going to meetings and I have met Greg, who is my counsellor. I can do this, Steren.' Star nodded again. 'I'm doing it for you, and I'm doing it for me,' she held the photo up, 'and for him by the look of it too. I know it's going to be hard, and I will need your support.' Estelle then looked at her daughter's big bump. 'From now on I'm going to be the best damn grandmother to this little mite and to Skye and, of course, the best mum to you.' She smiled. 'I was right about a St Patrick's Day baby, wasn't I?'

'Yes, incredibly.'

'The American, was it?'

'He's English, but yes, he lives in America.'

'So, my prediction? Which one of these men is the shaker, and which one is the breaker?'

'It's not black and white mother.'

'Is it ever?' The wise woman smiled.

'I think I love Jack and knowing that I can't be with him does break my heart. But he is still with his girlfriend and he thinks this is Conor's baby.' Star cradled her bump.

'Oh, Steren.' Estelle Bligh's voice cracked with emotion as her daughter went on.

'I could also say he was the shaker too, as he stirred up sexual feelings I had long buried and thought I would never experience again. Conor took and shook up the mantle ably on that front to make me realise what I'd been missing on an intimacy level, too. And what a lovely, kind guy to hold me through it. I hope I haven't hurt him. If I have, he hasn't shown it.' Star sighed deeply. 'Mum, what should I do?'

'Oh, darling. Tell Jack the truth. Then it's up to him what he does with it. You can't live a lie like I did for all those years. I loved your father. I loved him so deeply. I should have shouted louder for his time; despite his sacrifice.' Her voice tailed off. 'But I put him first, instead of me *and* you.'

'That is so sad.' Star put her hand on her mother's knee. 'But what if Jack doesn't care?'

Lyrics from Enya's haunting 'May it Be' filled the room. The two women's sapphire-blue eyes locked in understanding. 'Then at least you know.'

Star got into her car and waved back to her smiling mum, who had come out on to the decking to see her off. She automatically checked her phone for messages but remembering the signal was so rubbish at the static home park she threw it back in her bag. As she parked up behind her shop, a couple of texts beeped in. One was Kara saying she hoped everything had gone well with Estelle, and the other was from Jack. Star's heart leaped with anticipation.

And then, just as quickly, her heart plummeted a million miles to the bottom of an ocean of depression. She cried out in pain at the heartless message. 'Getting married? No! No! *No!*'

Chapter 56

Kara pushed open the white wooden gate to Bee Cottage. Seeing her dad down at the end of the garden she walked slowly towards him.

'All right, our Kerry? Why aren't you at work?' Joe Moon asked. 'I'm just checking the bees are warm enough.' He smiled. 'Got to keep old Harry's Honeysuckle Honey going or he'll be telling us off from above, won't he?' Then on noticing the expression on her face, he knew it was time. 'Get yourself in the shed, pet, the heater's on,' he said.

Joe Moon let out a loud, 'Oof!' as he plonked himself down on the threadbare green armchair in the big old shed. Kara felt as if she was reliving times with her Grandad Harry, Joe's father, who would make exactly the same noise as he sat down there. He would then look out of the open door and down the long, beautifully tended garden to the pretty cottage at the end, inevitably making some comment or other about the chickens, which would be scratching around in their pen.

As he switched Harry's old portable radio off, Kara shut the door, pulled out the old fold-up chair, and sat down opposite him. Without saying a word, she handed him the letter from her birth father.

'The Reverend Matthew Nesbitt,' he said, without even opening it.

Kara's mouth fell open. 'You knew, Dad? You knew and you kept this from me?' She went to get up.

'No, no. Stay and hear me out, Kerry Anne. I only found out the truth myself last week. Doryty sent me an email telling me about that man; said she thought the secret would come out, now she'd learned that he had died. I think she wanted to warn me, shield me from the blow. I admit, it was a very great shock, but I've had time to adjust.'

'That's not like her – and why didn't you tell me as soon as you knew?'

Joe Moon said chokily, 'Because I wanted you to believe that you were my own precious daughter for just a few days longer.'

'Oh, Dad.' Kara jumped up and went to his side. He pulled her onto his knee as if she were five years old again and held her to him as if he would never let her go, his face in her luxurious mane of red hair.

'You will always be my daughter,' he said huskily. 'I love you so much, Kerensa Anne. Your name even means love, for God's sake, as the minute I saw that beautiful little squished-up pink face of yours, that is what I felt for you. Pure and simple love.'

Kara unfurled herself, got up and stood leaning against the long workbench to her father's side.

'I don't know why he had to tell me.' She was upset and on the verge of tears. 'We could have just carried on as we were, in ignorant bliss.'

'Oh, darling. It could have been worse. If, all those years ago, your mother had told me she had had an affair and that you weren't mine, we might never have had this special bond. To me, you *are* my daughter.'

'Maybe he just wanted to absolve his own guilt before

he died.' Kara pulled herself together and took a deep breath.

'Yes, and who are we to judge him, or to work out what was going through the mind of a dying man?'

'It makes me so sad that Grandad wasn't really my grandad either.'

Joe said warmly, 'Now there *is* proof that it doesn't matter that you are not mine by birth. You were everything to that man and he to you.' It was true. Then: 'Have you told your sister yet?'

'Which one?' Kara replied flippantly.

There was a silence while Joe thought about this. 'What – do you mean this fellow Matthew had more children?' he asked, looking astonished.

'Just the one. It turns out that Star is my sister too – well, like Jen she is my half-sister, and she's younger than me by six months.'

'Well, I'll be jiggered!' Joe's mouth was wide open. 'Un-be-liev-able! And she has always been like a sister to you even though neither of you knew the truth. See? It's all OK, it really is.'

'Do you mean that?'

'What do you think?' Joe Moon got up and ruffled his daughter's hair. 'Right, I need to go and pick Pearl up from the hospital. I don't like her being on that scooter of hers when it's cold like this.' They walked down the garden arm in arm. 'Come for dinner later, if you want to.' Joe kissed his daughter on the cheek. 'Just got to go in and get my keys. I love you,' he called after her, watching her leave through the gate.

And when she was safely gone, Joe walked into his cosy low-ceilinged kitchen, reached for the worktop to steady himself. Then he began to weep.

Chapter 57

On hearing the wind chime, Star turned down the music in her workroom and walked through to the shop.

'Hey, Kar, come on through,' she said.

Kara sat herself on the high stool in the corner of the room. 'I went to tell Dad but Doryty had got to him first – which was a good thing, I suppose.'

'How are you feeling now?'

'Discombobulated.' Kara smiled. 'I love that word.'

Star made a funny little noise. 'You're so sweet.'

'Hardly.' Kara waited. 'I spoke to Jen too.'

Star gasped. 'I didn't think about your real sister who isn't your real sister now!'

'It's mad, isn't it, but she is still my half-sister, as we share the same she-devil of a mother. I was thinking: we now have to make a decision. Should we start finding out about our new relations, or do we keep the reverend's secret safe between us? For my part, I don't think I want to know. Not yet anyway. How about you?'

'I was thinking just the same. I've got to get my head around him first, let alone a whole new bloodline.'

'Jen was quite funny about it, and surprisingly understanding as it turned out. Joked that at least I had one sister – you – who could treat me properly now. She's coming to Dad's for Christmas as Markus has to see his children from his previous relationship and even the word "stepmum" brings her out in hives.'

Star laughed. 'That's Jen for you, but she did finally come good though, arranging your trip and sorting the lease on your shop.'

'She did. I meant to ask, how's Estelle doing?'

'Like a different woman now she's on the wagon. Still on the normal cigarettes but if it gets her through giving up the drink and the weed, then she can worry about that later. It's her peace of mind that she's working on first.'

'Is she excited about the baby?'

'She really is.'

'You're getting bigger day by day.'

'I know. Bigger – and more bitter.' Reaching for her phone, Star put the message from Jack on show and passed the handset to Kara.

'Oh, mate, how horrible. What an absolute wanker!'

'I'm in bits. Estelle had just said that I should find out the truth and there was this message moments after.'

'Did you send a reply?'

Star tutted. 'Give me some credit. I've embarrassed myself enough, don't you think? How can I have misjudged someone so greatly? *I'd rather you didn't contact me again.* I mean, what the fuck? That's just cruel. And it also means he must have seen my other messages and just ignored them.'

'I'm so sorry. Your poor heart is sitting in that chest of yours wondering what on earth is going on. At least it's just bruised and not broken.'

'But I feel broken, Kar,' she said tearfully. Her friend jumped down to her side. 'I thought there could be just one happy ever after in my life, just one.'

'But on a positive note your mum is getting better, and

Skye is happy, and Conor is great and will always have your back, and I'm your bloody sister, for God's sake.' Kara's upbeat voice tailed off in a wobble. 'And I know our dad died but at least you now know who he was and—'

'Yes, yes, I know all that, but I love Jack. I *love* him, Kar. But I will get through this. For Skye's sake, for the new baby's sake.'

'You need to get through it for your own sake too.'

Star sniffed and sat up straight. 'And get through it I will. Here.' She handed Kara the red ring box. 'Can you give this to Joe,' she held Kara's gaze, 'to your *dad*, I mean.'

'I have to look – is that OK?' Kara peeked inside. 'Wow, it's gorgeous! You're so clever.'

'Thanks.' Star's voice was feeble. 'Kar, when will I be good enough for somebody to want me, like properly want me?'

'Mate! It's not you, beautiful you. Don't ever lose sight of that or who you are. These men, they don't deserve you. It's their loss – and what do you always say to me? "The universe will work its magic when the time is right." And let's not forget, it's Christmas next week.'

'Whoopee do,' Star replied flatly.

'And . . . Pearl and Dad have said that you, your mum, Skye and Auntie Flo are welcome at Bee Cottage, if you fancy it. Dad said he couldn't think of anything out of the ordinary to do to propose, so decided that Christmas Day will be The Day. Pearl is going to expect it on her Christmas Eve birthday, but he wants to do it when there are lots of people around, including her sister, brother-in-law and the two kids so that we can all party on into Boxing Day.'

'I thought you said Pearl hated a fuss?'

'Ah, that's what she says, but she's one of those people who say it and don't really mean it.'

Star laughed. 'I love Pearl.'

'So do I. She's the mother I never had.'

'See? We don't have to share the same blood to love somebody. Thanks for the invitation: I'll ask the Bligh-Sibley contingent later and see what they say. But for now, I'd better get on. I've just had an email in for a last-minute bespoke request for a necklace. The customer has a good budget, and it will keep me busy.'

'You are creative and clever AND beautiful and if it counts, I love you very much.'

Star smiled. 'That counts for everything.'

'And I'm holding on to Auntie Flo's words that she said the other day: "Everything will be all right in the end. If it's not all right, it is not yet the end." I love that!'

'She got that from a film, what is it? Oh yeah, *The Best Exotic Marigold Hotel*.'

'Oh, and there was me thinking she'd got it from the Bible. She's such a character, that auntie of mine. She comes out with all sorts.'

Kara laughed. 'I hate to say this, Star, but I also think that John Lennon said something very much like it – argh, which makes me think of Jago – nightmare! Aw, I love Flo and she really is one of a kind. Right. I'd better get going.' Kara reached for her handbag. 'I'm having dinner at Dad's so will sneak him the ring then. Exciting.'

Star opened her laptop to see the screensaver of the Blaise Pascal quote she had put up straight after meeting Jack. 'Fuck you, Jack Murray!' she snarled at it. If his heart had decided on a violent, jealous woman rather than a genuine and friendly person like herself, then that was his bad judgement. Searching for a photo of her and Skye at Penrigan beach last summer, she swiftly changed the screensaver.

Then, going to all the unanswered sent emails to Jack, she firmly pressed delete. She cupped her bump through her dress. A new start was needed. No men required. She had managed before, she would manage again, and now that Estelle was hopefully on the road to sobriety, her mum could be a support to her now, rather than the other way around.

She opened up the email entitled **VERY URGENT Christmas Order** and reread it:

Hello, I got your details from your website and I love the idea of you picking a relevant crystal with meaning to put in a bespoke necklace. Sorry it's SO close to Christmas, but I need it for 23 December if at all possible. I realise this could be a big ask, however I am willing to pay whatever it takes for your time and creativity.

My partner is just the most beautiful woman I have ever met, so she deserves an equally special necklace. Her eyes are the colour of the ocean, her heart the colour of kindness. She doesn't really believe in herself, so I guess the message I want to convey is that she should. I also want to be able to tell her that this crystal will offer her peace and calm, and will protect her forever from negative emotions. I don't have much of a clue about design so I would like you to create something that you yourself would love to own, then I think we are in with a chance of her loving it too! Her birthday is in March and I see you make birthstone jewellery. I will leave all that malarky up to you.

We have both finished work for Christmas now, so email is the best way to contact me as I don't want her to get one whiff of the surprise. I am happy to pay upfront directly into your bank account. Anything up to £500 is fine. If you could let me know as soon as possible whether you can do this, I would be most grateful.

    Best regards and thank you, from
    Sid

Star went to her book of birthstones and turned to March. 'Perfect!' she said aloud, already having had aquamarine, the birthstone for March, in mind before Sid had even mentioned when his beloved's birthday was. Auntie Flo had, in fact, bought some earrings for her thirtieth birthday with that very stone in.

Reading down the meanings and energies of the stone, she thought it couldn't be more perfect. *Hold the aquamarine in your hand and as you enter a state of meditation you will visualise your worries and tension washing away into brilliant turquoise tides against the inner beach*, she read. She then automatically moved down to the 'Love and Relationships' section, and it was there that she found what she needed for herself:

Aquamarine works to enhance clear, constructive communication because of its power to cleanse and energise the throat and heart chakras.

*   The energies of aquamarine will help you become more sensitive to the needs and feelings of your partner. It will help you tune into their emotions, and they don't even have to say a word for you to know how they are feeling.*

Bless Sid, there were still some good men in the world. She started to type.

Dear Sid

Thank you so much for your order. I would love to take it on. I can design a timeless but unusual silver and aquamarine (your partner's birthstone) design for half of your budget. I will invoice you now and if you could send payment online today, I will begin work as soon as possible. Please let me know if you would like to see the designs before I go ahead and also where you would like the finished necklace sent. With postal deliveries being unreliable this close to Christmas, I am happy to deliver within a ten-mile radius of Hartmouth.

Star Bligh

The reply was immediate.

Dear Ms Bligh

Thank you so much. I trust you with the design. I will get the money transferred to you right away. And I will let you know in due course the best place for delivery.

Yours gratefully,
Sid

Star connected her phone to her Bose speaker and, putting the haunting melody of Enya's 'If I Could Be Where You Are' on repeat, she checked to see if she had a suitably sized piece of aquamarine and began to sketch out some designs.

Chapter 58

Pearl Baptiste walked into Bee Cottage and engulfed Joe Moon in a loving hug. He was hoping she wouldn't feel the jewellery box that he had just shoved in his pocket as she pressed against him. He adored the ring but as an afterthought was going to take it back down to Star to get it engraved with their names before he wrapped it and hid it under the Christmas tree.

'Blimey, what have I done to deserve this?' he asked, coming up for air.

'Just for being you, my Joey.'

Just then, Bob the Dog came bounding in to greet her, and jumped up at the woman's thighs. 'He's going to be a handful, this one,' she said, giving him a stroke.

Joe planted his hand on her voluminous bottom in a resounding smack. 'No more than you are, my love.'

'Oi, mister!' Pearl laughed her loud infectious laugh. 'How are you feeling about everything today?'

'A bit better.'

'She loves you, Joe, and that's all that matters. You've been more of a parent to her than most birth fathers are, I tell you that for nothing.'

'But what about grandchildren?'

'What about grandchildren? How lovely that will be. Me and you will be the best grandparents ever to those little

315

Dillon babies when they come. I may not be blood, but I love your daughter, no, let's make that daughters, now that Jen has shown us her true light, at last, and with Star being related to Kara, she's a daughter too. We're all part of the same big, happy family.'

Bob the Dog started barking relentlessly. 'Here.' Pearl opened a tin of dog food and put some down for the noisy hound.

'We spoil him,' Joe warned her.

'What's the harm, he's only just finding his paws here, so we need to show him a whole lot of love too.' As Pearl got up, she noticed the bulge in his trousers. 'Ooh. Is that a dog bone in your pocket or are you just pleased to see me?' Playfully, she went to grab the bulky object.

'Oh no you don't,' Joe said, play-fighting with her, 'it's private.'

They were having fun, but then Pearl managed to grab the little red jewellery box and as she was lifting it above Joe's head in triumph, the ring suddenly shot out and flew up into the air, in the direction of Bob the Dog's food bowl.

'Oh my God, Joe, what have I done! Is that what I think it is?' Pearl gasped and put her hand to her heart.

Joe's face was stern. 'Yes, it was what you thought it was, with *was* being the operative word.' He lifted up the now empty dog bowl to check it hadn't rolled under it and then started shaking with laughter. 'He's only gone and bloody eaten it – and I wanted it to be so special.'

As Pearl fell into a bout of hysterical infectious laughter, Joe managed to splutter, 'It's not funny. I wanted to make it romantic and lovely and in a special place.'

'It *is* in a very special place! In Bob the Dog!' They both collapsed again, but eventually Pearl wiped her eyes then gave her future husband a tender peck on the lips. 'We will never forget this moment.'

She was right, Joe thought.

As Pearl watched wide-eyed, he went down on one knee on the kitchen flagstone tiles and said, 'Sod a special place. Anywhere is a special place with you, Pearlette Joy Baptiste. From the minute I saw that beaming smile of yours in the car park of the Ferryboat and you went on to tell me that the name of your perfume was Desperation, I knew you were an amazing woman. I don't want to spend a day of my life without you, so will you please do me the honour of becoming my wife.'

Pearl helped him up off the floor, and with her beautiful brown eyes melting into his, she said, 'Yes, of course I will – but we'd better ring the vet before we start on the celebrations.'

Chapter 59

'They could have flattened the earth down.' Skye looked down at the new grave, still not quite believing that her Granny Bligh had slept with a Catholic priest, and that here lay her grandfather.

'It will flatten with time,' Estelle said, noticing the temporary wooden cross that had a small brass plaque with just the words *Reverend Matthew Nesbitt* and his dates of birth and death on it.

'I wonder if anyone will be ordering a proper headstone for him?' Star said, pulling her scarf tighter around her in the cold. 'I was rather hoping that there might still be some cards or wreaths on here so we could have a snoop.'

'Steren, I don't want to know anything about Matthew's family.' Estelle was firm in her delivery. 'I found out online that his parents had died, and he was an only child, so . . . let's leave it that way, shall we? For me, doing that honours his memory and also honours my promise to him.'

'I agree, and Kara does too.'

Star noticed the look of relief that spread across her mother's face.

'I thought Kara might meet us up here today?' Estelle quizzed.

'We're coming up together on Christmas Eve – just the two of us. She had a last-minute Christmas order in for

Crowsbridge Hall today, and being honest I think she wanted to visit on her own, in peace.'

Estelle nodded in understanding.

'I do want to tell Auntie Flo though,' Star told her mum. 'My bond is so great with her that I can't not.'

Estelle Bligh sighed. 'If we are to be one close family, which I want us to be now, then she should know. It would be lovely to spend some time with her, now I'm not hiding behind my addictions or lies. There is so much I have yet to learn about my mother, and Flo, for that matter, while there is still time.'

Star asked gently, 'How are you getting on with your support group, Mum?'

'It's bloody hard breaking the habits of so many years, but now I've gone through the first really tough bit, I'm strangely beginning to enjoy it. One day at a time and all that, but at the moment sobriety is suiting me. I've even come off my benefits, and whilst I wait for my clairvoyant readings to pick up – don't faint – I've got a job two days a week working in the health shop in Penrigan.'

Skye giggled. 'The health shop, Granny? You'll be stopping smoking soon.'

'I'm contemplating patches, but contemplation is as far as I've got.' Estelle kissed her granddaughter on the forehead.

'Good,' the young girl said seriously. 'I like having the new you around.'

Estelle felt so moved that for a moment she couldn't speak.

'And around I shall be, for you two and the new little baby Bligh who will be coming in just a couple of months.'

'Have you had any feelings or seen whether it's a boy or a girl?' Skye asked.

'Nooo.' Estelle dragged on the word and then, shutting her

eyes tightly, she intoned, 'I see a man with two names. On the pier. Steren, it is your time now.'

Skye took both her mum's and gran's hand. 'Come on, you witches. Goodbye, Grandad Nesbitt,' she acknowledged the grave in front of them. 'Maybe I should become a nun, to keep these two on the straight and narrow, what do you reckon?'

Chapter 60

'What's going on?' Star asked Pat Dillon in reaction to the commotion at the top end of the market.

'Some work's being done up at Tasty Pasties, by the look of it,' the woman told her.

'They've put hoarding up around the sign and are closing for the whole day on Wednesday. Bad timing if you ask me, what with this week's festivities an' all. Mrs Harris came down for some extra carrots and onions earlier, but she was holding her cards very close to her chest when I asked her what was happening. I reckon it's been sold already.'

'That was quick. Especially as it's freehold, that one. Philip Gilmour must be laughing. He's sold it just in time for Christmas so he can run off into the sunset with wads of cash and the new boyfriend Charlie told me about.'

Pat's eyes filled with tears.

'Oh Pat, I'm sorry – I wasn't thinking. Are you sad about Darren?'

'Yes.' She swiped at her eyes and said angrily, 'Charlie laughs about every other bugger – oops. See? I say everything wrong my bloody self! You can't say this, and you can't say that.'

'It's OK,' Star soothed. 'The PC police aren't listening. But I know what you mean, you do have to think before you say anything these days. Where is Charlie anyway?'

'Just on his way back from the wholesaler. We've had so many pre-orders in for Christmas we're working sixteen-hour days at the moment. It's hard getting through it without Daz. What am I going to do, Star?'

'It's a tricky one.'

'Tell me about it. I love me old man, course I do, but those twin boys are my bloody life.'

Star was thoughtful for a second. 'I think the answer is time. As time passes he will realise he's missing Daz. I said something indirectly to him the other day. Probably shouldn't have, but maybe all these things might sink in. He's obviously not prejudiced towards Philip, so I don't really understand his issue. And also, him having to work so hard without Daz on the stall at the moment, that's another thing to make him think.' She looked into Pat's eyes and said kindly, 'Try not to worry too much.'

'Bloody men! I mean, Star, what do we need 'em for really? I think once we've procreated we should just throw 'em out so they can run off and sow their seed elsewhere. I'm sure they'd love that. Just think: we wouldn't have to put the toilet seat down or pick up wet towels or hear the words "What's for dinner?" ever again. Then us ladies, we just make sure we have a good network of friends and a brothel full of firm, toned young men on every street corner.'

Star laughed out loud. 'Good on yer, Pat. That sounds like a great plan. Ouch.' She winced and put her hand on her abdomen.

'You all right, darlin'? Go in and sit down. Take the weight off for a minute.'

'I'm fine, just a little twinge. I've still got around twelve weeks left, so we don't want him popping out just yet.'

'Oh, I didn't think you'd found out the sex?'

'I didn't and I know I shouldn't say this, but I do really want a little boy. I hope if I keep saying it, he will be one.'

'I always wanted boys. Lovely they are. Mind you, I'm biased and don't know no different. You at your auntie's for Christmas again this year?'

'No, we're going to Bee Cottage. Pearl is a great cook and she wanted a houseful, so Joe has invited me, Mum, Skye and Auntie Flo. Billy, Kara and Jen will be there. And Pearl's sister, husband and two kids are coming in the evening.'

'Blimey, a right old knees-up.'

'I know – and guess who'll be the nominated driver.' Star was awkward for a second. 'I hope you're OK about Daz joining us too?'

Pat looked sad. 'I was waiting for him to say what he was doing.'

'Shit, sorry, Pat, with days to go I just assumed he'd have said something to you by now.'

'It's all right. I'd guessed already and Billy and Kara are going to come to us in the evening now, so we're not on our tod all day.'

At that moment a young lad wearing a fake moustache and beret riding an old-fashioned bicycle with a big basket in the front braked sharply in front of them. He had a string of onions around his neck and his mouth was crammed with braces. He handed Star and Pat a piece of paper and in the worst French accent possible said, 'Bone jaw, mad hams. I invite you to zee opening drinks at zee new and improved Tasty Pasties on zee twenty-third of December at five-thirty p.m.' Then he was off again, stopping at each unit as he made his way down the hill.

Star looked closely at the flyer. 'Intriguing. We shall have to go.'

'You bet we will. French, eh? Maybe, it's gonna be a deli or something?' Pat frowned. 'I bloody hope they keep selling them pasties though. I will miss 'em if they don't.'

'Snail pasties, nice.' Star laughed.

Pat was amused, but just then Charlie Dillon's voice could be heard calling his wife's name from inside the fruit and veg shop. 'Talk of the devil,' she said. 'He must have parked out the back. OK, I'd better get in there. Ta-ta, luv.'

'Take care and if I don't see you before, I'll see you for a frog's leg or two on Wednesday.'

'Ooh la la – you're on. *Au revoir*!' Pat wiggled her big bottom in the usual faded tatty jeans she wore for the market and sashayed her way inside.

Chapter 61

'*Non, je ne regrette rien,*' Florence Sibley warbled. She was getting cobwebs off the ceiling with her feather duster whilst belting out her favourite Edith Piaf track when Star struggled up the wooden steps to the flat.

The old lady clutched her chest. 'Ooh, Steren love, you didn't half make me jump. Wait a minute – let me turn this noise off. What are you doing here on a Tuesday anyway?'

'I finished work and I – well, I wanted to have a word.'

'That's nice. I'm just back from doing the church flowers and then suddenly saw cobwebs in every corner.'

'Hello, hello, hello, hello.'

'Hello, Boris.' Star put her finger in to stroke his head. He promptly pecked her. It hurt.

'Ow! You are such a naughty boy.'

'Naughty boy, naughty boy.' The budgie started flying around his cage in a whirr of blue and yellow feathers.

'Tea?' asked Florrie, when suddenly a screeching sound came from her ears. She frowned in concentration as she adjusted her hearing aids.

'Have you got any herbal tea, Auntie?'

'You know I don't buy that expensive muck. Tastes like floor sweepings. I've got milk or water, tea, coffee or lemon squash.'

'I'll have a hot lemon squash then, please.'

The two sat down by the fire with their drinks, Star as usual sitting in her great-uncle Jim's armchair.

'Funny you were singing in French just then,' she remarked. 'Tasty Pasties is reinventing itself with some kind of Franglais theme, we think. The grand opening is on the twenty-third – that's tomorrow, isn't it?'

'Yep, then it's two days until the big day,' her auntie said cheerfully. 'I need to go downstairs and get myself a new dress as we are going to Bee Cottage. For once I'll make an effort.' She beamed. 'I'm looking forward to a bit of a party. Are you sure you're OK to give me a lift home in your condition?'

Star caressed her bump. 'Of course. Skye is coming to get you and I will take you home whenever you're ready, or you can always stay with us. You can have my bed and I'll get in with Skye.'

'No, I like my own bed, you know that. Anyway, what's the matter?' the old lady asked perceptively. 'I can tell you're not here for small talk.'

Star took a deep breath. 'It's actually very big talk, Auntie Flo. I have shared everything with you through my life as you know, but I had to think twice about telling you this.'

'Is it about Estelle?'

'Yes, but it affects all of us. Estelle is doing so well, by the way. She's still sober and has got herself a job at the health shop on William Street, so hopefully you will see more of her. She is getting the bus in, which stops just up the road from here. She wants to see you, Auntie.'

'Good, that's the best present I could ever have. I can't wait to catch up with her at Christmas, now that she will be able to hold a conversation that's not full of vitriol against the world.' Florence Sibley had hopes but no illusions.

'It will be a test for her with lots of alcohol flying around, but she's up for it.'

'Steren, stop avoiding the real issue now, please.'

The young woman cleared her throat. 'You know you told me how sad it was that the Reverend Nesbitt from Penrigan Catholic Church had died from cancer far too soon?'

'Yes, such a sorry business.'

'Also, you know how closed Mum has always been about telling anyone who my father was?' Star braced herself. 'Well, it was him. The Reverend Matthew Nesbitt was my dad.'

'Jesus, Mary, Joseph, Mother of God!' Florrie put her drink down with a shaky hand.

'Estelle has thrown up some challenges to this family before, but dearie me – a reverend?'

There was a pause while Star waited for the news to sink in. It wasn't long before Florrie spoke again.

'He should have known better,' she said angrily. 'He betrayed his faith. No wonder God took him early. I am just so pleased it wasn't my vicar. I mean, the duplicity of it all! The sheer hypocrisy! How could he preach the word of the Good Lord with a clear conscience and have done such a thing? It beggars belief. I am very upset.'

'I shouldn't have told you.' Star's voice wobbled.

'No, no, you did the right thing. I just need time to absorb it. Mind you, I bet your mother was flaunting herself in front of him and in that red suede miniskirt she used to wear. You could practically see her knickers,' Florrie snapped.

Star's 'she wasn't actually' fell on her deaf ears.

'The basic fundamentals of our dear Lord's Prayer,' Florrie went on. 'Luke chapter eleven, verse four: "Lead us not into temptation."'

'Hear me out, please, Auntie. It's a very sad tale, if truth be told.'

'I don't know if I'm more cross at him or her to be honest,' Florrie ranted on.

'*Auntie!* Please – just listen for a second. The Reverend Nesbitt – my father – wrote me a letter, to be given to me by his solicitor when he died. He wrote that it happened like this: Mum went to the church to find solace after Granny Lilian died.'

'She did?' Flo's voice softened.

'She had lost her way. Like I imagine you did too. The reverend wrote especially to explain all of this, to state his side and ultimately ask for forgiveness, I believe. He told me she had been frightened and felt so alone. He met her over a period of years, Auntie. As a friend. They were the same age, they would chat in the church and he made her feel safe. And say whatever you will, and I know it wasn't right on his part, but Estelle had no faith or allegiance to anyone but herself. They fell in love.'

Florence Sibley was listening with her full attention now.

'They made love – once,' Star continued quietly, 'and created me. When Matthew chose God, not me or Mum, it did break Estelle's heart. But for many years he had given her peace and solace, and then when I was born I hope that she found happiness from having his child. Now that he's dead, I pray that she will let him go and allow herself to grow. This revel- ation has taught me that life isn't perfect. Love isn't perfect.'

'And we are all human.' Flo sniffed, her Christian spirit of charity and kindness restored. 'Poor Estelle,' she murmured, 'and poor you, Steren.'

'I actually feel blessed that I was created from a loving place and I can hold that knowledge forever now.'

Florrie nodded. 'And I have it on good authority that Matthew Nesbitt was a lovely man. He did so much for the community, and it makes sense now that he did an awful lot for single mothers especially.' The old woman managed a little laugh.

Florence Sibley heaved herself upright, kissed the crown of her great-niece's golden head then, before going through to the kitchen to put the kettle on again, she asked, 'Are you burying all of this with him? Not going to take it further?'

'No, we've decided to leave things be. We see no point in stirring up anything within his family. And Mum kept his secret right to the end.' Star reached out a hand to her great-aunt. 'I think you need to sit down again. You see, I've got something else to tell you.'

'What is it? Oh dear, I'm not sure I can take many more surprises.' Florence Sibley sat herself down, uttering a silent prayer to be able to cope with whatever this new shock turned out to be.

'It appears that the Reverend Matthew Nesbitt is also Kara's father. Before Mum, he er . . . spent time with Doryty Moon.'

'*What!*' Florence screeched, which made Boris join in from his perch. 'Oh my goodness – if the Pope knew!' She went on grimly, 'Somehow his story doesn't seem so beautiful and romantic now. Kara, that poor girl . . . she loved her grandfather so much and adores her dad – and to have that snatched away from her is terrible. And how awful for that dear man, Joe Moon.' Florrie sniffed. 'I never did like that wife of his – Doryty Moon always thought she was too good for Hartmouth. Did the dirty on Joe, passing Kara off as his own, as well as deserting him later on. It's a wicked world, Star love.'

'I know. But evidently it was also a one-off with Doryty. A single moment of temptation. However, when she found she was pregnant she was more hard-faced than Mum, who'd really loved him and he her. Doryty made sure she fleeced him for maintenance on the quiet.'

'She was a right tart, that one. Would drop her drawers for anyone, I reckon.'

'Auntie!'

'Well, it's true.' Florrie pursed her lips. 'But the reverend should have known better in both instances.'

'Yes, he should, but he didn't. We are where we are, and nothing can be changed.'

Flo managed a smile. She got up from her chair again with difficulty, releasing a succession of little sounds. 'Oops, windipops, it's not easy being my age.' While Star suppressed her laughter the old lady went on, 'Well, you're from good stock, my girl, and at least we know that now. But I would not love you less whoever your real father was, and let's face it: with Estelle we knew he would never have been an accountant.'

'I love you, Auntie Flo.'

'Till death us do part, my dear child. Till death us do part.'

Chapter 62

Kara popped her head into Star's as she made her way to Passion Flowers. 'Busy, isn't it?' she said.

'Morning. I know, but we mustn't complain.' Star stretched her aching back.

'I won't, and you know what? Your Skye is so efficient, bless her. She has got me totally organised. I honestly don't know what I'd do without her now. But how are you managing?'

'I sent all my overseas orders out a while back, just got to deliver a local one at lunchtime to Penrigan. This guy is so funny. He's called Sid, and I'm struggling to get a sense of his age. Anyway, he's so precise about his instructions. His partner is at home in their house, so he asked if I minded meeting him at Penrigan Pier as he's pretending to go for a walk on the beach. She has no idea of the gift he has in store for her.'

'Hmm, that's a bit odd,' Kara said thoughtfully. 'Why can't he come here?'

'He doesn't drive and it's fine, I said I'd take it to him. It's such a lovely piece, though I say it myself, and I can't wait to see his face. Tegan is working for me today and tomorrow, so she can cover for me later. He said he'll be there for midday prompt.'

'Ah, OK. Fair enough. Christmas Eve tomorrow, I can't believe it. It's lovely to have Billy by my side this year.'

'I bet.' Star's expression was wistful.

333

'Sorry, there I go with my big size nines again.'

'It's fine. I'm used to being man-less at Christmas.' Star brushed it off. 'And there is a party at Mum's static home park tonight, where we will be going in and out of everyone's homes. They light a massive bonfire in a pit, with someone guarding it to keep everyone safe. It will be lovely. Mum has made a massive effort cooking and offering free readings. And then of course we are all coming to your dad's on Christmas Day, which will be fun.'

'My dad's exactly,' Kara stated. 'When the madness of Christmas is over, I'd like to talk so much more about all that business with you.'

'We can start at the graveyard tomorrow. I thought we could go early, before the madness starts down here.'

An emotional Kara nodded. 'I made a little Christmas wreath for him. No one need know who left it there.'

'Aw, that's nice.' Star put her arm on her friend's shoulder. 'And we will be talking about it forever now or as long as we need to, don't worry. OK, I'd better get on. So much to do before the customers start arriving,' Star said.

'Me too. I've got hotel flowers to deliver all over the place and I think we need to go and be nosy at Tasty Pasties tonight, don't you?'

'Hell, yeah!' Star grinned mischievously.

'Billy has been a bit weird about it. I'm sure he knows something, but won't say.'

'Well, we'll all know later. I walked up there earlier and amongst the bashing about inside, behind the whited-out windows, there were some amazing cooking smells wafting out into the air.'

'Yum! Right, I'm off. See you later.' The wind chime signified Kara's departure.

Star walked through to her workroom and switched on the local radio. *'It's going to be a crisp, freezing cold but sunny day across the south-west coast today,'* said the weatherman's voice. *'Not looking like a white Christmas this year, I'm afraid, but hallelujah for no rain until the New Year, people.'*

'Yes, hallelujah,' Star repeated sarcastically. As if 'no rain' was all she had to worry about. The enormity of bringing up a baby on her own had hit her again last night. She had lain awake for hours going over the reality of it all. Yes, she had been blasé about everything being all right, but she had a business to run and a crying, feeding, needy new baby to look after, a task that she knew would be all-consuming. Estelle could do her bit, but her mother was just finding her feet again, plus there was the big issue of who she could trust to run STAR Crystals & Jewellery for her. She could buy in some ready-made jewellery, but didn't want the quality of her pieces to suffer. Tegan had said she'd love to help out in the holidays and could also cover market-day Saturdays, but Star knew she needed to get this all organised and in place before the baby came. There was so much to sort out.

Checking the calendar for the hundredth time this month, she felt slightly calmer. There was all of January and February to go, and she could get a lot done in two months. She was a grafter, always had been. Hard work didn't scare her.

Convincing herself again that it would be OK, she lifted the beautiful aquamarine necklace she had made out of its pretty golden gift box and gave it a polish. Holding it up to herself, she admired the way it looked against her skin in the mirror. *I would like you to create something that you your-self would love to own,* Sid had requested. What a sweet and clever thing to say. It had made her put even more love and passion in than usual. The design was simple. The heart-shaped bluish-green stone sparkled as it hit the light. Star had encased the aquamarine within an elegant four-claw silver setting, which she had made into little hearts that sat around the stone, the pendant suspended from a delicate silver chain, which also glittered in certain lights. Aquamarine worked its powerful magic best when set right against the skin, so she had laid it flat just above her increasing cleavage to steal the effect before wrapping it.

The morning flew by in a flurry of customers collecting orders and other customers searching desperately for last-minute gifts on the racks of earrings, rings and necklaces on display around the cluttered shop. Tegan worked hard, wrapping gifts in the beautiful Christmas tissue paper that Star had ordered specially, and as an extra incentive, the pretty hand-painted star and moon gift boxes were offered free for any spend of ten pounds or over.

'So, you're all OK with everything whilst I pop this order over to Penrigan?' Leaving the girl on her own for an hour at this busy time felt a bit unfair.

Tegan nodded enthusiastically. 'Yes, I'm sure. I've sussed the till now properly and got the price list you gave me, so I'm all good.'

'Call me anytime. I won't be long.'

Star layered herself up with scarf, hat and gloves and made her way outside to her car, where the bright midday sunshine had defrosted the windscreen. As she drove to Penrigan along the winding coastal road, she began to think of all that had happened throughout this year. One drama had followed another. Her emotions had been spun into a vortex like the famous Bermuda Triangle: down Hartmouth Head, along Penrigan Pier and fired right back out again.

As she sped round a corner and caught sight of the long sandy beach and the familiar iconic structure of the pier, she relaxed. The world was a beautiful place full of exquisite nature and lessons. She now needed to stop wasting her emotions on could-have-beens like Jack Murray. Conor wasn't the love of her life but was now a great friend, which was always a bonus. She and Jack had been – in his words – 'the best one-day stand' he'd ever had. That still hurt, but she must forget him now. Her priority had to be the little being growing inside her, a brother or sister for her beloved daughter Skye. Whether it had been love between her and Jack Murray she would never know and would just have to deal with it in the best way she could. He was going to be marrying his jealous little actress next month anyway.

Star let out a whimper of despair. Who exactly was she trying to kid with all these rational thoughts? '*Je ne regrette rien*' Edith Piaf had been singing at Auntie Flo's the other day. Maybe the singer didn't regret anything, but Star realised that she herself did. In fact, now that Jack was getting married, she would just have to live a life full of regret. Regret for not having had the courage to tell him that it was his baby she was carrying; for not having had the courage to tell him exactly how she felt about him, even before she knew that this baby was his.

She pulled up at the Penrigan Beach car park at ten minutes past twelve. She was late.

When she checked her phone, she saw there was a text from an unknown number. *You'll find me sitting on the fifth bench along on the left-hand side of the pier. Sid.* Realising that was Molly and Ronnie's bench, Star brightened up.

Walking along the pier, she did her usual thing of looking out to sea and not down at her feet in order to avoid the dizzy terror of seeing through the slats and feeling as if she was about to fall through them into the dark waves below. The sun was shining brightly. Gulls were soaring on the wing in the light breeze, cawing in delight at this brief respite of winter warmth, which had brought out some walkers who might be carrying something to eat.

As she approached the covered bench, Star could see a trendy pair of red trainers poking out, which was a surprise. Sid had seemed an older name to her, but she had obviously got that wrong, unless this person had a particularly young taste in footwear. As she approached the bench the man poked his head around, then stood up. Star was slightly taken aback by his appearance. He was wearing decent jeans and a navy ski jacket, but he had a blue beanie hat pulled right down to his designer sunglasses, plus he had a scarf draped round the bottom of his face and neck. He could easily have passed as some sort of gangster disguising himself for fear of being outed on one of those live crime investigation programmes on TV.

He held out his gloved hand and said in a muffled Welsh accent, 'I'm Sid. Have you got the necklace?'

'Yes, here it is.' Star handed him the little golden gift box and turned to leave. He was so strange she didn't really want to spend one more minute here, let alone hang around to see him open the box and bask in his pleasure in the necklace.

'Wait! One second, please.' The man held his hand out.

Star stopped and stared, bemused, as the man pulled a sticky label from his pocket, stuck it on the box then handed it back to her. She gazed at the handwritten message in disbelief, then feeling a tingle spread through her from the top of her head to the tip of her toes, she read aloud: '*The heart has its reasons which reason knows not. My reason is you.*'

The man took off the glasses, then pulled away the beanie hat and scarf to reveal the familiar bearded face she had been longing so badly to see again.

'You frightened the shit out of me then, you bastard,' she said shakily. 'And I've never heard such a rubbish Welsh accent.'

'I thought it would be romantic.'

Star laughed then burst into tears. 'Oh, Jack.'

'We're not very good at this, are we?' he said, and guided her to sit next to him on the bench. He cradled her into him. 'Let me explain, OK?' Star nodded.

'I don't care that you're pregnant with another man's child. I don't care that you are in a relationship. I care about *you*. In fact, Star Lilian Bligh, crazy as it sounds, I am in love with you.'

'But you're getting married?'

'No, I'm not. I found the message that conniving little bitch Riley sent you. We had already split. I was working out the best way to contact you and then, when I saw that spiteful message, I knew I had to come and see you face to face, because if I had received something like that, I would never have spoken to you or trusted you again. Look, Star, I know you're with Conor and you have a whole new life ahead of you with your baby, but I had to tell you how I felt. I would never have found peace within if I hadn't done so. You are a beautiful, gifted, kind and generous person, and if I can work that out after spending just a few hours with you, then that must mean you are one special human being.'

'I'm not with Conor.' The statement was short and factual.

Jack pulled away from her, his hazel eyes wide. 'He left you and you're pregnant? No, no, that's so wrong.'

'I think you had better be ready for the next surprise. We split because I'm pregnant with somebody else's baby. And I'm in love with the father.'

'Oh.' Jack felt his throat tightening with emotion.

Star got ready to pull the pin on the grenade, which was her heart. 'It's your baby, Jack,' she whispered, her voice barely audible.

'My baby?' he echoed.

Star nodded. 'I didn't know I was pregnant for ages. I'd met Conor by then, and assumed it was his, but the midwife examined me and I learned that I was a lot further on than I'd thought. This baby can only be yours, Jack.'

Speechless, full of joy and excitement, Jack leaned forward and put his lips on hers. The bristles of his beard scratched against her soft cheeks as she gripped his head firmly, as if to keep him from escaping. Breathless and passionate, loving and meaningful all in one glorious toe-curling moment of joyous togetherness. They kissed.

'Star Bligh, I need to make love to you, right now!'

'Yes,' Star replied just as feverishly, 'but not here. Where are you staying?'

He pointed up at the Penrigan View Hotel.

'Are you sure it's safe for the baby, having that much sex in one go?' Jack propped himself up on one arm and stared down at a very flushed Star.

'It's a bit late to worry about that now. God, that was so

good.' She lay back and did a mad snow angel effect under the covers. 'Why call yourself Sid, by the way? That's such a random name to come up with.'

Jack laughed. 'It just came into my mind – and then I realised why. It was the name of Kara's terrapin, Sid Vicious, do you remember? He wasn't there this time around.'

'Of course I remember,' Star told him, 'and it's not a name to bring up in conversation. You see, he suffered a very sad demise in the jaws of James Bond.'

'Oh no,' Jack snorted. 'That is quite funny though.'

'On a serious note,' Star went on, 'I've just given you the news that you're going to be a father and you have taken it so bloody well. You don't have to stay with me, you know. Just for the sake of the baby.'

Jack shook his head. 'You need to stop this. I really, really want to be with you, Star Bligh. Nobody else, just you. The baby is the icing on an already delicious cake. Are you hearing those words loud and clear, madam, because I mean them.'

'But what about your job? And do you want to live with me straight away? And—'

Jack put his finger to her lips. 'We will work it out. I had no idea that this was going to happen. I assumed you were with Conor, so I'm booked in the hotel here until Boxing Day, when I promised to go and see my parents and sisters for a couple of days – and then I'm all yours, if you'll have me? My job can be overseen from the London office, which basically means I can work from home anywhere I want to. They offer paternity leave too, so I will be able to help you when the baby comes. We both know my dream is to write, and that could be worked around joint parenting too, I'm sure.'

He kissed his happy girl on her forehead. 'There's always

a solution, always. I am yours. I've left New York now. My plan was to come and say my bit to you, then retreat to my parents' house in Bristol until I worked out where I wanted to live.'

'Hmm. I know of a beautiful estuary town called Hartmouth.'

'Ah, well, that's a consideration. And I've heard a gorgeous pregnant blonde girl lives there who is looking for her knight in shining armour?'

'Just the red trainers will do.' Star smirked. 'By the way, I love the necklace I made for myself.' She fingered it on her neck. 'Aquamarine works so well for me – for us, in fact, in its message of love. And then for you to add that Blaise Pascal note, well yes, I'll give you that, that part was romantic.'

'Tick.' Jack grinned.

'The heart certainly has its reasons which reason knows not, but our hearts are at last together and now there is a third little heartbeat in the mix, it's just perfect.'

Jack gently put his hand on her ever-growing bump. 'Do you know the sex?'

'No, I wanted a surprise.'

'You're good at firing those off.' Jack kissed her on the lips. 'Any names yet?' He then gave a groan. 'Oh no, they are going to be way out like Star and Skye, aren't they?'

Star laughed. 'I do quite like Storm for a boy.'

Jack made a face. 'Let's discuss it when he or she comes out, shall we? They say a name suits a face and we will just know, I'm sure. Drink?' He got up and walked naked over to the minibar.

'Fizzy water, please, and then I really have to go back to Tegan at the shop. She was fine when I texted her, but I need to get back to cash up with her, at least.'

Jack put the drinks on the side and got back into bed. 'I don't know why on earth I didn't tell you what was going on in my head the last time I was here. I suppose I decided there was no point because of Conor and the baby. But then, when you showed me Molly and Ronnie's inscription – *There's never an end to the sea, so why for you and me?* – it stuck with me. Actually, who am I kidding. I never stopped thinking about you from the moment I met you, Star, I really didn't. I'm so sorry that I hurt you, my angel.'

'It was as much me as you. I should have had the courage to come out with it and tell you what I thought, but I assumed you would reject me. I wasn't confident enough to think you would love me back, especially as you were living with Riley. Old Blaise Pascal must have been shouting down at us, saying "bloody sort it out, you two".'

They both started laughing.

'What do you think your parents will say?' she asked.

'I'm thirty-seven, Star, there's not much they can say apart from "Congratulations", I hope, and no doubt they will be relieved that I won't be moving back in with them. Look, don't worry, I just know they will be thrilled to hear that I have finally become a father. They will be grandparents again. My mum will be over the moon.'

They stared at each other pillow to pillow.

'We are going to be parents.' Jack put his finger gently on Star's nose. 'How mad and brilliant is that?'

'It won't be plain sailing.'

'But there will be nobody jumping ship and I promise you that with my whole heart.'

'*If you do not love too much, you do not love enough,*' Star suddenly quoted, then whispered, 'I understand that now.'

Jack pulled her towards him. 'And so do I.'

343

Chapter 63

As Frank Sinatra and Bing Crosby's silky tones began to flood down across Ferry Lane Market, stallholders, customers and locals alike looked around wondering where the music was coming from. The two old crooners sang together, dreaming of a white Christmas. And then, right on cue, there was snow! Lots of magical white flakes were pouring from a large snow machine behind the back of Tasty Pasties, and for those who didn't realise, it really did look like the real, wondrous thing. Skye and Tegan rushed out of their respective shops and hugged in the street. The Christmas lights twinkled, and the excited chatter of intrigued folk filled the air.

As Kara locked up her unit, she spotted Star walking towards her, arm in arm with a familiar-looking man.

'Is it really you, Jack?'

'Hello, Kara.' He kissed her on both cheeks.

'It's a long story,' Star told her, 'but this one does have a happy ending, at last. Now come on, let's go up and see what's happening. We don't want to miss the grand unveiling.'

A grinning Billy appeared and, at the sight of Jack, made a quizzical face at his girl. 'I've no idea what's going on yet, but Star looks happy so that's what matters,' Kara breathed in his ear.

When a small crowd had gathered, Conor and Darren appeared at the door of Tasty Pasties.

'What the bloody hell is going on?' Pat Dillon queried to Charlie who shrugged his massive shoulders.

In silence Conor and Darren looked at each other, then counted down from three. When they pulled away the red blanketing that had been shielding the old Tasty Pasties sign, a collective gasp went around the captivated audience. There, replacing the familiar depiction of a Cornish pasty, was a beautifully hand-painted image of a Burlesque dancer, with a pink neon sign to match Frank's saying simply MONIQUE'S.

Conor nodded for Darren to turn the music off. He then picked up a handheld microphone from the top of the speaker.

'Welcome, everyone, to Monique's. When I arrived in Hartmouth just under three months ago, I was jobless, a little bit sad and not sure where my life was heading. But I'm a prime example of how fate can turn on a sixpence. I found a job and a great friend in Billy on the ferry, despite my seasickness.' A hum of laughter went round the crowd. 'And I also found a beautiful girl, who I am now proud to call my friend.' He smiled at Star, not even flinching at the sight of Jack who, on this comment, gripped her hand territorially. 'I'm proud to say that my son Niall is here with me for the Christmas holidays and made a fine Pierre on his bicycle, delivering the leaflets, I hope you can agree.' The gawky, metal-mouthed teenager stood by the side of his dad and smiled awkwardly.

'So, back to Monique's,' Conor continued. 'I've always had my finger in many pies—'

'Oi, oi!' Charlie Dillon shouted.

'Stop that!' Pat Dillon swiped him on the arm.

The crowd laughed again.

'But this new venture is not going to be one of them.' He

looked towards Star, whose brow furrowed slightly. 'As I said, my time down in this beautiful town of yours has been amazing, but in January I shall be moving on again.' Billy did a thumbs-up as the Irishman caught his eye, while beside him Kara was feeling slightly aggrieved that her partner had not told her this news. Conor then looked over to Star, who was wearing a strained smile.

'Please don't worry, the pasties will always be on the menu, and of course, our very own Mrs Harris will remain at her post.'

At the mention of her name, the plump assistant appeared in the doorway wearing a new Monique's pinny and, smiling broadly, she waved at them all as if she was the queen.

'I mean, we had to keep her on,' Conor confided to them all in a stage whisper, 'as she does have the secret pasty recipe and Philip Gilmour is now locked away somewhere safe, screaming to get out and claiming that we have stolen it. Anyway, my friends, I must stop gabbling and give you the facts. Big Frank has bought the place, and will be bringing in somebody to manage it. The only French thing about it is Monique's name because she is so lovely, and of course the odd croissant or two will be served. Market stallholders, you will no longer have to go all the way down the hill to get your coffees now.' There was a hurrah from the crowd. 'Monique's will be offering takeaway food similar to Frank's and there are a few more eat-in seats too.'

At that moment, all six feet four of Big Frank appeared in the doorway with a huge tray balanced in his hands, full of hot pasties on one side and warmed mince pies on the other. Monique, wearing her trademark bright red lipstick, was right behind him with a tray of mulled wine, teas and coffees, which Conor swiftly took off her and placed on one

347

of the outside tables that had been set up next to the snow machine.

'Do help yourselves, all. We are open tomorrow for Christmas Eve drinks, pasties and mince pies, and then will be fully up and running from the start of the new year.'

With Kara now deep in conversation with Jack, Star went to get a mulled wine for him and a cup of tea for herself.

'I hope it's not down to me that you're going, Conor. I thought we were good?' She let out a funny little nervous laugh. Pulling his big shoulders back and swallowing down the lump in his throat, the handsome Irishman put his hand gently under her chin and lifted it.

'You, my lovely girl, worry too much.' He nodded in the direction of Jack, who was still chatting away to Kara. 'I take it that's him?'

'Yes. That's Jack.'

'Make sure he treats you right, OK? One false move and I'll be back to make pastry out of him.'

Star laughed. 'Well, you always said you were here for a porpoise.'

'You loved that one.'

'I did.' She bit her lip. 'Where are you going, anyway?'

'Back to London. My cousin Sean has a landscaping business, going to help him for a bit, until I can afford to set up on my own again. And Maeve, well she's all up for me seeing a lot more of Niall, but would rather me be in London than Cornwall as it's so much easier for him to fly straight into Heathrow.'

'Well, that's such a positive. I wish you so much happiness, Conor, and I'm so pleased that your boy is here with you now too for Christmas.'

'Me too,' Conor said quietly, willing the stinging in his

eyes to retreat. 'Now go back to your fella, he's waiting for you.'

Star picked up the drinks and headed back to Jack.

'Cheers.' The couple clinked paper cups and couldn't stop smiling at each other.

'If you've been a good girl this year, I hear that you even get a special present the night before Christmas Eve,' Jack said, giving her an intimate look.

'Another one?' Star said flirtily, leading him by the hand down the side alley of her shop and up the stairs to her flat.

Chapter 64

Christmas Day

Joe Moon came bursting in through the back door with two old fold-up garden chairs from the shed, then began counting on his fingers. 'Me, you, our Kara, Billy, Darren, old Flo, Estelle, Skye, that Jack fellow. Or is Billy going home for his Christmas dinner? I forgot. That still doesn't seem many.'

'Don't you be telling my sister you forgot her, now.' Pearl swiped him with a tea towel.

'Oops.' Joe laughed. 'Of course, your Ireany, John and the kids are coming in the evening.'

'Yes. And Billy *will* be here for dinner, he's going to Pat and Charlie's with Kara later on.' Pearl tutted. 'And what about your second daughter, Joey?'

Joe bit his lip. 'My memory. Jen messaged me earlier. She's driving down from London and left later than she thought, so she said we should just start without her.'

'Right. So, set out ten places, which is plenty for this kitchen table, especially with the amount of food I'll be piling on it, and Jen can slip in when she arrives.' Pearl then checked inside the oven. 'No need to worry we'll run out of food. We've got a big enough turkey to feed the whole market.'

She laughed her big infectious laugh. Hearing it, and smelling the roasting meat, Bob the Dog appeared in the kitchen, his tongue out and tail wagging madly.

'Still no sign this morning?' Pearl asked, stroking him. 'I'm beginning to think we missed it.'

'No, I've checked every single poop, all for the love of you, my lady. Poked them with a stick but still no sparkle.'

'The vet said it should have come out the day after. I hope it's not stuck inside him somewhere.'

'Look at him, there's nothing wrong with you, is there, boy?' The big Labrador jumped up at Joe's legs, and ignoring his owner's sharp, 'Down,' he proceeded to lick the startled man's face, much to Pearl's amusement.

'Don't encourage him, Pearl,' Joseph Moon managed to say, mopping his face and trying not to laugh.

'It's a lost cause now,' Pearl said indulgently. 'He's nine. It's like trying to discipline someone your age in dog years. Mind you, I like it that you're still a naughty boy.'

Joe Moon grabbed a handful of his fiancée's bottom and gave her a smacking kiss on the neck, causing her to squeal loudly.

Joe chinked his fork against his champagne flute. 'Before we all sit down to stuff our faces, I would like to propose a Christmas Day toast.'

'And then say Grace, I hope,' Florence Sibley muttered under her breath. Estelle, about to tell her aunt to shut up, instead bit her tongue and poured fizzy water into her wine glass. Skye stayed looking down at her phone.

Suddenly there was a knock at the door. 'Must be our Jen,' Joe said, 'but why's she knocking?'

On Joe's shouted instruction to come in, the door flew open. Darren and Billy looked at each other as their father suddenly appeared in the now cramped kitchen. Pat Dillon for once stood quietly behind him.

'Happy Christmas, everyone, and sorry to interrupt but I've come to collect something extremely important.' Darren's eyes began to well up as his dad took a deep breath. 'Son, there will always be a place at our table for you, come rain or shine, Christmas or otherwise, and I mean that.'

Darren looked at Pearl, who was nodding and gesturing, 'Go!'

'Are you coming, Daz?' Pat Dillon's voice was wobbling.

Darren stood up at exactly the same time as Billy. Kara reached up and squeezed his hand.

Billy checked with Pearl and saw her nod before answering, 'We both are, Mum and Dad, but before I go, Kara and I have an announcement to make.'

'Oh my days! Here it comes!' Pearl clapped her hands together excitedly.

'We are having a baby Dillon,' Kara told them all.

Star gasped. '*Yes!* We can be mummies together like we always wanted to be. When are you due?'

'Not sure. I know you're supposed to wait to tell people, but I literally just did the test before we left and we are so excited.' A beaming Billy leant down to kiss Kara on the cheek.

'That's really fantastic.' Joe felt overcome with emotion. He turned to Charlie and Pat. 'Come on, have a glass of something with us to celebrate our new grandchild.'

Pearl rushed to get them a drink.

'To Kara and Billy!' they all toasted.

A shocked and delighted Pat Dillon downed her glass in one.

Kara then tapped on her glass of fizzy water. 'So many toasts are required today. Mine is to Star and Jack, and I wish them every happiness together, bringing their new baby into the world.'

'To Star and Jack!'

Star turned to Jack. 'Can you cope with all this lot, do you think?'

He kissed her hand. 'With you by my side I can cope with anything.'

Joe took a huge glug of his champagne and stood up. 'I want to say something too.'

Flo raised her eyebrows. 'Kerry Anne, you are the best daughter a father could ever have wished for. Living nearby and working on the estuary for many years, this family has water running through its veins, so blood would not have been thicker, whichever way. Our love has grown from a mutual understanding and respect and, like your grand-parents before me, it will never falter. In fact, what has come to light has made me feel even luckier. Our bond is stronger than the tides, without it even being a natural one. And how wonderful to bring Star and Skye into the family unit too, with Star being your sister 'n' all, now.'

'Thank you,' Kara whispered.

Pearl downed her flute of champagne in one before surprising everyone there by saying, 'So, Billy Dillon, are you going to make an honest woman of our lovely Kara before this baby comes then?'

Kara spoke up. 'We don't want to outshine your wedding, now do we?'

Estelle spoke up. 'Weddings, babies, it's all happening, isn't it? You give me hope, Joe: it's never too late, is it?'

'No, it isn't, Estelle, and may I say how fine you are looking. Your hair is great like that.'

Estelle found herself blushing.

Darren cleared his throat. 'As we are all having a say, I'd like my turn, please.' He addressed Charlie. 'Dad, thank you for coming. I can't say I haven't been hurt by your actions, because I have. But knowing you as I do, I'm aware it took a lot for you to come in and face everyone like this and for that I'm really pleased and proud of you. I have, however, decided to move away from Hartmouth.'

Kara grasped Billy's hand.

'I'm not going far though – only to Devon. A picturesque little place called Cockleberry Bay.' There was a sigh of relief from the Dillon family. He went on awkwardly, 'I'll be going to live there with my new boyfriend,' adding, 'Phew, it sounds weird but so bloody liberating saying those words.'

'Anyone we know?' Star asked nosily.

'You all do, actually. Let's just say I call him my Tasty Pasty!'

A tutting Auntie Flo got up to refill her glass with tap water.

'Well, I propose a toast to my twin brother,' Billy said. 'Proud of you, mate. To Darren *and* his tasty pasty!' The words echoed around the kitchen and Joe replenished everyone's glasses.

Star really wanted to say something too. 'I didn't know you'd proposed already, Joe,' she said. 'Did you like the ring, Pearl? Joe had a big input in its design. He wanted to use your namesake stone, diamonds and white gold. And the little shell flower was down to me.'

355

'What, this one?' Flo, noticing a sparkle around the back of the kitchen tap, lifted the beautiful piece of jewellery in the air.

Pearl and Joe were now falling about in hysterics, the big lady's infectious laugh setting everyone else off without having a clue what was going on.

Once he had managed to contain himself, Joe wiped his eyes and explained, 'We thought Bob the Dog had eaten the ring. Well done, Flo.' A unified toast of 'Well done, Flo!' went around the room as Pearl popped open another bottle of champagne.

Joe tapped his glass again and made eye contact with everyone around the room.

'To Star and Moons, to babies, boyfriends and weddings. To old friends and new beginnings. Happy Christmas, everyone!'

A resounding, 'Happy Christmas!' filled Bee Cottage.

'Woof, woof,' said Bob the Dog.

Epilogue

'I am so happy it's a boy,' Star said, looking up at Jack lovingly from her hospital bed as their tiny tot slept soundly in his baby bed alongside her. 'He looks like you with all that black hair.'

'Poor little mite,' Jack teased. 'If he's going to be short with wonky teeth like me too, I'm not sure that a huge name like Storm will fit the bill.'

'It's fine – I know exactly what I want to call him.'

'Scare me,' Jack dared her.

'Matthew James Murray.' Star delivered each name slowly and deliberately before explaining: 'Matthew for obvious reasons and Jim is short for James, so Flo will be so happy that her late husband, my wonderful great-uncle Jim, is getting a nod. Plus of course, James is your dad, too.'

'I love it.' Jack kissed his girlfriend on the cheek. 'Dad will be made up and I think it sounds very distinguished.' As the baby began to stir, he carefully lifted the little bundle and handed the tiny boy to his mum.

'Hello, Matthew Murray,' she cooed, then on kissing him gently on the top of his soft little head, she awkwardly positioned him for a feed.

Jack produced a jewellery box from his pocket. 'We kind

357

of forgot it was *your* birthday today too, didn't we, with all of this going on.'

'Oh, Jack. Open it for me, can you?' And then: 'A ring? Aw. Aquamarine to match my necklace. It's beautiful.'

Getting down on one knee next to the hospital bed, Jack said, 'To celebrate two special birthdays today, I think the only thing that will trump that is an engagement, don't you? Star Lilian Bligh, I'm so happy that your heart had a reason which reason knew not. Will you marry me, and of course not forgetting Skye in all of this, make our precious little Murray family complete?'

'I will.'

Read on for an extract from

RAINBOWS END
IN FERRY LANE
MARKET

The third book in Nicola May's brilliant Ferry Lane
Market series . . .

HODDER

'I would rather die of passion than of boredom.'
Vincent van Gogh

Chapter 1

'To be honest, I'd rather celebrate with a mariachi band and burgers down the front at Frank's *Café*.'

'What – you'd prefer that over a marquee in my beautiful grounds with caterers and a four-piece string quartet? Glanna, *really*?' Penelope Pascoe tapped her freshly manicured nails on the handset.

'Yes, *really*, Mum.'

'Well, you're only forty once, dear, that's all I'm saying, and the Penhaligons at Crowsbridge Hall are expecting to attend a big event.'

'Good to know that your posh neighbours are on the guest-list for *my* party. Thanks for that.' Glanna Pascoe blew out an exaggerated breath, then checking herself in her hall mirror, ran her hands through her expensively highlighted blonde crop and wiped a smudge of mascara from her eyelid.

Penelope Pascoe tutted down the line. 'It would be lovely to have you back home for your birthday. Plus, if the predicted Indian summer bestows itself upon us, the pool should still be warm too.'

Glanna didn't allow the familiar manipulation to get to her. 'My home is here in Hartmouth, not at Riversway with you, Mum.' She glanced at her watch. 'I've got to go; I'm meeting someone at six.'

'Ooh, a date?' Penny asked excitedly. 'I always hoped that

when you hit the big four zero, you'd grow up, find love, have a family and live happily ever after.'

'Bingo! All your dreams coming true, just like that.' Glanna couldn't help but smile through her sarcasm. 'I can see it now. Middle-class utopia.' She became staccato in her delivery. 'Two children – a boy and a girl, of course – Mind*less* Chef deliveries four times a week, and a couple pretending that monogamy is what they both want and should abide to.'

Her mother sniffed. 'You're a stroppy madam today, aren't you?'

'You've wound me up, that's why. Anyway, I don't think even you can class my very married therapist as a date.' Glanna pushed her chunky brown tortoiseshell glasses back on to the bridge of her prominent nose. 'And how many times do I have to tell you that I'm happy as I am?'

'Well, I'll bet that shrink of yours will tell you the same as me. Nobody can be happy single, darling. We all need somebody.'

'Says the woman who's exhausted every dating app in Cornwall.'

'Exactly! I'm not the one denying that I'm sick of rattling around this mansion with a sex-drive that's off the scale for a woman of my age.'

Glanna grimaced. 'Anyway, I have Banksy. Far less trouble than any partner.' The sleeping black whippet let out a little snore from his kitchen-based basket as if acknowledging his important role.

'You'll be a sad lonely old spinster at this rate,' Penelope Pascoe muttered, then more loudly: 'Not everyone will hurt you like Oliver did, you know.'

'Mother! Enough! I've got to go.'

'I was thinking maybe you could pop over to Riversway for dinner this Saturday, if you fancy it?' the indomitable woman continued.

'Um, I can't, sorry. I'm taking photos at Kara Moon's wedding.'

'Oh. That's the ferryman's daughter, isn't it? I do hope they're paying you enough.' The woman didn't stop to take a breath or to give time for Glanna to admit that she was doing it in exchange for a month's worth of fresh flower displays for the reception desk of the Hartmouth gallery, her much-loved business where she exhibited and sold not only the works of some quite well-known local artists but also various pieces of her own.

'And, darling,' Penelope went on, 'if you hear from your father, I want to talk to him. He hasn't been in touch for over a week and that's so not like him.'

'OK. I'll tell him. Goodb—' Desperate to finish the call, Glanna began fidgeting.

But Penelope Pascoe always had to have the last word. 'Think about a nice grown-up party please, darling, for all of our sakes,' she trilled, and hung up.

Chapter 2

'It annoys me that you never start the conversation.'

After she'd got that off her chest, Glanna made a face at the soft-bellied bald man opposite her and wondered if it was a prerequisite to being a counsellor that you had to have kind eyes and an expressionless face. She also wondered if Myles Armstrong put a hint of mascara on his lashes as surely no one could flaunt such beauties without make-up.

'You know that's not the drill,' Myles said, suppressing a smile.

Glanna reached down to stroke Banksy who, having managed to stealthily poke his long snout into her handbag and finish all his treats, was now lying innocently next to her feet, eyes firmly closed, his jewel-encrusted collar sparkling.

'Mum's pissing me off again. She's such a bloody snob.'

Saying nothing, Myles flicked a piece of fluff from off his jeans and cocked his head to the side in anticipation of his feisty client's next comment.

He had liked Glanna Pascoe the minute he had met her just under a year ago. On their first meeting, the tall willowy woman, dressed like she'd walked straight off the Green Fields at Glastonbury, had breezed in and without requesting whether it was OK for the black whippet trotting at her heels to stay with her, had sat down and announced drolly, 'Hi. My name's Glanna, which my mother tells me means "pure" in Cornish.' The corners of her mouth had then fleetingly upturned, and she had given him the cool look he had by now become accustomed to from her huge, doe-like brown eyes. Eyes that had been smudged not only with smoky eye-shadow but with an underlying sadness too.

It had taken Glanna a while to trust the forty-something professional. However, in time, the mild-mannered therapist had succeeded in gently coaxing out the information he required to start working with his new client.

Where mental health was concerned, everybody was different, but due to Glanna's brief stint in rehab and ongoing support, Myles Armstrong could tell that she had already put a lot of work into herself and was well on the way to being sorted. The truth was, she was his favourite kind of client. Troubled but intelligent. She challenged him in a good way. In fact, she reminded him of a thoroughbred racehorse, sleek and beautiful but with the ability to turn and buck him off at any second.

He was pleased with her progress and hoped that the time she had spent in therapy with him had brought her close to the stage where she would be able to form healthy relationships and make the decisions that were right for her. Plus, of course, keeping herself sober along the way.

It had been an exciting but also toxic journey that had led Glanna to be sitting here mending her mind at the age of thirty-nine and three-quarters.

Cornish-born and bred, as soon as she'd left school after her A-levels, the young woman's life had consisted of travelling to far-flung places with her friend Carmel. Like Glanna, Carmel too had been bankrolled by her family until she met and married the Earl of Newham after getting pregnant by him during his yacht party in Ibiza. She subsequently went off to live in her new husband's huge pile in Dorset, popped out two more kids and was regularly seen in four-page features in *Country Lives* magazine and the like.

Throughout her twenties, when not travelling, Glanna intermittently returned to the family home, Riversway, nestled along the banks of the River Hart and across the estuary from Hartford where her gallery business was located. At Riversway, she would spend her time sketching in the wooden art studio right at the edge of the water that her dear dad had built specially for her. For pocket money she'd do the occasional shift at the café in the grounds of Crowsbridge Hall, the local National Trust property.

It was only after her mother's constant nagging that Glanna should do something constructive with her life that, at the grand old age of thirty, she had headed to London where she became a mature student and obtained a first-class degree in Fine Art at University College in Bloomsbury. Funded solely by Penelope Pascoe, of course.

But even with a distinct proof of education under her belt, Glanna had chosen to remain in the city and continue to live a student lifestyle. Vodka binges, drug-taking, and a constant flow of partners of both sexes became her norm. This, combined with her irascible, unreliable personality had caused her to neglect her artistic talent and instead get hired, then fired from various jobs, including working in an exclusive boutique and as a receptionist of a casting agency.

Back in Cornwall, Penelope Pascoe, who was busy focusing on her role as society hostess at Riversway, would blindly fund her troubled offspring's chaotic life, ignoring the danger that Glanna was in and prolonging the situation by bailing her out every time. Thus, through the first three years of her thirties and still supported purely by the ugly currency of money instead of love, Glanna Pascoe's cycle of addiction and indulgence began to spiral out of control.

Now, in Myles' pleasant treatment room, Glanna glanced through the open double doors to view the estuary twinkling below. It was a hot July day and the water, as still as a mill pond, reflected the deep blue of the cloud-free sky. She could just make out the familiar yellow and red outline of the *Happy Hart* ferry landing across the quay at Crowsbridge. A few boats were making their leisurely way out of the harbour towards the ocean. This serene scenario was, Glanna knew, the relative calm before the storm. For once the kids broke up from school near the end of July, and the 'haves and have yachts' descended on Hartmouth, it would turn into a bustling hive of activity for young and old alike. Great for her gallery, not so great for getting around the town or finding a seat in one of her favourite eateries.

'Glanna, are you with us today?'

'Sorry, Myles. It's just that now I'm coming up to forty, it's making me think about my life.'

'Go on.'

'Mostly, where have my thirties gone.' She looked to the outside again and sighed. 'I've wasted so much time.'

'Time is never wasted if you've learned from it. We are all a work in progress, Glanna.'

The woman in front of him smiled weakly. 'I keep thinking of my years at university, with everything that came after that, then meeting and living with Oliver before coming back here on my own . . . In the autumn, it will be two years now I've lived in Hartmouth and run my business. It's just flown by in a haze.' She reached down to stroke the whippet and made a funny little noise. Myles heard her gulp. 'And Mum's getting on my nerves too. Going on again about me settling down.' Glanna's voice turned into a whine. 'What if I don't want to settle down? What if I am happy being single and childless?'

'Well, are you happy?'

There was a lengthy pause. 'Yes! Yes, I am.'

'You took your time there, Ms Pascoe.'

'Don't go all therapist on me, please Myles.' The sage man remained silent. 'Anyway, I don't want to talk about it now.'

'That's fine.' Myles waited.

'Oliver encouraged me to freeze those eggs,' Glanna went on in a rush. 'I wish he hadn't, it makes me feel guilty.'

'"Those eggs"?'

'OK, OK. *My* eggs.'

Myles nodded slowly. 'But guilty, for what? For whom?' This was only the second time she had ever mentioned this, and his trained ears honed in attentively.

'It's like there's little pieces of me sitting there waiting for something to happen, which isn't *going* to happen, and I don't like that. I'm angry. Angry that I've started something that's not going to be finished. Angry that Oliver managed to persuade me so readily.'

'And the feelings of guilt?' Myles pushed.

'Oh, I don't know,' Glanna said impatiently. 'For what could have been, I guess. And for today's society making women feel guilty for not wanting to be breeders. As though if we dare to not follow the sacred path to fertility, we should be banished to a life of living with twenty cats and have the word "odd" tattooed on to our foreheads.'

'No one can *make* you feel anything, Glanna. You do that all by yourself.'

'Yeah, right, but when someone fires off the loaded question, "So, do you have children?" I just want to reply, "No, I bloody don't. I don't like the little bastards. I like my freedom. I like my peace and quiet. I like to have money. I DO NOT WANT children." Instead, I smile sweetly and just say, "No, not yet".'

She scratched her head manically, then started to fiddle with Banksy's lead. The whippet let out a sleepy sigh. 'I really did love Oliver, you know.' Her voice cracked. 'I get it, that he wanted a family. And who was I to stand in the way of his dream?'

'Tough stuff.' Myles nodded.

'What – to realise that me on my own wasn't enough for him, you mean?' Glanna checked her watch and stood up, causing Banksy to give a little whimper of dismay for being so rudely awoken. 'I need to go.'

'You've only been here twenty minutes.' Myles noticed the rare glisten of tears catch the light from behind his client's glasses.

'I'll pay you for the hour.'

'I didn't say it because of that.' His voice was kind. 'It's your session to do what you want with, but I've got a free slot next Wednesday at seven if you did want to come back and finish this one off.'

With an agitated bark from Banksy at the unexpected jerk on his glitzy collar, Glanna rushed for the door and without turning around, said, 'I'll let you know.'

Chapter 3

'Get your summer strawberries, ripe and juicy, two quid a punnet, three quid for two,' Charlie Dillon bawled, his family's fruit and veg stall already in full market-day swing as Glanna walked down the hill from Monique's *Café* with one of her favourite takeaway coffees in hand.

A heavily pregnant Kara put down the bunches of sunflowers that she had just carried out from inside her shop, then on seeing Glanna beckoned her over to her bloom-filled market stall.

'Hey, Glanna. How's it going?'

'Good, good, thanks. Just grabbed one of Monique's Morning Macchiatos. They're potent enough to perk a sloth up, I reckon.'

'Tell me about it. God knows what the Donatos put in them. My Billy has one and tells me he could ditch his tug and just push the ferry right across to the other side of the estuary all on his own.'

'I see how you got in that state now,' Glanna said directly, causing the pregnant woman to laugh loudly and her voluptuous breasts to shake to the happy beat.

'He's on a complete sex ban at the moment.' Kara pointed to her stomach. 'Last thing I want to happen is for these two little bundles to be prodded out before the wedding – not that I feel in the mood anyway.'

'Twins? I didn't realise.'

'Yes, we thought it might skip a generation but alas, we have been blessed with double trouble. At least I shall only have to do this once, hopefully.'

'The wedding or the babies?' Glanna joked, taking a tiny sip of her scalding coffee.

Kara laughed and moved her hand to her ample hip. 'Saying that, if Billy has his way, Penrigan United won't have to advertise for any future players.'

'Anyway,' Glanna brusquely changed the subject, 'what time do you want me tomorrow? And still the same brief as our first chat?'

'Around six, if that's OK. And please no formal photos, I hate them. So just some casual shots inside and outside of Frank's *Café* with the estuary behind us. I'd quite like some black and white ones, too. If there's just a couple of good ones for me to put up in the flat and a handful for my lot and Billy's family to choose from, I'll be happy.'

'Sure, whatever you like.' Glanna glanced at the sun. 'Looks like it's going to be a scorcher tomorrow, so that's a bonus.'

Kara grimaced. 'For whom? I'll be wearing a kaftan, not the planned dress at this rate. Oh, and just shots of me from the boobs up if you can manage that.'

Glanna laughed, then said, 'You look stunning, Kara, or maybe I should say "glowing". That's the right adjective to use for a pregnant woman, isn't it?'

'Growling, more like. I'm so bloody tetchy and knackered. We'll be home and tucked up before this fat lady sings if I have my way.'

'Best make sure your Billy doesn't have one of these coffees first then.' Glanna put her takeaway cup on Kara's stall and picked up a long-stemmed red rose from one of the metal buckets on the ground, pressed it to her nose and inhaled its sweet scent. 'Can I just ask why you didn't wait to do it until after the birth?'

'Why did I want to be a big fat teetotal bride, you mean?' Kara grinned.

'Well, since you've put it like that . . .' Glanna smiled back at her.

'My Billy's got a bit of an old-fashioned streak, wanted the two bubba Dillons to arrive in wedlock. God knows why we didn't do it in the spring. The next thing is to try and agree on suitable names to go with the surname. I'm just thankful that we already have a Bob the Dog in the family, as even though it's not spelled the same, I know how my fiancé's sense of humour works.'

'Bob Dillon – ha ha! How about Doris and Dennis?' interjected the blonde and ethereal Star Murray as she walked around the front of her jewellery stall next to her best friend Kara's flower stall, to tidy a display of necklaces. 'I can see the pair of them running around now. Two little gingers with *big* personalities.' As she spoke, the black-haired baby with podgy bare legs hanging down from the blue and white striped papoose she was effortlessly wearing, let out a blast of bubbly wind. 'Matthew Murray, have you no manners in front of the ladies?'

'Bless him.' Kara went over and gently stroked his downy hair with one finger. 'Doris and Dennis, what's your mummy on about, eh?' She turned back to Star. 'And how do you know it's not going to be two girls or two boys, Madam Murray? Or that they might not be gingers like me but have their daddy's dark hair and colouring?'

'Sorry to interrupt you lovely ladies,' Glanna broke in,

'but this macchiato is calling and I'd better open up. I'm already late on parade this morning.' She went to put the red rose she was still holding back in the bucket.

'Keep it,' Kara told her. 'See you tomorrow. I'm having a few days off after the wedding, but I'll be sure to sort your first flower display for the week after.'

'That's kind.' Glanna looked at her rose. 'I haven't been given one of these in a while, and there's no rush for my flowers – although saying that, as you know I do have my new show called "Seascapes in All Seasons" running from the end of next week so it would be nice to put on a bit of a display.' She had put up posters all around the small town of Hartmouth, and in the local area, as well as advertising the show on her website. Bidding them both goodbye, she headed off to open her shop.

Kara watched her go. 'Oh, to be so tall and willowy.'

'She always looks a bit sad to me,' Star said thoughtfully, then screwed up her face. 'Poo! I'd better get inside and change this one's nappy!'

Chapter 4

'Oh, so you're wide awake now, are you, mister?'

Glanna Pascoe stroked Banksy's soft ears as he blinked at her from the cosy dog basket under the reception desk-cum-counter of the Hartmouth Gallery. The contented canine brushed his cold nose against her hand, then yawned widely and stretched.

It was almost two years ago to the day when she had noticed his sweet little black pointed face looking longingly at her from behind the bars of his Westmorland Whippet Trust cage. And it had taken her a mere three seconds to decide that Banksy, the dog previously known as Wilbur, was the perfect pet for her. So, after an inspection from the charitable trust, her home above the gallery at Flat 4, Ferry Lane, Hartmouth found itself with a new, sleek and handsome four-legged inhabitant. Albeit a little shy and sometimes sly where food was concerned, Banksy was a perfect companion for the recently single Glanna. He also was a blessing with regards to her physical and mental health as boy, could he run when she took him out for his regular walks up on Penrigan Moor.

'Alexa, play "Changes" by David Bowie on repeat,' Glanna ordered, then draining her coffee, she glided through to the kitchenette and cast the takeaway cup into the recycling bin. The stable-style back door led on to a small concrete yard with an outbuilding in which she stored her overflow of stock and her beloved electric-blue, electric bike. Standing there, with Banksy at her side, she closed her eyes and sucked in a breath of fresh summer air, the seagulls' cries echoing above her.

Oh, how different her life was now, Glanna thought, from the one she had led in London. But that was the old Glanna, and now that the new Glanna was at last beginning to find her feet, she found that she actually quite liked her.

Single, with just Banksy at home for company, she could see things much more clearly these days. Could see how she'd taken a life of privilege for granted – the travelling, the freedom, her studies – all funded without any effort on her part. She had never had to worry about money. Had never experienced hardship and poverty. Instead, she had partied the years away. She couldn't deny that the drinking, drug-taking and sexual encounters had been a whole lot of fun, most of the time. She'd enjoyed men, and even the odd woman too would light her fire, usually when she was high on cocaine and when even her inhibitions had lost *their* inhibitions. It wasn't unknown for her to wake up with three other bodies in the bed after a night of debauchery.

Before long, the drink was taking away far more than it was giving her. The hangovers and fall-outs with her companions began to take over the good times. Her once alabaster-clear skin became blotchy, her face puffy. Her mind wasn't focused. Despite looking in the mirror and flinching at the sight, she didn't stop. But with every high came a low and the lows were getting ever lower and more frequent.

It is said that everyone must hit their rock bottom in order to start climbing to the top. In Glanna Pascoe's case, her rock bottom came when she drove straight into the back of a parked Range Rover in the heart of Fulham, regaining consciousness to find the emergency services cutting her out of her Alfa Romeo Spider. The doctors said the fact that she had been twice over the alcohol limit and her body was not tensed up, had saved her from more serious injury. The physical damage consisted of two badly bruised ankles and a deep cut above her eye, where a scar remained to this day. The mental damage was still a work in progress. She had not driven a car since.

Standing in court, as the magistrate dished out a two-year driving ban and forty hours' community service, she could still remember the sight of her mother, huge sunglasses covering all emotion, and her father with his hand on his heart trying to convey his feelings of love for her. It was only thanks to her solicitor telling the court that his client wholly regretted her actions and had already spent twenty-eight days in a dedicated addiction facility that she managed to escape a custodial sentence.

Glanna wasn't fazed by the not-driving bit, it was the community service that had hurt her the most. Scrubbing giant graffiti off underpasses was sacrilege to her as she knew that the street artists who had created them would have put their heart and soul into the illegal but colourful masterpieces.

She had also had to accept the brutal realisation that once she was no longer the resident party girl and cocaine cash cow, the hangers-on had long since gone. Not one of her so-called 'friends' had remained to pick up the shards of her broken body or mind. And that hurt. It hurt a lot.

'Ch-ch-changes . . .' Glanna began to sing along to the iconic Bowie track that had got her through many a dark day of alcohol cravings. Where she would repeat over and over again her coping mantra: 'S.H.O.W. – Sickness, Hangover, Obesity, Waste', until the urge for a drink had gone off and she could breathe again.

Going back inside, Banksy trotting behind her, she took an orange duster from the cupboard under the sink, then went through to the gallery and started flicking it randomly around. Glanna didn't find one bit of satisfaction in either tidying or cleaning – probably because she'd never had to do it. Oliver, for some reason, loved both – and in fashionable Clapham, south-west London, it was he who had kept their flat in order. Back in Hartmouth, Glanna regularly thought about getting a cleaner, but her mother's helpers had always been so chatty and nosy, and she really couldn't do with having to make endless chitter-chatter or deal with somebody snooping around her private affairs. When she moved into her Ferry Lane apartment, she had resigned herself to being her own Mrs Mop.

The Hartmouth Gallery was very much Glanna's sanctuary. Painted bright white, the unit had a huge, curved window, where the big, dramatic oil paintings were displayed. At the back of the shop were various shelving areas where she not only placed her own work but also the works of other local artists. The plain white walls of the gallery were covered with watercolours in varying shapes and sizes, while on the main shop floor stood several smart black easels holding white-framed prints.

The main shop led through to a hallway where a steep

flight of stairs had a chain across with a notice attached, marked *Private*. And up those stairs was where Glanna and Banksy lived, each one devoted to the other, and where Glanna had her own separate art studio, filled with light.

To find out more, order *Rainbows End in Ferry Lane Market* by Nicola May now!

Looking for more from Nicola May?

Sign up to the Nicola May newsletter for exclusive updates, extracts, competitions and news at WWW.HODDER.CO.UK/LANDING-PAGE/NICOLA-MAY/

Or scan the QR code below

Stay Social and Follow Nicola:

@NICOLAMAY1

@AUTHOR_NICOLA

@NICOLAMAYAUTHOR

WWW.NICOLAMAY.COM

Bookends

When one book ends, another begins...

Bookends is a vibrant new reading community to help you ensure you're never without a good book.

You'll find exclusive previews of the brilliant new books from your favourite authors as well as exciting debuts and past classics. Read our blog, check out our recommendations for your reading group, enter great competitions and much more!

Visit our website to see which great books we're recommending this month.

Join the Bookends community:

www.welcometobookends.co.uk

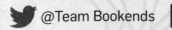 @Team Bookends   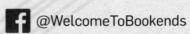 @WelcomeToBookends